THE MAN IN THE CROOKED HAT

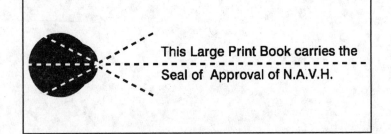

This Large Print Book carries the
Seal of Approval of N.A.V.H.

THE MAN IN THE CROOKED HAT

HARRY DOLAN

THORNDIKE PRESS
A part of Gale, a Cengage Company

Farmington Hills, Mich • San Francisco • New York • Waterville, Maine
Meriden, Conn • Mason, Ohio • Chicago

Copyright © 2017 by Harry Dolan.
Thorndike Press, a part of Gale, a Cengage Company.

Thorndike Press® Large Print Bill's Bookshelf.
The text of this Large Print edition is unabridged.
Other aspects of the book may vary from the original edition.
Set in 16 pt. Plantin.

LIBRARY OF CONGRESS CIP DATA ON FILE.
CATALOGUING IN PUBLICATION FOR THIS BOOK
IS AVAILABLE FROM THE LIBRARY OF CONGRESS

ISBN-13: 978-1-4328-4961-0 (hardcover)

Published in 2018 by arrangement with G. P. Putnam's Sons, an imprint of Penguin Publishing Group, a division of Penguin Random House LLC

Printed in the United States of America
1 2 3 4 5 6 7 22 21 20 19 18

To Michelle, with gratitude

1.

On the shore of the Huron River, Michael Underhill sits in the grass with his back against a tree. He watches the sunlight glinting on the water. He listens to the burble of the current.

The woman is next to him, her back against the same tree. You could see them from the river, if you were out there in a canoe. But it's late in the season. There's no one on the water.

Underhill picks up a leaf from the ground beside him.

"Sometimes I think too much," he says in a quiet voice. "I remember this thing that happened, an accident. Just dumb. I was driving to the grocery store on a Saturday afternoon, coming up to an intersection. I had the green light. There was a fire truck idling on the cross street. He had the red, so he was waiting. But he must have gotten a call, because suddenly he turned on his lights and siren."

The leaf is yellow and dry. Underhill twirls it by the stem.

"Now I have to decide. Hit the brakes or go on through. It happened fast, but I remember thinking: *This is not good.* I hit the brakes. And I stopped in time, right at the intersection. But the car behind me didn't. It slammed into me — I can still remember the sound. The driver was a kid. I think she was nineteen."

He holds the leaf steady and looks at the veins.

"No one got hurt, and even the damage to my car wasn't too bad. I had to take it in and have them replace the bumper and the taillights. The girl's car was worse, but it wasn't my problem. I wasn't at fault. What the whole thing amounted to was a bad afternoon and some phone calls to the insurance company and a week of inconvenience while my car was in the shop. But I kept thinking about it. It didn't have to happen. I could have made a different choice. When the driver of the fire truck turned on his siren, he didn't move out into the intersection right away. I could have gone through and there would have been no harm. No damage. No hassle. So why didn't I go through?"

Underhill closes his hand around the leaf and feels it crumble. The woman is silent beside him.

"It still bugs me, even though it happened years ago," he says. "And this thing today, I know it's going to be the same. I'm going to wonder if it might have turned out differently. If I had taken a different tack. If I had talked to you in a different place. It'll bother me for a long time. In my defense, I think I handled it pretty well. I was friendly. You were friendly. We struck up a conversation. It's broad daylight in a public park. You shouldn't have been nervous. I didn't think you were nervous. And I worked my way up to it — to asking you the question. It wasn't a hard question. There's no reason it should have made you suspicious. If you had given me a straight answer, that would have been the end of it. I would have smiled and gone away. No harm. All you had to do was tell me the truth."

He opens his hand and lets the pieces of the leaf fall to the ground.

"But I could see that you weren't comfortable," he says. "You didn't trust me. That wasn't right. I didn't deserve it. And then pretending you didn't remember. That's just clumsy. Anyone would have seen through that. What was I supposed to do? Let it go?

How could I? By then we'd gone too far. You were starting to be afraid of me. You shouldn't have been afraid of me."

Underhill gets up from the ground and brushes his hands over the front of his shirt. A cool wind touches his face. The woman doesn't stir.

Out in the river, a fish breaks the surface of the water.

"You shouldn't have been afraid of me," Underhill says again.

The woman's camera is lying in the grass where it fell. Underhill lifts it by the strap, swings it back and forth to build momentum, and hurls it out into the middle of the river.

He returns to the tree and crouches down. He touches a lock of hair that has fallen over the woman's forehead. He takes her earrings from her ears, takes her wedding band. Throws them out into the water. They don't go as far, but it's far enough.

He stands on the shore, wondering if there's anything else he should do.

"This is as much on you as it is on me," he says after a while. "I'm not going to feel bad about this."

One last look around. His hat is in the grass. He picks it up and puts it on his head and walks away.

2.

Eighteen months later

If you wandered through midtown Detroit that spring, you saw the flyers.

You saw them if you went to the Shinola store on Canfield Street, or Third Man Records, or any sort of hipster hangout. One on every stretch of bare brick wall. You saw them on the campus of Wayne State University and at each entrance to the public library. You saw them in front of the DIA — the Detroit Institute of Arts — taped to the granite base of Rodin's *Thinker.* At least until the maintenance workers came to peel them off.

They were sheets of white paper, eight and a half by eleven, printed with a composite sketch of a man's face — a man wearing a fedora. There were two lines of type above the sketch. The first asked: HAVE YOU SEEN HIM? The second was an e-mail address.

You may have spotted the person who put

them up. He would have been carrying a sheaf of them under his arm, and a roll of white duct tape. You might have wondered about him. He wore good clothes, but sometimes he wore them carelessly. One sleeve rolled up and one left down. Shirt-tails untucked. His hygiene left no room for complaint, but his shaving was haphazard. He moved at his own pace, half a step slower than everyone around him. If you got close enough to see his eyes, you might have suspected he wasn't getting enough sleep.

If you tried to engage him in conversation, it would have been hit-or-miss. He could be friendly, but he might not have patience for small talk. He was a difficult person to get to know.

His name was Jack Pellum.

That Tuesday, Jack had one important thing to do, and two unimportant things.

The first unimportant thing was an appointment with Dr. Eleanor Brannon at her office on Selden Street. He arrived twenty minutes late.

Dr. Brannon heard his knock and greeted him at the door. She offered him one of the two chairs in the room and took the other. The low table between them held a box of tissues and a vase of spring flowers. Jack moved the vase aside to make room for his stack of flyers. The duct tape went on top.

There were pleasantries. Wasn't it a fine sunny afternoon? It was. Did Jack have any trouble finding the office? None at all.

Dr. Brannon opened a file in her lap and put on a pair of reading glasses.

"You were seeing Dr. Kershaw," she said.

"Yes."

"And it turned out the two of you had different styles of communication."

Jack settled back in his chair. "Is that what he told you?"

"Not in so many words. He said you threatened him."

Dr. Brannon's voice was mild. Unconcerned.

"Really?" Jack said.

"You told him —" She consulted the file. "You told him you wanted to rip out his heart and eat it. . . . That's quite colorful."

"It's not true."

"No?"

"I said I wanted to cut out his heart and fry it in a pan. I never said anything about eating it."

Dr. Brannon may have wanted to smile. Jack couldn't be sure. If she did, she resisted.

"And you weren't making a threat," she said.

"I was trying to make a point. He kept telling me that his office was a safe place. I could say anything I wanted there, without fear of being judged." Jack paused, tapping the arm of the chair. "I don't think he understood me."

Dr. Brannon turned a page in the file. "So, as I said, you had different styles of communication. Why did you go to him originally?"

"My father thought I would benefit from talking to someone."

"You're thirty-five years old."

"Yes."

"So you're not bound by your father's wishes."

"No, but I have reasons to take his wishes into account."

"What reasons?"

"He's paying my rent, for one thing."

Dr. Brannon looked up at Jack. "You don't have money of your own? You're not working?"

"Not for a while."

"I understand you used to be a police officer."

"I was a detective."

"But not anymore."

"I quit. The year before last."

"Why?"

"You know why," Jack said. "It's in the file."

"I'd like to hear it from you."

Sometimes Jack's hands make themselves into fists without his realizing. He opened them now and flexed his fingers.

"My wife died," he said.

"Olivia."

"Yes, Olivia."

"She was murdered."

"She was strangled on an afternoon in October," Jack said, "and left propped against a tree by the shore of the Huron River."

"I'm sorry," said Dr. Brannon.

Jack never knew how to respond to condolences. He kept quiet.

"And after that," the doctor said, "you didn't want to be a detective anymore."

"After that, I desperately wanted to be a detective. But the only case I cared about was hers, and no one would let me anywhere near it. My lieutenant told me to take some time off."

"And you haven't gone back."

"I can't see the point."

"It might do you good, to be working. Some people find that work helps them cope with grief."

Jack flexed his fingers again. "Is that where we are now? You're going to ask me how I'm coping?"

"Does that word bother you?"

"I don't care about the word."

"Do you think you're dealing well with your wife's death?"

"Should I be honest?"

"Please."

"I don't think that's any of your goddamn business."

The profanity left the doctor unfazed. She turned some more pages.

"Yet you're here," she said. "Do you want to tell me about George Hanley?"

"Jesus, is that in the file?"

"You were arrested for assaulting him two months ago. You broke his nose."

"That's not entirely accurate."

"Which part?"

"I wasn't arrested."

"Why don't you tell me what happened."

Jack leaned forward, let out a long breath. "Look, that was a mistake. I wasn't thinking clearly. You have to understand, when you're investigating a homicide, sometimes there's very little to go on. And then maybe you start reaching. For anything. Olivia was a photographer. A freelancer. One of the

16

things she did, she worked for Ford, photo-graphing cars for their brochures. That's a good job. It pays well. After she died, George Hanley got hired to replace her. So, in a sense, he benefited from her death. That gave him a motive."

"Did Mr. Hanley have a criminal record?"

"No."

"But you thought he might have killed your wife to pick up some freelance work."

"I just wanted to talk to him," Jack said. "I'm afraid I didn't come across very well. He didn't like the tone of my questions. He got angry. We both did."

"You hit him."

"It went further than I intended."

"But you weren't arrested."

"No."

Dr. Brannon took off her reading glasses. "Even though you shouldn't have been questioning him in the first place. You had no authority. And you caused him grave physical harm."

"I don't know how grave it was."

"He didn't call the police?"

"Oh, he called them, and they came," Jack said. "They put me in the back of a squad car and drove me away. If you want to call that an arrest. Nothing happened to me. From what I heard, Hanley wanted to press charges at first, and then later on he didn't."

"What made him change his mind?"

"I imagine someone talked to him. You know who my father is, right?"

Dr. Brannon nodded. "He's a judge."

"He's a federal judge on the Sixth Circuit Court of Appeals."

She raised an eyebrow. "So you're saying he made the assault charge go away."

"I'm pretty sure he made the assault itself go away. If you went looking, I think you'd find that there's not a scrap of documentation. No incident report, no witness statements. It never happened. I'm surprised he didn't send someone to scrub it from that file."

Dr. Brannon balanced her glasses on the arm of her chair. She smoothed her hair from her forehead. It was dark but turning silver. She was probably ten years older than Jack. Short, slender, well dressed in a silk blouse and a navy blue skirt. She seemed calm and benevolent and Jack wanted to like her.

She said, "Do you think your father is looking out for your best interests?"

"I'm not here to talk about my father."

"Yet he's come up twice now. Tell me about him."

"He's not an easy man to explain."

"Tell me the first thing that comes to mind."

"He used to play catch with me when I was a kid."

She smiled. "Tell me the second thing that comes to mind."

Jack hesitated. Studied the flowers on the table between them. Finally he looked up and met her eyes.

"This past Christmas, my father wanted to know about my plans for the future. I said I was thinking about going back to school, to study law."

"All right."

"Then about six weeks ago I got an acceptance letter from the law school of the University of Michigan. They're holding a place for me there in the fall."

"Congratulations."

"You're not following me," Jack said. "I didn't apply. I wasn't that serious about it. My father made it happen. He took care of it, like he took care of the assault. That's only the beginning. Last week I got my private investigator's license."

The doctor tipped her head to the side. "You didn't apply for that either?"

"I didn't have to. It came in the mail — because a while back I happened to mention that it was an option I was considering, becoming a P.I. I got business cards last week too: *Jack Pellum Investigations.* They showed up on my doorstep. I've already been getting calls from potential clients. Apparently I advertise online. If you google 'Detroit private investigators,' my name comes up first."

Dr. Brannon looked thoughtful for a moment. "It sounds like your father wants to help you. I'm not saying he's going about it in the right way. But it sounds like his intentions are good. Would you agree?"

"Probably."

"What do you think he wants for you?"

"He says he wants me to be happy."

"You sound skeptical."

"I think he'd take happy if he could get it. Otherwise he'd settle for normal."

"What do you want?"

"That's a large question."

"Yes."

"And again I'm not sure if it's any of your business."

It seemed to Jack that Dr. Brannon wanted to sigh. But she managed to hold it in.

"All right," she said. "What do you want from *me*?"

He let a few seconds pass, making up his mind.

"I might like to come here and talk to you.

Occasionally."

"For what purpose?"

"To keep my father off my back."

"You could get the same result by pretending to come here," she said. "What would we talk about?"

"It doesn't really matter."

"Would we talk about Olivia?"

"Possibly."

"I don't know if I can help you."

"I don't expect you to."

Dr. Brannon closed the file, and her eyes turned sad and kind.

"Your wife died, for no good reason," she said. "People die and leave us behind and we have to find a way to go on. You're coming up against the human condition, Mr. Pellum. You could meet with me and talk about her and it might make you feel better. Or it might not."

"It doesn't matter," Jack said.

After he left Dr. Brannon's office, Jack made his way up Woodward Avenue. The temperature stood in the sixties, but he had the sidewalk mostly to himself. He put up some flyers at the Majestic Theatre and crossed the street to tape one to the gate of the Whitney House. He knew from experience it wouldn't stay there long, but you do what you can.

His walk ended at the DIA — the site of the second unimportant thing he had to do that afternoon. He sat on the steps in front of the museum and waited. Schoolkids milled around nearby. Two of them had rolled-up posters from the gift shop. They fought a duel up and down the steps, using the posters as swords, until a sour-faced teacher came by and told them to knock it off.

Around then a school bus drove up to the curb and the kids started getting on, and Jack looked across the street and saw a woman watching him uncertainly. He gave her a little wave to encourage her. She waited for a gap in traffic and crossed over to his side. Her clothes were upscale casual: cashmere sweater, black jeans, designer handbag, leather boots. She wore her blond hair in a ponytail. Jack put her age in the mid-thirties.

He rose as she came up the steps.

"Mr. Pellum?" she said. "I'm Kim Weaver."

Jack gave her a smile. Low-grade, professional. "Nice to meet you."

She put out a hand and he took it briefly and they stalled after that. She looked around, taking in the steps and the pillars at the entrance of the museum.

"We could go inside," Jack said. "But I thought we might talk here."

The last of the schoolkids went down to the bus, leaving them alone, and Kim Weaver made her decision.

"Here is fine."

They sat on the steps, with Jack's leftover flyers between them.

"I've never done this before," Kim said. "Hired a detective."

"I'm new to it myself," Jack told her.

"I wouldn't have known who to call. But then I saw your billboard."

"My billboard?"

"The one on the interstate, near the airport."

"Oh, that one. Sure."

"And now here we are. You're not what I expected."

"I'm not?"

"I thought you'd be older and, I don't know, smelling of cigar smoke."

Jack gave her the smile again. They watched the school bus ease away from the curb and roll up Woodward. When it was out of sight, Kim got to her point.

"It's my husband," she said. "I think he's having an affair."

"Okay."

"It's such a cliché. You must hear it all the time."

"What's his name?"

"Doug."

"What makes you think he's having an affair?"

"A few things. Lately he's been working more. Or he says he has."

"What does he do?"

"He sells real estate. The past few months, he's been spending more time at it. But he's not making more sales. Sometimes he works until ten or eleven at night. I know he's not showing houses that late. He says he's doing paperwork, but if I drive by his office he's not there. Then there's his phone. He started locking it, so you have to key in a number —"

"A passcode," Jack said.

"Right. He never did that before. It makes me think he's keeping secrets. And then there's a woman, Gwen Davis, another agent. She started working at his company last year, and she's the type he would go for. I've seen the way he acts around her. There's something going on. I'm not blind."

"Have you asked him about it?"

"He denies it. Says I'm being paranoid."

"What about the phone?"

"He says the passcode is for safety, in case

it gets stolen. Which sounds reasonable, right?"

"Sure."

"So I put a lock on my phone too. And I gave him the code, in case he needed it. Like in an emergency. But he wouldn't give me his code. He said he wouldn't play that game. He said I should trust him. You're married, aren't you?"

The question caught Jack by surprise. He wondered for a moment why she would make that assumption, but the answer was obvious. He looked down at his left hand. He still wore the ring.

"I used to be," he said.

Kim Weaver turned away, embarrassed. "I don't mean to be nosy. I've been married for five years, but Doug and I knew each other for another three before. I didn't want to rush into it. I took it seriously. I wanted to be sure. It's not the way I thought it would be. I don't like it, feeling this way. Like it was a mistake."

She went quiet and they sat together watching the traffic on Woodward. An elderly couple came out of the museum behind them and made a slow descent down the steps.

Jack thought about Dr. Brannon and the question she had asked him.

"What do you want?" he said.

Kim Weaver pulled the sleeves of her sweater down over her hands, as if the day had turned cold.

"I want to live a good life," she said. "I want the world to be fair. I want a husband I don't have to doubt. I want to feel like I made the right choices."

"What do you want from *me*?"

She bent forward, resting her elbows on her thighs. "I guess I want you to follow Doug around and see if he's sleeping with Gwen Davis. I want you to see if they're doing it at her apartment or in a hotel or in some empty house with a FOR SALE sign in front of it. I want you to get up close and look through the window and maybe take pictures, because if I don't have proof, he'll keep denying it, and I don't think I could stand it, going on this way."

Jack nodded. "I'll do that for you, if you're certain it's what you want."

"Will you?"

"Absolutely. I'll skulk around, and I'll take pictures. But you have to be certain."

"You don't think it's a good idea."

"I won't say one way or the other. But there are things you might want to take into account."

"Such as?"

"His dignity. And yours. And mine. I don't care so much about mine, but it's something to consider. It's part of the mix. Let me ask you this: What would you do if you found out you were right, if I got you proof that he was cheating?"

"I'd leave him. Divorce him."

"You could do that now."

"But shouldn't I be sure?"

Jack shrugged. "You sound like you are. I'm pretty sure, just from what you've said. And I'm not the one living with him. But forget about cheating. Leave it aside. Is he treating you the way you want to be treated? Is he acting like he cares about you?"

"No. He's distant and cold."

"So why stay with him? Do you have children?"

"No."

"Then it's easy. Do what you want."

Kim searched for a response to that, and didn't find one. Jack shifted his feet to a lower step, stretching his legs. Down on the street, a silver Town Car drifted by slowly. Beside him, Kim's hands came out of the sleeves of her sweater and dug through her handbag for a tissue. She wiped away some tears. Not many, not in front of a stranger. Jack wanted to reach over and pat her shoulder. He didn't.

The tissue went back into her bag. Kim sniffed and started to get up and then noticed the flyers lying on the step. She tugged one of them out from underneath the roll of duct tape.

"Who's this?" she asked. "A missing person?"

"Sort of," Jack said. "He's someone I need to talk to."

Kim let herself smile. "You must handle a lot of missing person cases."

"Why do you say that?"

"You're not making any money off of wives with cheating husbands." She tapped the flyer. "What's his story, the man in the hat?"

"I don't know. Does he look familiar?"

"I can't say he does."

"All right."

"But at the same time, I feel like I've seen him before. You know what I mean?"

"Yes."

"There's not much to him. He could be nobody. Or anybody. I might have passed him twice on the street today. But if I saw him again tomorrow, I might not remember. Does that make sense?"

"It does."

She returned the flyer to the stack. "I hope you find him," she said.

She stood, and Jack did too.

"I'm glad we had this talk," she said, adjusting the strap of her handbag on her shoulder. "But then again, I'm not glad about it at all."

"I know."

She thanked him and said good-bye and turned away. Jack watched her walk down the steps and head off at a crisp pace along Woodward. He was still watching her when the silver Town Car came by again. He figured it must have circled the block. It stopped and let out a passenger from the backseat before driving on.

The passenger was tall and rail thin and wore a tailored black suit. He had gray hair and a stern, grim face. If you were casting him in a film, he might play a scarecrow or the angel of death.

He was Alton Pellum, Jack's father.

Jack sat down again and waited. His father approached him, but not directly. He went to the statue of Rodin's *Thinker* first and casually tore the flyers from the base. He wadded up the tape and crumpled the paper and stuffed everything in the pockets of his jacket.

When he reached Jack, he eased himself down on the step beside him.

"Lovely woman, the blonde," he said. "Is

she someone you're seeing, or is that too much to hope?"

"It's strictly professional," Jack said. "She had a job she needed help with."

"I trust you took it."

"I already helped her. What brings you here?"

Alton Pellum clasped his hands together over one knee. "I come here quite often," he said. "I go around the neighborhood and count your little posters. It's the only way I have of assessing your well-being."

"It can't be the only way."

"What's another?"

"You could ask me how I am."

"Very well. How are you, Jack?"

"I'm fine."

Jack's father frowned. "That's uninformative, and probably a lie. Have you gone to see that new doctor?"

"I saw her today."

"And?"

"She's good. Better than the last one. I think she's someone I could talk to."

Jack watched the knuckles of his father's hands turn white.

Alton Pellum said, "Why do I think you're telling me what I want to hear?"

"Would you rather I told you things you didn't want to hear?"

"Yes, if they were true."

"Then I will endeavor to tell you only true things from now on."

"That would be a welcome change. We worry about you, your mother and I."

"I don't want you to worry."

"Nonetheless, we do," Alton Pellum said. "Have you been getting enough sleep?"

"More or less."

"Have you been exercising?"

"Yes."

"Have you been eating properly?"

"Yes."

"Your mother would like you to come for dinner."

"Yes."

"So you'll come?"

"No. I was acknowledging that she would like me to come."

"Don't be a smart aleck. She'd like to fix you a home-cooked meal. Perhaps roast pork or lamb."

"Her lamb is terrible," Jack said.

"That's an exaggeration. It's also irrelevant."

"She made it for Christmas and I could barely chew it," Jack said. "I ate it anyway and it sat in my stomach for three days. I would rather she shaved the wool off a lamb and fed me that."

"She doesn't have to make lamb."

"Whatever she makes will be heavy and bland. She's not a good cook."

"We'll go to a restaurant then. The main thing is, she'd like to talk to you."

"She's not a good conversationalist either."

"Now you're being flippant," Jack's father said. "I don't think you realize how hurt your mother would be if she heard you saying these things."

"I do realize. I just don't care that much about hurting her feelings. Or yours."

Anger turned Alton Pellum's grim face grimmer and he got up on his feet. Jack picked up the tape and the flyers and did the same. His father's breath rumbled in his throat and the old man's dark eyes glared.

"That's fine, Jack," he said softly. "You have chastened me with your truth-telling. I am defeated. Your mother would still like to see you. We will keep her innocent of your true nature. You'll have to pretend you're a good son and find something to say to her. Can you do that?"

"I could," Jack said, "but it would be an effort."

"We'll make it as painless as possible. We'll meet at a restaurant of your choosing. We could do it tonight, get it over with. Then you could go on about your life."

"Tonight's no good."

"Some other night then. But soon."

Alton Pellum started down the steps without another word, his back straight, his head held high. Jack followed him. The silver Town Car was waiting when they got to the street. Jack held the door while his father climbed in.

Jack shut the door but the car didn't move. The window came down and his father leaned toward him, his anger gone, replaced with weariness.

"Are you sure you can't make it tonight?" the old man said. "It would mean a great deal to your mother. To both of us."

"I'm sorry, Dad. I really can't. I've got something important to do."

3.

The Park Bar in downtown Detroit attracts twenty-somethings who work nearby and people going to shows at the Fox Theatre and the Fillmore. It's a big room with a square bar in the middle and booths along each wall. It's moderately crowded even at six on a Tuesday night.

Jack Pellum bought a Coke at the bar, claimed a booth, and used his phone to check his e-mail. There were a handful of new messages to the address on the flyers: iveseenthehatman@gmail.com. The first one was typical: *Have I seen him? Yeah I saw him in an alley once, fucking your sister.* The others were equally useful: *Is that Jimmy Hoffa?* they said, or *Have you found Jesus?* or *Stop taping your shit to my wall, asshole.* He deleted them one by one.

Around quarter after six Jack heard a voice he recognized calling out to one of the bartenders for a beer. He looked up and

34

saw Carl Dumisani, all six feet of him, broad-shouldered, bulging a little at the stomach, but solid. He wore a blue suit, the jacket folded over his arm. White shirt and suspenders. Loose tie. He dropped some bills on the bar and picked up his mug and carried it over. Eased himself into the booth across from Jack.

He took a slow drink and looked Jack over. Carl had gentle brown eyes and skin the color of caramel. Jack had spent a lot of time with him once. It was Carl who had trained Jack when he became a detective. They rode together for five years before Jack quit.

Carl Dumisani put his mug down and said, "We're back to the flyers again, Pellum?"

They were on the table next to Jack's phone.

"I guess we are," he said.

"Thought you were gonna stop."

"I did. Held out for about three weeks."

"I guess that's better than some people do." Carl reached over and took one from the top of the stack. "Honest to god, you might as well put up a sign that says, *You ever seen a white man in a hat?* See if that works."

"There's an idea."

"Seriously, you ever get anything off these?"

"Not yet."

"Maybe that's 'cause there's nothing to get." Carl put the flyer back. "This can't go on, Pellum."

"Don't try to fix me, Carl."

"I wouldn't. You're my boy, you know that. Even when you're broken. But it's not up to me." He had a deep voice, and Jack could hear the regret in it. "You go on as long as you want," Carl said. "I won't stop you. But you and me, meeting like this, it has to end. The word has come down."

"From who?"

"From the lieutenant, and she got the word from the chief, and I don't know where *he* got the word but I can guess. Probably from a man wears a black robe."

Sometimes Jack gets a sick feeling, a tightness in his chest, like he's breathing air but there's not enough oxygen in it. But it always passes. If he holds out, he can make it pass.

"Okay," Jack said. "We can deal with this. We've been careless, meeting at the same time every week, in the same place. Someone was bound to notice. We can change things up."

"No. You're not hearing me. It's done."

"I know it's a risk for you —"

"And I'd take the risk, you know I would, if I thought it was doing you any good. But it's not."

"I can talk to my father —"

Carl Dumisani reached over and touched Jack's arm with his thick fingers. Jack had seen him do it before, to people they interrogated. It was meant to soothe them.

"We're not bargaining, kid," Carl said. "This is the last time. You want to do this or not?"

Jack didn't answer. He was dealing with the thing that was pushing down on his chest. He worked on controlling his breathing. He told himself he wasn't in danger. He wasn't going to die. It only felt that way.

"We don't have to do this," Carl said. "You know that, right? You can come back. I'll put in a word for you. Not that it'll matter. The only thing that'll matter is your father, and we both know he's got the juice to get you back in. You and me can partner up again. I'd be happy to. You should see the clown they put me with."

He meant it. Jack knew. But it didn't matter. The offer didn't tempt him.

Jack waved it away. And the other thing, the feeling in his chest, it passed.

"This is the last time," he said. "I understand. Let's do it."

Carl drank from his mug, watching Jack over the rim. Jack could see his disappointment.

"Okay," Carl said. "There were four new homicides in the city this past week, and one in Dearborn." He pulled a small notebook from his pocket and consulted it. "The Dearborn one is easy. Guy got into a fight with his brother-in-law, beat him with a wrench. Called 911 himself and confessed. Safe to say, the man in the hat was not involved."

Jack nodded his agreement. "I read about that one in the *Free Press.*"

"Now, the other four," Carl said. "Two of them were gang-related. Both victims were young men. Nineteen and twenty-three. Both had priors for drug offenses. Both were shot. One black. One Hispanic. We don't have any suspects yet, no one's talking, but it doesn't sound like the man in the hat to me."

Carl waited to see if Jack would contradict him. When it didn't happen, he continued.

"The next one is a black female victim in her thirties. Tamika LaSalle. Her body was found in an abandoned house on Eight Mile. It had been there a few days."

"I read about that one too," Jack said.

"I figured you would. Now there's a superficial similarity with Olivia's case, in that Tamika LaSalle was strangled, but that's where it ends. La-Salle's killer used a ligature — an extension cord. We found it wrapped around her neck. Her body was hidden in a closet, not left out in the open. Different MOs. The other difference: La-Salle had a history of arrests for prostitution. She had a pimp: a man named Jamal Hudlin. He's the one we're focusing on. I think he did it. A friend of the victim says she wanted to leave him. And he has a temper. He's done time for assault before. But if there's any reason to connect him with Olivia's death, I can't see it. Do you think I'm wrong?"

Jack thought it over, longer than he had to.

"You're not wrong," he said. "What about the last one?"

Carl took another drink of beer, brought the mug down to the table, flicked his fingers against the handle.

"The last one's weird," he said. "I don't even want to tell you about it."

"Come on, Carl."

"I'm afraid you're gonna cling to it and waste your time obsessing over it. But it's really nothing. It's a suicide."

"I haven't read about any suicide."

Carl resigned himself, looked down at his notebook. "Happened on Friday in Corktown. Didn't make the papers. White male, thirty-three years old. Daniel Cavanaugh. He was living alone. Distraught over the death of his wife. She had one of those awful kinds of cancer that kill you young. Leukemia, I think. He cut open the ceiling in his living room and tied a rope around a wooden beam and hanged himself. A neighbor found him."

"That's a shame," Jack said, "but why would I obsess about it? Is there something you're leaving out? Did he look like the man in the hat?"

Carl smiled faintly at the idea. "I don't think so. Not particularly."

"Then what's special about this case? Could it have been staged? Is there any doubt it was a suicide?"

Carl shook his head. "Everyone agrees Cavanaugh was depressed. And he had tried it once before, with pills."

"Did he leave a note?"

Carl fiddled some more with the handle of his mug. "That's the thing that's a little strange. He left two. He painted them on the walls of his living room, in letters a foot high. He was a writer. I guess he had a flair for the dramatic. One of them said, *What's so great about any of this?* Sort of an all-purpose sentiment if you're gonna kill yourself."

"What did the other one say?"

Carl sighed. "The other one is the one you're gonna get worked up about. But I swear to you, I don't think it means anything. It's just a coincidence."

"What did it say?"

Carl lifted his broad shoulders, let them fall again.

"It said, *There's a killer, and he wears a crooked hat.*"

4.

Jack Pellum knew a little about Corktown. When he was a child, his father had taken him to ball games there.

Tiger Stadium used to sit at the corner of Trumbull and Michigan Avenues. The structure is gone, torn down years ago, but the ball field is still there — the infield and the outfield, surrounded by an empty lot. The stadium gates still stand along Michigan Ave, but they're not locked; they don't keep anyone out. People play baseball on the field sometimes. Kids fly kites there too.

Jack drove out that way on Wednesday afternoon. He drove south on Trumbull and turned right onto Leverette Street, where Daniel Cavanaugh and his wife once lived. He left his car on the street and walked through the neighborhood. The houses on Leverette were narrow and squeezed together, some of them so close you'd have to turn sideways to walk between them. They had steep roofs and tall brick chimneys, and the people who lived in them were not afraid of color. The Cavanaugh house was painted deep red. Its neighbors on either side were blue and yellow.

Jack had a key to the house. Carl Dumisani had brought it with him to the Park Bar the night before.

"I know you're gonna go there," Carl had said, sliding the key across the table. "This will save you from having to break a window."

"I thought you were done helping me," Jack had replied.

Carl's smile had been gentle. "This is the last time. Don't make me regret it. I'll need the key back. I have to return it to Cavanaugh's next of kin."

Jack left the key in his pocket and moved past the red house. He wasn't ready to go in yet. He came to the end of the block and turned the corner, and a little way on he found an alley that ran parallel to Daniel Cavanaugh's street. He followed it and had a look at Cavanaugh's backyard: long and skinny and closed off with a chain-link fence. Plenty of trimmed grass and a small brick patio with a pair of green Adirondack chairs.

What did that say about Cavanaugh?

Maybe he mowed his lawn before he killed himself. What did that mean? Probably nothing.

Jack walked out of the alley and back around to Leverette Street. A small girl rode a tricycle along the sidewalk. Her mother trailed behind her. Jack moved into the street and went around them, came to the Cavanaugh house again, and stepped up onto the porch. The white-painted railing gleamed in the sunlight. He leaned against it and reached into his pocket for the key and looked around to see if anyone was watching him. He noticed a guy in his twenties sitting on the steps of the house directly across the street. He hadn't been there before. He wore jeans and a gray T-shirt and a fedora with a thin brown band.

Jack remained calm.

There are many people with hats in the world. This Jack knew. If you paid attention, you saw a lot of them. And even if you believed that one of them killed your wife, you had to keep your cool. You couldn't let them rattle you.

As Jack watched, the guy in the hat took out his phone and looked at the screen and did whatever people do on their phones. The day went on around him. The girl on the tricycle laughed as she worked the pedals. Her mother turned her around and sent her in the other direction on the sidewalk. The guy in the hat looked up from his phone and saw Jack staring. He stared back. He was definitely not the person who had killed Olivia, Jack thought. Too young, too lean in the face. His skin a shade too pale.

The guy returned his attention to his phone. Some instinct told Jack that he should cross the street and talk to him. But before he could, he heard a voice call out, "Are you a friend of Danny's?"

Jack turned and saw her on the porch of the house next door: a white-haired lady in a tracksuit and tennis shoes.

"Not exactly a friend," he told her.

She took that in, but it didn't discourage her.

"I found him, you know," she said.

"That must have been a shock."

"Oh, it was. But I think he wanted it that way, on account of the newspaper."

Jack started to ask her what she meant. He didn't need to. She came down from her porch and approached him, talking all the way.

"We used to quarrel, me and Danny. He had a subscription to the *Free Press,* and they delivered it every day. They're supposed to bring it to your doorstep, but they never do. They toss it from the street. Half the time, Danny's paper ended up on my lawn."

"I see," Jack said.

"Well, I couldn't have that," said the woman. "I like things tidy. So we quarreled. I told Danny he had to straighten them out. He did, for a while. The papers stayed off my lawn. Until this past Friday."

She stood beside Jack now, on the porch of the Cavanaugh house. She barely came up to his shoulders.

"Well, on Friday I'd been feeling a little under the weather," she said, "and I never set foot outside my door until dusk, but when I did, what do you suppose I found?"

Jack played along. "A copy of the *Free Press* on your lawn."

"That's exactly right. And what do you suppose I did? I'll tell you. I marched right over here with that paper and knocked on Danny's door. But he didn't answer. Now I could see the light on behind the curtains, and I thought sure he must be home. So I went to this window right here and put my face up close to it and there was just enough of a gap between the curtains to see in, and what do you suppose I saw?"

"Did you see his body?"

"Now, I know that's what you'd think, but

you have to understand what a tiny space I had to look through. The only thing I could see was a chair turned on its side on the living room floor. A wooden chair from the kitchen. That was bad enough. Enough to make me worry."

"Is that when you called the police?"

"Not then. First I went to get my keys. Christina — that was Danny's wife — she and I used to be friendly, and we traded keys in case one of us got locked out. So I came back here and unlocked this door, and that's when I found him."

She turned solemn then, and quiet, but only for a moment.

"A horrible thing to see," she said. "Everything still and silent in there. But I'd swear poor Danny swayed a little, back and forth on the rope. I don't know how long he would have been there if I hadn't found him. That's why I thought later he might have done it on purpose."

"Done what?" Jack asked her.

"The newspaper. Don't you see? I think he threw his paper on my lawn so I'd come over here. Poor man. He wanted someone to find him." She touched the front window of the Cavanaugh house, solemn again. Jack watched her run her fingers slowly down the glass.

"How did you know Danny?" she asked.

"I didn't know him," Jack said.

She looked him up and down. "Are you with the police then?"

"I'm a detective," he said. Technically it was true.

Her eyes twinkled. "I thought you might be," she said. "You have that look about you." She stepped closer to him and lowered her voice as if they were conspirators. "Do you need to go inside the house? I could get my key."

Jack drew the key Carl had given him from his pocket. "I've got one," he said, nodding toward the door. "I should get to it."

A look of disappointment passed over her face. She'd been hoping to go inside with him and talk some more, Jack thought. She parted from him reluctantly, telling him to let her know if he needed anything. He watched her return to her house, then slipped the key into the lock.

The door was tight in the frame, and he had to put his shoulder to it to get it open. He passed through and pulled it shut behind him and he was alone in the quiet of Daniel Cavanaugh's living room.

The curtains filtered out the afternoon sunlight. Jack didn't want to open them, so he switched on a lamp in the corner.

The lamp threw his shadow onto the south wall of the room. It would have done the same for the shadow of Cavanaugh's body, he thought.

He looked around and tried to piece it together, what Cavanaugh had done.

Here's the room, with not much in it. A flat-screen television on a stand. A leather sofa on the east wall. A mahogany coffee table that Cavanaugh pushes against the sofa to make space so he can work.

He brings a chair in from the kitchen, stands on it, cuts a neat square from the drywall of the ceiling. The square exposes a wooden beam — one of the floor joists of the bedroom upstairs. He drills a hole through the beam so he can tie off one end of the rope. With the other end, he fashions a noose.

There's dust on the floor from his drilling. He doesn't bother to clean it up. He leaves the drill and the drywall saw on the coffee table.

Then there are his suicide notes. Two of them, just like Carl said.

On the south wall: *What's so great about any of this?*

On the east wall, over the sofa: *There's a killer, and he wears a crooked hat.*

The words are written in letters a foot

49

high. Painted in red on a background of pale blue.

In the lamplight, the red resembles blood. Is that on purpose? Cavanaugh is a writer. He has a sense of drama. Or maybe he used what he had on hand: the paint looks like the same shade of red that's on the exterior of the house.

The paint can and the brush are set aside neatly in a corner, with the square of drywall from the ceiling underneath them.

Here's Cavanaugh. He's ready now. His wife is dead; it's been more than a year since she passed. He climbs onto the chair, tightens the noose around his neck. Kicks the chair away.

Maybe it's fast. Or maybe he has time to regret it, time to struggle and kick, time to dance in the air.

He's gone now; they've taken him away. The rope too. The chair is upright near the foot of the stairs that lead to the second floor.

Jack can picture Cavanaugh's shadow on the wall, but that's gone too. The only shadow there is his own.

Jack left the scene behind and went upstairs. Two bedrooms and a bath. The bedroom at the front of the house was the one where

Cavanaugh slept. A queen-size bed, unmade. Half a glass of water on the nightstand. The closet was full of men's clothes. Cavanaugh hadn't held on to his wife's things.

The bedroom at the back was set up as an office. A desk facing a wall, a laptop on the desk. Jack didn't pry into the laptop, but not for lack of trying. It needed a password.

Another wall had built-in bookshelves. The titles were mostly fiction. Jack scanned one of the shelves: Neil Gaiman, Clive Barker, a lot of Stephen King. He came to a hardcover copy of a novel called *The House on Night Street.* The author's name on the dust jacket: Daniel Cavanaugh.

Jack opened the book and looked at the first line, even though he already knew it. He'd just read it downstairs: *There's a killer, and he wears a crooked hat.*

Carl knew it when Jack talked to him the night before. It wasn't difficult to suss out. All you had to do was run a Google search.

"He's a writer and he's about to sign off," Carl had told him. "So the last thing he does, he writes out a line from his book on the wall. Maybe then people will remember him. That's all it is. There's nothing more to it than that."

Jack closed the book. Maybe Carl was

right. Maybe the killer in Cavanaugh's novel had nothing to do with the face on Jack's flyers. But he needed to know for sure.

He spent some time going through the drawers of the desk, but found no answers. The afternoon was fading when he went downstairs and switched off the lamp in the living room. When he left, he made sure to lock the door behind him.

The tricycle girl and her mother had gone inside. A boy of ten or twelve walked a terrier along the sidewalk. Jack looked to the house across the way and noticed two things: the guy in the hat was gone from the porch, and a FOR SALE sign hung from a post on the lawn.

Jack crossed the street and climbed onto the empty porch. Got up close to the front window. No curtains to block his view. No furniture inside, only bare floors.

It meant nothing. Maybe the guy knew the people who used to live there. Maybe he had lived there himself. Maybe he had simply needed a place to sit.

Jack had a pocket full of business cards. He took one out and wrote *Please call me* on it and wedged it between the front door and the jamb.

A silly gesture, he thought. Might as well toss the card into the wind.

Sometimes a guy in a hat is just a guy in a hat.

5.

Jack's wife smoked cigarettes all through her twenties, but when they got engaged she promised to quit.

She kept her promise, mostly. Sometimes she cheated. Jack knew, and she knew that he knew, and they didn't talk about it. They lived in an apartment in the Brentwood building on Prentis Street, and every now and then he would find an open pack: on a high shelf in a kitchen cupboard, in the pocket of an old coat in the closet. He never bugged her about these discoveries and she never smoked inside. That was their unofficial bargain.

One night when they'd been married four years, Jack woke and found Olivia's side of the bed empty. He checked his phone for the time: 12:56. He called her name, waited, called it again louder.

He got up and pulled on the pants and shirt he'd worn the day before. Took a quick tour of the apartment. No Olivia. He went to a window and looked down on Prentis Street. She was there on the sidewalk with a cigarette. He watched her breathe out a stream of smoke.

Jack left the apartment and descended two flights of stairs. The door to the street creaked on its hinges when he went out, and Olivia spun around, startled. She saw him, hid the cigarette behind her back, and laughed.

Jack would like to believe he laughed too, but that's not the way he remembers it. The smoking bothered him more than he wanted to admit. He kept their bargain, though. He pretended not to notice when she dropped the cigarette and crushed it beneath her shoe.

"Where are we living?" he said.

It was an in-joke between them, a bit of code, a question Jack asked Olivia when she did something he considered unwise. When she didn't lock her car, when she left her purse unattended in a shop or a restaurant.

She smiled and rolled her eyes at him. "I know where we're living, Detective Pellum."

"We're living in Detroit," he said, "and it's late. Too late to be out alone on the street."

"I'm not alone," she said, nodding over

her shoulder toward the corner. A few people stood there talking, hands stuffed in pockets. Patrons from the Bronx Bar on Second Avenue.

"It's cold," Jack said, because he was beginning to feel it. He didn't have a coat. Olivia didn't either.

She said, "Which is it, Detective Pellum? Too cold or too late?"

She was trying to be playful. Jack didn't answer her. He was watching the people on the corner. One of them stood apart from the others. A man in a peacoat and a fedora. Medium height, medium build. He was staring at Olivia and Jack. Jack could feel the stare like a touch.

Olivia tugged his sleeve, put her arms around him. "You're right," she said. "It's cold. Warm me up."

The man in the peacoat turned away abruptly and slipped through the bar crowd. He disappeared around the corner.

Jack decided to follow him. Even now he's not sure why.

He eased Olivia away from him. Said, "Go inside. I'll be up in a minute."

"What's wrong?" she said. "Where are you going?"

He headed for the corner.

"Jack!"

He turned back. "Go inside. Please."

She scowled and shook her head in frustration and went in. Jack passed through the bar people and rounded the corner. The man in the peacoat had crossed to the other side of Second Avenue; he was walking south at a brisk pace.

Jack called out to him, "Hey! Hold on. I want to talk to you."

The man in the peacoat sped up, didn't look back. Jack jogged across Second. "Hey!" The man turned the corner onto Canfield Street and Jack lost sight of him again.

There's a block on Canfield that belongs to another time. The houses were built in the late eighteen hundreds, with a lot of carved wood and elaborate stonework. They represent a fine sampling of architectural styles — Queen Anne, Second Empire, Gothic Revival — most of them lovingly restored. Even the street recalls an older era; it's paved with cobblestones.

When Jack turned the corner, the man in the peacoat was nowhere to be seen. No footsteps echoed on the cobblestones. Jack walked along in the light of the streetlamps, listening, checking parked cars, trying to peer between the houses. He covered the whole block. There were people living in most of the houses, some of them had porch lights on, but the last house on the south side of the street looked deserted. It had wide stone steps in front that led up to two doors. The bricks of the building's façade were dark and stained and beautiful. Jack thought the man in the peacoat might have gone inside, but all the windows were intact and the doors were secured with heavy padlocks.

Jack stood on the steps in the night, a visitor to a haunted mansion. He waited there, thinking the man might come back. But he was gone.

That was the only time Jack ever saw him. Later on, when he needed to remember him, he couldn't. The things he remembered best were inessential: the man's coat, his hat.

Jack knows now that he should have searched for the man longer. He might have found him. But it was only a feeling that made him follow him in the first place. He didn't know. He had no real reason to believe the man was important.

That was a Saturday night in October, the year before last.

Three days later, Olivia was murdered.

Jack still lives in the place he shared with

her, the apartment on Prentis Street. He has given away some of her things, mostly clothes and shoes. Like Daniel Cavanaugh did. Other things he's kept. He has a papier-mâché mask of her face, an art project she made in college. He has souvenirs from her travels: a necklace from Nepal, vintage postcards from a shop in Vienna.

He has her photographs. They cover the walls, some framed, some not. He has pictures of trees and sky and every place they ever visited. He has portraits she made of musicians who played at venues in the city, or at the Palace of Auburn Hills. He has pictures of auto shows, museum events, restaurant openings, street festivals.

He has ads she shot for businesses in Detroit. He has one for a start-up called Motor City Keys, a company that makes pianos and ships them to China, because it turns out the Chinese can't get enough pianos. It's one of his favorites, a study in black-and-white — a luminous row of piano keys and a pair of hands playing them. There's a ring on one finger of the left hand, a signet ring that shows two knights — like the chess pieces — facing each other, one black, one white.

That ad appeared in papers all over the state. It even ran once on the back cover of

And he has pictures of Olivia, ones that he took himself. He has her in Hart Plaza near the riverfront, standing beside the statue of Antoine de la Mothe Cadillac, the explorer who founded Detroit. He has her at a courtyard café in Paris. He has her lying across their bed on a Sunday morning, one arm dangling, her chin on her pillow, staring into the lens.

He has the coffee mug she drank from every day, and a pack of Virginia Slims she bought and never opened, and a silver lighter inscribed with her full name, *Olivia Makinnen.* On Thursday at eight in the evening all three of these things were sitting on the low table in his living room. The mug was half full of lukewarm tea. Jack was lying on the couch, reading a copy of Daniel Cavanaugh's book.

You could call it a thriller, or a horror novel, or you could call it a slasher film transcribed on paper. There was a fortune-teller in it, and a nerdy paranormal expert who had visions, and a spooky kid who might have been the reincarnated spirit of a G-man from the nineteen twenties, and all of them came together to track down the killer in the crooked hat. The setting was a small town in Michigan referred to as

Harmony. Jack was pretty sure it didn't exist.

He had started reading the book in the hope that it might reveal something useful about the man who killed Olivia. But if there was any truth in it, then reality was a far stranger enterprise than he had previously thought. The killer in the hat was a kind of supernatural being who abducted his victims and took them to a run-down clapboard house that was bigger on the inside than it was on the outside. He kept them there in a hidden room for days until they lost hope, then released them and stalked them through the house's endless, twisted hallways before finally doing them in.

Around twenty after eight Jack folded down the corner of a page and closed the book. He got up and stretched and took Olivia's mug to the kitchen. Poured the tea down the sink. When he returned to the living room, he heard a ping from his cell phone that meant he had a new text message. He fished the phone from his pocket and pressed the home button. The message came from a number he didn't recognize. It was brief, only four words:

I've seen him too.

6.

When Jack saw the message, no chill ran down his spine, no hairs stood up on the back of his neck. He'd had false alarms before, in earlier days when he put his phone number on his flyers. He'd heard from pranksters, scammers, bored people trying to entertain themselves.

He dropped down onto the sofa and typed a message back.

Who is this?

A few seconds passed.

My name's Paul Rook. You left your card for me.

And who are we talking about? Who have you seen?

You know. Him. The dude in the lid. The

cat in the hat.

What's his name?

I don't know his name, Jack. No one knows his name.

What are you after?

You wanted me to get in touch. This is me getting in touch.

Do you want money?

What makes you think this is about money?

Then what do you want?

I want to know if you're serious. I want to know if you realize what you're up against.

What am I up against?

Something deadly. And you're trying to provoke him. You can't hang his picture everywhere and expect he won't notice.

Jack read the last message twice and thought about the implications. He hadn't put up any flyers in Corktown. They were all in midtown, in his own neighborhood. Which led him to believe that Paul Rook had come looking for him. It would have been easy. He had Jack's name. The only thing he would have needed was an Internet connection.

Still there?

Jack tapped out a quick reply:

Still here.

Then he added:

I'm not afraid of provoking him. He killed my wife.

He waited for a response from Paul Rook, thinking he might have lost him. Then:

She's not the only one.

Who else?

Another delay, as if Paul was thinking something over.

Too many to list in a text. Do you want to talk?

When? Where?

Depends on how cautious you are. We could meet tomorrow afternoon at the Scarab Club. That's a safe, public place.

The Scarab Club was a few blocks from Jack's apartment, on Farnsworth Street behind the DIA.

What if I'm not cautious?

We could meet now. I'm right outside.

Jack went to the window and saw Paul Rook across the street, leaning against the fender of a rusted white Chevrolet. The guy in the hat from the day before. He looked up at Jack and waved.

Paul Rook was twenty-six years old. He didn't live in Corktown but he had been a friend of Danny Cavanaugh. He had a small apartment downriver in Lincoln Park, three hundred square feet, and he made his money from a collection of part-time jobs: working the cash register at a dollar store, delivering pizzas, driving for Uber.

All this Jack learned eventually. First Paul wanted to talk about the man in the hat. He came into the apartment and dropped a heavy-looking messenger bag by the door. Jack offered him a seat, and a drink, but he didn't want either. He drifted around the room, looking at the photos on the walls as he told his tale.

"The end of my junior year in high school, that's when I saw him," Paul said. "Nine years ago. We lived in Dearborn. My father was kind of a sketchy character. *His* dad had worked a good job on the line of the River Rouge plant, but the best my father could do was a gig as a cashier at an auto parts store. Plus he drank, so if business got slow at the store, he'd be the first to get his hours cut back.

"My mom stayed home when my sister and me were young, but when we got older she started taking part-time jobs, mostly child care. All through my junior year, she worked for a woman who lived a few blocks from my high school. She had a toddler, and my mom would go to her house three or four days a week to look after the kid, and I would visit sometimes after school. The kid would be in his playpen or down for a nap, and me and my mom would watch reruns of *Law & Order.*

"The people who lived on that street had detached garages, and you would get to them from an alley that ran behind the houses. When I walked from school to visit my mom, I went through that alley and cut between two garages along a flagstone walk that led through the backyard to the house. That's where I saw him. We passed each other on the flagstones. It was a sunny day, and I remember he had a printed shirt on — a Hawaiian shirt — and linen pants and dark sunglasses. And his hat. I'd never seen him there before, but he acted like he belonged. He could have been a neighbor. I never gave him a second thought. Until later.

"On Friday, two days after I saw him, my mom finished work around ten p.m. She always worked late on Fridays. She walked through the backyard to the alley, where she'd left her car. She had to park there. You couldn't park in front on the street. That's where they found her body, lying between her car and a line of trees that grew behind the alley. He knocked her down and hit her in the head with a hammer. He took her purse and left her there. The police never found him."

Paul turned to Jack for his reaction. His face was even leaner than Jack remembered, and he carried acne scars on his cheeks.

"You don't know that he did it," Jack said.

Paul closed his eyes, disappointed. "Here we go."

"You saw someone in sunglasses and a hat," Jack said, "and then your mother got killed, and you connected the two events because they happened close together."

"You think I haven't heard this before?"

"You took him for a neighbor when you saw him. Maybe that's all he was."

Paul Rook opened his eyes. His voice was calm, but Jack could sense an edge in him, a coiled energy he was holding in check.

"When I found the card you left, I looked you up," Paul said. "I read about your wife. All the news reports I could find. And other things. Websites. There's a whole network online, people with time on their hands and a fascination with unsolved murders. You can find things you shouldn't be able to find. Bits and pieces, sometimes whole case files. And in everything I read, there's no mention of the man in the hat."

"That doesn't mean anything —"

"No mention," Paul said, "because I'm guessing he's just someone you saw around the time your wife died, and you put the two events together."

Jack waved at the air, brushing his point away. "The police know about him, believe me. Sometimes they withhold things from reporters, they leave things out of the file."

Paul smiled, but there was a sadness in his eyes. "I told the police about the man I saw too. They reacted the same way you did. He could have been a neighbor or someone visiting a neighbor. The cop I talked to was nice about it. 'I can't go looking for a fella in a Hawaiian shirt and sunglasses. I need more.' But I couldn't give him any more. I saw the man once. That's how he is. When you see him, you don't pay attention to him, and later on you wish you did. The dude's elusive. He doesn't get caught."

Jack touched a photograph of Olivia on the wall.

"Suppose you're right," he said. "The man you saw is the one who killed your mother. That was nine years ago. What are the chances that the same man killed my wife?"

"It's him," Paul said.

"What's the connection? What's his motive?"

"He kills people. He doesn't have motives."

"That's not the way it works," Jack said. "If he was a serial killer, there would be commonalities. How old was your mother when she died?"

A pause. "Fifty-two, I think."

"My wife was thirty-one. That's a big difference. Your mother was bludgeoned, my wife was strangled. Another difference. If the same man killed them, you would expect to find a thread connecting them."

Paul shook his head impatiently. He picked up his messenger bag from the floor and laid it on the sofa.

"I know all this," he said. "I used to think this way. I thought about motives. At first I told myself my mother was killed for the money in her purse. But if he wanted to rob her, she wouldn't have resisted. I told myself there'd be a pattern, maybe I could find other women killed in the same way, with the same kind of weapon. Maybe I could make sense of it."

He opened the bag and took out a bundle of files — manila folders held together with rubber bands — and set them on the coffee table.

"But that's wrong," he said. "There's no thread. You don't get anywhere looking for threads. But if you look for *him,* if you're patient, you can find him. People see him. He's there, on the edges of things. He plans, he watches. That's when you have a chance to get a glimpse of him. I've looked at cases, unsolved murders, all around southeast Michigan, and I've found sightings of him. Some of them go back years. The earliest one I've found was twenty years ago. It happened about thirty miles from here, in a town called Belleville. I think the man in the hat got his start there. The victim was a high school student, a seventeen-year-old boy."

Paul stood over the files. Tense. Waiting. Jack asked him the obvious question, the one he was waiting for.

"What was the victim's name?"

"Alex Cavanaugh," Paul said. "He was Danny Cavanaugh's brother."

7.

The city of Belleville tends to crowd around the edges of Belleville Lake. All the best houses have a view of the water. The Cavanaugh house on Hull Road was bone-dry, a mile or two from the shore.

Jack found it on Friday afternoon around five o'clock. It was the second Cavanaugh house he tried, after the lady at the first one set him straight.

"Danny Cavanaugh never lived here," she told him. "You want Ed Cavanaugh, his dad. Ed's my husband's second cousin, though between you and me I don't see much resemblance, thank the lord. I think you'll find him at home, though I don't know what mood he'll be in. Good luck with him."

Jack left his car in Ed Cavanaugh's gravel drive and climbed the steps of his white-washed porch. There was an old brass knocker mounted on the front door, but when Jack used it no one answered, so he swung around to the back and tapped on the screen door. He could see into the kitchen. No one there.

The garage out back stood open, with a Dodge pickup parked inside. Jack took it to mean someone was home. He wandered across the yard and found a dirt path that led through a gap in a low wall made of piled fieldstones. The path took him to a copse of trees that grew alongside a dry creek bed. There was a picnic table on a stretch of grass and a small cooler on the table. Jack lifted the cover off. Ice and beer inside.

As he replaced the cover he heard a gun-shot.

He reached automatically for the pistol he'd once carried on his belt, and when he didn't find it he put his hands up slowly and looked around. The echo of the shot faded and he heard a voice from above.

"I wasn't aiming at you, jackass."

An empty beer bottle landed at his feet.

Jack looked up and saw the shooter through the branches of an oak, a patch of orange climbing down from a deer blind.

"Twelve-point buck," the man said. "I had him in my scope. Wanted to get it just right. Then you blunder in and I have to rush the shot. Missed him clean. Son of a bitch."

The shooter reached the ground. Orange vest and camouflage and heavy boots, a rifle slung over his shoulder. He laid the rifle on the picnic table and took a fresh beer from the cooler.

"You can lower your hands, boyo. You're not under arrest."

Jack lowered them. The shooter twisted the cap from his bottle and took a long pull.

"I'm sorry I startled you," Jack said.

He watched the shooter swing a leg over the bench of the picnic table and sit.

"You didn't startle me," the man said. "You startled the deer." He had a stubble of gray hair on his head, and a long, weathered face. His voice was raspy.

Jack gave the man his name and said, "I'm looking for Ed Cavanaugh."

"You found him."

"I'd like to speak to you about your son, if I could."

Cavanaugh took another drink and squinted at Jack across the table.

"My son's dead. He put a rope around his neck. We buried him in the ground, day before yesterday. If you're here for that, you're too late."

"Sorry. I didn't mean Danny. I meant your other son, Alex."

"Well, then you're way too late. He died years and years ago. That's not a story I'm inclined to tell. What's your interest?"

Jack thought about how much to reveal, how much Cavanaugh needed to know.

"I'm looking into a case, a woman murdered about a year and a half ago." *A woman, not my wife.* "Her name was Olivia Makinnen. The case might be related to your son's death. Or it might not. I need to find out."

Cavanaugh had another go at his bottle. Jack tried to decide if he was drunk. He'd done all right climbing down the tree.

"You got a badge, Mr. Pellum?" Cavanaugh said.

Jack shook his head. "I used to be a detective in Detroit. I'm working private now."

"I used to be a patrolman with the Belleville P.D.," Cavanaugh said. "They made me retire. They make you retire?"

"I quit. For personal reasons."

"You think that gets you something, telling me you were on the job once?"

"I'm not counting on it," Jack said. "You'll talk to me or you won't."

"My Danny lived in Detroit. Did you know him?"

"I never met him. I've read his book."

"What did you think?"

"I liked it."

"That's the polite answer. What did you really think?"

"It was kind of wild. Outlandish."

Cavanaugh chuckled. "That's a good word. Danny liked tall tales. I used to tell him campfire stories. The weirder the better. He told me that book did all right. He thought he could do better. But he never wrote another one, because of his wife getting sick. It wrecked him, I think." Cavanaugh had frown lines around his mouth. They deepened. "When I was a boy, the priests told us killing yourself was a sin. The sin of despair. What do you think about that?"

"I think if it's a sin, it's a forgivable one," Jack said.

"You ever been tempted?"

"Yes."

"Me too. But we held on, didn't we?" Cavanaugh looked up into the branches of the oak, then at Jack again. "Sit down, boyo," he said. "Do you need an invitation? What do you want from me?"

Jack sat and took a photograph from his shirt pocket. "This is Olivia Makinnen. I'm wondering if you recognize her."

The photo was one he had taken himself, on a summer trip: Olivia standing at the end of a dock on Lake Michigan.

76

Cavanaugh shook his head. "She doesn't look familiar."

Jack showed him another photo, a shot of Olivia from one of her high school yearbooks.

"Are you sure?" he said. "Maybe your sons knew her when they were young."

Cavanaugh shook his head again. "Did she grow up around here?"

"She grew up in Virginia."

"Then why would you think —"

"I don't, but it's the obvious question to ask." Jack put the photos back in his pocket. "I'd like to show you something else. I'm wondering if you ever saw a stranger hanging around, in the days before your son Alex died." He took out one of his flyers and unfolded it on the table in a patch of sunlight. "He might have looked something like this. He would have been younger, though, back then."

Cavanaugh picked up the flyer and laughed, a coarse laugh that turned into a cough.

"That's the boogeyman," he said when he recovered. "Is that what you came here to ask me? If I ever saw the boogeyman?"

"This isn't a joke —"

Cavanaugh wiped his mouth on his sleeve. "No, it's not," he said. "I've seen a picture like this before. A little cruder, maybe. Danny drew it when he was thirteen years old. He said he saw him, a man in a hat, the day his brother died."

The last part Jack knew. He'd heard it from Paul Rook.

"I didn't know he drew him," Jack said. "Do you still have that picture?"

"No, and it wouldn't do you any good. Danny wasn't much of an artist."

"Are you sure you don't have it?"

Cavanaugh returned the flyer to the table. "I'm sure. Danny got rid of his drawings a long time ago. He was a kid whose brother died, and then he grew up and put that away. He took the man in the hat and wrote him into a book. Maybe it helped him deal with losing Alex. Who knows? But it's history."

"You're certain you never saw anyone like this back then?" Jack said. "Forget about the hat. He may not have been wearing it. Maybe you saw him though. Someone lingering. Someone out of place. Or if you didn't see him back then, maybe you've seen him more recently. A stranger watching you, for no good reason."

Cavanaugh tilted his head, confused. "Recently? You think he'd come back? Why?"

"I don't know," Jack said with a shrug. "Maybe to check on you. I don't know what his motives are."

Cavanaugh turned his bottle in a circle. He ran a thumbnail over the rough surface of the table. "Look," he said, "I never saw any stranger lurking around back then. And no one's been watching me. I don't know what else to tell you."

Jack could see he was losing him. He folded his flyer and tucked it away.

"All right," he said. "But I'd still like to talk if you have the time. About Alex. What sort of person he was. Anything that happened back then. Whatever you can recall."

Cavanaugh stood up and polished off his beer. Jack stood with him.

"I can't help you," the older man said.

"I know it might be hard to remember. It's been twenty years —"

Jack saw a warning in Cavanaugh's eyes. The man placed his bottle on the table, the movement smooth and measured. If he'd been drunk before, he was sober now.

"It's not that I don't remember," Cavanaugh said. "My son was murdered before he could graduate high school. He never got a chance to live his life. I remember him. I remember all the things that happened around the time he died. There's not a day goes by that I don't think of him. But I don't want to talk about him. I don't talk about him with people I know, so why would I talk to you?"

By the time Jack walked back to his car, a film of gray clouds had covered up the sun. The green of the lawn had turned dull. He looked at the Cavanaugh house — two stories of shambling white clapboard — and wanted to go inside. He wanted to see where Danny Cavanaugh and his brother had lived. He imagined Alex Cavanaugh's room, preserved the way he'd left it, waiting for him to come and find a clue to the identity of the boy's killer. But that was probably wishful thinking. Jack could have tried to go in through the screen door at the back, but before he could decide, a dark blue sedan pulled in to the gravel drive and parked beside his car.

The sedan had the look of an unmarked police cruiser, and the woman who got out wore a badge on a lanyard around her neck. Her clothes said detective: pale blouse, dark blazer and slacks. She had the face of a heroine out of an Irish fairy tale: smooth skin, a wide mouth, a faint scattering of freckles across the nose. Wavy brown hair held in check with clips and pins. When she got close, Jack could see that her eyes were green and her badge said CHIEF OF POLICE.

"What's your name?" she asked him. Halfway between an official inquiry and a friendly one.

"Jack Pellum," he said.

"Are you a friend of Ed's?"

"No, but I just came from talking to him."

"Did you do something to anger him?"

"I don't think so."

"A neighbor called in to report a gunshot. But I guess he didn't shoot you. You look to be intact."

"I am."

"Did you shoot him?"

"No."

"You can tell me if you did. I might even be sympathetic. There've been times I wanted to do it myself."

She said it casually, with nothing but a hint of a wry tone in her voice to let him know she was joking.

"I'm not armed," Jack said, trying to match her tone. "He was up in a tree with a rifle. Said he fired at a deer, a twelve-point buck."

She laughed. A pleasant, rolling laugh. "I doubt it. Did you see this twelve-point buck?"

"No. He said he missed."

81

"He better have. He knows very well it's not hunting season." She looked across the yard at the distant trees. "Is he still back there?"

"That's where I left him."

She sighed and brushed at a lock of hair that had gotten loose from a clip. Jack thought she would go looking for Cavanaugh, but she turned back to him.

"What were you talking to him about?"

Jack leaned against his car. "I had some questions about his son."

"That's a delicate subject," she said. "His son just died."

"Not Danny. The other one."

"That's delicate too. Did you get any answers?"

"Not really."

She looked down at the gravel and up at Jack again. Decided he was unimportant.

"I need to have a word with Ed. You can go."

Jack said nothing. She nodded a good-bye and headed across the lawn, moving with a relaxed authority.

After a moment, he called to her. "Could I talk to you sometime about Danny and Alex? Did you know them?"

He thought he saw the slightest hitch in

her stride, then she paused and looked back. "I didn't know them," she said.

8.

Jack drove east from the Cavanaugh house and followed Hull Road for half a mile until it came to an end. From there he headed south, then switched back to the west until he arrived at an empty lot with a large white stone in the front and a wooden post that might once have held a mailbox.

He got out and felt the wind and heard the calls of finches from somewhere in the trees along the edges of the property. He shut the car door quietly, trying not to disturb them. There had been a house here once. Jack could see some stones in the overgrown grass that would have been part of the foundation.

He had photographs of the place from Paul Rook's files. They showed a clapboard house a lot like the Cavanaughs', but this one had graffiti painted along the side, and broken windows, and shutters hanging at odd angles.

This was where Alex Cavanaugh died.

Jack waded through the tall grass and found what was left of a wooden fence at the back of the lot. He climbed over and the ground sloped downward and there was a tangle of brush and a pair of apple trees. The ground between the trees had been tended: someone had come back here with a rake and a weed trimmer. There were flowers planted inside a rough circle of stones, bluebells and violets and morning glories that snaked their way up a small wooden trellis. Jack found words carved into the trunk of one of the trees: ALEX WE LOVE YOU.

He stayed there for a few minutes, listening to the birdsong and feeling the calm of the place. He didn't know if it served any purpose. Alex Cavanaugh wasn't there. If some trace of the boy's spirit remained, it didn't speak to him.

Jack walked back to his car and sat with the engine off and the windows rolled down. He had papers from Paul Rook's files on the seat beside him. He'd spoken with Paul for hours the night before, and Paul had told him about more than a dozen murders — each one with a witness who claimed to have seen a man in a hat. The sightings took place at different times, sometimes on the day of the murder, sometimes in the days before. Never at the scene of the crime. In a few instances there were drawings, composites based on the descriptions provided by witnesses. The men in the drawings resembled each other vaguely, or not at all. The hats were usually fedoras, but in one case the man in the hat wore a ball cap.

Paul and Jack had lined up the drawings on the floor of Jack's apartment and stood over them.

"You're seeing what I'm seeing, right?" Jack said.

"What?" said Paul.

"Someone could look at these and say they're not the same person."

Jack could almost feel Paul tense beside him.

"You don't have to believe me," Paul said.

"I'm not saying I don't believe you."

"Eyewitnesses are never perfect."

"That's just another reason to doubt that these are the same man."

"He's real."

"I'm not saying he's not real."

They went round and round. Paul kept coming back to the Alex Cavanaugh case. It was the earliest one he'd found, and he thought it must be the key to everything.

Paul had discovered it by accident, after

reading Danny Cavanaugh's novel. He connected the villain — the man in the crooked hat — with the man he'd seen before his mother died. He became even more convinced after reading an interview Cavanaugh had done in a magazine called *Mystery Scene*, right after the publication of his book. He gave Jack a copy with the important part highlighted.

Tell me about him.
The killer?
The killer. Where did he come from?
I never reveal that in the book. He's a man with no past.
That's not what I meant. How did you come up with him?
I made him up.
Of course.
I'll let you in on a secret. I made up everything in this book.
Sure. But the inspiration must have come from somewhere.
Are you asking me where I get my ideas?
[Laughs] I guess I am.
I don't have a good answer for that.
Lie to me then. Tell me a story.
All right . . . It was summertime. I was thirteen —
That's a start.

— riding my bike through the neighborhood and I saw a man whose car had broken down.

That's it?

He had a flat tire and was changing it. I stopped to watch. I remember him taking off his hat and wiping his brow. When he put it back on, it was crooked — one side lower than the other. I remember watching him struggle with the tire iron. And one of the lug nuts got away from him. It rolled along the street and would have gone in a storm drain, but I caught it and gave it back to him.

And then?

I think he thanked me and I got back on my bike.

And that's where you got your killer?

No, that's just a story. You wanted a story.

I wanted to know where your killer came from.

I told you. I invented him. I made him up.

Jack was skeptical, but Paul had insisted the story was real. "It's the first thing I asked Danny about, when I tracked him down and convinced him to talk to me. He didn't make it up for the interview. It happened — the day his brother died."

As far as Jack could discover, Danny Cavanaugh had never discussed his brother's death in print. But he had talked to Paul, and Paul had written everything down. Jack had copies of his notes.

It happened in August, a few weeks before what would have been Alex Cavanaugh's senior year in high school. Danny and Alex had bedrooms next to each other on the second floor of their house. Alex had a habit of slipping out at night — something Danny had recently discovered. He'd been awake and restless one morning at four a.m., had looked out his window and seen his brother crossing the moonlit lawn, coming back from wherever he'd been.

Danny knew better than to ask Alex about it. He could guess what the answer would be: *None of your business, you little punk. And you better not tell Mom and Dad.*

On the night of August tenth, Danny made a plan to follow Alex and find out where he went. He lay awake for hours in his clothes under the covers, listening for his brother's footsteps in the hallway. He finally drifted off to sleep a little after two a.m.

Sometime after that, Alex Cavanaugh

crept through the hallway and down the stairs. He might have left through the back door in the kitchen, but he would have risked being heard by his parents, whose bedroom was directly above. More likely he left through the door at the front of the house.

Either way, he crossed the backyard and passed through the gap in the stone wall. He walked through the woods and over a field and wound up at a house with graffitied walls and broken windows. The house had belonged to a family named Sturridge until they abandoned it. It had stood empty for three years.

Alex brought his camera with him, a Pentax K1000, a camera that would be considered old-fashioned today, since it used actual film. He had taken a class in photography in the spring, and had learned to print black-and-white photos in a darkroom.

He had a tripod, and he set it up on the lawn of the Sturridge house and focused in on some of the broken windows. He took several shots using long exposures in the moonlight. They came out brilliantly when the police had the film developed later on.

At some point that night, someone struck Alex Cavanaugh on the side of the head with a blunt object, possibly a broom handle or a metal pipe. This initial blow was followed by several more, delivered to the back of Alex's skull while he lay on the ground. The weapon was never recovered.

In the morning Danny Cavanaugh woke to his mother shaking him, asking him if he knew where his brother had gone. The next two days saw a stream of visitors to the house: friends of his father's from the police department. His father sat him down and spoke to him very seriously. *We can't have secrets, Danny. This is too important. You're not going to get Alex in trouble, but you have to answer me: Did he have a girlfriend we didn't know about? Did he ever talk about running away?* Danny had nothing useful to tell him.

On the evening of the twelfth, Danny heard his parents talking in their bedroom. His father told his mother that they'd had a lead from one of Alex's friends, a kid named Bobby Wilson. Bobby admitted that he and Alex would occasionally meet up at night at the Sturridge house, to talk and drink, sometimes to smoke a joint. Danny's father had just come from the house. He confessed to his wife that he'd gone there fearing the worst: he thought he'd find Alex dead. But there'd been nothing but some beer cans and cigarette butts and girlie magazines. So there was still hope.

The next morning a pair of detectives from the department went back and made a more thorough search of the property. They found Alex out behind the ruined fence between the two apple trees. He was lying facedown, with his camera and tripod beside him.

Jack sat in his car and watched a blue jay hop through the grass beside the remnants of the foundation of the Sturridge house, and it occurred to him that it might be useful to talk to a friend of Alex Cavanaugh's. He ran a search on his phone for a Robert Wilson and there weren't any in Belleville, but there were too many to sort through in the surrounding towns and cities. So he tried again, searching for "Wilson" and "Belleville" and found something promising about a mile away from him on Bemis Road.

He started the engine and drove west, scanning the road ahead. He saw an antique shop first, and then an old silo and a barn and a sign for Wilson Stables. He turned in on a long, unpaved drive that led up to a sprawling farmhouse. In a paddock near the barn, a girl of about thirteen walked a brown Arabian in circles. Jack strolled over and put a foot up on the low rail of the fence. The girl and the horse stopped about twenty feet away, eyeing him with a measure of suspicion.

He waved. "Do you know Bobby Wilson?"

"He's my uncle," the girl called back.

"He isn't here, is he?"

She shook her head and pointed toward the house. "You can talk to my mom."

Jack nodded thanks and headed for the house, but before he got there a lanky black-haired woman came out the front door and down the steps of the porch. She was dressed to ride, definitely in the Western style, not the English. Lots of denim, red bandanna tied around her neck.

"You don't look like a horseman," she said.

"No?"

"I have a sense for these things." She extended a hand and Jack introduced himself. She was Regina Wilson, Bobby's sister, and when he asked her if he could speak to her about her brother and Alex Cavanaugh, she invited him onto the porch and offered him a chair.

"Bobby is what you'd call the black sheep of the family," she told him. "He got out of this town as soon as he could. My parents made him apply to colleges and he got into Michigan State. They dropped him off at the campus in the fall and as soon as they left he hopped on a Greyhound bus. Ended up in Texas, working on an oil rig. He got married down there, had a kid, got divorced. Lived in New Orleans for a while, tending bar. Spent some time on a fishing boat in Florida. I couldn't tell you where he is now."

"When's the last time you saw him?" Jack asked.

"A few years ago our father passed away," she said. "Bobby showed up for the funeral. He was driving an RV, one of those big Winnebagos. I guess that's what he does now: he keeps moving. He stayed for two days and then took off, like he was scared of sticking around here. I know what it is: he's afraid he'll get roped into this place. As if I'd want him. He never liked working here, even as a kid. Didn't like the smell. Thought it was all beneath him, shoveling horseshit. He took a dishwashing job downtown instead."

A wistful look in her eyes as she spoke. She missed her brother, even if she didn't approve of him.

"What about Alex Cavanaugh?" Jack said. "Did he come around here?"

She smiled. "Sure. He hit on me once, but I was a year older. I was dating a college boy."

"But Alex and Bobby were close."

"They were thick as thieves, starting in middle school. My parents thought Alex was a bad influence."

"What did you think?"

"I thought Bobby was bad enough on his own, but the two of them definitely encouraged each other. It started with little things. My mom had chronic pain in her back and she would get Tylenol with codeine from Canada. Bobby and Alex would steal those pills and take them and think they were getting high. Then they graduated to boosting bottles from my dad's liquor cabinet, and you can imagine where it went from there."

"Help me imagine," Jack said.

There was a rusted milk can on the porch. Regina Wilson rested a booted foot on the lid. "The usual teenage boy stuff," she said. "Vandalism. Knocking over gravestones at the cemetery. Throwing eggs at houses on Halloween. And then some shoplifting. Bobby had a collection of CDs that I know he never paid for."

"And Alex wasn't worried about breaking the law? His father was a police officer."

She laughed. "That would work in his favor, wouldn't it? If he got caught he'd probably be let off easy."

"What about sneaking out at night?" Jack

asked her. "I understand Bobby and Alex would meet up at the Sturridge house."

"A lot of kids went to the Sturridge house. I used to go there with my friends. We'd light candles and drink beer and try to scare each other with stories about Scotty Sturridge and how he went crazy and shot his little sister in the head in one of the bedrooms upstairs."

"Is that true?"

"It sounded true if you told it right. Sometimes he cut her throat and collected her blood in mason jars. We were teenagers making stuff up. I don't think there ever was a Scotty Sturridge. Nothing tragic happened in that house, just the boring kind of tragedy that happens all the time. The Sturridges were poor people who couldn't afford to pay their mortgage. They got foreclosed and moved away and the bank couldn't get anyone to buy their crappy house. So it sat there empty and high school kids found it and tried to make it exciting. But the appeal wore off pretty fast. Put a bunch of drunken teenagers in a house they're not responsible for and pretty soon they're knocking holes in the walls and throwing up on the floor and peeing in a toilet that can't be flushed because there's no running water. It stopped being cool.

People stopped going."

"But Bobby and Alex still went there."

"Once in a while. Not very much at the end."

Jack watched a caterpillar crawl up the side of the milk can.

"What was it like when Alex died?"

"People got scared, like you'd expect," Regina said. "My dad put Bobby on a short leash, wouldn't let him go anywhere except school or his job. Started looking in on him in the middle of the night — no more sneaking out. Not that he would have. Bobby wasn't the same. He kept to himself, that year after Alex died. I think he was marking time until he could finish high school and leave home."

She tipped her head back, remembering. "Everything was different that year. Everybody kept a closer eye on their kids. The cops boarded up the doors and windows of the Sturridge house, and no one with any sense went there anymore. But once in a while some asshole would break in just for the thrill, and then somebody started a fire, and eventually the bank paid to have it torn down. People wanted that to be the end of it, but it wasn't the end. They were still scared, and they were angry too, because nothing had changed. Alex Cavanaugh was still dead and nobody knew who did it or why."

"Have you thought about that — who killed him?"

She brought her boot down off the milk can and faced Jack squarely. "I don't have a clue, and anything I could tell you would be on a par with those stories we invented about Scotty Sturridge. There were plenty of rumors flying around at the time."

"Do you remember any of them?" he asked her.

A little pause, and then: "I can think of two. The first was that Alex had been killed by a convict, someone his father had sent away to prison. Which was silly, because Ed Cavanaugh was never more than a traffic cop. He spent his time writing speeding tickets."

"What was the second?"

A rueful smile. "Some people thought it was a serial killer. *Silence of the Lambs* and all that. 'Alex was a bad boy, so I ate his liver with some fava beans and a nice Chianti.' Which was slightly more plausible, because of the other one."

Jack didn't follow her at first. "The other one?"

"The other boy," she said. "I don't remember his name. He was killed about a month

after Alex, six or seven miles from here, over
in New Boston. You didn't know about
him?"

9.

Jack checked his phone when he left Wilson Stables and found a message from his father:

Your mother and I are dining at eight this evening at Giovanni's. You could join us.

Jack thought about his reply on the short drive north to Main Street and typed it after he'd found a parking space:

Thanks but I can't make it. I'm having dinner in Belleville tonight.

He walked along Main, considering his options. A place called the Bayou Grill caught his eye; it served Cajun food and had a model of a giant alligator on the roof. But the hostess told him he'd have to wait thirty minutes, so he went with Tanager's Pub two doors down.

Tanager's had only a ten-minute wait. Jack

spent the time at the bar. He ordered a Coke from a bartender with sleeves of tattoos on his arms: dragons and knights, a whole mythology. He thought about Bobby Wilson, wondered where the man might be tonight. Maybe in a place like this. Jack had no way to contact him, not even a cell phone number. "The last number I had for him got disconnected," Regina Wilson had told him. "But if he calls me, I'll let you know."

Jack looked around the restaurant. It had a lively crowd and flat screens mounted high on the walls tuned to a baseball game, and in one corner a white-haired heavyset man strummed a guitar and sang covers of songs from the seventies. He did one by Paul Simon and another by James Taylor, and a waitress came and led Jack to a booth and he ordered the fish and chips and a salad. The food was better than he expected and he took his time with it. He scanned the crowd while he ate, returning to the faces of the middle-aged white men until he realized he was looking for the man in the hat. Sometimes he believed he would recognize him if he saw him, and other times he had his doubts. If the man was there, he didn't reveal himself.

Around the time Jack finished his meal,

Ed Cavanaugh came in and perched himself on a stool at the bar. He wore a gray sweater and the same camouflage pants he'd had on earlier in the day. The tattooed bartender poured him a beer and a shot of Jack Daniel's, and he downed the shot fast and asked for another. The waitress refilled Jack's Coke and brought his check and told him there was no rush. She cleared away his plate and he sipped the Coke and watched Cavanaugh drink. Jack counted two beers and five shots and then the bartender balked at a sixth. Cavanaugh said something Jack couldn't hear, and the bartender nodded along like he'd heard it a million times, and Cavanaugh tipped over his beer glass and the bartender wiped the bar and waved a waitress over and whispered something to her. She went away into the kitchen and Jack got up and dropped some money on the table and moved to the bar, three stools down from Cavanaugh.

The waitress came back with a silver-haired man in his sixties who looked like he belonged in a different restaurant in another city altogether. He had on a tailor-made suit and a silk shirt unbuttoned at the collar and a wristwatch that cost as much as the suit. He waved the bartender back and put a hand on Cavanaugh's shoulder.

"Ed, I don't want to have a problem," he said.

"I don't have a problem," Cavanaugh answered. "Your man here has a problem. He's forgotten how to pour a drink."

"Ed, you know there are limits. There have to be. After a certain point I can't serve you any more."

"I know my limits, Tanager. We're not there yet."

"I think we are. What if I get you a table — you can have some dinner. Maybe some coffee. Then I'll get someone to drive you home."

"I'll go home when I'm ready. My truck's outside."

"That's no good. I wouldn't feel right about letting you drive."

Cavanaugh looked pointedly at his shoulder. "How would you feel with a broken finger?"

The silver-haired man, Tanager, withdrew his hand. He looked around at the crowd. Some of them were watching. The guy with the guitar started in on a Neil Young song.

"Don't be that way, Ed," said Tanager softly. "I don't want to have to call Keely."

Cavanaugh smirked. "Jesus Christ. Keely. Go ahead, call her. Am I supposed to be afraid of her?"

"She won't be alone, Ed," Tanager said with a sigh. "She'll bring help and they'll haul you out of here and you'll embarrass all of us. Let's avoid that. I'll drive you home myself."

Cavanaugh climbed down from his stool and leaned into the other man. "I'd rather walk home than ride with you."

"That's fine," Tanager said, "but you'll need to give me the keys to your truck."

Cavanaugh's eyes glared and he swayed on his feet. Jack watched him roll his shoulders and knew he was thinking about throwing a punch. Jack stood up and walked over and said, "I'd be happy to drive you home, Mr. Cavanaugh."

Cavanaugh turned to him, annoyed by the interruption, but after a moment recognition set in. The older man's glare softened a little.

Tanager frowned in confusion. "Who's this now?"

"I'm a friend of Mr. Cavanaugh," Jack said. "That's all you need to know."

"Well, I suppose —" Tanager began.

Cavanaugh pushed him aside, but not too roughly. "I suppose you can go fuck yourself," he said. "My friend and I are leaving."

Ed Cavanaugh's truck was parked down the

street in front of a pharmacy. Jack got to the driver's door first and held out his hand. Cavanaugh snorted and dug in his pocket and surrendered his keys.

They drove to Hull Road with the windows down, Cavanaugh with his head back in the passenger seat. It was dark, and clouds obscured the stars. When they reached Cavanaugh's house he climbed out and bent over double and threw up on the gravel of the driveway.

When he had recovered, Jack gave him his keys and held the screen door open for him while he unlocked the other. Cavanaugh left the keys on the kitchen table and went through to another room. Jack took his silence as an invitation and decided to stay. He saw a loaf of bread on the counter and opened Cavanaugh's refrigerator and gathered cheese and bologna and butter. In a few minutes he had a sandwich grilling in a skillet on the stove. While he waited for the bread to brown, he took a closer look at Cavanaugh's key chain. There were five things on it: three silver keys that presumably opened the house and the garage, the key to his pickup, and a woman's diamond ring with a gold band.

Jack flipped the sandwich over and filled a glass with water from the tap. He turned off the burner and put the sandwich on a plate and took everything into the next room, including the key chain. Cavanaugh was sprawled in a cushioned armchair with his boots off and his feet up on an ottoman. On an end table beside the chair was a chessboard with the pieces laid out to begin a game. Jack shifted the board aside so he could set down the glass and the plate within Cavanaugh's reach.

The older man eyed them warily, reached for the sandwich, took a bite.

"Could use some mustard," he said.

Jack headed back to the kitchen.

"Not the yellow," Cavanaugh called after him. "The brown spicy kind."

Jack found a jar of deli mustard and a knife and brought them back. He sat on the sofa across from Cavanaugh while the man fixed the sandwich to his liking. On the arm of the sofa was a shoe box full of photographs. Jack thumbed through them while Cavanaugh ate. There were shots of Danny Cavanaugh at his wedding: toothy smile and shaggy hair. He must have grown it out when he left home, because in the pictures of younger Danny he had a crew cut. Here he was at nine or ten, with an older boy who must have been his brother; they stood side by side holding fishing poles. Here he was at his high school commencement, with his arm around a girl who looked familiar. She had brown hair tamed by pins and clips; she'd grown up to be the chief of police. Jack turned the picture over and looked at the back. Someone had written, *Danny and Keely, graduation day.*

"You're a nosy one, aren't you?" Ed Cavanaugh said.

Jack returned the photos to the box and listened to the night wind blowing against the windows while Cavanaugh finished his sandwich. He put Cavanaugh's key chain on the lid of the box. The old man ate the last bite and washed it down with half the glass of water, and the two of them passed a moment in silence until Cavanaugh said, "She died."

Before Jack could ask him what he meant Cavanaugh pointed at the key chain. "My wife," he said. "That's her ring. I bought it for her when I asked her to marry me. You're thinking it's valuable. You think I should be more careful with it. I should lock it away."

"No —"

"A diamond's only a piece of stone," Cavanaugh said. "They're not even that rare, not as rare as the people who sell them would like you to believe. Try selling one secondhand and you'll find out how much they're worth." He looked off at nothing, lost in a memory. "I met my wife when we were in high school. I gave her my class ring after our second date. It was too big for her. She wore it on a chain around her neck until we were married. Then she put it on her key chain. Kept it there all her life. And when she died I started carrying her ring around with me. It's been five years now. She had a heart attack. She was younger than me, took better care of herself. It shouldn't have happened, but she's gone and I'm the one left. Things don't go the way they're supposed to. I know that isn't news to you, even if you try to hide it."

"What have I tried to hide?"

Jack felt Cavanaugh's dark eyes stare into him.

"I looked you up today after you left. That woman who got killed, Olivia Makinnen, she was your wife. You kept that to yourself. When I was a boy in Catholic school, the nuns would have called that a lie of omission."

"I would have told you," Jack said, "but I didn't think it made any difference."

"You didn't want me to think you were a crackpot who couldn't let go of his wife's death. Someone desperate to find a connection between her and my son."

Jack spread his hands, accepting the older man's judgment.

"You're pretty sharp for a drunk," Jack said.

"I'm probably not as drunk as you think."

"The connection's real. It's the man in the hat. Danny saw him. I saw him."

Cavanaugh made a sour face. "We're talking about two murders that happened almost two decades apart. It's not the same man."

"I had my doubts too, at first. But then I heard something that changed my mind."

Jack had heard it from Paul Rook the night before — something that convinced him he needed to learn more about the death of Alex Cavanaugh. Something that had brought him here, to Belleville.

"Danny saw him again," Jack said to Ed Cavanaugh. "Out of the blue one day. Danny walked out his front door to get his newspaper, and the man in the hat was standing on the sidewalk in front of his house, as real as life. When he saw Danny he didn't speak, he just walked away down the block. Danny wanted to follow him but he couldn't. His wife called for him. She was sick from chemotherapy and he had to tend to her. But he remembered, and he told a friend about it, and the friend told me."

Ed Cavanaugh looked away, at the darkness outside the windows.

"Even if it's true, if he saw him, what does it have to do with your wife?"

"It's the timing," Jack said. "Danny saw him in the fall. Not last fall, the one before — right around the time my wife died. It can't be a coincidence. It can't."

"You don't want it to be," Cavanaugh said, fixing his eyes on Jack again. "But we'll let that lie. I don't know what you expect from me. Do you think we're best friends now because you made me a sandwich? Do you think I'm gonna sit here and reminisce with you — I'm gonna talk about Alex, tell you stories, and you'll hear some gem, some detail, the one fact you've been missing, something that'll make everything else fall into place? And even though no one in twenty years has ever been able to say who killed my son, *you'll* be able to say, *you'll* know, because you're so much smarter than everybody else. Is that what you think?"

"No," Jack said. "You already told me you don't want to talk about Alex. I didn't come here for that. But maybe you can help me with something else. I heard today that there was another victim, a boy from New Boston,

110

killed a month after Alex. I could go looking, and it won't be hard to find his name and whatever news stories were published at the time, and I might even be able to find a cop in New Boston willing to talk to me about the case. But if you know about it, you could save me some trouble."

"Why would I know about it?"

"Because you're a cop, and you've had twenty years to think about what happened to your son back then, and if there was a similar case it wouldn't have escaped your notice."

Ed Cavanaugh shook his head and clicked his tongue against his teeth. He eased himself up from his chair and gathered his plate and glass and took them to the kitchen. Jack heard him puttering around in there, running water in the sink, washing up.

Maybe he was thinking things over. Jack let him have some time. He rose from the sofa, drifted through the room. Stopped to look at the chessboard. He picked up the white king, put it down again.

No more sound from the kitchen. Jack turned and saw Cavanaugh leaning in the doorway with his arms crossed. Watching him.

"That was my father's board," Cavanaugh

said. "He loved the game. He taught me to play, but I never took to it the way he wanted me to. I still play now and again, but I don't really have the mind for it. He had better luck with my sons. With Alex especially. Alex loved to play."

Cavanaugh uncrossed his arms and let out a heavy breath. "I never got anywhere, looking into what happened back then," he said. "Maybe you will. But you'll need to do better than you're doing so far. I don't know where you're getting your information, but you haven't got the whole story. There wasn't just one other boy who died. There were two."

10.

Hull Road is peaceful at night. Jack found out for himself.

Ed Cavanaugh showed him the door around eleven thirty. He left Jack with the names of the other two dead boys, Timothy Caslake and Dylan Vernen. Cavanaugh had newspaper clippings and his own rambling handwritten notes, all collected in a black three-ring binder. He let Jack borrow it.

Jack walked west in the dark with the wind at his back. He figured it would be less than two miles to Main Street, where he'd left his car. He set an easy pace, his feet shuffling over the grass at the roadside. Cavanaugh's neighbors were spread out. Once in a while Jack saw a porch-light like a distant star.

After half a mile he thought he glimpsed a deer running through a field south of the road, but it might have been only the wind stirring the tall grass.

He heard the car long before it reached him.

He glanced back and saw the headlights coming on slow. Stopped and stood further out on the shoulder to let it pass. The driver rolled by him and bits of gravel skittered over his shoes. After a few seconds, he saw the flare of brake lights and the driver stopped and made a three-point turn.

She rolled the window down as she came back — the chief of police. Jack walked over to meet her.

"I could write you up," she said.

"I wish you wouldn't."

"You're walking on the wrong side of the road. It's dangerous."

Jack looked east and west, taking in the emptiness. "Obviously."

She nodded toward the passenger seat. "Get in. I'll give you a ride."

He stood with the black binder under his arm. "Is that an order or an invitation?"

Her wide mouth smiled. "Does it matter?"

He went around the front of the car and got in, and she drove east, back toward Ed Cavanaugh's house. Jack looked at her profile in the light of the dash. She looked young, confident, relaxed. They rode along in the quiet, no radio, nothing but the hum of the engine.

"You never introduced yourself to me," Jack said. "You know, before."

"Didn't I?"

"I'd remember if you did."

They passed the Cavanaugh house. It loomed against the cloudy sky.

"I'm Keely Tanager," she said.

"Tanager like the pub?"

"Like the pub."

They bounced over a rut in the road, came to a stop sign. A branch drifted through the intersection like a tumbleweed. Keely turned left.

Jack said, "Can I ask you something, Chief Tanager?"

"Go ahead."

"Why did you lie to me today?"

"I didn't lie to you."

"You told me you didn't know Alex and Danny Cavanaugh," Jack said. "But you went to school with Danny."

"That's not really a lie, is it?"

"It seems like one."

"But it's not really lying if you do it to someone who's not entitled to the truth."

Keely made another left and they drove on for a while in the dark. They crossed some railroad tracks and started to see the lights of downtown.

"I knew Danny Cavanaugh," she said. "I

liked him. I went to his funeral two days ago. When I talked to you earlier, I had no idea who you were. So I didn't feel guilty about lying. Then Ed told me you were a private investigator working on a murder in Detroit and trying to connect it to his son, and I figured you hoped to swindle him somehow, except he hasn't got anything worth taking."

"That's not what I want —"

She lifted a hand from the steering wheel. "No. I've looked a little deeper since then, so I know about your wife, and I'm sorry, I really am. But it leads me to believe you're on some kind of mission. You want to find her killer and maybe take revenge, and I can't see it ending well. So frankly I'd rather have it end somewhere else. Not here."

She slowed and pulled over to the curb in front of Tanager's. The door of the pub opened and two young couples spilled out. Music came with them, not the guitar music from earlier in the night, but something livelier, with a beat.

Keely Tanager pressed a button to unlock Jack's door.

"Good night, Mr. Pellum," she said. "Take care driving home now."

Jack told her good night and got out. She pulled away from the curb and made another three-point turn and headed south. He felt the wind pick up as he walked to his car and tossed Ed Cavanaugh's binder onto the backseat. It landed beside a pile of flyers. Jack wondered if it might rain, held out his hand, didn't feel any drops. Keely Tanager's taillights got smaller and he looked around and inhaled the night air and decided he would do what she wanted: go away, leave her city in peace. But first he would tape a flyer to every lamppost in sight.

After Olivia died, Jack attended a few meetings of a grief counseling group. They met in a church basement, and they would sit in a circle in folding chairs and try to comfort each other. A sweet old man would talk about his wife, how he still had dreams about her and in the dreams the two of them did ordinary things: they sat at the table after breakfast, each with a section of the paper, or they went to the grocery store and held hands as they walked through the aisles. He said that sometimes he would wake up and, for a moment, he would forget that his wife was gone. He'd feel her there in bed with him, and it would last until he turned over and touched the empty sheets.

Jack would have liked to have that happen, even once. He woke up on Saturday and heard rain falling outside and knew he was alone. He rolled out of bed, showered, wiped the steam from the mirror, and considered his face. The beard had progressed beyond a suave three-day stubble. If he let it go, he knew what was coming. He knew the stages: unemployed, homeless man, biblical prophet. None of them suitable for dealing with people. He put a fresh cartridge in his razor, lathered up, and did what needed to be done.

He got dressed and brewed coffee. Scrambled two eggs. Cut up half a cantaloupe. He ate standing up and loaded the dishes into the dishwasher. The counter and the stove had begun to look a little suspect. He wiped them down.

He devoted the next few hours to reviewing Ed Cavanaugh's notes and news clippings. He cleared a space on a wall in the living room and pinned up photos of Timothy Caslake, Dylan Vernen, and Alex Cavanaugh. They didn't look much alike; that was the first thing he noticed. Caslake had sandy-blond hair, blue eyes, a handsome, square-jawed face. Vernen and Cavanaugh had dark hair, Vernen's a bit unruly, Cavanaugh's in a crew cut. Vernen's face was round with a weak chin. Cavanaugh had a long face like his father's.

Tim Caslake and Alex Cavanaugh had been seventeen when they died. Dylan Vernen had been nineteen.

Caslake had been murdered first; Cavanaugh nine months later; Vernen a month after that. All three had died from blows to the head. On a handwritten page in his binder, Ed Cavanaugh had noted that the attacks differed in their severity. Dylan Vernen suffered the least violence; he had been dispatched with two blows to the back of the head. Tim Caslake had it the worst: broken ribs and a broken arm, in addition to severe head trauma. Alex Cavanaugh fell in between.

All three had been killed outdoors, and their bodies were discovered lying facedown in wooded areas. Caslake and Cavanaugh had their arms folded underneath them; Vernen's arms were at his sides. In each case, the killer took the victim's wallet and keys.

You could drive yourself crazy, Jack thought, looking for similarities and differences. In the movies, serial killers sent messages to the police claiming credit for their victims, or they left some token at each crime scene, a tarot card or a symbol drawn on the wall. In the real world, things were rarely so clear-cut.

The whole thing was a fool's errand, Jack thought. He looked from Cavanaugh's notes to the stack of manila folders that Paul Rook had given him. What were the chances that all these cases were related to each other — and to Olivia? Because Olivia was the one he cared about. Paul's files were a hodge-podge: some of them a few pages, some of them an inch thick. The file on the death of Paul's mother, Bonnie Rook, was one of the most extensive. Jack had looked through it, and as far as he could tell, the case had been worked competently. Nothing leapt out at him — no leads for him to follow, even if he wanted to pursue the matter. And he didn't want to, because he couldn't see how it could be related to Olivia.

The same was true of the other murders that Paul had collected. If you set aside the sightings of men in hats, it seemed unlikely that these deaths had anything to do with Olivia's.

Alex Cavanaugh's death was the only exception. And even there, the only real link was the man in the hat. But Jack had been struck when Paul told him that Danny Cavanaugh had seen the man in the hat twice, once on the day his brother died and again about a year and a half ago. Just before Olivia was murdered.

It couldn't be a coincidence. He remembered saying as much to Ed Cavanaugh the night before, and he remembered Cavanaugh's reply.

You don't want it to be.

Which was true. Jack wanted Alex's murder to be connected to Olivia's. It gave him hope that if he solved one he might be able to solve the other.

He spent some more time with Ed Cavanaugh's notes, sitting on the floor with the black binder on his lap. Around four o'clock he put it aside and stretched out on the sofa to think.

Though Jack doesn't dream about Olivia, sometimes he can summon up her voice in his head. He knew what she would say if she saw him now. *Detective Pellum is on a case. Or he's ready for a nap. I never know which.*

It turned out to be neither. Jack floated along on the edge of consciousness, but he didn't fall asleep. And he didn't have any revelations about Alex Cavanaugh. After a few minutes, he sat up and yawned. He grabbed a jacket and left the apartment and took a walk down Cass Avenue. Raindrops shone on the storefront windows, but nothing was falling now. He picked up a pulled pork sandwich and waffle fries from Slows

Barbecue, and when he brought them home he saw Paul Rook waiting for him on the steps of the Brentwood.

He invited him up and Paul wanted to know all about what he'd learned in Belleville. Jack filled him in and let him have half the sandwich and fries, and afterward Paul went to look at the photos he had tacked to the wall.

"That's Tim Caslake, with the blond hair," Jack said. "And the other is Dylan Vernen. I'm surprised Danny Cavanaugh never mentioned them to you, since they were killed around the same time as Alex."

Paul stood with his hands in his pockets. "I remember them," he said. "Danny did mention them."

"You might have told me," Jack said. "It would have saved me having to find out on my own."

Paul shrugged. "They're in the file," he said. "There's a newspaper story that talks about them. More than one story, I think. Didn't you read the file?"

Jack laughed quietly to himself. Paul's file on Alex Cavanaugh was thick as a phone book. "I haven't gone through the whole thing yet," he said. "I guess it serves me right. Are there any other surprises in there?"

"I don't think so," Paul said. He turned away from the wall and sat on the sofa and started paging through Ed Cavanaugh's black binder. Jack joined him.

"I did some research on them," Paul said. "Caslake and Vernen. It would have been right after I talked to Danny for the first time. Do you think they're important?"

"They could be," Jack said.

"But I couldn't find any connection between them and the man in the hat," Paul said. "No one saw him when they were killed. I'm not sure they're important at all."

Jack reached for Olivia's lighter on the coffee table. He flipped the top up and snapped it closed again.

"We need to get clear on some things, Paul."

"What things?"

"Like what we're doing. What we're trying to accomplish."

"We're trying to find the man in the hat."

"No, we're not," Jack said. "That might be a consequence, but it's not the main thing we're trying to do. That kind of thinking makes you blind."

Carl Dumisani had taught him that, on his first day as a detective. *You don't want to be blind,* he'd said. *Can't do this job if you're blind.*

Paul looked skeptical.

"We're trying to find the truth," Jack said. "The truth might lead us to the man in the hat, or it might not. He might have killed Caslake and Vernen and Alex Cavanaugh. He might have killed your mother and my wife. He might have killed all of them or some of them or none. He might just be someone we've made up, out of different sightings of different men, bystanders who never killed anybody. We have to keep an open mind until we know the facts. Otherwise we're blind. Do you understand?"

"Yeah. Okay."

Paul didn't sound entirely convinced, but Jack let it go. He returned the lighter to the coffee table and picked up a pad of paper and a pen. Started making a list of things he needed to do.

Paul went back to paging through Ed Cavanaugh's notes. The light in the room faded, and he switched on a lamp. After a time he said, "If we're keeping an open mind, then what about Alex's friend, Bobby Wilson?"

"What about him?" said Jack.

"He's not the man in the hat. I mean, Danny saw the man in the hat and didn't recognize him. But he would have recognized Bobby, because Bobby was a friend of Alex. So Bobby is not the man in the hat.

Can we assume that's a fact?"

"I think that's safe, yes."

"But Bobby could still be the one who murdered Alex. Alex was killed at the Sturridge house, and we know that Alex and Bobby used to go there together."

"That's a good point," Jack said. "Bobby should have been considered a suspect. I don't know if he was. He may have been cleared. I'd like to talk to him, but he may be hard to find. There are others I'd like to talk to as well, people who knew Dylan Vernen and Tim Caslake."

Paul closed the black binder. He raised a hand to his face and drew his fingers over the acne scars on his cheek and down to his chin.

"I could go with you," he said.

Jack tried not to show his surprise. "I don't know if that's a good idea," he said.

"I feel like I should do something," said Paul. "Something real. I've felt it ever since Danny died. That's why I went to his house. But even then, what did I do? I sat across the street and watched, thinking the man in the hat might show up there. I was waiting, but you can't just wait for him. He doesn't do what you want, just because you want it."

Paul put the binder aside. "But I'm glad I

125

went there," he said. "because that's what brought me here. Now I feel like I can do something important. Finding out the truth, I mean. Like you said."

"Look, whatever I find out, I'll tell you," Jack said. "I promise."

Paul's scarred cheeks flushed red. "I get it. You don't think I'd be any good."

"That's not —"

"It's okay," Paul said. "You may be right. I'm not always good at talking to people. What about this: Take me along once and if it doesn't work, that's the end of it. I won't ask again."

He sat steady with his head held up, waiting for an answer. Specks of dust floated in the lamplight beside him. Jack watched them and tried to think of a graceful way to refuse.

In the end he nodded and said, "All right."

11.

Michael Underhill is lying on his back on a floor made of plywood. The woman lies beside him.

The floor belongs to an unfinished wood-frame house on Washington Street in Chelsea, Michigan. You could walk in, if you wanted. There are no doors or windows yet, only openings. You could come in on the ground floor and stroll through the shells of rooms. The interior walls have been framed in, but if you step between the two-by-fours you can pass through them. They are insubstantial, the ghosts of walls to come.

The stairs are real and solid. Climb up to the second floor and when you reach the top you can see blue sky through two rectangles of empty space — the windows of the master bedroom. The light of a Sunday morning comes through. Underhill closes his eyes against it.

"Sometimes I think about how unlikely

everything is," he says. "If the earth had been a little farther from the sun, it would have been too cold. All the water would have turned to ice. If it had been closer, it would have been too hot. The water would have boiled away. There'd be nothing alive."

He sits up, bracing himself with his left arm. The floor is rough against his palm.

"There are seven billion people on this planet," he says, "and only five thousand of them live in this city. But I'm here, out of all the places in the world. Or look at it another way: I come from a long line of ancestors, going back to the first human beings, the first primates, the first fish that crawled out of the ocean. That line could have been broken a million times, but it wasn't. If any two of my ancestors had missed each other, if they'd failed to get together, I wouldn't exist."

His hat is on the floor, a loose nail beside it. Underhill picks up the nail and slips it in his pocket. Gets to his feet. The woman doesn't move.

"I think about all the decisions I've made," he says. "Even the small ones, day-to-day. When to go out, when to stay in, where to be at any given time. If I had done one thing differently, you and I might not be here. We might never have met."

He feels a breeze from outside. Shifts his weight from one foot to the other. The floor creaks.

The woman is silent.

He nudges her thigh with his toe. "Have you been listening? Are you asleep?"

She opens one eye and smiles. "I'm awake," she says. "I like hearing you talk."

Then both eyes are open and Anna Haley rolls onto her side, grabs Underhill's hat, and puts it on her head. She reaches for him and he takes her hand and pulls her up, and then she's against him, her arms wrapped around him.

"You found me," she says. "We found each other. Doesn't matter how unlikely it was. We're gonna live together. In this house. And we won't ever have to be alone."

He feels the words on his neck, and he believes them. She could say anything, and he would believe it. She loves him. There's no accounting for it, but there it is.

She knows nothing about Olivia Makinnen or any of the other bad choices he's made. Sometimes when he's alone he imagines telling her everything. He thinks about how to explain it in a way that she would understand, how each step made sense at the time, there was a logic. Sometimes he believes that she would accept it, she would accept him, just as he is.

Part of him realizes that this is idle fantasy. He can never tell her.

He used to believe that if he could go back, he would do things differently, he would change. But now, as he holds her tight in his arms, he knows it's not true. All his choices are a part of him. They led him here. And here is the only place he wants to be.

After a time Underhill lets go of all these thoughts and takes Anna's hand and walks her down the stairs. They pass through the place where the kitchen will be, then through the opening where the contractor plans to install sliding glass doors. There are no steps leading out, only a temporary wooden ramp that takes them into the back-yard.

He says, "Would you still love me if we couldn't afford this house?"

The question makes her laugh. "Would we be very poor?"

"We might be."

"I'd still love you."

"What if we had to live in a trailer?"

"Even then."

They walk through the yard. The ground is uneven and marked with patches of grass.

He says, "What if you had to sleep on the floor?"

"Why would I have to sleep on the floor?"

"There's only one bed in the trailer, and it's narrow."

"So you're sleeping in it?"

"I don't see why both of us should have to sleep on the floor."

She laughs again. He savors the sound.

"I would love you," she says, "even if it meant sleeping on the floor."

There are dandelions growing in the grass at the side of the house. Some yellow, some gone to seed. He scuffs through them and the seeds waft into the air.

He says, "What if we had to change our names and move somewhere far away?"

"Would we be fugitives?" she asks.

"Probably."

"On the run from the law?"

"That's usually how it works."

"Would we be guilty, or would it all be a misunderstanding?"

"I'm not telling."

"Could I pick our new names?"

"Yes."

"Then yes."

They come to the patch of dirt where he parked his car. It's in the shade near the attached garage. Nearby is a dumpster full of scrap wood and construction debris.

"Last one," he says.

"Go."

"Would you still love me if I didn't wear my hat?"

She still has it on. She touches the crown as if to hold it in place.

"I like this hat," she says.

"I know."

"And you look good in it."

"That's not the issue. What if I stopped wearing it?"

"Would you wear a different hat?"

"No."

"So you'd be hatless."

"Yes."

"And I'd have to look at your head."

"Yes."

"Well, I love your head."

"So it wouldn't matter," he says, "if I threw the hat away right now?"

Anna takes it off. Hands it over. "Do it," she says.

She doesn't believe he will. But he throws it like a Frisbee and it spins through the air and lands in the dumpster. A strange thing to do, yet she doesn't ask him why. She leans in and kisses him, a long kiss on tiptoe with her fingers in his hair.

■ ■ ■ ■

Michael Underhill believes he is on the verge of something. You could call it *happiness* or *fulfillment,* but he thinks of it as *real life.*

He believes his real life will begin when he moves into the house on Washington Street with Anna Haley.

"Real" may not be the right word, but it's as close as he can come. Words are only tools, and he needs one to distinguish his future from his past. And if his earlier life was not exactly *unreal,* it was certainly *lacking.*

Underhill grew up in a small town in Ohio, an only child, raised by his mother. He did well enough in school but didn't shine. Went to college for three years before dropping out. Moved to Michigan just to be out of Ohio.

In his early years in Michigan he held a string of menial jobs — roofer, landscaper, busboy, waiter. The jobs taught him that work was unpleasant and best avoided. He decided if he ever came into any money he would skip town, light out, get as far away from the Midwest as he could. Then he did come into some money, and he spent part of it on a secondhand car that took him all the way to California.

He spent the rest living in Los Angeles, in an apartment complex in Westwood. The complex had a pool. He tried his hand at a bohemian life, lounging by the pool during the day, hitting the clubs at night. He experimented with cocaine. When his money ran out, he got evicted from his apartment. He slept on people's couches. He had affairs with struggling young actresses, and twice with older women. The second one was an ad executive and she bought him a new wardrobe and made him stop the cocaine. She kept him for almost three years.

After that, he found work as a bike messenger and an extra in movies and TV shows. He lived in a two-bedroom apartment with three roommates. The others moved out one by one, and new ones came in. Underhill stayed. He got older and lost some of his charm.

When he was thirty-four he received news that his mother had died. She'd had a stroke one night while watching television. Her body went undiscovered for a week.

He had long since sold his secondhand car. He borrowed money from his roommates for a plane ticket home, packed the best of his clothes, and never looked back.

His mother's house was full of newspapers and magazines and commemorative plates she'd bought from QVC. There were eight cats and one litter box. He took the cats to the Humane Society and hauled his mother's furniture to the curb a few pieces at a time for people to scavenge. A neighbor got the plates in exchange for helping clean the house. He put the place on the market and accepted the first offer. He cleared enough to pay for his mother's funeral, with a few thousand dollars left over.

The money got him out of Ohio and back to Michigan. He hung around Ann Arbor for a while, wandering the campus of the university during the day, sleeping at the Y at night. He dated an assistant professor for a few weeks and she took him to a play in Chelsea and he wound up moving there. He fell in with some actors at a theater called the Purple Rose. He picked up a job now and then building sets or running the lights during shows. The people at the theater found him entertaining. He had stories about working in Hollywood.

On the day he turned thirty-seven he was living in a rooming house on Summit Street. He climbed up on the roof that night and sat under the stars and thought about how close thirty-seven was to forty. He thought about how little he had and how little, really, he'd done. He told himself he wanted to change. And he could; he just needed some luck. And money. No matter what you wanted, it usually came down to money. Looking up at the scattered stars in the dark blue sky, he thought of a number: a hundred thousand dollars. If he had that much, he thought, he could invest it. He could turn it into something real.

There are ways to get your hands on a hundred thousand dollars, if you're willing to do whatever it takes. Underhill was. Less than six weeks after that night on the roof, he had the money he needed.

He used it wisely. He bought a three-bedroom house a block away from where he was living. He hired a contractor to fix it up and hung around while the man worked, peppering him with questions. He sold the house at a profit and bought another. The second time around, he did a lot of the work himself. He refinished the hardwood floors, retiled the bathrooms, installed new coun-tertops in the kitchen. He held on to the house and rented it out.

Underhill owns five houses in Chelsea now. He has flipped some others over the years. When he started, he thought it would be easy. He thought he would reach a point when he could sit back and wait for the rent checks to roll in. He has learned better. There's always something demanding his attention. Furnace maintenance, plumbing issues, broken appliances. He's careful in his choice of tenants, but sometimes he makes mistakes. They keep pets they're not supposed to; they let their children break the windows and draw on the walls; they skip out on their leases. Sometimes you'd like to kill them.

He has never done that.

He has killed very few people, really, in the big scheme of things.

The years have flown by. He's forty-six now. He wanted to change his life, and he has changed it. He has found Anna Haley. He's having a house built for her now. For the two of them. It's the first time he's ever had a house built new.

And now they climb into his car and drive away from it. There's a picnic basket in the backseat. Anna is the kind of woman who plans a picnic and brings a basket. They drive north out of Chelsea, past the Jiffy Mix plant, through the countryside to the shore of a pond. They spread a blanket on the grass.

The basket holds a feast. Fried chicken

and deviled eggs, coleslaw and tuna salad, cucumber sandwiches, cheese and apples, carrot sticks and hummus, grapes both green and red. There is a large mason jar of iced lemonade, slices of lemon floating at the top. China plates and silverware and glasses.

They eat their fill and clear the rest away and lie back on the blanket, shoulders touching, her hair tickling his ear. They look at the sky and she asks him what he thinks the clouds look like, because she is the kind of woman who thinks about what the clouds look like. He makes his best effort. There's a whale and a hawk and a sailing ship. Later in the afternoon Anna fetches her guitar from the car and plays him a song, her own composition. Her singing voice is rich and earthy. She tells him the song is unfinished. To him it sounds perfect.

She plays gigs when she can, just her and the guitar, mostly in little cafés. That's how Underhill met her, in a café in Chelsea called Zou Zou's. A tiny space with a dozen chairs and twenty people gathered on a Friday night. He stood against the wall and watched her and listened. When the place closed down and everyone else left, the two of them lingered on the sidewalk outside, talking.

That was almost a year ago. These days they spend as much time together as they can. He has his business and she earns her money performing and teaching kids to play guitar. But kids are fickle; they stay interested for a time and then give up. She's looking for steadier work.

Sitting cross-legged on the blanket beside him, she says, "I had a second interview on Friday."

"Where?" he asks.

"At the hospital. It's a part-time opening, for a music therapist. Twenty or thirty hours a week. Playing songs for sick people."

"Would you get to play your own songs?"

"I don't think so. You play whatever they want to hear. A lot of them are old, maybe they're dying. They want to hear something familiar. Ideally, you get them to sing along."

"And that's a real thing? Music therapy?"

"Sure. It's for the patients, and the families too. People visiting. You play them something they know. Sometimes you play classics. 'Oh! Susanna.' 'Michael Row the Boat Ashore.' Stuff you'd sing around a campfire."

" 'Kumbaya'?"

"You bet. I can play the hell out of 'Kumbaya.' "

"And you think you'd like doing that?"

"I do," Anna says. "I need a regular gig. I'm getting older. I don't know how much longer I want to go on suffering for my art."

Underhill always smiles when she talks about getting old. She's thirty-two.

"Do you think you'll get it?" he asks.

"I hope so."

"You don't sound sure."

"The HR woman at the hospital likes me. She said it's down to me and one other person."

"When will they decide?"

"The end of next week."

"I bet you'll get it."

"I don't know. The other guy — I'm not supposed to know who he is, but I saw his resumé on the HR woman's desk. His name is Chris Treadwell. I looked him up. He's got a degree from U of M, and he's done music therapy before. He volunteers at old folks' homes. He runs marathons."

"Does the job involve running?"

"No, but the point is, he's impressive."

"He sounds all right," Underhill says, wrinkling his nose. "But is he dazzling? Because *you* are dazzling."

Anna laughs. "I don't know how far dazzling will get me. I'm secretly hoping he drops out."

"It could happen."

"Fingers crossed. Maybe he'll get a better offer. Maybe he'll go running and get hit by a bus. I really want this job."

Underhill closes his eyes, feels the warmth of the sun on his face.

"I bet you'll get it," he says again.

12.

Tim Caslake's mother made pies.

She had two pies cooling on her kitchen counter (blueberry and cherry) and a third in the oven. It was, all together, an abundance of pies and she was sorry she couldn't offer any to Jack and Paul.

"They're for work," she explained.

She waited tables at a diner near the airport, and for years the owner had bought supermarket pies and passed them off to his customers as homemade. Then a new owner came in and updated the decor and overhauled the menu and asked Beverly Caslake if she knew how to bake.

"I couldn't tell you how he knew to ask," she said.

Jack could guess. Beverly Caslake had what you would call a maternal figure: not fat, but plump; soft and pleasing in its curves. She wore her hair in what used to be called a beehive. Jack's grandmother had worn hers that way too. So had a lot of housewives, he thought — the kind of women who owned aprons and used them, who cooked roasts and casseroles, who mixed drinks for their husbands when they came home from work. Mrs. Caslake wasn't of the same generation, but she had the same spirit. She looked like a woman who would know how to bake.

She had invited Jack and Paul to have a seat in her kitchen. She served them coffee and put out a plate of cookies. Her husband was on a fishing trip up north. Her daughter, who looked to be a little younger than Jack, breezed through and grabbed a cookie and disappeared out into the yard.

Paul sat very still at the table and left his coffee untouched. He had dressed like a kid on his first job interview: dark shirt, narrow tie, khaki pants with a well-defined crease.

Jack asked Beverly Caslake to tell him about her son.

"Tim was a sweet boy," she said. "Right from the beginning. A beautiful child, always smiling. I can picture him running around the yard when he was three or four, silky blond hair like an angel. He would pick flowers from the garden and bring them to me. Daffodils."

She stood by the counter, keeping watch

on the pie in the oven.

"His teachers loved him," she said. "They'd make a point to tell me how well-behaved he was. Always raised his hand in class. He wasn't shy. He had all sorts of friends. He joined the Cub Scouts. Played Little League — got elected captain of his team. Then in high school he went out for football, and the first year he tried out he didn't make it. He was heartbroken. But he trained harder, lifted weights, pulled himself up by his bootstraps. He was second-string quarterback in his sophomore year and first-string as a junior."

She beamed at Jack, remembering. "A smart boy too, always getting A's. He studied Latin and took AP history. But he was down-to-earth, didn't put on airs. You could talk to anyone who knew him, you wouldn't hear a harsh word. His father and I never went to college, but we had big hopes for Tim. We knew he would shine. He should have gone far."

Jack could hear pride in her voice, and sadness too. But it was an old sadness. He asked her if she would mind talking about the night Tim died.

"There was nothing special about it," she said. "I remember it was a cold night. November. A week before Thanksgiving. We

144

had an early snow that year, but it didn't stay. Tim had football practice that day, and by the time it ended the sun had gone down. He started off for home in the twilight. He always walked home from school, unless the weather was bad, and then he would catch a ride or I would pick him up. That night, his coach saw him head off on foot. It should have taken half an hour; it was less than two miles if he cut through the woods.

"When he didn't get home in time for dinner that night, I didn't worry. High school boys make their own plans, and they don't always call their mother. Kids back then didn't have cell phones. Around eight o'clock I started calling around to his friends' houses, but no one could tell me where he was. At nine his father met up with the coach at the high school, and the two of them followed the route Tim would have taken through the woods. They found him after less than a mile. His body was lying just west of the railroad tracks."

Jack knew the spot. Ed Cavanaugh had marked it on a map in his notebook. It didn't strike Jack as the kind of place where you would run into someone at random. He thought Tim Caslake's killer must have waited for him there.

"I know it's been a long time, Mrs. Caslake," Jack said. "But I wonder if you remember anything unusual that might have happened in the days before Tim died."

"Unusual?"

"Was his mood different? Did he seem troubled? Do you remember anyone taking an interest in him? Someone unfamiliar. Someone who might have been following him."

She frowned. "If there'd been anyone like that, I would have told the police."

Jack took a flyer from his pocket and unfolded it on the table. "Do you remember seeing anyone who might have looked like this?"

He didn't expect her to say yes, but he thought he had to try. She leaned down to study the paper and shook her head.

As he refolded the flyer, the timer on the stove started beeping. Beverly Caslake pressed a button to silence it and pulled on a pair of oven mitts and opened the oven door. A rush of heat and the scent of apples and cinnamon filled the room.

"One last thing," Jack said. "I'm sure the police asked you at the time, but I wonder if you can think of anyone who had a conflict with your son. Anyone who might have wanted to do him harm."

146

She set the pie on a trivet on the counter, shaking her head all the while. "There was no one like that," she said, "no one who wanted to hurt Tim."

Jack nodded and pushed his chair back from the table. Paul did the same. He'd been silent the whole time, but he chose that moment to speak.

"There had to have been at least one person."

It was a graceless thing to say, and he realized it a moment too late. Jack watched him flush red. The heat in the room seemed to swell. But either Beverly Caslake hadn't heard or she pretended she hadn't. She drew the oven mitts from her hands and laid them on the table.

"Everyone loved Tim," she said.

The Caslake house sat at the end of a long driveway on Tyler Road in the city of Romulus. The side yard was bordered by birch trees and a few shortleaf pines. If you looked up, you were likely to see passenger jets cutting their slow way across the sky. The Detroit Metropolitan Airport was less than four miles away.

Jack and Paul had come in at the side door; they left the same way. There was a brick patio in the shade of the house, with a propane grill and four cheap lawn chairs. Beverly Caslake's daughter sat in one of the chairs smoking a cigarette. She had four earrings in each ear and a tattoo of a compass on the side of her neck, and her hair was cut short and spiky and dyed bright yellow. She wore a loose-fitting sundress and white socks and engineer boots. Jack remembered her name from Ed Cavanaugh's notes: Jennifer.

She called to them as they walked by. "You're the private eyes."

Jack smiled and asked her if she had a minute to talk. She took a drag on her cigarette, looked at the house, and made a face to let him know she didn't want to talk where her mother might overhear. She led Jack and Paul across the yard to a tiny pond surrounded by a ring of stones. A few koi fish swam in the water.

Jennifer Caslake looked Jack over. "You I can see as a private eye," she said. She turned to Paul and took in his dark shirt and tie. "You look like you want to sell me a car stereo."

Paul cast around for a reply, took too long, and finally came up with: "Are you in the market for a car stereo?"

That got him a smirk, and his cheeks flushed red again. Jack stepped in with a question for Jennifer. "How much did you hear of what your mother had to say?"

"Enough," she said.

"What did you think of it?"

"I thought every word was true," she said. "Tim was an angel. He saved kittens from trees and helped old ladies cross the street. He peed sunshine and shat rainbows. If he'd lived, he'd probably be the president by now. You believed all that, right?"

"Not exactly," Jack said.

"Well, you should. We can't speak ill of the dead."

"I could stand to hear a little ill," Jack said. "Just to round out the picture."

Jennifer hesitated, studying the ash growing at the end of her cigarette. "I was only thirteen when Tim died," she said. "I don't know everything about him." She flicked the ash into the pond. "I know he didn't like it here. In this town. He thought he deserved better. My dad is a maintenance supervisor at the airport. That's what he's done all his life. Tim didn't think much of that job. He wanted to play football — like, for real, in the NFL. But there was no way."

"No?"

"It was a pipe dream. He was the second-best quarterback at Romulus High, and they only let him play because the other guy got sacked and landed on his elbow. Tim played in six games and lost half of them. He might have gone on to play in college, but I doubt it. I think he would have joined a frat and studied economics or business administration. He'd be soft around the middle now, balding, working as a mid-level manager. And the thing is, if that's where he had ended up, you wouldn't want to be working under him."

"Why not?"

"Because he was kind of a dick. My dad used to take us for ice cream in the summer. You never knew when: he'd just announce it in the evening after dinner, and Tim and I would race out to the car. Whoever got there first would get to sit up front. Tim would always win, but one time the ground was wet and he slipped and I beat him. He was mad, he said it wasn't fair, but my father let me have the front seat. Tim didn't do anything — not then. A week later he let me win again; he laughed about it. We went to the Dairy Queen and got our ice cream, and afterward as I was climbing back into the car, he slammed the door on my finger." She held up her right hand for Jack to see. There was a white ridge running through the nail of the index finger. "I've had that ever since," she said.

She dropped her cigarette onto the rocks by the koi pond and stepped on it with the toe of her boot. She looked around for another one and realized she'd left her pack on the patio. Paul had been standing quietly, listening, with his hands in his pockets. He brought his left hand out and it held an old-fashioned cigarette case. He flipped it open and offered it to her.

The smirk was gentler this time. "Aren't you a smooth one?" she said, and tucked a cigarette between her lips. Paul's right hand came out with a Zippo lighter. He flicked it with his thumb and it caught on the first try.

Jack observed this little scene and waited for Jennifer to breathe out a stream of smoke. Then he said, "Maybe it was an accident, slamming your finger in the door."

Jennifer ran her tongue over her teeth. "Maybe it was. Tim was prone to accidents. At least, that's what I heard. At school, if you scored better on a test than he did, he might accidentally trip you in the hall. If you were gay, he might accidentally write 'faggot' on your locker. If you were a poor kid and you saved your money to buy a new shirt, he might accidentally run into you and spill your lunch tray all over the front of it."

She shrugged her shoulders. "Those were the little things," she said. "I heard about one girl, sort of a science nerd, the kind who wears glasses and when she takes them off you realize she's gorgeous. Tim asked her to go to a dance. Her parents didn't want her dating, so she turned him down. Before long her phone number was on the walls of the boys' bathrooms. Somebody started a rumor that she had slept with half the football team. She couldn't walk down the hall without getting catcalled. Eventually she transferred to another school."

"Do you remember her name?" Jack asked.

"This was twenty years ago. I don't remember any of their names." Jennifer waved the hand that held her cigarette. "This is all gossip, stuff I heard secondhand. You wanted to know about Tim. He was my brother and I loved him and I'm sorry he's gone. But I'm pretty sure he wasn't a saint."

13.

"I used to put up pictures of Olivia. After she died."

"I think that's common. You wanted to see her. To remember her."

"I don't mean at home," Jack said, "although I did that too. I put pictures up around the neighborhood."

"Why?" Eleanor Brannon asked.

He had called her Monday morning to schedule an appointment. She told him she could see him right away if he wanted. She'd had a cancellation.

"I did a lot of things at the time, trying to figure out who killed her," Jack said. "In those first few months, I talked to everyone I could think of, everyone who knew her. I traveled to Virginia to see her family, her friends, people she grew up with. But none of that helped. It didn't bring me any closer to finding out why she died. And then I started to think she must have had a secret life. The people I really needed to talk to were the ones I didn't know about. So I put up flyers with her picture on them, and asked people to call me if they knew her."

"Did it work?"

He shook his head. "I got some calls, but most of them were from people I'd already spoken to, people who wanted to know how I was doing. The others were strangers who thought it was a joke, or called for the novelty of it. I realized it was hopeless. The only people who would call — apart from those who were just curious — were the ones who knew Olivia and wanted me to know that they knew her. But the ones I was looking for were the ones who knew her but didn't want me to know it."

Jack felt his hands gripping the arms of the chair; he made an effort to relax them.

"I know what this sounds like," he said. "This is how crazy people talk."

"I don't think you're crazy," said Dr. Brannon.

"There's one thing that happened, because of the pictures. I was in a restaurant called Traffic Jam, right around the block from my apartment. I had some flyers with me and the waitress saw them and said, 'I know her. That's Cindy.' And then my heart starts racing and I'm convinced that I've finally discovered Olivia's secret. She had another identity where she was named Cindy. You can guess what happened next."

"I don't want to guess."

"The waitress called Cindy over."

Dr. Brannon took a moment to work it out. "Cindy was another waitress at the restaurant."

"Exactly," Jack said. "So Cindy comes over and she looks a little like Olivia. It's a passing resemblance. Maybe at a certain angle, from a certain distance, you could mistake them."

"And you thought that's what the killer did. He saw Olivia and mistook her for Cindy. All the while you've been looking for someone with a motive to kill Olivia when you should have been looking for someone who wanted to kill Cindy."

Jack couldn't help but smile. "That's some first-class paranoid thinking," he said. "I'm impressed. But no, that's not what I thought. It's not plausible. I could go out this afternoon and find ten women who looked more like Olivia than Cindy did. And you could speculate that the killer really meant to murder one of those ten. You could really fall down a rabbit hole, thinking that way. That's not the mistake I made. I made a different one."

"Which was?"

"I went on a date with Cindy. She gave me her number that day in the restaurant, and a week later I called her and we met for a drink at the Bronx Bar. She showed up in a black dress and heels. She looked better than the Bronx Bar deserved. We talked about baseball — who the Tigers were playing and whether they had a chance to make it to the World Series. That was enough to distinguish her from Olivia right there, because Olivia would go to a game now and then, but she never wanted to talk about it. She didn't see the point.

"Anyway, Cindy and I had two drinks apiece and I heard her thoughts on Miguel Cabrera and Prince Fielder and whether Verlander was overrated, and then we went around the corner to my apartment and she took off those heels and walked into my bedroom, blissfully unaware that I had a dead wife. And the dress came off and she looked less like Olivia than she had before and I knew I would be all right. It had been almost a year since I slept with anybody. That's long enough, isn't it?"

"I don't think there's a rule," Dr. Brannon said.

"For me, it was long enough, and Cindy was sweet and eager. And it was fine. I mean, it didn't change anybody's life, but it was good."

Dr. Brannon nodded thoughtfully. "So it wasn't a mistake."

"No," Jack said.

"Because you said it was. You called it a mistake. Did you feel bad about it after?"

"No."

"Did you think it was wrong?"

"No."

"But it didn't change your life."

"Well, I didn't really expect it to," Jack said.

"But it could have. You said she was sweet. It might have led somewhere."

"She was a waitress."

"People fall in love with waitresses all the time."

"I wasn't in love with her."

"Fair enough," Dr. Brannon said. "Let's leave her out of it. Do you think you'll fall in love again?"

"That's an awfully theoretical question."

"Some people, they fall in love, they lose the one they love, they figure that's it, they had their chance, there won't be any more. Maybe they think they're not entitled to any more. Maybe they think it would be an affront to the person they loved. A betrayal."

Jack looked away from her, at the sunlight

falling on the low table between them.

"You're sounding like a shrink now."

"How am I supposed to sound?"

He shifted in his chair, rubbed his chin. "Maybe this was a mistake. Maybe I shouldn't have come here."

"Yet here we are," Eleanor Brannon said. "The last time I saw you — I thought it really would be the last. I figured you'd never set foot in here again. But you called me, and you came. I assume there's a reason. I assume you'll let me in on it eventually."

"I just wanted to talk."

"We could've talked about anything. You wanted to talk about your encounter with Cindy."

Jack felt the roughness of the stubble on his chin. The sunlight glowed on a corner of the table. He tried to convince himself she was wrong. He couldn't quite manage it.

After a time he said, "It happened again."

"What happened?" she asked.

"Another *encounter,* I guess you would say."

"With Cindy?"

"No. Not with her."

It went like this.

On Sunday night Jack turned on his stereo

158

and synced it with his phone and opened up a playlist that Olivia had made for him. At twenty after eight he was listening to a Jason Isbell song called "Traveling Alone."

Jack was writing out some notes from his interviews with the Caslakes earlier in the day. He had a frozen pizza warming in the oven.

The first text came in at 8:22. He heard the ping and reached for his phone. The message said:

You're not here, I hoped you might be.

He didn't recognize the number. The next message said:

I don't know where you live, So this is really the only place I could look for you.

Then:

I came here yesterday too. Thinking you might walk by.

Then:

I sound like a stalker. I'm not a stalker, I promise.

Then:

I'm at the DIA. On the steps, where we talked. In case you're in the area.

Then:

This is Kim, BTW.

Jack started to type a message back, then turned off the music and called her instead. She answered after the second ring.

"You're there," Kim Weaver said. "I didn't think you were there."

"Are you okay?" he asked her.

"I am. I just sound like I'm not."

"Stay where you are," he said. "I'm not far away. I'll come to you."

"You don't have to. I think it's gonna rain. We could meet somewhere. I have a car."

"Are you sure you should drive?"

"Why not?" she said. "Oh. I'm not drunk. I haven't had anything. I have a bottle of wine, but it's in the car. I don't even have a corkscrew."

"I've got one," Jack said. "Do you know where Prentis Street is?"

"I could find it."

He gave her his address. "You can park on the street, or there's a store down the block. Marcus Market. The sign says parking is for customers only, but they won't tow you."

"Are you sure?"

"They're closed now anyway."

"I mean, are you sure I should come?"

"No. But come anyway."

She found a parking spot on the street. Jack went down to meet her and brought her up. The apartment door clicked shut behind them and what followed was an awkward silence. Two people realizing they didn't know each other. Now that we're here, what do we do? Jack took the wine and went to find his corkscrew. Kim looked around, saw the pictures of Olivia on the wall, had a question ready for him when he came back with the open bottle. "Who is she? She's beautiful." He didn't want to tell the story, but he fumbled through it. Kim was appropriately shocked and dismayed. *My god, that's terrible, I'm so sorry, I had no idea.* Then more silence and awkwardness while she decided if she would stay or try to make a graceful exit. Jack poured the wine and she stayed.

They wound up sitting on the floor by the sofa, wineglasses on the coffee table, slices of untouched pizza, rain pattering against the windows. He could tell that she wanted to talk about her husband — and that she thought she shouldn't. You don't tell your troubles to the man with the murdered wife.

But he encouraged her and eventually she opened up.

"I had it out with him," she said. "The same day you and I talked. I told Doug I knew he was cheating. He denied it. He always denied it. So I lied to him. Told him I wasn't guessing, I'd hired someone to follow him — which was almost true. That did it. He confessed."

She sipped her wine. "If you can believe it, he acted hurt," she said. "Like I was in the wrong for not trusting him. I thought he would want to try to work things out. That's what I kept worrying about — would that be the right thing to do, to give him a chance, or would he lie to me again? I didn't want to go through all that. But he didn't want another chance. He turned it around on me, told me I had shattered his faith. He couldn't be with someone who would spy on him."

Jack's cell phone pinged. He glanced at the message on the screen and left it alone. Kim seemed not to notice.

"So now I'm talking to a lawyer," she said. "Doug's not going to make it easy. He wants to keep the house, but we own it together and I doubt he can afford to buy my share. In the meantime he won't move out, and I don't see why *I* should. I have friends who would let me stay with them, but I don't want to be dependent on anybody. I don't want to be the sad girl. For now, I've moved into the spare bedroom, but I don't like it. I don't like being in my house anymore. Like tonight. He's there. I had to get out."

She went on for a while longer: about what the past few days had been like, and the things she needed to do, all the steps it would take to untangle her from her old life. At some point Jack's phone pinged again and he ignored it, and she said, "You can look at your messages if you want."

"It's not important," he said.

"I'm taking up your time, and maybe you've got other things to do."

"It's my father. He wants me to have dinner with him."

"You should go then. I don't want to keep you."

"Not tonight. He wants to arrange something. One night this week."

"Oh."

"He thinks if he keeps asking me, I'll have to say yes."

"You're not going to say yes?"

"I don't think so."

"Why not?"

"It's complicated."

"You don't have to tell me."

"It's sort of a long story."

She reached for the wine. "You're right. I don't want to sit here and listen to you talk about your problems."

Jack let her top off his glass. He got up and opened one of the front windows. The rain was falling steadily, but not very hard. A few beads clung to the wire of the screen.

"The day my wife died," he said, "she left here around eight in the morning and drove west for about an hour, to Hudson Mills Metropark. She took her camera. The fall leaves were turning colors. She planned to spend a few hours there, taking pictures along the Huron River.

"I was still in bed when she left. I'd been getting over a cold. I slept past noon, took a shower, got dressed. My head felt clearer than it had in days, so I decided to go in to work. I was a detective in the Third Precinct then. I ended up staying late, doing paperwork, getting ready to testify at a trial coming up the following week. Around seven o'clock my partner came looking for me, told me there was an investigator from the state police who wanted to talk to me, a guy named Ben Thurman.

"He was an older guy, in his fifties, and he was smart. He'd come to tell me my wife was dead, and sometimes, in a situation like that, you approach it indirectly, you work your way up to it. You get the husband alone in a room and ask him if he knows where his wife is and when's the last time he saw her. You watch how he reacts. You make him ask you what happened. Thurman didn't do that. He told me straight out. They'd found my wife's body, a hiker had found her in the park, and it looked like a homicide.

"I didn't believe him. Maybe they made a mistake. I wanted to see her. Thurman told me there'd be a time for that later. They were confident in the identification, based on her driver's license photo. They were working the scene now. The medical examiner had removed the body. I'd be able to see her, of course, but right now he needed my help. He wanted me to come with him, answer some questions.

"My partner was watching out for me. He wasn't going to let anyone take me anywhere. But I agreed to talk to Thurman there, in an empty conference room at the precinct house. He started with the basics: Olivia's job, her routine, what time she had left that morning, where she intended to go. Information you would need to establish a timeline. Then he moved on to other things: Did she spend a lot of time by herself? Was it normal for her to go to a park alone?

Could she have been meeting someone there? What did she say to you this morning? What did you say to her? What did you do after she left?

"Thurman was subtle. He didn't accuse me of anything. But he'd circle back to certain points. Like the fact that I'd called in sick that morning, but later decided to come in and work. He was curious about that. I knew why. It meant there was time I couldn't account for — the time when I claimed to be sleeping. Time I could have used to drive to Hudson Mills Metropark.

"I knew what he was thinking. If I'd been in his place, I might have thought the same thing. But it still made me angry. I came very close to telling him to go to hell. I didn't have to. The cavalry came and did it for me."

"The cavalry?" Kim said.

"My father," said Jack. "He's a judge. He showed up because my partner called him. He brought a friend, a criminal defense attorney, one of the best in Detroit. They shut the interview down. Ben Thurman never tried to talk to me again."

"Isn't that a good thing, if he thought you were guilty? Wasn't your father looking out for you?"

"I'm sure he was. But I can't help thinking about what happened after. Thurman never came close to finding Olivia's killer. Maybe he tried his hardest, maybe he followed every lead he had. Or maybe he decided I was guilty and he wouldn't be able to touch me. So why bother to work the case at all?"

Jack had been standing by the window all this time, looking down at the street. At some point Kim Weaver had come to stand beside him. He felt her arm brush his.

"You blame your father for that," she said. "That's why you don't want to have dinner with him."

"That's part of it," he said.

"What's the rest?"

Jack studied the beads of rain on the window screen. "The rest is . . . It's how he's acted ever since. How they've both acted — my mother too. They came to Olivia's funeral and stood by me and since then I don't think they've ever said her name. They want to pretend she never existed, that this unpleasantness never happened. Having a murdered wife is bad form. They're willing to overlook it, as long as no one ever brings it up. And that's not the worst of it. I'm supposed to ignore the worst of it — the one thing that they would never admit in a million years, even to themselves. But I can see it, every time I look at them."

"What?"

"They think I might have killed her."

Jack and Kim stood together with their arms touching, listening to the rain. Down on the sidewalk someone walked by under a big black umbrella. It could have been anyone: man or woman, young or old. Jack's mind went automatically to the man in the hat. He thought idly of going down there in the rain to get a closer look. But Kim was right beside him. He could feel the warmth of her. He turned to her and she lifted her face up to him and their eyes met. Hers were blue, like Olivia's. He leaned into her and watched those eyes close. He closed his too. Her mouth tasted like wine.

14.

On Sunday night Michael Underhill was carrying a big black umbrella, but he was nowhere near Jack Pellum's apartment.

He was on Maynard Street in Ann Arbor, rain falling all around him. Across the street, Chris Treadwell ducked inside an Indian restaurant called Madras Masala. Underhill had found his address online, parked on his street, watched his house. It was an old Victorian, run-down, split up into apartments. Treadwell had come out around seven o'clock. Underhill had followed him on foot, eight blocks weaving through downtown, until he reached the restaurant.

Now Underhill stepped into the shelter of the Nickels Arcade. He leaned against a wall and shook the rain from his umbrella. The shops of the arcade were closed. He was alone. He figured he had a long wait ahead of him but he didn't mind. He could always entertain himself. He let his thoughts drift:

to bits of music, songs he'd loved growing up, Billy Joel and Tom Petty and Bruce Springsteen. He went over snatches of conversations he'd had with Anna Haley, and things he wanted to say to her.

He thought about Chris Treadwell. Reviewed what he'd learned about the man online. Treadwell had studied classical guitar in the music department at the university, and he had soloed with the Detroit Symphony Orchestra. He also played the violin and the piano. He seemed overqualified to be a music therapist.

The rain slowed and picked up again. People came out of the restaurant but none of them were Treadwell. Underhill heard laughter and turned to see a pair of teenage boys dashing in out of the rain at the other end of the arcade. One of them a little taller than the other, both dressed in jerseys and shorts, sneakers on their feet. Their voices echoed: "Whew!" "Holy shit!" "You almost bought it, bro. That motherfucker looked like he wanna run you over."

Underhill turned back to the restaurant. Hummed to himself. Listened to the footsteps of the boys as they came closer. One of them stopped at the door of each shop and rattled the handle. The other one said, "We need beer. Ain't no beer in here."

They reached Underhill's end of the arcade and peeked out. A flash of lightning lit the sky. The shorter of the two boys jumped back, laughing. The taller one kept his cool. They both took up positions across from Underhill, facing him, mirroring his pose, their backs braced against the wall.

"Look at this guy," the taller one said. "Lurking. Looks like a perv."

"Could be a cop," said the shorter one.

"Could be both. Check out his coat."

Underhill was wearing a trench coat and a ball cap with a John Deere logo.

"He might be a narc," the shorter boy said.

"Are you a narc?" said the taller one.

Underhill ignored them.

"Could be deaf," the taller one said.

"Are you deaf?" said the other. He waited a beat and repeated it louder. *"Are you deaf?"*

Underhill kept his eyes on the restaurant across the street. "I'm not deaf," he said quietly.

"The man's not deaf."

"Definitely not deaf."

"Maybe he's not a narc either. Maybe he could help us out."

"Maybe he's got beer."

"Where would he keep it, in his pockets?"

"Weed, then. Maybe he's got weed."

"Ask the man."

"Hey, man, you got any weed?"

Underhill didn't look at them. "No," he said.

"Man's got no weed. What good is he?"

"Disappointing, bro."

"No weed, no beer."

"He could get us beer."

"He ain't gettin' us beer. Man's not friendly. He's not even civil."

"We could ask."

"*You* ask."

"I'm not getting you beer," Underhill said.

The shorter boy poked the other with his elbow. "He's not getting us beer."

"Shit."

"We'll have to get it ourselves."

"I guess."

"Raining, though."

"Raining hard."

"Not letting up."

"Man's got an umbrella."

"It's sittin' right there, goin' to waste."

"We could borrow it."

"You think?"

"Ask him."

"Yo, how about you loan us your umbrella?"

Underhill turned to them. "No."

"How come?"

"I need it."

"We need it too," the taller one said.

"We need it more, really," said the other.

"Maybe we could take it. Bring it back when we're done."

"No."

"Maybe we could take it and not bring it back."

The umbrella was leaning against the wall. Underhill didn't reach for it. He did nothing. The taller boy took a step toward it. Then another.

Underhill brought his hands out of the pockets of his coat.

"You boys are amusing," he said.

"Yeah?"

"But you really should be careful about messing with people you don't know."

"Why's that?" the taller boy said.

"Because they could be dangerous and unpredictable."

The boy's eyes narrowed. "You supposed to be hard? You don't look so hard."

"That's the unpredictable part."

The taller boy stood still. Underhill stared at him, unblinking. Seconds ticked by. The rain fell steadily. The shorter boy shifted his weight from one foot to the other, nervous. The taller boy turned to him and laughed. "You heard the man," he said. "He's dangerous. Let's go."

The two of them ran out into the rain, heading south, whooping and hollering, their sneakers slapping the pavement. Their voices faded in the distance and Underhill put them out of his mind. He watched the traffic on Maynard Street, the water flowing in the gutters. A pigeon came into the shelter of the arcade, hopped and fluttered along, found a perch on a little shelf in front of a shop window.

Across the street, a woman stepped out of Madras Masala, young and pretty, a long coat belted around her slender waist. Chris Treadwell came out behind her, opened an umbrella, held it to shield her from the rain. They walked together, hip to hip, north on Maynard.

Underhill picked up his umbrella and followed them.

Bright lights on Liberty Street — the marquee of the Michigan Theater. Treadwell and the woman headed west, past a yogurt shop and a Mexican restaurant. Then three blocks north to a quiet street with tall hedges and old trees. They went up onto the porch of a gray two-story house — not Treadwell's; it must have been the woman's — and lingered there talking. Underhill passed them by and found a place to wait in the shadow of a spreading oak. He could see them, but their words reached him only indistinctly. The conversation seemed lively. Treadwell was a compact man, not much taller than the woman, but he was full of energy. He paced around the porch as if telling a story. He acted things out, spread his arms, slapped his forehead, touched the woman's shoulder. The woman responded in kind, shaking her head in mock disbelief, punching his arm playfully.

Underhill tried to puzzle out their relationship. They were friendly, obviously. Even flirty. Maybe they were on a first date. Maybe Treadwell would pick a moment and lean in to kiss her — or she would kiss him. They would make out a little on the porch, in the romance of the night and the rain running down from the eaves, and she would invite him in. He would be with her for an hour, or two, or all night, and Underhill would miss his chance.

Or it could go differently. Treadwell has bad breath, he's a disappointing kisser, the woman has to get to work early in the morning. He never gets through the door. She sends him on his way.

Hard to know what to do.

Underhill stepped out from the shadow of the oak. The rain pattered on the fabric of his umbrella.

Anna Haley was a fine musician. She could get a job without his intervention.

He walked east to the end of the block, went on until he came to the end of another.

Anna wanted the job at the hospital very badly. She deserved to have what she wanted.

Underhill reached inside the front of his coat, felt the cool steel of the crowbar he was carrying there.

He could keep walking, east and a little north, and come to the place where he'd left his car. Or he could wait awhile. He could step around the corner, stand right here, with his back to the hedge.

The hedge would conceal him from Treadwell, if Treadwell came this way.

It would conceal him, but not the umbrella. The umbrella was too tall. He closed it and laid it on the ground.

The rain fell, not so hard now. The bill of his cap kept it out of his eyes.

Underhill decided he would wait for ten minutes. He counted off the seconds in his head. Sometimes his mind drifted and he thought about what he would say to Chris Treadwell, or whether he would say anything at all.

When he had counted ten minutes, he decided he would give it a little longer.

Twelve. Fifteen.

After twenty, he heard footsteps, wet on the sidewalk. They came closer.

Underhill opened his coat and drew out the crowbar.

15.

Jack drove alone to New Boston on Monday afternoon. Paul Rook was supposed to come with him, but he sent Jack a text at the last minute: *Working. Can't make it this time.*

The Vernen house stood on the south side of Judd Road. It was long and low, one story, with ragged vinyl siding and gray trim that needed a new coat of paint. It had a long, screened-in porch at the back, and that was where Jack spoke to Dylan Vernen's parents — the three of them gathered in wicker chairs around a small glass-top table.

"It's cool out here in the evenings," Irene Vernen said.

Her hands drew a shawl close around her shoulders, as if she were feeling the cool. Bone and sinew those hands — and the skin covered in fine, delicate wrinkles. The same wrinkles marked her cheeks and her high forehead. A sharp white line ran through the middle of her scalp — the part in her iron-gray hair. The hair grew down past her shoulders. She had a golden cross on a chain at her throat.

"Dylan used to sleep here when he was a boy," she said. "He liked the fresh air."

Her husband made a noise then. Not quite a grunt, but not a word either — at least not a word that Jack could understand. It must have meant something to Irene Vernen, though. She patted her husband on the knee and said, "You're right, Wes. That was in Kansas."

Wesley Vernen looked at least eighty years old, perhaps ten years older than his wife. He had puffy, liver-spotted skin and thin white hair slicked back from a craggy brow. His eyes were distorted behind thick-framed glasses and the left side of his face drooped noticeably. He wore a red flannel shirt and corduroy pants, and his wife had tucked a blanket around his legs.

"We moved here from Kansas when Dylan was seventeen," Irene Vernen explained. "That's where Wes and I met, in Wichita." She pronounced it *Witch-taw.* "Our house there had a porch like this one too, and Dylan would sleep out there in the summer on an old Army cot. He shared a bedroom with his two brothers — he was the youngest — and he liked to go off by himself."

She leaned over to fuss with her husband's blanket, then patted his knee again.

"We were blessed with six children in all, Mr. Pellum," she said. "Three boys and three girls. Wes had a job at the IGA supermarket in Wichita, worked his way up from stock boy to store manager. They transferred him to a store here and we had to relocate. By then our three oldest had moved out: Arthur and Hal and Louisa. Dylan had a bedroom all to himself here." She touched a bony finger to the cross at her neck, thoughtful. "But he did come out here to sleep sometimes, Wes. I remember that."

Wesley's mouth opened and some indecipherable sounds came out. His wife nodded along and poked at his knee. "That's true, Wes. We left the Army cot behind in Wichita, but Dylan had that old sleeping bag, you remember, and he would bring it out here now and then when it got too hot in his room."

Wesley looked unconvinced, but he flicked his fingers against the arm of his chair. A dismissive gesture. He didn't care to argue.

"I understand that Dylan went to high school in Romulus," Jack said. He'd learned as much from Ed Cavanaugh's notes. "Could you tell me if he knew Tim Caslake?"

Irene touched her husband's arm. "That's the other boy from the school who died." She turned to Jack. "Dylan didn't have many friends at school," she said. "The move here from Kansas was hard on him. He always struggled in his classes. When I look back, I think he might have had a learning disability. Dyslexia or something like that. But we never got him tested. He had to repeat his junior year at Romulus High and I think it embarrassed him. He kept his head down. I don't think he knew the Caslake boy."

"Dylan would have been a senior when Tim Caslake died," Jack said. "It would help me to know if they had any friends in common."

Irene came up with a couple of names of Dylan's friends, and Jack wrote them down. He knew Dylan's brothers and sisters might be able to give him more; Jack had their names, and before he left he would ask for their phone numbers. For now he said, "There was another boy killed around the same time as your son — Alex Cavanaugh, in Belleville. Is it possible Dylan knew him?"

Irene's shoulders rose and fell beneath her shawl. "I don't think he knew anyone in Belleville." She turned to her husband. "Do you?"

Wesley made a noise and tried to lean forward in his chair. His right hand reached toward the glass-top table. Irene had placed a mug of coffee there for Jack, though he hadn't touched it. Beside it sat a tumbler of ice water. She picked up the tumbler and tried to hand it to her husband. He waved it away. More incomprehensible noise. Jack thought it sounded like a complaint.

"You know you can't have coffee, Wes," Irene said. "You've had your coffee for the day." To Jack she added, "Wes had a stroke three years ago. His doctor is very particular about what he can eat and drink. He's not supposed to have coffee at all, unless it's decaf — but if it's decaf, he doesn't want it. So we compromise. He gets one cup of regular in the morning. But that's all. If he's thirsty he can drink water." She offered her husband the tumbler again. He turned away from it, letting out an angry sigh.

Jack talked some more with her about Dylan, about the day he died. He had graduated from high school by then and gone to work at the supermarket with his father. Irene thought he was happy with the job. Wesley made no comment; he seemed to have tuned out of the conversation. On a Sunday morning in September, the family went to church: Wesley and Irene and the two daughters who still lived at home.

"Dylan didn't come with us," Irene said. "I knocked on his bedroom door and got no answer. Which was typical. He liked to sleep late on Sundays. He got bored at church and we'd given up on making him go."

They went out for lunch after the service and returned home around two o'clock. Dylan wasn't there. They weren't alarmed. He was nineteen years old; he could take care of himself. His car and his bike were in the garage, but he could have walked into town. He had done it before.

They held out till midnight before they phoned the police, and the police said Dylan would probably turn up by the morning. He didn't. They made calls to the few friends he had, and to his coworkers at the store. No one had seen him. They went around to his favorite haunts: a pizza joint, a bar where he liked to shoot pool, a few others. New Boston is a small town; they ran out of places fast.

When he'd been gone two days and part of a third, his father took a walk through the woods behind their house, to an old private cemetery half enclosed by a wrought-iron fence. Dylan had been known to go there when he wanted to be alone.

Wesley Vernen found his son's body lying facedown in the grass over one of the graves.

"Wes came back to the house," Irene said, "and I swear he looked like the life had drained out of him. He fell on his knees right here in this room and told me what he'd found. I called the police, and I wanted to go see Dylan, but I had to stay here with my girls. Wes walked back to the cemetery and sat on the ground with our son and waited. They found him there — a detective and a patrolman, the first ones to come along. The detective opined that Wes would have done better to stay clear of the crime scene. Civilians made his job harder, tromping around, obscuring the clues. Wes nearly punched him in the mouth. The patrolman had to get between them."

The scene had been photographed and searched. No murder weapon was ever found. The police in New Boston talked to the police in Romulus and Belleville and tried to draw connections between the three dead boys. Irene and Wesley Vernen gathered their family together and buried their son.

"And we waited," Irene told Jack. "We waited to find out who was responsible for killing our boy. And people around here waited for it to happen to some other boy. But it didn't. It never happened again."

■ ■ ■ ■

The cemetery was something over a third of a mile behind the Vernen house. Irene walked Jack to the edge of the woods and set him on the path, but from there he went by himself. The path was notional in places: Jack lost it twice and had to find it again. He might have missed the cemetery itself, but he spotted a vine-grown section of the wrought-iron fence leaning against the dead trunk of an ash tree.

He counted twenty-three gravestones. There might have been more buried in the grass. Some of the names were worn away by time and weather. The dates — the ones he could read — went back as far as the early eighteen hundreds.

A pot of chrysanthemums rested beside a stone engraved with the name Melvin Kossuth. Irene had told Jack to look for the stone. It marked the grave where Dylan Vernen died.

Dylan wasn't there, of course. He was buried in a different cemetery, a few miles south, in a town called Flat Rock.

Jack stood over the flowers and listened to a flutter of wings above him in the trees. He looked around at fallen leaves and dead branches littering the ground. Fat gray squirrels darted and rustled among the leaves. He scanned the black fence, ornamental points at the top of the posts jutting up like spears. He tried to imagine the man in the hat leaning against the fence, waiting for Dylan.

Jack imagined him here in the daylight, talking to Dylan, putting him at ease. Then Dylan looks away for a moment and the man reaches for his weapon. Maybe a length of pipe; maybe it's been resting against the fence, unnoticed all the while.

It might have happened that way, Jack thought. Or Dylan might have been killed in the dark of night. No one saw him on Sunday morning. His mother knocked on his door and received no answer. Maybe Dylan had snuck out the night before — the same way Alex Cavanaugh had snuck out. Maybe the man in the hat was watching; maybe he followed him here.

No way to be sure. Dylan's body had been exposed to the elements for more than two days before it was found. Jack knew, from Ed Cavanaugh's notes, that the coroner had been unable to fix the time of death precisely.

Jack crouched down and touched the petals of the chrysanthemums. They were warm from the sun. He wondered if Dylan's killer had ever revisited this place.

Jack had done his trick for Dylan's parents: showed them his picture of the man in the hat. Irene had run the tips of her thin fingers over the paper, like a blind woman trying to feel the contours of his face. She returned it to Jack and shook her head. Her husband squinted at the image from behind his thick eyeglasses. The tip of his tongue poked out between his lips.

Jack held the paper closer for him to see, and the old man took hold of it with his left hand. His right one came off the arm of the chair and he made a beckoning gesture with his fingers. It took Jack a moment to figure out he wanted a pen. Jack let him have one — gave him his notebook too so he would have a firm surface to write on. Wesley Vernen laid the notebook on his thigh and the flyer on top and scratched something out on the paper. He went slow and the letters were very small, and the fingers of his left hand, holding down the paper as he wrote, blocked Jack's view.

When he took his hand away Jack saw what he'd come up with. Five letters in shaky uppercase. Almost a whole word. COFFE.

Irene Vernen saw it too. "Now, Wes, I told

you," she said. "You've had your coffee for today. You can't have any more."

16.

At home on Monday night, lounging on the sofa, Jack Pellum got a call from an unfamiliar number. He took a chance and answered.

"I've done some sleuthing," a woman's voice said.

He sat up. "Who is this?"

"Mata Hari. Was she a detective? No, she was a spy. Name some lady detectives."

Jack played along. "Kinsey Millhone. Cassie Maddox. Miss Marple."

"None of those ring a bell. This is Jennifer. Jennifer Caslake."

She sounded giggly. Maybe drunk.

"What's going on, Jennifer?"

"I've been asking around, looking at old yearbooks —" She seemed to cover the phone. Jack heard a muffled laugh, heard her speak to someone on her end. "Stop it," she said. Playfully. She came back. "The point is, I've been sleuthing. I've got a name for you. Lisa Saladino."

"Okay."

"I googled her," Jennifer said. "She works in Ann Arbor, at the university. I can give you her phone number."

"Who is she?"

"Who do you think? She's the girl I told you about. The one Tim harassed. Maybe you want to talk to her."

Lisa Saladino taught electrical engineering at the University of Michigan. Jack drove out to see her early Tuesday afternoon. She had a small office on the north campus, enough room for two chairs and a tall filing cabinet and a steel-gray desk with a dent on the front as if someone had kicked it.

"I haven't thought about Tim Caslake in years," she said. "But since you called, I can't get him out of my mind."

"I'm sorry to bring up bad memories," said Jack.

"They're not all bad. I knew him a long time. I remember in grade school, playing with him at recess. Standing up on the swings and then jumping off. Fearless. You'd get arrested if you let a kid do that today. I remember Tim's mother made his lunch. Always something good. She baked him cupcakes, brownies, and he would share them with me."

"I've met her."

"She was nice. I don't know what happened to Tim. We didn't stay friends. Some people, you fall off their radar. By the time we got to high school, I don't think he remembered that we had a history."

"I understand he asked you to a dance, and you turned him down," Jack said. "Your mother didn't want you dating."

"That's one version, I suppose."

"Have I got it wrong?"

Lisa sat sideways behind her desk. Her clothes fit her loosely, the practical wardrobe of a professor of engineering. Her hair swept in two curves down to her chin, framing her face and emphasizing the length of her neck. She wore retro glasses with black plastic frames.

"Well, it's a minefield, isn't it," she said, "when you're sixteen and a boy asks you out. That's what it feels like. If you don't want to go with him, and you don't want to hurt his feelings, you have to find a graceful way to say no. But some boys, some men, don't want to take no for an answer. So you tell them whatever you have to. The truth is, I was dating someone else at the time."

"Did Tim know?"

"Not when he asked me. But I told him, and even then he thought it shouldn't matter. He was Tim Caslake, why would I turn him down? So I told him I was grounded, my mother wouldn't let me go to any school dances. I thought that would end it."

She tipped back in her chair. "The irony is, I don't think he really wanted to go with me. Tim dated cheerleaders. I wasn't his type. Maybe he asked me in order to prove something to himself. I don't know. But when I turned him down, it got ugly.

"I'm not sure how far he intended to go. It started with my name and number on the wall of the boys' locker room. Then kids started calling my house late at night. Not just boys. Some girls too. The timid ones would breathe for a minute and then hang up. The bold ones would say things. Foul things. I won't go through the list. Then the rumors at school: I would sleep with any boy who asked, and also I was a lesbian, so try to make sense of that. Before long I was feeling sick every morning. I couldn't eat breakfast without throwing up."

"So you transferred to another school," Jack said.

"Not exactly. My parents decided to keep me home. My mother tried homeschooling me. She wasn't very good at it, but it was better than dealing with the other kids. We went on that way for a few months, from the end of my sophomore year and into the following fall. Then Tim got killed around Thanksgiving, and after the Christmas break I went back to school." Lisa paused and laid a hand on the blotter of the desk. Her left hand, a gold ring on the third finger. "It was a relief," she said. "Not that Tim died, but that things went back to normal. Am I allowed to say that?"

"Of course you are," Jack said. "Let me ask you something else, if I could. Did you know a boy named Dylan Vernen?"

She looked out the office's lone window. "The name sounds familiar."

"He went to your high school. He was murdered the year after Tim."

"I did know him," she said, turning to face Jack. "I mean, just to say hello. We weren't friends. He was shy. You got a sense he was always watching, taking things in."

"Can you think of anything he had in common with Tim Caslake?"

"What do you mean?"

"If the same person killed both of them, they must have had something in common."

"They went to the same school. Is that enough?"

"Maybe."

She thought about it. "They weren't alike. You couldn't see Dylan treating people the way Tim did. Dylan and I were in biology class together. We sat next to each other in the lab. One time we had to dissect frogs. They were dead, of course, smelling of formaldehyde. Other boys in the class made a joke out of it, like they were competing to see who could be more callous. Dylan was different. He didn't even want to touch his frog. His hand trembled trying to work the scalpel. Like he thought it was cruel, cutting it open. I don't think he had a mean bone in his body."

Jack nodded. "A couple more things. Did you know Alex Cavanaugh? He lived in Belleville, went to a different school. But he was killed around the same time as Tim and Dylan."

"No," she said. "I didn't know him."

"And the guy you were dating, when Tim asked you to the dance, who was that?"

"Why?"

"I'm just curious," Jack said.

Lisa Saladino took off her glasses. She looked at him with keen brown eyes.

"You're not just curious," she said. "You're trying to work out who killed Tim."

"That's true."

She tapped a stem of the glasses against her chin. "You want to find someone who had a motive."

"Yes."

"Like revenge. That's a motive. Tim made my life miserable. So if you think about it, I had a motive."

The brown eyes were alive. Jack realized he'd had part of her attention before. Now he had all of it.

"I don't think you killed him," he said.

"Why not?"

"You seem too well-adjusted."

"Ha. His name was Richard Sheridan. The guy I dated back then."

"What was he like?"

"He was sweet, kind, gentle."

"Yeah?"

"And well adjusted. He didn't kill Tim Caslake."

"Are you certain?"

She held up her left hand. The one with the ring.

"I sure hope he didn't. I wound up marrying him."

17.

The Belleville Police Department is housed in an unassuming brown-brick building on the corner of Main Street and Huron River Drive. Jack sat down in the waiting area near the sergeant's desk at ten minutes to four. He had a four o'clock appointment with Keely Tanager.

There were two other people waiting. One was a grand old lady in silk and pearls. She sat with her knees together and read a copy of *People* magazine, licking her fingers to turn the pages. Every once in a while she dug around for something in a pricey leather handbag. As far as Jack could tell, she never found what she was looking for.

The other was a Hispanic kid in his twenties, black T-shirt and jeans, his hands cuffed in front of him, arms resting on his knees. He behaved himself, mostly. He delivered a tortured monologue, his voice rising and falling, punctuated by pauses to shake his head and rub his face. "I didn't do it," he said. "I didn't. . . . Why would I do that? That's disgusting. . . . I didn't do it. What do I look like? I'm a civilized person." His name was Jerry. Jack knew because sometimes he would get too loud and the desk sergeant would call out, "Be cool, Jerry."

Jack had a flyer in his pocket. He had shown it to Lisa Saladino before he left her. He had the crazy thought that she would say, *What are you doing with a drawing of my husband?* and he would have his killer, the case would be solved. But she just looked it over with a blank expression. It was the one that Wesley Vernen had written on, and before Lisa returned it to Jack she pointed to the word — COFFE — and asked, "What's this? Is it supposed to be his name?" "It's nothing," Jack said.

But now he wondered if it meant something. Your mind could go on tangents like that, if you let it. Wesley had written COFFE. It made sense to assume he meant COFFEE. It fit the moment: he'd wanted coffee. But it was still an assumption. What if he'd meant to write COFFEY? That could be someone's last name. What if it was the name of the man in the hat?

Could Wesley Vernen have recognized the face on the flyer? Jack tried to recall the old man's reaction to the picture. You couldn't read his eyes, really, not behind those thick glasses. Jack thought about it there as he waited, with Jerry beside him shaking his head. "I didn't do it. I swear to god. Why would I lie to you?"

At four o'clock the desk sergeant called out "Mrs. Abernathy" and the old lady put her magazine aside and stood. The sergeant let her through a swinging half door and pointed her down a hallway and she passed out of sight. A few minutes later she came out, accompanied by Keely Tanager. Keely held the swinging door for her and walked with her across the lobby to the exit. A breeze from outside stirred the pages tacked to the bulletin board behind the sergeant's desk.

Keely came back, her shoes clicking over the tiled floor. Jerry looked up at her.

"I didn't do it," he said. "You have to know I didn't do it."

"Be cool, Jerry," Keely said.

She told the sergeant she was stepping out for a few minutes, then lifted her chin at Jack.

"Let's take a walk."

They went out into the sunlight and crossed Huron River Drive to a small park with benches and a bandstand. Jack smelled lilacs and fresh-cut grass.

He said, "I've begun to wonder if Jerry did it."

Keely Tanager laughed. "Let me put your mind at ease. He did. It's open-and-shut."

"What did he do?"

"He went to the Frosty Boy for an ice cream cone. He didn't have any money. They wouldn't give him the cone, so he did something he shouldn't."

"He got violent?"

"No, he unzipped and took a pee on their floor. He's done it before. He's off his medication again. We'll get him straightened out."

"What about Mrs. Abernathy?"

Keely bent to pick up a candy wrapper in the grass. "She's all right. She came in to report a crime. She thinks someone's been using her car without her permission. They take it when she's not looking and then bring it back. She's never caught them at it, but she's been writing down the mileage from the odometer. She says the numbers go up, even when she doesn't drive it."

"Do you think she's just confused?"

"Maybe. But she has a habit of leaving her car doors unlocked. And she tends to lose her key, so she keeps a spare in the glove box. She's had cars stolen before, over the years. But if someone's taking it and bringing it back — that's a new wrinkle."

They were walking around the perimeter of the park. They came to a trash bin and Keely threw away the candy wrapper.

"You didn't come in to talk about petty crime in Belleville," she said.

"No," said Jack. "I came to ask a favor. I wonder if you'd let me have a look at the case file on Alex Cavanaugh."

Keely nodded as if she'd expected the request.

"Why would I do that?" she said.

"Call it professional courtesy."

"You're assuming we belong to the same profession." She turned to look at him. "Is that what you did in Detroit? You gave private investigators access to murder files?"

"What harm can it do?" Jack said. "It's a twenty-year-old case."

"What hope do you have of solving it?"

"Not much," he admitted. "But my chances are better if I can see the file. And it's not just Alex Cavanaugh. I've been looking into Tim Caslake and Dylan Vernen too. I don't know how much you know about them —"

"I'm familiar."

"All I've had to go on are Ed Cavanaugh's notes. They're not enough. I need the files.

The police in Romulus and New Boston —
they're not going to want to help me. But
they'll share the files with you."

Keely smiled. Jack liked the look of her
profile.

"So now I'm supposed to get you three
files?" she said. "You don't ask for much,
do you."

"You wouldn't really be doing it for me,"
he said.

"Then what would I be doing it for?"

"To satisfy your own curiosity. You must
wonder what happened to Alex. You were
friends with his brother."

"You don't want to bring Danny into this."

"Why not?"

"It's presumptuous. You don't know anything about him." Keely's smile had gone
away. She shook her head. "Look, of course
I'm interested in Alex's case, and the others
too. Do you think I haven't looked at those
files? I have. When I took this job, I had it
in mind that I could dig into Alex's murder,
maybe solve it. But then reality set in. There
are new crimes happening every day, more
than enough to fill my time. Most of them
aren't as exciting as a decades-old murder,
but they have to be dealt with all the same.
A lot of this job is dealing with the small
stuff, with people like Jerry and Mrs. Aber-

nathy. You can't go back and fix everything. If you think you can, you're dreaming."

Jack touched her arm and they stopped. Faced each other.

"I understand," he said, trying to stay calm. "You have responsibilities. The thing is, I don't. Dreaming's all I want to do."

Keely sighed and looked to the sky. Jack thought she was trying to summon patience.

"Listen to me," she said. "I never found anything in those files. Some cases are unsolved for a reason — there's nothing to go on. Even if I could get them for you, I don't know what you'd do with them."

"They could save me some wasted effort," said Jack. "Today I came across a name: Richard Sheridan. He was the boyfriend of a girl Tim Caslake harassed. He could have had a motive to kill him. If I had the Caslake file, I'd know if the police ever questioned him. Maybe they cleared him. Maybe he's not worth worrying about."

He took the flyer from his pocket, the one Wesley Vernen had written on. "Here's another thing. The other day I talked to Dylan Vernen's father. He had a stroke; he has a hard time communicating. When I showed him this picture, this is what he wrote down. I thought it meant he wanted coffee, but maybe I'm wrong. Maybe he was giving me a name. Do you know anyone named Coffey?"

"No," Keely said.

"Maybe there's a Coffey mentioned in one of those files."

"I doubt it."

"But there could be," Jack said. "I need to see them. I'll tell you what else I need —"

Keely arched an eyebrow. "There's more?"

"I need to know if there were other boys killed around the same time in the same way, high school boys whose bodies were found in the woods. Not just here in Michigan, but in other states too. The FBI keeps a national database of homicides. It's called VICAP —"

"I know about VICAP, Jack."

"Then you know it could be useful here."

"I also know you can't run a VICAP search."

"But you can."

Keely frowned and started walking again, heading back toward the police station. Jack kept pace with her.

She said, "If I ran a search for you and something came back, you'd only have more cases to wade through. You can't solve the ones you've got now. But you want more."

"You know how it works," he said. "The more information you have, the more likely you are to find some common thread."

"That's assuming there's a thread to be found."

He started to reply, but she held up a hand to stop him. "Let's leave it there," she said. "You've made your pitch, and I have to get back to work. I'll think about it, the files and the search. I'll see what I can do — what I'm willing to do."

"Thank you."

"Don't thank me. I haven't decided yet."

18.

On Tuesday night, Michael Underhill walked through the second floor of his unfinished house. The contractor and his men had gone home for the day. The plumbing had been roughed in: plastic tubes instead of metal pipes. Red for hot water, blue for cold. The tubs had been installed. The sinks and vanities were downstairs in boxes.

Underhill went through the house, breathing the smell of wood and sawdust, picking up the detritus the workers had left behind. Paper coffee cups, fast-food wrappers, a stray glove, loose nails. He gathered it all in a small cardboard box. He went down to the basement and back up again, then tossed the box into the dumpster outside.

Cool night air and starlight. He strolled over bare ground marked with the tread of a backhoe and heard the clucking of chickens. He kept a coop near the back of the lot, one of the benefits of small-town living. The clucking grew more urgent as he approached. He scooped feed corn from a wooden bin and tossed it through the wire mesh. While the birds were eating, he unlatched the door and went in and collected their eggs in a plastic bowl.

He walked past an old tractor and came to the edge of the lot. He crossed the property line into the backyard of a ranch house. Nothing much: two bedrooms, one bath, small kitchen. He had bought it when he decided to build the new house. He lived in it for now. When the new house was ready he would fix up the ranch and sell it.

He opened the glass slider and stepped inside. Put the eggs on the kitchen counter. He didn't expect to see Anna Haley in his living room.

"There you are," she said.

"Here I am. How long have you been here?"

"Not too long."

She looked like she'd been crying. He went to sit with her on the sofa.

"What's the matter?"

"Bad day," she said.

Underhill put an arm around her. "What happened?"

"I got a call from the HR woman today,

about the hospital job."

"The music therapy thing? I thought they weren't making a decision until the end of the week."

She rested her head against his chest. "Something happened. Something terrible."

"You didn't get it?"

"It's not that. Something happened to the other candidate, the one I told you about. Chris Treadwell. He was attacked."

"When?"

"Sunday night. Somebody beat him up pretty badly. He's in the hospital."

"Here in Chelsea?"

"No. He lives in Ann Arbor. He's got a broken jaw — they had to wire it shut. One of his arms is broken too, and one of his knees is shattered. He's already had surgery on it, and he's going to need more. After that, he'll need months of physical therapy, maybe years."

"My god."

"The HR woman told me he'll have to move back home to recover — his family lives in North Carolina. So obviously he can't take the job."

Anna was crying now. Underhill could feel her shaking. He kissed the top of her head.

"It's all right," he said. "Everything's all right."

"I know," she said. "I've got you, and you've got me, and nothing can touch us, not deep down, not if we hold on to each other. But I just don't understand the world sometimes. He had forty dollars in his wallet. Somebody beat him half to death for forty dollars."

"People do crazy things."

"The HR woman, she talked to his mother. His mother said he's awake. He can communicate. He can write things on a pad. And what he's saying is —" Anna broke off, sobbing. Underhill rocked her gently.

"What's he saying?"

She sniffed, sat up, wiped her face. "He's saying he's grateful. Can you believe that?"

"Grateful?"

"Because of his hands. Some guy was beating him in the street, and all he could do was hope that nothing happened to his hands. He was afraid they were going to get stomped. But they didn't. His hands are okay. Once his broken arm heals, he'll be able to play the guitar again. And he's grateful for that."

Underhill laid his palm against the side of Anna's neck. His thumb stroked her cheek. He kissed her brow.

"Well," he said, "I guess that's a good way to look at it."

■ ■ ■ ■

Jack stayed up late Tuesday night thinking about Richard Sheridan.

Sheridan was a dentist with a practice in Ann Arbor. He had two children with Lisa Saladino, a boy and a girl. Based on the photos Jack found on social media, they looked to be around five and seven. Sheridan coached his son's soccer team. He gave his daughter piggyback rides. He grilled in the backyard. He played in an amateur hockey league and followed the Detroit Red Wings.

He would have been seventeen or eighteen when Tim Caslake was murdered, which would make him thirty-seven or thirty-eight now. He looked older in the pictures; he had thinning blond hair that did him no favors. Jack tried to picture him in a hat. Tried to picture him at a distance, at night. He got nowhere. Sheridan's face stirred no memory.

He imagined Danny Cavanaugh at thirteen, riding his bike, stopping to watch the man in the hat change a tire on his car. Could he have seen Richard Sheridan that day? Sheridan would have been only four or five years older than Danny, not a man at all, just a high school boy.

You're trying to force it, Jack thought. You want to believe that Sheridan killed Tim Caslake, because of what Caslake did to Lisa Saladino. You want to believe he went on killing, just because, because he liked it. You want to believe he murdered Alex Cavanaugh and Dylan Vernen, then took a break to go to dental school and marry his high school sweetheart, and then he picked up again, with Paul Rook's mother, with Olivia, with a dozen unrelated victims that Paul collected in his files.

You want to believe all that, because you don't like the alternative: that Richard Sheridan had a motive to kill Tim Caslake but not the others. That you have a solution to one murder, but only one.

Not the one you care about.

We're not looking for the man in the hat. That's what you told Paul. *We're looking for the truth.* But that was pretty talk. You're looking for the man you saw that night, the one you followed through the streets, the one you couldn't catch, the one you blame for Olivia's death.

It was after midnight when Jack went to bed. Light from a lamp on the street below cast the shadows of tree branches onto his ceiling. The wind moved the leaves. He didn't sleep. At one o'clock he threw his blanket off and got up and found a folder of old medical bills. He looked for a bill for a filling Olivia had replaced a few months before she died. He found it. Her dentist was a woman named Patel with an office in Dearborn Heights, not Richard Sheridan in Ann Arbor.

Back in bed Jack watched the gray leaves on the ceiling. He thought of Wesley Vernen, who had written COFFE on the flyer. It's not a name, he thought. You're silly to think it's a name. You're reaching.

Not a name. But maybe it's an offer. Maybe Wesley Vernen was proposing a transaction. *You bring me coffee and I'll give you what you want. I'll tell you who he is, your man in the hat.*

That's thin, Jack thought. Thin as paper, thin as a strand of silk. It won't lead anywhere. It'll only waste your time.

The shadows moved on the ceiling. Time was the one thing he had. Tomorrow he would go see Wesley Vernen; he would try to get answers from a man who couldn't talk. The idea made him smile. He rolled onto his side, pulled up the blanket, and drifted off to sleep.

On Wednesday afternoon Irene Vernen

worked in her yard. Jack watched her from across the road. She used a shovel to dig up a patch of ground on the east side of the house, then hauled bags of fertilizer from the trunk of her car and cut them open and dumped them out. She used a rake to mix the fertilizer in with the soil. She worked in the sun, with her gray hair tied back in a blue bandanna. Once in a while she took out a second bandanna and wiped the sweat from her face and neck. Jack got worried for her. He thought somebody should really go over there and help her.

He kept an eye on her from his car, all four windows rolled down, two tall cups of coffee in a cardboard takeout carton on the passenger seat beside him. He'd found a place to park that wasn't too conspicuous — not directly across from the Vernen house but about seventy yards up the road to the east, a spot where the shoulder widened out and you could pull off. He had stopped in New Boston first, looking for a coffee shop. He had a hard time finding one. He saw a gun shop and a liquor store and a place that sold gifts and greeting cards, but for coffee he had to go to a convenience store at a Mobil station.

He sipped from one of the coffees and watched Irene Vernen carry black plastic pots from the front steps of the house to her garden. The pots held seedlings. Tomatoes, Jack guessed. A woman like Irene would plant tomatoes. She'd share them with her lady friends. She'd make sauce and put it up in jars and store it away for the winter.

Jack checked his watch. Quarter after two. Irene's planting could take a long time. He put his coffee aside, leaned back against the headrest. A kid on a bike rode past, coasting along, standing on the pedals. Jack watched him recede into the distance, swing around in the empty road, and come back again. He stared at Jack as he rolled by, a black kid, maybe thirteen. Jack kept track of him in the side mirror. The kid came to a stop sign and blew through it. A minute later he had reversed course again. Jack watched his approach in the mirror, heard a slow squeal of brakes as the kid glided up beside him.

"Hey," the kid said.

"Hey."

"You picking berries?"

"No."

"Sometimes people come here to pick berries. There's blueberries growing wild, if you can find 'em."

"Do you live around here?" Jack asked.

"Down the road a way."

"You go to school?"

The kid looked at him warily. "There's no school today."

"I bet there is," Jack said.

"How would you know?"

"Doesn't matter to me."

Off in the distance, Irene Vernen coaxed a seedling from a plastic pot.

Jack pointed a finger at her. "Do you know that lady?"

"Yeah," the kid said. "That's Irene. My grandma knows her. Is she in trouble?"

"Why would she be in trouble?"

" 'Cause you're sitting here watching her."

"She's not in trouble. I came to talk to her husband."

"Yeah? What's stopping you?"

"I want to talk to him alone. I plan to give him coffee and his wife won't like it. She doesn't want him drinking it."

The kid's eyes narrowed, as if he wondered if Jack was putting him on.

"That's fucked-up."

"I know."

"He's like a hundred years old. Why shouldn't he have coffee if he wants it?"

"I'm with you."

With one foot planted on the road, the

kid rolled back on his bike, then forward again.

"You're not lying to me," he said.

"No," said Jack.

"You're not waiting for Irene to leave so you can go in there and rob them."

"I'm not going to rob them."

"You swear?"

"I swear."

The kid squeezed the brake levers on the handlebars. Released them. "You should come back tomorrow night."

"What happens tomorrow night?"

"Bingo at Saint Stephen's. Seven o'clock. My grandma goes. Irene too. Her husband'll be alone."

Jack nodded. "Thanks."

The kid braced his foot on the left pedal of the bike. "Dude's a hundred," he said. "He should get to have whatever he wants." He pushed off, found his balance, pedaled down the road. When he'd built up enough momentum, he let go of the handlebars and spread his arms out at his sides. He kept on that way and didn't come back.

Jack stepped out of his car and eased the door shut. He walked along the roadside to stretch his legs, came to a long ditch with cattails growing out of still water. A turtle sunned itself on a broken rock.

The afternoon crawled along. Irene Vernen knelt on the ground, fussing over her seedlings, patting the dirt into place around them. Jack decided he would wait a little longer, then head home and think about coming back tomorrow. He returned to his place behind the wheel of the car, rolled up his sleeves, fanned himself with his notebook.

Irene stood and brushed dirt from the knees of her denim pants. She used a hose by the side of the house to clean her hands. She went inside by the front door, and Jack let a few minutes pass and started the car. He powered up the windows and ran the air conditioner. He was ready to leave when Irene came out of the house in fresh clothes, got into her car, and backed out of the driveway.

She drove west, away from Jack. He cut his engine and took the untouched coffee and crossed the road, walking along the southern shoulder to the Vernen house. He went around to the back, thinking he might find Wesley Vernen sitting on the sunporch. When he arrived there, the screen door was unlocked but the wicker chairs were empty.

Another unlocked door let him into the kitchen. He called out, "Mr. Vernen?" Not too loud, not too soft. He left the coffee on the kitchen counter and passed into a sitting room and found Wesley Vernen lying in a recliner with a thin blanket over him, head tipped to one side, mouth open, snoring.

Jack took in the room, full of old-people things. Side tables cluttered with framed pictures and bowls of potpourri. Wall shelves with porcelain figurines and dusty unlit candles. A cheap reproduction of a painting of Jesus, long brown hair, eyes gazing up at heaven. A china cabinet for the good dishes and silver that would rarely be used. Overstuffed furniture upholstered in patterns three decades out of date.

Wesley went on snoring. Jack decided to explore a little. Dylan Vernen had been absent from the house for twenty years, but there might be traces of him still.

There was no second floor. You got to the bedrooms by passing through a hall off the sitting room. The first one he came to had two narrow beds with iron bed frames. The curtains on the windows had started out white and yellowed with age; there were patterns of flowers woven into the lace. Jack remembered that the Vernens had moved here from Wichita, bringing Dylan and the two daughters who still lived with them. This seemed to have been the girls' room.

Further on he found a bathroom with a

rusted claw-foot tub. A plain white shower curtain with little dots of mold. A window with four panes of glass, one of them cracked, all of them streaked with grime.

Across from the bathroom Jack found a large bedroom that must have been Irene and Wesley's. A queen-size bed halfheartedly made up with an embroidered bedspread. A crucifix on the wall above the carved wooden headboard. Closets standing open. Unwashed laundry in baskets on the floor.

One last door at the end of the hall. Jack pushed it open and caught a whiff of mothballs and cedar. A single bed that must have been Dylan's was pushed against one wall beneath a window. White sheets and a tan blanket. Nothing to suggest a personality. The walls were covered in striped wallpaper, blue and white. Jack found a few pinholes where Dylan might have tacked up posters.

No clothes in the closet, only a few bare hangers on a rail and three stacked cardboard boxes. The one on top held mementos: a pennant with the logo of the Kansas City Royals, Dylan's high school diploma, a yearbook from his senior year, Matchbox cars, a cheap plastic trophy from a grade school bowling tournament, a compass, a sack filled with pebbles and seashells and a single buffalo nickel, old birthday cards.

Jack put the first box aside and hauled out the second. He opened the flaps and found a collection of oddities: a pouch of chewing tobacco, tins of sardines and Vienna sausages, Snickers candy bars, Oreo cookies, a bottle of bourbon with nothing left but the dregs. Jack smiled. He thought he must be looking at Wesley Vernen's secret stash, all the things his wife wouldn't let him have.

The third box held more secrets. A layer of paperbacks on top: Sidney Sheldon and Peter Benchley. Underneath them, a cache of dirty magazines. *Penthouse, Playboy, Hustler.* The covers were dated within the last few years. So they were Wesley's, not Dylan's.

Jack returned the boxes to the closet and took one thing with him when he left the room: Dylan's yearbook. Passing through the sitting room, he heard the even rhythm of Wesley's snoring. In the kitchen the takeout coffee was cold. Jack thought he could brew some fresh. There was a coffeemaker on the counter. He looked through random cupboards and found filters but no coffee. He checked the freezer. No luck. He decided Irene must have squirreled the coffee away somewhere, to save her husband from its temptation.

In the end Jack poured the takeout coffee into a mug and heated it in the microwave. He found a carton of cream in the fridge. A bowl of sugar. He went looking for a spoon and the first drawer he opened was stuffed with pot holders and dish towels. The second held matches and toothpicks and Scotch tape and batteries and a nickel-plated revolver with pearl inlays on the grip. The gun surprised him, but only a little. He had some experience with searching people's houses. He'd come across guns in stranger places. Opening the cylinder, he saw that the revolver was loaded, six rounds in six chambers.

He put it back and tried a third drawer and found the silverware.

The coffee, cream, and sugar went onto the table beside Wesley's recliner. Jack shook the old man's shoulder gently. A catch in the snoring and Wesley came awake, slowly at first, eyes blinking, the back of a ruddy hand wiping drool from the corner of his mouth.

Jack took a chair and tried to look casual. Unthreatening.

"You remember me," he said. "We talked on Monday."

Wesley Vernen stared at him.

"I thought we might do better one-on-

one," Jack said. "You wanted coffee last time. I brought you some."

Wesley looked around. Saw the mug but didn't reach for it. He twisted to look behind him, as if his wife might be waiting there, watching.

"She's not here," Jack said. "She went out."

He sat quiet while Wesley spooned sugar into the coffee, everything in slow motion, the white grains drifting down like snow-flakes. The old man blew into the mug and took a cautious sip.

He went on that way, blowing and sipping, his lips making wet noises, his breath whistling faintly from his nose. After a while he took a break, resting the mug in his lap.

Jack drew the flyer from his pocket, the same one he'd been carrying around. He bent forward and held it out for Wesley to see.

"I showed you this the other day. I think this is the man who killed my wife. He may have killed your son too. I want to find him. If you know him, if he looks familiar at all, you can tell me. If you don't, that's okay too. Just take a look."

Wesley had another sip of coffee and put the mug aside. He moved with exaggerated care, as if everything he did were part of a ritual that had to be performed in just the right way. He worked a lever at the side of the recliner to lower the footrest. Leaned forward. Accepted the flyer. Brought it close to his face. Lowered it to the blanket on his lap. Jack offered his notebook and pen.

The old man took the pen. Laid the flyer on top of the notebook. Pressed the point of the pen to the paper below the word COFFE. He made a mark there, the black ink smearing. The mark turned into a letter J. Then two more letters, I and M.

Jack waited.

The next four letters came more smoothly. B-E-A-M.

Wesley looked up from his work, stone-faced, eyes steady behind the thick lenses of his glasses. Jack laughed softly, bitterly, shaking his head.

"I guess I deserve that," he said, "for thinking I could come here and get anything out of you. I'm an idiot."

The old man sat impassively, watching him.

"I tell you what. I'll bring you a bottle of Jim Beam. I'll go buy it for you right now. But you have to give me something first." Jack tapped the face on the flyer. "I need one unambiguous answer. Do you know who this man is? Or not?"

The eyes behind the lenses didn't blink.

"You get the bottle either way," Jack said. "Whether you tell me yes or no. But it has to be one or the other."

Wesley Vernen looked down at the flyer and up again. And nodded yes.

"You're saying you know him?"

Another nod.

"Who is he?"

Wesley shook his head from side to side.

"I have to get the bottle first. Is that the way it is?"

Nod.

"You don't know him," Jack said. "You don't know a goddamn thing."

The old man sat back in the recliner. The notebook, pen, and flyer slid off the blanket and onto the floor.

"You're a miserable old bastard and you don't know anything," Jack said. "I'm wasting my breath with you."

Silence. Jack looked around. Saw little tasseled pillows on a sofa. He could take one and put it over Wesley Vernen's face, just to get his attention. He could take the revolver from the kitchen and press the muzzle to Wesley's craggy forehead.

But what would be the point? How much more life did the man have left in him? How much could he care for it? It's hard to threaten a man who has nothing to lose.

"I'm driving to the liquor store in town," Jack said. "I'm coming back with a bottle of Jim Beam. You'll tell me something or you won't. Then I'm done with you."

No reaction from Wesley. Small sounds were magnified in the quiet. The ticking of a clock on one of the wall shelves. A housefly flitting against a window screen.

Outside, a car pulled into the driveway. Irene Vernen returning.

Jack bent to retrieve his notebook, pen, and flyer from the floor. He stowed them in his pockets. He gathered the coffee mug and sugar and cream.

Wesley's eyes followed him.

"I'll be seeing you." Jack said. "Maybe not today. Maybe tomorrow night."

The sound of a car door slamming.

In the kitchen, Jack returned the cream and sugar to their places. Rinsed the mug and spoon and set them in the drying rack. He grabbed the cardboard takeout cup and Dylan's yearbook.

He slipped out through the sunporch just as Irene Vernen opened the front door.

19.

Wednesday night. Kim Weaver lay on her side in Jack's bed, blond hair loose over one of his pillows. Jack touched a tiny mole between her shoulder blades. He traced two fingers over the curve of her hip.

"Is it late?" she asked.

"I lost track," he said.

She turned onto her back. His fingers found the soft place below her navel.

She said, "Should I go?"

"No. Stay."

"It's perfect here. Except that I'm a little cold."

He got up. "I'll close the window."

"Just partway," she said. "And cover me up."

He drew the top sheet up to her shoulders, touched her temple, told her to sleep.

He put on sweatpants and a T-shirt and settled in on the sofa in the living room. He had a gift from Keely Tanager: copies of the police files on Tim Caslake, Alex Cavanaugh, and Dylan Vernen. The Cavanaugh file would have been easy, since the Belleville police handled the case. The other two should have taken longer to get. Jack concluded that she must have had copies of them all along.

Keely had run his VICAP search as well, looking for cases of males, fourteen to twenty-one, murdered by blunt-force trauma to the head, bodies found in wooded areas. She'd set the time frame for five years before Tim Caslake and five years after Dylan Vernen. She'd run the search twice: once for Michigan and the surrounding states and once for the entire continental U.S. Jack had the printouts. The smaller search had yielded less than a dozen results, the larger more than a hundred.

Jack delved into the Caslake file first. Tim Caslake had been the first boy killed, and detectives from the Romulus Police Department had interviewed a wide circle of his friends and classmates. From the summaries of the interviews in the file you could get a sense of how their investigation had evolved. In the early interviews, with Tim's friends on the school football team, the investigators wanted to know how much money Tim usually carried, if he ever bragged about money, if people resented him for it. Clearly they considered robbery a possible motive for the killing — which made sense, because when Tim's body was found, his wallet and keys were missing.

As the investigation went on, the detectives began to get a fuller picture of Tim's character and habits. People said he had a sharp tongue, a cruel streak. If he didn't like you he would mock you, tease you, maybe shove you around. Once the investigators had a taste of stories like this, they went looking for more. They learned about what Tim had done to Lisa Saladino. They questioned her boyfriend, Richard Sheridan. They asked him to account for his time on the day Tim Caslake died. He told them he had gone straight home after school. His family backed him up.

Not the most solid of alibis. Jack thought the investigators should have pushed a little harder. But as he read on, he understood why they hadn't. Lisa Saladino's case wasn't unique. Tim Caslake had a pattern of reacting badly to rejection. There were other girls he had tried to humiliate. The detectives questioned them, and their boyfriends. They spoke to the girls' fathers as well. But they found no one to zero in on as a suspect.

Around two in the morning Jack's attention started to drift; the words on the pages began to turn fuzzy. He got up and went to the window and looked down on Prentis Street. A few college kids lingered on the sidewalk, ejected from the Bronx Bar, not wanting to go home. Jack listened to their chatter.

"And then Sheila tells me the coat belongs to her cousin."

"No way."

"And I tell her no worries, vodka doesn't leave a stain."

"Is that true?"

"That's verified. That's like fucking climate change. That's science."

He went back to the sofa and picked up Dylan Vernen's yearbook. He remembered the kid on the bike asking him if he planned to rob the Vernens. He had denied it. He hadn't meant to take anything, but he had taken this. He wasn't a thief, though; he would return it tomorrow when he brought Wesley Vernen his whiskey.

He flipped through the pages of the yearbook and found Dylan's senior picture. Dylan was a year older than the other kids in his class; he'd had to repeat a grade. In the picture he looked serious, his dark hair carefully combed, his eyes gazing into the camera.

In the same year, Tim Caslake had been a junior. Juniors didn't get individual portraits, only group shots taken with their homeroom classes. Tim smiled in his, standing at the edge of the image. Jack turned some pages, found the section for teachers and staff — the real reason he'd wanted the yearbook. He thought he might get lucky, he might find a coach or a janitor with a half-familiar face, or a goofy shop teacher everybody liked, the kind who wore his hat to have his picture taken.

Jack was scanning through the faces when Kim emerged from the bedroom. He made room for her on the sofa and she sat with her legs curled beneath her, her phone in her hand, wearing one of his button-down shirts.

"Am I intruding?" she asked.

"No."

"I just want to sit here. I don't want to distract you."

"Okay."

She laid her phone on the coffee table and picked up some pages from the Caslake file — notes from the detectives' interviews with Tim's parents — and started reading. When she came to the end she turned to the coroner's autopsy report. Her phone vibrated on the table. She left it alone.

"It's late for a call," Jack said.

"It's a text," she told him. "Doug's been texting me."

"Ah."

"You don't want to know."

"You can tell me."

"It's melodrama. It's not your problem."

"I like a good melodrama."

Kim pretended to look at the autopsy report, flipped a page. The phone vibrated again. She reached for it and pressed a button to power it off.

"I hate this," she said.

Jack put the yearbook down and waited.

"Not this," she said, pointing to him and back at herself. "I hate him. The way he's acting. He's a sad puppy now. He wants me back. He says he'll change. I know what it is. She dumped him. Gwen Davis, the one he was sleeping with."

"Did he tell you that?"

"He told me he's not seeing her anymore. I can guess what happened. Doug can be needy. He probably told her he wanted to see more of her. And she thought hard about what a future with Doug Weaver would look like and decided to pass."

Kim smoothed the tails of the shirt over her thighs. "So now he wants to know where I am. He's jealous. He's texting me in the middle of the night to prove his love. I'm sorry."

"It's okay."

"You're sweet. You didn't ask for this. I can go if you want."

"You can stay. Get some sleep."

"But you're staying up." She looked around at the files. "You've got a lot of reading to do."

"I'll come to bed in a little while."

She gestured at the yearbook on the sofa between them. "Is this part of it?"

"It belonged to one of the victims," Jack said. "I thought I might find the killer in there."

"But you didn't."

"No."

She touched the cover. "Maybe the killer signed it. People write messages in yearbooks."

Jack had thought of the same thing. He had checked.

"This belonged to a shy kid," he said. "Nobody signed it."

Kim lifted the cover and let it fall. "That's sad."

Before she left, she leaned in to kiss him and brush a hand through his hair.

He stayed awake for another hour. Spent most of the time with the Caslake file, but it didn't tell him anything. For a few minutes he switched over to the VICAP printouts but he was too tired to tackle them properly. The names of dead teenagers ran together in his vision. *Anthony Odum Joseph Lander Kevin Whiting Christopher Hammond Brian Crane Andrew Rensler Matthew Turnstone Joshua Kaplan Robert Barnevelder.* Too many of them. They would have to wait till the morning.

Jack closed the windows and brushed his teeth and went to bed.

Kim was curled up under the covers on the right side — Olivia's side. He climbed in beside her and wrapped an arm around her, his palm over her heart. She settled back against him and he felt her fingers on his wrist, on the back of his hand. She touched the gold ring on his finger.

"I'm not needy," she said softly.

Jack waited.

"You're supposed to say you know I'm not needy."

"I know you're not needy," he said.

"But I'd be happy if you would take it off sometimes."

Jack felt her heart beating under his palm. He said nothing.

"I'm not saying you shouldn't wear it. I would never say that. I know what this is, and what it isn't. But sometimes you could take it off. When you're holding me."

They lay together in the dark and he felt the warmth of her. He counted her heartbeats, ten of them, twenty, thirty.

He took his hand away from her and slipped off the ring and set it on the nightstand.

20.

Thursday night, eight o'clock. Irene Vernen was out playing bingo. Jack had driven past Saint Stephen's Church and noted her car in the parking lot.

The sun hung low in the sky. Gray light in the Vernen house. No lamps lit. Wesley Vernen, in his recliner, mumbled something in his sleep. His legs twitched beneath his blanket.

Jack poured him a third of a tumbler of Jim Beam and put the glass and bottle on the table next to him. He spoke the old man's name, shook him awake.

The familiar scene. Wesley looking around, wiping his mouth, lowering the footrest of the recliner. Spotting the glass. Reaching for it by slow degrees. Raising it to his lips. Sipping. Swallowing.

Leaning his head back in pleasure.

Jack said, "I was rude to you yesterday. I'm sorry. I should have been patient. The thing is, I haven't felt right since my wife died."

Wesley had another taste of the Jim Beam.

"I'll tell you something — and nobody knows this but me. The day she died, she left early to go to the park. She wanted me to go with her. I was getting over a cold, but it wasn't so bad. I could have gone. If I'd been with her that day, she would have been safe. But I wanted to sleep."

Wesley stared at Jack, curious, the whiskey temporarily forgotten.

"That makes me sound sympathetic. *Poor Jack, how awful he must feel, knowing he could have protected his wife.* But that's just a way of looking at it after the fact. That day, that morning, I was relieved when she left. I was glad. I liked having the bed to myself, the whole apartment to myself."

The old man's eyes blinked once behind his glasses.

"Don't get me wrong," Jack said. "I loved my wife. I remember loving her. That's the main thing I remember. But I also liked not having her around. Being alone. Maybe she felt the same way about me." He leaned forward and tapped a finger on the old man's knee. "And what I'm doing now, trying to find her killer, I couldn't tell you anymore if it's for her or for me. Maybe it's not for anybody. I started this thing and I can't let it go. You're probably wondering how you got tangled up in it, when I can't even know for sure that the same person killed my wife and your son."

Behind the recliner a curtain billowed on the wind. Jack brought out his notebook and pen. He took the flyer from his pocket and showed Wesley Vernen the face of the man in the hat.

"You were going to tell me his name," Jack said. "That's the deal we made. But I won't hold you to it. I don't think you know his name. Here's what we'll do instead. I'll write down a name and you can write whatever you want."

Jack opened his notebook to a blank page and wrote a name at the top. He turned it around for Wesley to read. The old man showed no reaction. He brought the tumbler to his lips and took a long, slow drink. Then another. He set the empty glass aside.

Jack watched him accept the notebook and rest it on his lap. Watched him grip the pen in a liver-spotted hand.

A minute passed. The tip of the pen hovered over the page.

Then it moved, haltingly at first. It wrote six letters: MELVIN. Jack read them upside down. The pen moved again, writing seven more letters underneath: KOSSUTH. The old man looked up, his mouth an expressionless line.

"I wasn't sure what you'd give me," Jack said. "But that's not what I expected."

Wesley drew a rough square around the name. Along the bottom edge he made a series of strokes that looked like blades of grass.

"I get it," Jack said. "I went out there, to the graveyard in the woods. Melvin Kossuth is a name on one of the stones. But he died a hundred years ago. He's got nothing to do with my wife or your son."

Wesley moved the pen again. Three letters this time. DIG.

"Are you serious? I'm supposed to dig up a grave now? Why?"

The old man scrawled out six more letters. BEHIND.

"Behind what? Behind the grave?"

The pen traced over the rough square.

"Behind the headstone?"

Wesley nodded once, sharply.

"What am I digging for? A body?"

Eyes closed in impatience, Wesley shook his head. He wrote a number on the notebook page: *6.* He followed it with two small slashes.

"Six inches. There's something buried six

inches down? What is it?"

Jack watched the old man hesitate, the pen suspended over the page. Wesley let out a frustrated breath, slashed a line under the word DIG and pushed the notebook away. It fell to the floor. He tossed the pen after it and twisted in his chair, gingerly, as if it pained him. He took hold of the bottle and the tumbler and poured himself a slug of Jim Beam.

Twilight in the woods. Jack followed the path. He had a flashlight from his car and he played the beam over the ground ahead of him.

He'd come close to doing violence to Wesley Vernen. Even now he wanted to go back and knock the man's drink from his hand, seize him by the collar, haul him from the chair, wring words out of him. But that would be cruel. Wesley had given him enough.

Jack stepped over tree roots and fallen branches, holding the flashlight in his right hand. In his left he carried a trowel. He'd taken it from a bag of garden tools on the Vernens' sunporch. He figured it would do the job. He only had to dig six inches down.

He'd brought along one other thing: the pearl-handled revolver from the drawer in the kitchen. He felt its weight in the pocket of his jacket.

He came to a dead ash tree, and another farther on, and then the flashlight beam found the wrought-iron fence. Jack followed the fence until he reached a break where the gate used to be. He passed through, stepped over a small granite marker half hidden in the grass, and saw the grave of Melvin Kossuth.

In front of the headstone: a clay pot of chrysanthemums to mark the spot where Dylan Vernen's body had been found. Behind it: grass and dead leaves.

Jack brushed the leaves away with his shoes. Balanced his flashlight on top of the stone. Kneeling, he plunged the point of the trowel into the ground and levered it back and forth to loosen the earth. He scooped out clumps of grass and tossed them away. He cleared a shallow trench the length of the stone and then went deeper. In the dry earth the work was harder than he had expected. He felt sweat trickling down his back.

Wesley had said six inches. It was closer to twelve. The blade of the trowel struck something metal.

Jack heard a rustling behind him in the woods. He sprang up, grabbed the flashlight, spun around. Dark now between the trees. The flashlight beam swept back and forth. He aimed it low, caught a glimpse of something black scurrying along the trunk of a fallen birch.

He waited, heart racing, listening to the night and hearing creaks and shufflings and distant murmurs. Breathing deep, he tried to loosen the tension in his shoulders and his arms. He looked down at his hands: the flashlight in his left, the revolver in his right.

Strange. He didn't remember drawing it.

He returned it to the pocket of his jacket. The flashlight beam trailed over the hole he'd dug behind the gravestone. A flash of silver in the black. Jack knelt again and used the trowel to widen out his excavation. He traced the outline of a round metal container with a lid — a tin for holding Christmas cookies.

He worked it free of the dirt.

The lid was on tight. He had to use the trowel to pry it loose.

Inside, a key ring with two keys. A brown leather wallet.

A flush of heat ran through him.

He opened the wallet. Saw a driver's license behind a little plastic window.

Timothy Rowan Caslake.

Behind him, a twig snapped. A voice said, "What have you found, Mr. Pellum?"

21.

Jack dropped the wallet into the tin. Rose up slowly, turning. His right hand reached for the revolver and drew it out of his pocket.

"You look frightened," Irene Vernen said. "What's the matter?"

He could see her in the dim — in the light of a half-moon and the beam of the flashlight lying in the grass. She stood twelve feet away. Gray hair tied in a scarf. Bulky fleece jacket worn over a dark blouse and tan slacks. Her hands in the pockets of the jacket.

"Stay there," Jack said. "Are you alone? Is Wesley with you?"

"Goodness, no. Wes is in no condition to be tromping around in the woods."

"Let me see your hands."

"What for?"

Jack aimed the revolver at her. "Just do it. Now."

"You're not a policeman, Mr. Pellum. Is that Wes's old gun?"

"Right now. Your hands."

"That old thing's a relic. There's something wrong with it — with the whatchamacallit, the firing point. No, that's wrong. The firing *pin*."

Jack drew back the hammer of the revolver with his thumb. Irene Vernen didn't flinch. He aimed at the ground and squeezed the trigger. No kick, no shot, nothing.

"You're very excitable, Mr. Pellum," Irene said. "Wes was like you once, if you can believe it. Time has mellowed him, but he can still be unpredictable. He thinks about dying and he has regrets. He worries about the state of his soul. I believe that may be what's happened here. But it's only a passing mood. He's a changeable man. As soon as he sent you on this little errand he regretted it. He phoned me. I can usually make sense of his talk, but this time he was so agitated I couldn't understand him. I knew I needed to come home, though, and when I got there he was calmer."

"I have a hard time picturing him agitated," Jack said.

"It happens. Liquor doesn't help. I wish you hadn't given it to him. And I wish you hadn't mentioned that name. Rensler. It brings back bad memories."

Rensler. Jack had never heard it said aloud. It sounded harsh in the night air of the cemetery. *Andrew Rensler.* It was the name Jack had written in his notebook and shown to Wesley Vernen.

"How did you come across that name?" Irene asked.

Jack looked down at the revolver. A glint of moonlight on the barrel. He returned it to his pocket.

"I found it on a list of murdered boys," he said.

He had passed over the name on the VI-CAP list the night before, but this morning he had studied the list more closely.

"Andrew Rensler lived in Haysville, Kansas," Jack said. "He had his skull bashed in with a wooden stave when he was fourteen. Haysville is right outside of Wichita. Andrew died three years before Tim Caslake. You and Wesley were still living in Wichita then."

"That's true," Irene said.

"How many boys has your husband killed?"

The question seemed to jar her. She took a step back and leaned against the cemetery fence.

"Is that what you think?" she said.

"That's my first guess. If it's not right,

I've got another."

"Wes is a gentle soul."

"He seems harmless now. I can't say what he was like before."

"He's always been gentle."

"Then it must have been Dylan," Jack said. "I've been thinking of him all along as a victim. As quiet and shy. Someone told me he didn't have a mean bone in his body."

Irene Vernen nodded eagerly. "That's true. He didn't. It was a sickness. It came over him. Dylan was kind. He had a sensitive soul. The world is a harsh place for a sensitive soul. A boy like Dylan sees too much. Feels too much. He wants the world to be fair. I ask you, Mr. Pellum, do you think the world is fair?"

"No."

"No. Andrew Rensler was a little monster, the kind of child who tears the wings off flies. He went to Dylan's school. We knew his family. They were country people. His father owned a bait shop. He would set traps for beavers and muskrats. He would skin them and sell their pelts."

The corners of Irene's mouth turned down in distaste. "There was a stray cat in the neighborhood of Dylan's school," she said. "The kids would see it at recess, hunting birds at the edge of the school yard.

Andrew Rensler saw it. One day he brought something in his backpack, something he'd stolen from his father: a steel leg trap, the kind that snaps shut when an animal steps into it. He used a can of tuna to lure the cat. It worked the way he wanted, except for the screaming. It was an experiment, you see. He wanted to know if the cat would gnaw off its own leg to get free. Like muskrats do. But the poor thing just kept shrieking, until Andrew Rensler stomped the life out of it.

"Dylan saw him. He came along too late to stop it. And he couldn't forget. It preyed on him for weeks. He knew what he had to do. But he struggled. There were two Dylans, a meek one and a strong one. The strong one prevailed. He followed Andrew home one day after school. Caught him alone in the woods. Dylan remembered picking up a heavy branch. And standing over the body after. He didn't remember what happened in between."

She paused. Jack filled the silence. "How did you find out?"

"He confessed to us," Irene said. "Five, six weeks later. I was gathering laundry one morning and found a jackknife in the pocket of his pants — nothing we ever bought for him. I asked him where it came from and

246

he wouldn't say. He looked guilty; I thought he'd stolen it. I sent him to talk to his father and Wes got the story out of him. He got lies first — Dylan said he'd found the knife in the woods. But eventually he told the truth. He'd taken it off Andrew Rensler's body."

"You never called the police?"

She let out a long breath. "You don't have children, do you, Mr. Pellum? When you do, I hope the worst doesn't happen. I hope you never have to make a choice like we had to make. But if you do, I think you'll find that your first instinct won't be to call the police."

"What did you do?"

"We turned to our church. Dylan needed help. Our priest agreed to counsel him. It really was a sickness, Mr. Pellum. An affliction of the spirit. We prayed for relief, and we believed our prayers were answered. Dylan felt better. He told us so. He felt as if a burden had been lifted from him."

"And you moved up here, to Michigan."

"We thought it would help. We didn't want to keep Dylan in the place where he'd been afflicted. We wanted him to have a new beginning."

"You wanted him to get away with what he'd done."

Irene's brow knitted in frustration. "No. We thought he'd been healed."

"But he wasn't healed," Jack said. "He murdered Tim Caslake."

Frustration turned to contempt. "Tim Caslake was a despicable person. A bully. An abuser."

"And when he died, you knew exactly what had happened. But you still didn't call the police."

"We weren't sure. Dylan denied it at first. We wanted to believe him. Then I caught him kneeling in his closet one afternoon. I asked him what he was doing. He said he'd seen a mouse. I looked in the closet the next day and pried out a loose baseboard. In the space behind it, I found the Caslake boy's wallet and keys."

Jack looked down at the hole he'd dug, the silver tin. "They wound up here," he said.

"I didn't know," said Irene. "Wes was supposed to get rid of them."

"What did you do with Dylan, after Tim Caslake? Did you send him to a priest again?"

She shook her head. "We didn't know the priest here. Not very well. We couldn't trust him. But we prayed with Dylan and we watched over him. He was better, after the

Caslake boy. We thought he'd worked it out of his system. There's no straight path, Mr. Pellum. Anyone can falter. Anyone can slide back into sin."

"But when Dylan slid back, people died. What about Alex Cavanaugh?"

The question made her shrink against the fence. "Alex Cavanaugh was a trial for us," she said. "When I heard about him, my heart broke. I was ashamed. We cried together, Wes and I."

"What did Dylan have to say?" asked Jack. "What awful thing had Alex done? Why did he deserve to die?"

Her eyes cut away from him. "I don't know. I wanted those answers. But Dylan wouldn't talk to me. He wouldn't talk to his father. I think he'd fallen very far. Wes and I were lost. We prayed for guidance but it didn't come. What do you do with a boy like that, when he's your son? He's yours, your responsibility. We knew we couldn't let it go on. But we had other children too, Mr. Pellum. Two more sons, three daughters. We had to think of them. Were we supposed to hand their brother over to the police? What would they be then? The brothers and sisters of a murderer. The shame would follow them all their lives. Wes and I — we couldn't do it."

Jack took a step toward her. "So you killed him."

Irene's shoulders came up. She seemed to draw into herself. "We had to. He was ours. I walked out here with him on a Saturday night. He liked to come to this spot. It was peaceful. Wes was waiting in the woods, with an old aluminum bat. Dylan and I stood there, on top of Melvin Kossuth, and I held my son's hand and told him I loved him. I said I wanted to pray and got down on my knees. He got down there with me in the grass. I spoke the Lord's Prayer aloud and Wes crept up behind him."

She bowed her head. Jack thought she wouldn't say any more, but after a moment she went on. "Wes didn't want to do it that way. He wanted to use a gun, so it would be fast and painless. But I knew that wasn't right. Dylan had to die like the others. If he died like them, no one would think he had killed them. That was the real test for us, for Wes and me: Could we take the hard road, could we follow it to the end? Wes did the hardest part, and when it was done, I couldn't even bear to look. I couldn't open my eyes, but I didn't want to leave here either. Wes had to lead me away. We left our boy behind. That night I couldn't sleep, and the next morning I sat in church and knew that we were damned. But Wes stayed strong. He led me through that day and the days after. We played the role of parents with a missing child, we told lies to the police, and when we judged that enough time had passed, Wes came out here and pretended to find our son's body."

Irene looked up and met Jack's eyes. Her expression seemed haunted. "I thought we'd be caught out," she said. "I thought the police would be able to read the guilt in our faces. When they didn't, when they left us free, I became convinced that something was waiting for us, some terrible curse, and it might not fall on us, it might fall on our family instead. I waited — for sickness, for cancer, for a fatal car crash. But the doom I looked for didn't come. Our children thrived. They found jobs, they got married, they had children of their own. What do you think that means, Mr. Pellum?"

"I don't know."

"I think it means that we paid our price. We sacrificed our son and the Lord accepted our sacrifice and blessed our other children." Irene Vernen stepped away from the fence. Her hands stayed in her pockets, where they'd been all along.

"Now you know the truth," she said. "What will you do with it? I think you're a reasonable person. You can see that no good purpose would be served by going to the police. The world doesn't need to know the truth about Dylan. His brothers and sisters don't need to know. We can have peace, you and I."

She nodded toward the broken earth behind the headstone. "The things you found there, they can go back in the ground. You and I can walk away from here together."

"That sounds fine," Jack said.

"Then you agree?"

"I'd like to."

"But something's stopping you."

"I have questions," Jack said. "I need to be sure about Alex Cavanaugh. If Dylan killed him, that's one thing. If he didn't, then whoever killed him may have also killed my wife. It's important for me to know."

"Of course Dylan killed him."

"But you said he wouldn't talk to you about it."

"That's right."

"What exactly did he say when you confronted him? Did he deny it?"

"He always denied it at first. With the Rensler boy, with Caslake —"

"But with them, he came around to the

truth," Jack said. "What about trophies?"

"Trophies?"

"The things Dylan took — Andrew Rensler's knife, Tim Caslake's wallet and keys. When they discovered Alex Cavanaugh's body, his wallet and keys were missing too. Did you ever find them?"

Irene sighed. "I never saw them. Maybe Wes knows. Maybe they're in the house, in some hiding place of Dylan's. We can search. We can look together."

"Sure," Jack said. "We'll walk to the house and look. Which one of us will walk first?"

"What do you mean?"

"The path isn't very wide. One of us will have to go ahead of the other. Will it be you or me?"

"What difference does it make?"

"No difference. Do you have a gun in your pocket?"

Irene's shoulders fell. "I'd hoped we were beyond this," she said.

Jack drew out the revolver again and tossed it on the ground. "I found that yesterday," he said. "Then tonight I searched the house to see if there were more. Wes was asleep. By then I had the idea he might be a serial killer. So you can understand why I wanted to have a look around. But no one's perfect. There might have been another gun and I missed it."

Irene's right hand came out of its pocket, holding a small black pistol.

"I carry this one in my purse," she said.

Jack nodded. "And you brought it here."

"I hoped you'd be reasonable. I couldn't be sure."

"That's fine. Leave it on the ground. We'll walk out of here together, like you said."

Stillness in the cemetery air. Irene held the pistol at her side.

"Now I don't know what to do," she said.

"Nothing's changed," said Jack.

"But it has. You don't trust me, Mr. Pellum. It's hard for me to trust someone who doesn't trust me. Do you understand?"

"Yes."

"I had my doubts, but I was willing to put my faith in you."

"You still can."

"I don't know. I don't think you're willing to let things be."

"Lay the gun down. We'll work it out."

"No. You won't rest. You said it yourself: you need to be sure about Alex Cavanaugh. I thought you would be sympathetic. I told you everything, because I thought when you understood you would show mercy. But I see you now."

"What do you see?" Jack said.

Irene Vernen aimed the pistol at him.

"You can't give me mercy," she said. "You want justice."

The sound of the shot was the loudest thing Jack had ever heard.

22.

On a Saturday afternoon, nine days after the thing that happened in the cemetery with Irene Vernen, Jack Pellum heard someone knocking on his apartment door.

It began quietly, like the pecking of a delicate bird. The volume increased over time, but it never became excessive. Loud knocking is coarse. It is the province of hoodlums and drunks.

Four raps and a pause. Four raps and a pause. On and on for three full minutes until he rose from the sofa and opened the door.

His mother said, "Jack, you look haggard."

He stepped aside and let her in. Alicia Pellum surveyed the room — heaps of files, newspapers, takeout containers. She took off a stylish suede jacket and laid it over the back of a chair and disappeared into the kitchen. Returned with a trash bag and started picking up styrofoam boxes and paper cartons of leftover Thai food. She moved with a smooth efficiency that had always fascinated Jack. She came from people who associated physical labor with virtue. At home she had a cleaning lady who worked five days a week.

When she finished she came to sit with Jack on the sofa.

"When's the last time you left this apartment?" she asked him.

He waved the question away. "I go out."

"When?"

"At night sometimes."

"You can't let them hem you in." By "them," she meant reporters.

"They don't come around anymore," Jack said. "Not like they did at first."

"There's a grubby man out there now, with a camera."

"He's nobody. A blogger."

"Your father could call someone."

"Don't be silly."

She drew away from him. She was unused to being called silly.

"Your father's been trying to call you," she said. "So have I."

"I turned off my phone."

"Why?"

"Because people kept trying to call me."

Jack's mother let out an impatient breath.

She sat straight and regal, her hands resting in her lap. The hands showed her sixty-odd years in a way that her face didn't. Her brow was smooth, her hair dyed auburn and cut fashionably short. Her eyelids had been tended to. Her jawline was delicate but firm.

She said, "You could get away from this, you know."

"Where would you like me to go?"

"I'm not saying I'd like you to go. I'm saying you could get away. You could visit your sister in California. Or your brother in D.C. He could help you find work."

Jack's brother was partner at a law firm on K Street.

"I'm not looking for work," Jack said.

"I never approved of this private detective business. That was your father's idea. He wanted to help you, and I don't think you realize what it cost him. People talk about that sort of thing. They see the ads, the billboards, for heaven's sake. It's vulgar. What do you suppose it does to your father's reputation?"

Jack's laugh started small. It grew until he shook, trying to hold it in.

"What's funny?" his mother said.

He wiped a palm over his face. "I'm sorry. I was thinking about her. She killed her own

son to save her family from embarrass-
ment."

His mother's eyes narrowed and she
scowled. "Don't you dare compare me to
that wretched woman."

The scowl made her face look ugly. She
let it pass.

"Listen to me, Jack," she said. "You've
nothing to prove to anyone. You solved four
murders. Maybe more, from what I'm reading. You could walk away from it if you
wanted. Find something else to do. Or you
could go back to the police, if that's what
you want. They'll take you. You're a hero."

Jack avoided her eyes. "There was nothing
heroic about it."

"You were always an impossible child,"
she said with a sigh. "Roll up your sleeve."

Instinctively, he drew his left arm across
his chest, away from her.

"You don't have to look at it," he said.
"It's fine."

"I was a nurse, you know. Before I met
your father."

"That was forty years ago."

"The signs of infection haven't changed
in forty years."

"It's not infected."

"Let me look and we'll know."

Jack gave in and unbuttoned the sleeve of

his shirt, pulled it up past his elbow. A patch of gauze on his upper arm, secured by tape. His mother peeled it away and examined what was underneath. Irene Vernen's bullet had left a shallow oval wound, long as a quarter flattened on a railroad track. A scab had formed over it, rusty brown in the middle, lighter at the edges.

"Does it hurt?"

"No."

"What about when you move your arm?"

"It's nothing."

His mother insisted on changing the dressing. He brought her fresh gauze and tape and sat patiently while she worked. Afterward he walked her to the door.

He embraced her and kissed her on the cheek, and when she had stepped into the hall she turned back and pointed at the outside of the door.

"I meant to ask you about that," she said.

On the white surface of the door, someone had spray-painted a message in black:

THIS IS WRONG

"It's been there for a while," Jack said.

"Who wrote it?"

"I don't know."

"You should have it painted over. Call

your superintendent."

"This building doesn't have a superintendent."

"Call a handyman then."

"When the time comes I'll do it myself. I'm in no hurry."

His mother frowned. "Sometimes I don't understand you. Why put it off?"

Jack ran a finger over the black paint. "I kind of agree with the sentiment."

More knocking, about an hour after his mother left. Jack looked through the peephole and saw Paul Rook through the fisheye lens. He wore the same hat he'd been wearing the first time Jack saw him.

Paul knocked again, tentatively, and looked off down the hallway. He tried a third time, then sat on the floor with his back to the wall across the way. He settled in, arms braced on his knees. Jack turned away from the door, then relented and let him in.

"I wasn't sure you were home," Paul said.

"I've been taking it easy."

"I called you a few times."

"I know."

"How are you?"

"I'm fine."

Paul rubbed the back of his neck. His

voice turned quiet, subdued.

"I understand if you're mad," he said.

"Why would I be mad?"

"I heard about what happened. I should've been there."

He sounded like a kid who had let down a friend. Jack couldn't help but smile.

"Don't worry about it, Paul. Really."

"I should've had your back. We were supposed to be in it together. But I went along with you one time, to talk to the Caslakes, and then I flaked out on you. I'm sorry."

"It's all right. You had work. I never expected you to be with me every minute."

Paul looked away, his cheeks flushing red. "It wasn't just work," he said. "I've sort of been seeing someone. We've been spending a lot of time together."

"Well, that's great," Jack said. "Good for you."

"It's someone you know."

"Yeah?"

"Jennifer Caslake."

Jack's surprise lasted only a moment. He remembered the playful way that Jennifer had talked to Paul. *You look like you want to sell me a car stereo.* And her response when he offered her a cigarette: *Aren't you a smooth one.*

"That makes sense," Jack said. "She was

flirting with you the day we talked to her."

The late afternoon sun shone through the windows overlooking the street. Paul walked over to one of them and leaned against the sill. Now that he had made his confession, he seemed to relax.

"Jen's cool," he said. "We hang out, listen to music. She takes classes at Eastern Michigan. Learning to write code. For designing games, stuff like that. She's trying to get me to apply."

"You should."

"Maybe. There's the money to think about — and the whole idea of going back to school." He shrugged. "But whatever I decide, I wouldn't start till the fall. So I'll have time, if you need me. I still want to help."

Jack dropped down onto the sofa. He felt tired. He'd felt tired ever since the night in the cemetery.

"I don't know, Paul. I think we may have been wrong. I think it's possible Danny Cavanaugh made a mistake. He saw someone the day his brother died, but it was just a man in a hat. It wasn't his brother's killer."

"You think Dylan Vernen killed Alex?"

"I can't be sure. But it looks that way."

Paul came away from the window and sat across from Jack.

"The man in the hat is real," he said. "I saw him. You saw him."

"We don't know who we saw," Jack said. "Even if he's real, I've got no leads. I've got no way to find him."

"There are other cases," Paul said, looking around the room at the stacks of files. "We could pick one."

Jack nodded. "We could. We might even find a killer. But if we did, I don't think it would be the man who killed your mother, or the man who killed my wife. I could look at every one of them — all those cases you found. I could get lost in them. But I think I've had enough. I don't want to get lost."

Warm in the room, and still, and quiet. Jack waited for an objection, for an argument. Paul opened his mouth to speak, closed it again, looked at the floor. A minute passed. He took off his hat.

"Maybe you're right," Paul said at last. "Maybe it's time to give up." He turned the hat over in his hands. "I bought this after my mother died. It's the same as *his* hat, as far as I can remember. It's like a talisman. I used to believe it would draw him to me. I was a kid. I believed the kind of dumb stuff that kids believe. Now I wear it as a message, to say 'Fuck you.' Like he's ever gonna see it."

He plucked at the fedora's brown band. "I hate him. I used to daydream about what I would do to him if I found him. I've spent too much of my life thinking about him. Danny Cavanaugh did too. He wrote a whole novel about him, about the man in the crooked hat. But it wasn't only a character in a book for him. It was more. It was everything bad, rotten. It was death." He looked at Jack. "You know Danny's wife died of leukemia?"

"I know."

"But one time he said to me, 'Where does leukemia come from, Paul?' 'It's cancer, isn't it?' I said. 'It just happens.' 'I think it comes from him,' he said."

Paul's mouth made a bitter smile. "Danny thought the man in the hat gave his wife cancer. He really believed that at the end. I think that's why he hung himself, because as long as the man in the hat was in the world, he couldn't have any hope."

23.

"I should have come sooner," Jack said to Ed Cavanaugh.

They sat in the shade at Cavanaugh's picnic table, a bottle of beer apiece. Sunday afternoon, warm sun, blue sky. Ten days after the night in the cemetery.

"I figured you were resting up," Cavanaugh said, "and you'd come when you were ready."

Jack touched the wound on his arm reflexively. "That's what I've been telling myself, that I've been resting. But it's not true."

"No?"

"It shook me. That's the truth. Did you ever get shot?"

Cavanaugh smiled a kindly smile. "Some people tried, a long time ago, but they missed."

"Here in Belleville?"

"In Vietnam."

"Then you've seen worse things than I have."

Cavanaugh ran a hand over his gray-stubbled scalp. "It's not a contest, boyo."

A bumblebee hovered near a corner of the table, decided not to make a landing. Jack picked at the label on his beer.

He said, "I've been dreaming about it — about that night."

"That'll happen," Cavanaugh said.

"It's always the same dream. In the cemetery with half a moon in the sky. Irene Vernen raises the pistol and without thinking I charge forward. She fires before she's ready, before she can aim, and the shot grazes my arm. I come in low, knock her down. The gun tumbles between the bars of the cemetery fence and into the brush. Neither one of us can reach it and she's seventy damn years old, so I hold her down. It's easy. She howls at first but the howls fade into crying, and I call 911 on my cell phone and wait for the police to come."

Ed Cavanaugh listened patiently and nodded at the end.

"That's not a bad dream," he said.

"No," said Jack. "I don't mind it."

"But that's not the way it was."

"No."

■ ■ ■ ■

Jack stood in the moonlight by the gravestone of Melvin Kossuth. He watched Irene
Vernen raise the black pistol and thought,
Move. Now. She made an effort to line up
the sights along the barrel and it saved him.
By the time she was ready, he was moving.
Not toward her, not away, but sideways, to
her left, toward a section of the wrought-
iron fence that had almost fallen over.

She fired a shot that would have hit him
center mass if he had stayed still. It slashed
his arm instead.

Her second shot came nowhere near him.
He reached the leaning fence and vaulted
over, landing hard on the other side, sprawling in pine needles and grass. Her third shot
tore a divot from the ground beside him,
but then he was on his feet. He pitched
forward, caught hold of a sapling, swung
around it, and took off into the woods.

He dodged through the trees, his breath
coming in rough gasps, a pulsing pain in his
arm. He heard another shot. Ran on in the
moonlight. Fell, scraping his hands. Got up
again. Blood trickled down his arm, soaked
his sleeve.

After a time — he didn't know how long

— he broke free of the woods and found himself in someone's backyard. Almost tripped over a child's red wagon.

He stood still and got his breathing under control. Listened. No sound from the woods.

Jack skirted along under the eaves of a dark house, came to a road, and stopped to get his bearings. The GPS on his phone showed him that he hadn't gone very far. If he went north and west he would come back to the place where he'd left his car, not far from the Vernens' house. He jogged along the shoulder under the stars, came to an intersection, and rounded a corner onto Judd Road — the Vernens' road. He heard a soft hiss: cattails swaying in the wind. He saw his car in the shadows by the roadside.

Then he heard a muffled crack. Another gunshot. He looked around wildly, thinking that Irene Vernen had followed him the whole way. But of course she hadn't.

The sound had come from the house.

It was seventy yards to the front door. He crossed the distance fast, but it seemed slow. The front door was locked. He had to run around to the back.

He knew what he would find. Wesley Vernen dead in the reclining chair. Irene standing over him, aiming the black pistol at her own temple. A final desperate move. A solution to an unsolvable problem.

That was not what he found.

"I should have known," Jack told Ed Cavanaugh. "Wesley had always been the strong one. She told me that at the cemetery. She could count on him to do what she wanted. She had given him the gun."

Cavanaugh waited, hands folded on the table.

Jack said, "I crossed through the sunporch and the kitchen and found Wesley sitting on the floor by his wife's body. Her blood soaking into the carpet. He didn't make a sound. He was weeping, stroking her hair.

"The pistol was there beside his hand. He reached for it when he saw me. Before I could do anything, he put the muzzle under his chin and pulled the trigger."

Jack bowed his head. Cavanaugh didn't say anything. He didn't rise, he didn't come around the table, he didn't lay a fatherly hand on Jack's shoulder. But he sat with him, the two of them sharing a companionable silence, until Jack lifted his head and said, "I owe you an apology."

"No, you don't."

"If I had done it differently —"

"You did fine."

"— they'd be alive," Jack said. "The police would have them. They'd be able to question them. Wesley might have been able to tell them something about your son. The way things stand, you're left not knowing."

Ed Cavanaugh turned away from Jack and looked off into the middle distance. A cloud moved in front of the sun and the weight of the gray sky seemed to settle on his shoulders.

"My son is gone," he said. "I've lived with not knowing who killed him for twenty years. None of it's your doing. You've got nothing to apologize for."

Jack drove aimlessly after he left Ed Cavanaugh's place. South on a long, straight two-lane, with farmers' fields on either side. Then west to a set of railroad tracks, the signal flashing as he approached, the barrier coming down. He waited out the passage of a freight train, then drove on another mile or two before turning around.

He drove east on winding roads, sometimes under open sky, sometimes in leafy shade. He had a gun on the passenger seat beside him, a Smith & Wesson revolver with a well-worn grip. A gift from Ed Cavanaugh.

"You might need it," Cavanaugh had said. "Better to have it than not."

"That's generous," Jack had replied. "I appreciate it. But you should hold on to it."

"I've got no use for it anymore."

"I wouldn't feel right —"

"For god's sake, boyo, we're not gonna stand here and be polite to each other all day. You're prone to trouble, and more likely to need it than I am. So take it and say thank you."

"All right. Thank you."

So now he had it as he drove east in the late afternoon, windows rolled down, one hand out to feel the wind. He came to New Boston without meaning to, but once he was there he made his way to the Vernen house. He drove by slowly, came back around, pulled onto the shoulder. Nothing much to see: boarded windows, a NO TRESPASSING sign on the front door. People get curious about a place where a serial killer lived. Jack looked at Irene Vernen's little garden and wondered what would happen to her tomatoes. There was a hose uncoiled on the lawn, as if a neighbor might have made an effort to water them.

Minutes passed in the idling car, and the only change was the drifting of the clouds over the roof of the house. Jack's thoughts wandered: to the cemetery in the woods, Irene Vernen's voice, *What have you found,*

Mr. Pellum? He thought of Wesley Vernen weeping beside his wife's body. He thought of what happened after. Needing to get out of the house. Sitting on the lawn in the dark, calling Keely Tanager on his cell phone. The only call he made that night; she made all the others. Then sirens and a circus of activity. Flashing lights in red and blue. Local cops, EMTs, state police. People talking to radios and to each other and sometimes to him. He didn't answer. The EMTs figured out there was no one to save. Someone put a blanket over Jack's shoulders, and he kept it there, even though he wasn't cold.

He remembered Keely on the lawn beside him. Sitting quiet for a long time. Then telling her the story, haltingly, the first of many times he would tell it.

Now, in the car, he was brought back to reality. A sheriff's cruiser drew up beside him. He heard a window rolling down, a hard voice saying, "Do you live in this neighborhood, sir?"

The deputy had a stern face to match the voice.

Jack said, "No, I don't."

"Do you have business here?"

"No. Sorry."

"Please move along then."

Jack nodded. The window rolled up. The

cruiser pulled away.

Jack looked at the revolver on the seat beside him, and the box of ammunition Ed Cavanaugh had given him to go with it. Careless. He opened the glove compartment and stowed everything out of sight. Then he put the car in gear and headed west back to Belleville.

Tanager's Pub was quieter than it had been on his previous visit. A light crowd for an early Sunday dinner, a lot of empty stools at the bar. No live music, just something instrumental and vaguely Celtic on the sound system. Henry Tanager, the owner, floated from one table to another, chatting with the regulars. He leaned in to say something charming to an elderly lady, a lock of his silver hair falling over his forehead.

Jack made his way to a booth in the back, under a framed poster of an Irish castle. Keely Tanager sat there reading a book — a hardcover with no dust jacket. She closed it and hid it away when he sat across from her.

"*Pride and Prejudice,*" he said.

"Pardon?"

"The book. I'm guessing it's *Pride and Prejudice.* It's been your favorite since high school. You reread it every couple years."

"No."

"Sense and Sensibility?"

"No."

"Right. It's not Jane Austen. Is it *Wuthering Heights? Jane Eyre?*"

"No."

"Is it something else by a Brontë?"

"It's not by a Brontë."

"Okay," he said. "Let me think about it. Don't tell me."

"I wasn't going to."

A waitress came and Jack ordered a Coke. When she'd gone he said to Keely, "I'm sorry I'm late."

"You could've stayed away. I don't have much to tell you."

"They haven't found any more bodies in the woods?"

"Not since the last time we talked."

Jack knew that the state police had been searching the woods behind the Vernen house. They had found a set of human remains in an unmarked grave near the cemetery fence. Based on dental records and items recovered with the body, the remains had been identified as Heath Warrington, a classmate of Dylan Vernen's at Romulus High. Heath had disappeared near the end of Dylan's senior year. The case had never been investigated as a homicide; Heath came from a troubled home, and authorities assumed he had run away.

"It would be nice to know if there are more victims," Jack said.

"The state police are on it," said Keely. "The lieutenant I talked to said they're moving with all deliberate speed — which was his way of telling me to get off his back. It's a complicated situation. Personally, I think they've found all they're going to find. It's not like there's a trove of unsolved cases of boys who went missing in this area twenty years ago. There aren't any others, as far as I know. But they'll keep searching. I think in the end they'll have to dig up all the graves in that cemetery, and sort out all the remains, just to be sure."

"What about the Vernen house?" asked Jack. "Have they found anything there?"

"They've been tearing the place apart from the inside," Keely said. "Prying up floorboards. Cutting holes in the walls. They found a money clip with Heath Warrington's initials engraved on it. They found the pocketknife Irene Vernen told you about, the one that belonged to Andrew Rensler, the victim from down in Wichita. His parents recognized it. The Wichita police are ready to close that case. They're looking at another case too, a boy who went missing during the time when the Vernens lived there, but so far they haven't been able to connect him to Dylan."

"What about Alex Cavanaugh?" Jack said. "Nothing of his has been found in the Vernen house? No wallet, no keys?"

Keely shook her head. "Not so far."

"Does that bother you?"

"Not especially."

"It bothers me."

"Tim Caslake's wallet and keys wound up buried in that cemetery," Keely said. "Alex Cavanaugh's are probably buried some-where too."

Jack was sitting sideways in the booth, his back against the wall, one leg drawn up on the bench. The waitress had brought his Coke, but he had left it untouched. Now he picked at the wrapper on the straw, pulling it apart at the seam. He wound the paper around the tip of his finger. Keely sat across from him in silence.

"When this thing started," he said, "I came here looking for Alex Cavanaugh's killer —"

"You came here looking for your wife's killer," she said gently. "You didn't care about Alex. He was a means to an end."

Jack unwound the straw paper. Nodded.

"That's fair. But I thought they were one and the same — the man who killed my wife, and the man who killed Alex. The point is, I meant to focus on Alex. But I got distracted along the way, by Tim Caslake and Dylan Vernen, because they all seemed to be related. That led me —"

"It led you to the truth," Keely said. "Just not the truth you wanted. Dylan Vernen died a long time ago, so he couldn't have killed your wife. So you don't want to believe that he killed Alex either."

Jack tossed the straw paper onto the table. "There are reasons to doubt that Dylan killed Alex. There's no evidence at this point that they even knew each other."

"That's true," Keely said.

"And if you look at the sequence, it doesn't make sense."

"What do you mean?"

It was something Jack had been going over in his mind. "Dylan Vernen kills Andrew Rensler down in Kansas," he said. "He leaves the body in the woods where it can be found. Then he kills Tim Caslake up here and does the same thing. *Then* he kills the boy they just found — Heath — and he changes his method. He conceals the body. He buries it."

"That's logical," Keely said. "He's getting

smarter. He can't leave all these bodies lying around. His parents are already on to him. He has to be worried about them, and about the police."

"Right. Then, supposedly, Dylan kills Alex Cavanaugh. But he doesn't bury the body. He leaves it where it can be discovered."

Keely's green eyes looked thoughtful. "I see what you're saying, but he could have had a reason. Suppose he meant to bury Alex, but someone drove by and spooked him. Or suppose burying Heath was too much of a hassle. He didn't want to do it again."

"Or maybe Dylan Vernen didn't kill Alex at all," Jack said. "Maybe he denied it when his parents asked him because he really didn't do it. And they killed him anyway, because they assumed he was lying. Why wouldn't they, given what they knew he'd done?"

Keely let a moment pass. Then said, "I think you're reaching."

"I know I'm reaching. It doesn't mean I'm wrong."

"If Dylan didn't kill Alex, there are two possibilities," Keely said. "The first is that some other crazy killer was roaming around southeast Michigan at the same time, and *he* killed Alex."

"That seems unlikely."

"I'm glad you think so. The second possibility is that someone had a motive to kill Alex, and he made it look like the work of a crazy killer. So you're looking for someone who had a compelling reason to murder a seventeen-year-old boy." She leaned toward him a little. Made her voice softer. "And since you don't really care about Alex for his own sake, you must believe that the very same person had a motive to kill your wife. Do I need to tell you how unlikely *that* is?"

Jack picked up the straw paper again, just to have something to do with his hands.

"You don't have to tell me," he said.

Keely watched him from across the table. Murmurs of conversation around them. Music in the air, something slow and wistful played on a harp.

She said, "You're not going to give up, are you?"

"I've thought about it," Jack said. "I really have. But no, I don't think I am."

24.

Ed Cavanaugh made himself dinner after Jack left. He peeled potatoes and sliced them thin and fried them in butter in a cast-iron skillet. He tossed some chopped onions into the pan next, and then a steak. He browned it on both sides and left it raw in the middle.

He ate the steak with ketchup and the potatoes with spicy mustard. He found that food had gotten blander as he got older. He needed something to give it taste.

He drank a beer with the meal, only his second of the day. He had been cutting back for the past week or so. His head felt clear.

Afterward he filled the sink with soapy water and cleaned his dishes. He left them to dry on a towel on the counter. He had a dishwasher but he never used it anymore. It seemed too much bother.

He walked through his house in the fading of the day. Upstairs he got undressed and stepped into the shower. He made the water as hot as he could stand. Steam on the mirror when he got out. He opened the window and waited for it to clear so he could shave.

In his bedroom he put on underwear and socks and a white dress shirt and his second-best suit. He left the best one hanging in the closet.

His pockets were empty. He poked around, here and there, and filled them with the things he needed.

Downstairs he opened the shoe box on the sofa and sifted through the photographs inside. He chose three to take with him.

A chorus of crickets outside. Cavanaugh backed his truck down the driveway to the road. His house, as he drove away, looked old and small. He listened to the rumbling of the truck's engine, rolled the window down to feel the wind. Slowed for the stop sign and took a right turn, then another, then a long gray stretch of road brought him to the lot where the Sturridge house once stood.

He took a flashlight and a folded blanket from the cargo bin in the bed of the truck and set out. The tall grass snatched at his ankles. He came to the ruined fence and braced a hand on one of the posts to climb over. Bits of rotted wood came away on his palm.

He descended the slope, careful of his footing, and came to the place between the two apple trees.

A burst of unexpected color in the night when the flashlight beam found the flowers growing in the circle of stones. Cavanaugh shifted the light to the trunk of one of the trees and read the words that were carved there. He remembered a day in the spring, months after his son Alex died. Remembered coming here and clearing the ground, he and his son Danny carrying the stones, his wife arranging them in a circle. She planted the flowers and Cavanaugh cut away a patch of bark from the tree and Danny took the knife and carved the letters — straight lines and smooth, patient curves — ALEX WE LOVE YOU.

Cavanaugh dropped the blanket on the ground and eased himself down. He brought out the photos from his shirt pocket: One of Alex as a boy, big smile, front teeth missing. One of Danny and his bride on their wedding day. One of his own wife, impossibly young, standing by a railing with Niagara Falls in the background. He had snapped the picture on their honeymoon.

Tears came to him. He didn't try to keep

them in. He let the sound out too, a moan that broke and heaved with his breath. There was no one to hear it.

When it passed he wiped his face with the heels of his hands. He wiped his hands on his sleeves. A wind ran through the clearing and stirred the petals of the flowers. Cavanaugh reached into a pocket of his suit jacket and brought out a Colt .38 semiautomatic. His best gun. He had given Jack Pellum the second-best.

From his other pocket Cavanaugh took an empty magazine and a handful of rounds. He fed the rounds into the magazine one by one, loaded the magazine into the pistol, heard it snap into place. He worked the slide to put a round in the chamber.

Long minutes crept by before he could go any further. He sat with his forearms on his knees, the gun held loosely in his hand. He thought of words. He ought to have words at a time like this, something to say to his family. In the end he could find only one.

He whispered it first: "Good-bye." Then said it louder.

It sounded hollow both times.

He pocketed the gun and rose slowly to his feet. Took a last look at the flowers and headed back to his truck. He left the photos on the ground, leaning against the stones.

■ ■ ■ ■

The truck rolled down Main Street, past the police station, past the Frosty Boy, past a diner and a jeweler's shop. Ed Cavanaugh found a place to park at the curb, a block away from Tanager's Pub.

The restaurant closed at nine o'clock on Sundays. Henry Tanager came out around nine thirty, his jacket slung over his shoulder, slick silver hair like a lounge singer. He stood on the sidewalk for a minute, taking the air, looking up at the sky. He rolled his shoulders and worked out the kinks in his neck.

His BMW occupied a prime spot in front of the restaurant. Tanager got in and drove north toward the lake. Cavanaugh let him have a good lead and then followed him.

The road ran past a string of houses on the shore of the lake. Cavanaugh came around a bend and saw three tall willow trees on a well-tended lawn. He glimpsed Tanager's house behind the tendrils of the trees as he drove by — a long structure of dark wood. He parked the truck on the roadside and walked back.

The smell of mint as he crossed Tanager's

lawn. Lights on in the house behind filmy curtains. Cavanaugh headed for the front door and then changed his mind. If you own a house on the lake and you come home on a clear night, you'll want to have a look at the water. He went through the side yard and came to the back and saw Henry Tanager smoking a cigar on a wooden deck by the shore.

A path of broad, flat stones crossed the backyard, but Cavanaugh kept to the grass. Tanager didn't hear him until he stepped onto the deck.

The silver head turned first, then the rest of him. The hand with the cigar moved to cover his heart. Tanager let out a nervous chuckle.

"Jesus, Ed. You scared me."

"Did I?" said Cavanaugh.

"I didn't expect you."

"I thought we should talk."

"Well, that's fine. But give a man some warning."

Cavanaugh stepped up to the railing of the deck. Both men looked out at the smooth plane of the water, at the dots of light on the far shore.

"I can't remember the last time you were here," Tanager said. "It must have been —"

"When Danny and Keely were teenagers."

"That's right. Those two, they were something."

"They were."

"You couldn't keep them apart."

Tanager's cigar had gone out. He laid it on the railing. The smell of it lingered, sour and musky.

"We did though," Cavanaugh said.

"What's that?" said Tanager.

"We kept them apart. They were sweet on each other."

"I don't know —"

"Sure you do. Anyone could see it. I know Danny thought about proposing, right after high school. He confided in his mother. I told her not to encourage him."

Tanager braced his arms on the railing and stared off into the distance.

"Well, that was probably wise," he said.

"I think he went ahead and asked Keely anyway, and she turned him down," said Cavanaugh. "Danny was awfully sullen when he went away to college. You can tell when a boy's had his heart broken. Do you know if he asked her?"

"How would I know?"

Cavanaugh leaned on the railing, mimicking Tanager's pose. The two of them stood less than a foot apart. Cavanaugh could smell the other man's sweat.

"I think he asked her. And maybe she wanted to say yes, and you made it plain you didn't approve."

Tanager sighed. "They were kids, Ed. They were too young to get married."

"My boy wasn't good enough for your girl."

"I never said that. I never said any such thing."

"You didn't need to," Cavanaugh said. "It was clear enough. I tried not to think too much about the reasons. I let myself believe it was because you were an arrogant prick. You and yours had money, and me and mine didn't have enough to suit you."

Tanager's expression darkened. "Hold on now —"

"You *are* an arrogant prick, so it was an easy thing to believe. I've let myself do that over the years — believe the easy thing. I let myself believe that an insane person killed my Alex twenty years ago. That it was random. That it happened for no good reason."

"But that's true."

"I don't think so anymore."

Something splashed out in the water. A frog, or a fish breaking the surface. Cavanaugh felt Tanager move beside him. He turned and saw the other man standing straight, facing him. Tanager's eyes held sympathy.

"I don't know why you'd say that, Ed. There's been nothing else in the papers, nothing on the news but stories about that lunatic — Vernen."

"Dylan Vernen didn't know Alex," Cavanaugh said.

"What difference does that make?"

"He knew the others. There's a connection, with each of the other victims. But not with Alex."

Tanager shrugged. "They lived a few miles apart. Their paths may have crossed. Who can say?"

"I've tried telling myself that, ever since I learned that Dylan Vernen was a killer. Maybe he saw my Alex somewhere. Maybe Alex looked at him wrong. Cut him off in traffic. Did some little thing that made him angry."

"There you go. That could have happened."

"I could believe it," Cavanaugh said. "But I've known for years that there's another explanation. There's someone who had a motive to kill my son. I didn't want to think about that. It was easier to believe there was no motive, because that meant it was completely out of my control. I was blameless.

There was nothing I could have done. Do you have your phone?"

Tanager's eyes narrowed in confusion. "What?"

"Your cell phone," Cavanaugh said. "I never had one myself, and now I've got no one to call anyway. I walked around my house today, through all the empty rooms, and I realized they were going to stay that way. Empty. There's no one to fill them. Not anymore."

Tanager's head tipped to the side. "Are you all right, Ed?"

"No. Of course I'm not. Do I seem all right?"

"Are you drunk?"

"Not today."

A pause while Henry Tanager thought something through. He made a decision. Clapped his hands together.

"Let's get you home," he said. "I'm worried about you. I think you need to rest."

Cavanaugh stepped back from him. "I'm not going home. You lied to me."

"Ed, you're not making sense."

"Before — you said you didn't expect me. That was a lie. I think you've been expecting me for a long time. You're the one. You had a motive to kill Alex. I've known —"

"Ed, please —"

"I've known all along, but I didn't know if *you* knew. That's the dicey part. I couldn't come out and ask you, could I? So I let it go. But today —"

"You're really scaring me now, Ed."

"Today's the day." Cavanaugh looked up at the vault of the sky and breathed deep. He drew the Colt from his pocket and aimed it at Tanager. "I came here thinking I would shoot myself —"

"For god's sake —"

"— or both of us. I didn't know if I could bring myself to kill you, no matter what you've done. But now that I see you, I think I can."

Tanager held up his hands, palms out. "I didn't kill your son."

"You did. You don't hide it well, now that we've come down to it. You look guilty as hell. You're sweating."

"You're pointing a gun at me."

"You were sweating before. If you have your phone, you can call Keely. Say good-bye. I already said good-bye to my family." Cavanaugh rested his finger on the trigger of the Colt. "You can tell Keely whatever you want. She won't be able to stop this. By the time she gets here, we'll both be dead."

Tanager made no move. He looked weak now, a sixty-year-old in shirtsleeves, stomach hanging a little over his belt. Ed Cavanaugh tried to read his eyes. He thought he could see things there. Fear, yes. Despair. Resignation. A pretense being dropped. When Tanager spoke, he sounded defeated.

"I don't want to call Keely."

Cavanaugh held the Colt steady. "Fair enough."

"Wait," Tanager said, moving his hands in a calming gesture. "Just wait. This is a mistake."

"No, it feels right."

"I'm not the one you want."

"Don't lie to me."

"I'm not lying. I didn't kill your son."

Cavanaugh hesitated, lowering the Colt a few inches, raising it up again.

"I didn't kill Alex," Tanager said. "But I can tell you who did."

25.

The city of Chelsea is sleepy, late on a Sunday night.

The traffic lights on Main Street blink yellow. The shops are dark. There's a lone man standing on a sidewalk, holding a leash patiently, watching a Scottish terrier sniff at the roots of a tree.

Chelsea is the home of sensible people, people who go to bed at a decent hour, people who have to get up and work on Monday morning. It looks like a town from the 1950s. There are flags flying from porches, flowers planted in window boxes. There's an old armory and a quaint post office and a public library built during the Great Depression. There are big stone churches with bell towers and signs in front that say JOHN 3:16.

In the daytime you'd see moms pushing strollers; you'd see older kids shooting baskets in driveways, and younger ones drawing with colored chalk on the sidewalks. But now the basketballs and chalk have been put away. People have locked up for the night. Only a few are still awake. One of them is Michael Underhill.

Ed Cavanaugh found his street without too much trouble. Tanager hadn't been able to give him an address at first — *It's not like we're friends,* he'd said — but eventually he had run a search on his computer. There'd been a string of addresses in the city of Chelsea, but this one was the most recent: a drab ranch-style house with an eagle ornament over the garage and a broken carriage lantern on a post by the driveway.

Underhill was watching television inside, and he wasn't alone. There was a woman too. Cavanaugh could see them through the frame of the big front window. He could see them best when they got up — to go to the bathroom (he guessed), or to fetch wine in long-stemmed glasses, or a bowl of popcorn. But even now he had a fair view of Underhill in profile, sitting with his arm around the woman's shoulders.

Michael Underhill looked utterly normal. His hair was starting to recede at the temples; he had a bit of fat under his chin. He had the sort of bland good looks you might expect in a cousin of a Hollywood star.

The woman was pretty, and younger than Underhill. Cavanaugh wondered about her. Was she his wife? Tanager had said nothing about a wife, but Tanager might not know.

It would be better if the woman was a girlfriend. Then she might leave. She looked vaguely hippieish: tortoise-shell glasses, hair parted down the middle. What sort of girlfriend would a killer choose?

There was a Volkswagen Rabbit parked in the driveway: purple with a COEXIST bumper sticker. Cavanaugh thought it must be hers.

He waited in his truck with the windows rolled down, the Colt .38 in his pocket. Once in a while he looked at the scene in the house: Underhill's face bathed in the television light. The program seemed to be a drama, but it must have had funny parts. Now and then Underhill laughed.

Cavanaugh waited so long that he began to doze. The night air was pleasantly cool. The back of his head touched the headrest and he drifted off.

And woke to the sound of a car door shutting, an engine starting up. He turned to see the Rabbit backing out of the drive, the woman at the wheel. He watched her in his side mirror as she drove to the end of the street, slowed for the stop sign, and turned the corner.

No sign of Underhill — and then he was back in front of the television. He would have walked her to the door, kissed her good-bye. Would he have come outside? Would he have noticed Cavanaugh's truck? No reason to think so. It wouldn't have stood out; there were other cars parked on the street.

Cavanaugh watched him through the window. He thought of walking to the front door, knocking, shooting Underhill as soon as he opened it. He would have done it but for the doubts that nagged at him. Tanager had given him a description of the man, and the description matched well enough, but he hadn't been able to find a picture of Underhill online. What if the man in the house wasn't Underhill? Perhaps someone else had recently moved in. Or what if Tanager was lying? Suppose he had offered up the name of someone innocent, to save his own skin.

Cavanaugh needed to talk to Michael Underhill, to look him in the eye, to know that he was guilty.

In the frame of the window, Underhill flipped through some channels. Got bored. He stood up and passed out of view. He was gone for several minutes, then passed by again, carrying a basket of laundry. A few minutes later Cavanaugh saw him return without the basket and gather the wineglasses and the popcorn bowl. The pattern continued — long periods of absence and then a glimpse — until Underhill closed the curtains around one o'clock. Then the lights in the house got switched off until only one remained, in a room at the eastern end of the house. Probably Underhill's bedroom.

The lone light stayed on for another twenty minutes. Then the house was dark. Cavanaugh watched it for half an hour and nothing changed. He gave it another half hour before he got out of the truck.

He crossed the street on stiff legs, tried the front door knowing it would be locked. He rounded the western end of the house and came to a glass slider in the back — also locked. He checked the windows. They were hard to get to, blocked by shrubs, but he found two of them open. A small one in the bathroom — too close to Underhill's bedroom. And a bigger one in the kitchen, open about six inches to let in the cool air.

Cavanaugh took his time, moving slow and quiet. He found a terra-cotta planter and carried it over to the spot between the shrubs and the window. Standing on the planter, he pried out the screen and leaned it against the house. He lifted the sash a fraction of an inch at a time, branches poking at the seat of his pants, a mosquito buzzing around his neck.

A younger man would have gotten through the window gracefully, relying on upper-body strength and flexibility. Cavanaugh began gracefully enough: he slipped off his jacket, leaving the gun in the pocket, and passed it through the opening. Draped it over the back of a kitchen chair. Then he flopped through the window headfirst, his belly on the sill. He wriggled. He turned the chair sideways and braced his hands on the seat to keep from landing on the floor. The chair legs squeaked on the kitchen tiles. Cavanaugh kept going. Knees on the sill now. Then one foot on the floor. Muscles in his arms beginning to strain. He dragged the other foot through and got it under him and pushed himself up to stand.

He took the Colt from the jacket and stood motionless by the window, listening, his eyes adjusting to the darkness of the house.

No sound but the ticking of a wall clock.

When at last he moved, the clop of his shoes on the tile seemed thunderous. He stepped out of them and passed through the kitchen in his sock feet. Then the carpeting of the living room, a thick shag. He stepped on something: a kernel of popcorn.

He stopped and listened again. The ticking clock behind him, and something else ahead. A washed-out sound. White noise. Static.

The carpet continued down a hallway. Bathroom on the left. A room on the right with a desk and bookshelves and a file cabinet. At the end of the hall, a door standing open. The white noise was louder. It had resolved itself into the sound of ocean waves. Something people used to help them sleep. Cavanaugh went through the door and saw the source: a clock radio by the bed.

Rumpled blanket on the bed with a figure underneath. A dark shape on a white pillow — the back of Michael Underhill's head. The ocean waves rolled on, masking the sound of Underhill's breathing.

No.

They masked the absence of Underhill's breathing. The dark shape on the pillow was a balled-up towel. Cavanaugh tore away the blanket. More towels and pillows underneath, arranged to make a human form.

Behind him, a closet door opened on well-oiled hinges. Cavanaugh sensed the movement and spun around, raising the Colt. A crowbar slammed against the inside of his wrist. The gun flew across the room, made a dent in the wall, and tumbled to the floor. Michael Underhill brought the crowbar up and jabbed the curved end at Cavanaugh's chin. Cavanaugh dodged, off balance, and fell back against the bed. He rolled aside as the crowbar swung down toward his chest, and it struck his shoulder instead. A stab of pain made him wince, but he reached for the clock radio, grabbed it with both hands, yanked the cord from the socket. Threw it at Underhill's face.

Underhill stepped back, swatting the clock away with the metal bar. Cavanaugh pushed himself off the bed and dove for the gun. Landed hard on the floor and felt something tear in his knee. He scrambled for the Colt, his fingers clawing at the barrel. He felt Underhill's foot on the small of his back as he wrapped his hand around the grip. He twisted round to aim the gun, and the crowbar came crashing down on his temple.

Ed Cavanaugh can feel that his eyes are shut tight, yet his field of vision is filled with a white glow. He thinks of tunnels of light. Of heaven. But he's not in heaven. He opens his eyes and the glow is still there, less intense. Now it's like looking at the sun through clean linen.

Gradually the glow begins to fade and he can see things. He's lying on his back, staring up at a ceiling. There's a crack in the plasterboard. It runs along and splits in two like a letter Y. He knows it. The ceiling is not Michael Underhill's. Cavanaugh is not in Underhill's house. He's in his own.

It's bright here, even though he knows it's nighttime. He sits up in his bed, the creak of the bed frame familiar. His wife is sleeping with her back to him, the way she always did. He should wake her. It's been so long since he's seen her. But that's not the way this goes; that's not why he's here.

He gets up and walks barefoot to the bathroom. The floor is cold. There are no lights on, but the glow has followed him in. He can see himself in the mirror over the sink. The stubble on his head is dark, not white. The lines on his face tell less of a tale. He's not seventy, he's twenty years younger.

The glow around him grows dimmer. He walks down the hall to a half-open door. His son Danny is asleep on his back, his glasses still on, one foot hanging over the side of his bed, a book tented on his chest.

Cavanaugh stands over him, lifts the stems of the glasses from behind his ears, folds the glasses up, sets them on the nightstand.

Into the hall again. Another door. Alex's room. Cavanaugh touches the door and it swings inward. Alex's bed is empty.

The glow has faded altogether. There's only the window and the light of the moon. The branches of a tree scratch at the window screen. The sound is like tires on gravel. Tires rolling slowly on gravel.

Cavanaugh crosses to the window. Down below, in the driveway, an unfamiliar car rolls to a stop.

He should be able to leap down there, to levitate, to pass through solid walls. Instead, he turns and walks in his bare feet through the hall and down the stairs and out through the back door. When he reaches the driveway, Alex is there, walking around the car, trailing his fingers over the headlights, the fender, the passenger doors, the lid of the trunk.

Alex circles once, twice, mumbling as he goes. The words aren't meant for Cavanaugh, but he can hear them: "Maybe it's nothing. Maybe I didn't. Maybe it's okay. I can't see anything, not even a scrape. Maybe it didn't happen. It happened so fast, so maybe it didn't happen."

On the third circuit, Cavanaugh steps in front of his son, takes hold of the boy's arms. "What's the matter?" he says. "What is this? Who's car? Where did you go? What did you do?"

Alex's eyes are wide. His mouth opens, closes, opens again. "I didn't mean it," he says. "I'm sorry."

"What did you do?" Cavanaugh asks again.

"I can't tell you. It's a bad thing. It happened fast."

"Tell me."

"I can't. You'll be ashamed."

"You can tell me anything."

"You say that, but it's not true. This thing, if it happened, it's too much."

"Tell me," Cavanaugh says. "We'll figure it out. If it's bad, we'll fix it."

"Not this. If it happened, you can't fix it."

"We'll deal with it together. You and me. Just tell me."

Alex bites his lip. Then: "Maybe we could take it back. I want to take it back."

"The car?" says Cavanaugh. "Okay. We'll take it back. Where did you get it?"

"I want to take it back. You believe me, don't you?"

"I do."

"That's the one thing I want. But we

can't, can we?"

"We'll do it," Cavanaugh says. "I'll help you. I promise."

"*Can* we do it, though? I don't think we can."

"I'll help you. I'll always help you. No matter what."

Alex looks confused. "What did you say?"

"I'll help you."

More confusion. "I can't hear you."

Cavanaugh holds on to his son's arms. He tries to speak very clearly. He tries to say, *You can count on me. No matter what you've done.* He tries to say, *You're not alone.* He tries to say, *I will never let you down.* But nothing comes. He can't say any of it. He can't speak.

Ed Cavanaugh came awake to the sight of a black circle amid bright light. His temple ached. Something plunked on his forehead — a drop of water. The black circle resolved itself into the opening of a faucet. He looked up at steep walls of white tile. He was lying on his back in Michael Underhill's bathtub.

The dampness on the side of his face might have been water or blood or both. Some of it trickled into his ear. He tried to sit up and scraped his scalp on the faucet. He cursed and it came out a mumble. A strip of tape covered his mouth.

Cavanaugh sat up again, more carefully. He had to strain to do it. His arms weren't much help: they were bound together with tape at the wrists. His legs were bound at the ankles. Dull pain in his injured wrist and knee. He managed to brace one elbow on the edge of the tub. He was shifting his weight, preparing to lever himself out, when he heard footsteps. His elbow slipped. He struggled to move it back into place.

Underhill entered the room, dragging a chair behind him. He watched Cavanaugh dispassionately for a moment, then lifted one foot and kicked with the heel at his shoulder. Cavanaugh fell back into the tub, his head striking the faucet. His vision blurred and he thought he would pass out, but he closed his eyes and breathed and when he opened them he saw Underhill sitting casually in the chair beside the tub.

Michael Underhill took pride in staying calm, even when people infuriated him. He was calm now as he leaned forward in the chair and looked into Ed Cavanaugh's eyes.

"I didn't ask for this," he said.

He rested his forearms on his knees. His fingers brushed the edge of the tub.

"I've moved on. I don't even think about

your son anymore. All of that, it's over."

He paused for a moment. An observer might have thought he was waiting for Cavanaugh's reply. But Cavanaugh could only stare up at him.

"I know," Underhill said. "It's not over for you. I can understand. But you have to see it from my point of view. I have a life. Time is passing. I have things I want to do. There's a woman — I think she and I could have a future together. And I want it. I want it more than anything. It's taken me a long time to get here. Too long."

Underhill felt tears welling in his eyes. He waited a moment until he had himself under control.

"The point is," he said, "I can't keep worrying about a thing that happened twenty years ago. And now you come here, the father looking for revenge. I can respect that. But honestly, what were you thinking? I couldn't let you kill me. You weren't even committed to it."

A spark of protest in Cavanaugh's eyes. Underhill dismissed it with a shake of his head.

"Come on. If you were serious, you wouldn't have left Tanager alive. You wouldn't have trusted him. You thought he wanted you to kill me — and you're right,

I'm sure he did. It would make his life easier. But how much faith do you think he put in you? He knew that if you tried and failed, it would come back to him. I would know that he betrayed me. And he's much more afraid of me than he is of you."

Underhill drummed his fingers, slowly, soundlessly, on the edge of the tub.

"He called to warn me. Of course. What was your plan? Shoot me in my sleep? Then what? Drive away, hope no one saw you? I guess it goes like that, sometimes. Mostly it goes some way you don't expect."

Underhill sat back in his chair. He wiped a palm over his chin.

"I don't want to do this," he said. "I don't want to *be* this anymore. I'm tired of it. There has to be another way. We don't have to be trapped in a goddamn feud. Do you want to be in a *feud*? It doesn't make sense, and it's not the only option. I mean, look at history. Look at the Vikings."

Underhill waved his hand in the air as if Cavanaugh had objected.

"I know," he said. "But listen. I read a book once about the Vikings. They had their own set of laws. If you killed someone, they didn't send you to prison. They didn't even have prisons. Instead, you had to pay a fine. They called it a *wergild*. You paid it to the victim's family. It was a way to keep the peace, so people wouldn't try to take revenge.

"I would do that. I would give you money, just to end this. It's not an insult. I know your son's life was worth more than money. But it's restitution. It's a way to make amends. Then we wouldn't have to be enemies. You could go. And I wouldn't have to do the thing I don't want to do." Underhill bent forward eagerly. "What do you say?"

The lights over the vanity behind him threw his shadow onto the tub. Ed Cavanaugh lay with his knees up, his bound wrists on his stomach. His mouth didn't move under the tape. Underhill searched his eyes. They glared back, unblinking.

Underhill pushed his chair away from the tub and stood.

"I know," he said softly. "It wouldn't work. You're right. . . . It's a pipe dream."

He knelt by the tub and used his left hand to move Cavanaugh's head to one side. Cavanaugh tried to resist, but it didn't matter. Underhill used his right hand to flip the lever that closed the drain. Then he spun the taps and watched the water run.

26.

Jack Pellum spent a week talking to onetime friends of Alex Cavanaugh.

He got their names from the case file that Keely Tanager had loaned him. They were classmates the police had interviewed after Alex's death. Jack tracked them down by trial and error, starting with addresses from twenty years ago; he found them through parents or siblings or Internet searches. He spoke to them in person when he could, on the phone if they lived far away.

He listened to their stories about Alex and tried to piece together a picture of the boy. Alex had been good in school, though not the best. He played softball and ran track. He dated girls and broke up with them, but he wasn't mean about it, he was sweet. He drank, sometimes too much. He got into mischief. Once he snuck into Belleville High with a group of friends late at night, gaining access through an unlatched window. They found a dolly in a janitor's closet and took turns riding it through the halls. They bounced on a trampoline in the gym. When the cafeteria staff came in the next morning, they were greeted with the word HELLO spelled out with plastic trays on the floor of the lunchroom.

The Sturridge house figured into some of the stories, but there was nothing Jack hadn't heard before. High school kids partying in an abandoned house. The worst that went on was someone getting sick and throwing up on the floor. Nothing to foreshadow what would happen to Alex; nothing worth killing a seventeen-year-old over.

Some of the people Jack spoke to had read about Dylan Vernen in the news, but none of them had known him back in the day. None could draw a link between Dylan and Alex.

When Jack asked about Alex's closest friends, two names came up over and over. One of them he already knew: Bobby Wilson. He paid a visit to Bobby's sister again, but she hadn't heard from him. As far as she knew, he was on the road, moving from place to place in his RV. She expected he would call in his own good time.

The second name that kept coming up was Virgil Parker. Parker owned a bakery on

Monroe Street in Greektown. Jack met with him there on a Monday evening after the shop had closed, the two of them sitting at a high round table while a young woman cleaned up behind the counter.

Parker was tall and lean, a light-skinned African-American with a shaved head and a gold stud in one ear. He put a glass of milk down in front of Jack, and beside it a frosted cookie on a paper plate. He said, "Have you ever had a black-and-white cookie, Mr. Pellum?"

"Not since I was a kid."

"You've never had one like this," Parker said. "You can't find a black-and-white anywhere else in this city. You can find something they *call* a black-and-white, but it's not the same. The guy I bought this place from, he used to sell one. Called it a half-moon. But the consistency was too dry, and it was dipped half in chocolate, half in vanilla glaze. The glaze would harden, and it would break off when you bit into it. A proper black-and-white, it's more like a cake than a cookie. It's frosted on top, and the frosting starts out creamy and stays that way."

Jack took a bite of the cookie, chased it with milk.

"That's good," he said.

311

Parker smiled. "Damn right it's good. It's one of my best sellers. That one's on the house, 'cause you're sort of a local celebrity. All these years, nobody ever came close to finding out who murdered Alex Cavanaugh. Not till you stirred things up with those Vernen people over in New Boston."

"I'm not sure how close I came," Jack said. "The truth is, I've got some doubts about whether Dylan Vernen killed Alex."

"Why's that?"

"It's hard to explain. But I'd be grateful if you could tell me whatever you remember about Alex. I understand you knew him well."

Virgil Parker sat quiet for a moment before nodding. "I knew him. I gave a lot of thought to him at one time, trying to figure him out. He meant something to me. I was in love with him."

Jack let his surprise show. "In love?"

"Totally."

"I haven't heard that Alex was gay."

"I don't think he was," Parker said. "I never worked up the courage to ask. Hell, I never admitted that *I* was gay. Not then. You could say I admired Alex from afar. Or not really afar — I admired him from as close as I could get. There was something about him. A gentleness. But he also had a touch of the bad boy."

"In what way?"

"He took chances I was afraid to take. Little things. He drank, he smoked. It seems silly now, but those things held a certain glamour for me. My mother was very strict. She didn't even let my father drink. But Alex had a hold on me. I don't think he ever knew it. He inspired me. Brought me out of my shell. There was this house —"

"The Sturridge house?"

"Right. I would sneak out at night and go there. It scared me half to death, the thought of my mother catching me. I would meet up with Alex, and usually Bobby Wilson would be there too. Do you know about Bobby?"

"I've heard of him," Jack said.

"They'd have parties in that house, with maybe a dozen people. I drank my first beer there. It was lukewarm and sour and I went home and brushed my teeth and I was still afraid my mother would smell it on my breath."

"How many times would you say you went to the Sturridge house?"

"It seems like we went once a week for a while. The parties — I only went to two or three. It wasn't my thing. But sometimes I would go just to meet up with Alex and

Bobby."

"What would you do?"

"What do boys do? Hang out. Talk about girls." Parker smiled. "Does that surprise you? I could talk about girls as well as anybody else. I did a lot of pretending back then. But sometimes the Sturridge place was only our first stop. Like a rendezvous point. From there we'd ride our bikes into town. None of us had a car, of course. Alex and Bobby had their licenses, but I didn't get mine till I was eighteen."

"What did you do in town?"

"Whatever Alex wanted. He was the ring-leader. He'd get a group together and sneak into the high school."

"I've heard about that."

"We never did any harm, just ran around in there like fools. We got into other places too. The public library. The A&W. We'd go in there — Alex, Bobby, and me — and drink the root beer. I don't know what the hell we were thinking. But if Alex wanted to do it, I was game. For the most part."

"There were limits?"

"Eventually, yes," Parker said. "Don't get me wrong. I think Alex was a good person, and whatever nonsense he got up to, it wasn't out of malice. He was looking for the thrill. He wanted to see what he could get away with. At the library, he'd go behind the reference desk and rifle through the drawers. If someone had stashed a couple dollars away, he'd take it. Or he might take a pen or a stapler, as a souvenir. Some nights we would walk around and see cars parked on the street, and he would try the doors, on the chance that they might be unlocked. If they were, he'd grab something: a pair of sunglasses off the seat, a flashlight from the glove compartment. It didn't have to be anything valuable."

Parker shrugged. "Like I said, I think he did it for the thrill. But it made me nervous. Alex and Bobby were white, and Alex's father was a cop. If they got caught, they would probably come out of it okay. But I was a black kid and my dad worked in a hardware store. I could have wound up in jail. I wised up after a while. We stayed friends, but I stopped sneaking out with them at night."

27.

Detroit is a city designed for driving, but Jack liked to walk its streets when he could. He had walked two miles to meet with Virgil Parker in Greektown, forty minutes at a moderate pace. He took it slower on his way back home, strolling to Cadillac Square, stopping for a hot dog at the Lafayette Coney Island.

When he started the long trek north to midtown, the sun had lowered out of sight. Crowds milled in front of the gates of Comerica Park; the Tigers had a home game against the Minnesota Twins. On Woodward Avenue he passed a long strip of torn-up street. It had been that way for a while, part of a plan to put in a light-rail line to connect downtown with midtown. The project had been going on for years. Jack doubted it would ever be finished.

He reached his building and climbed up to the third floor and found his door standing open, covered in a coat of white paint. He could still read the message underneath — THIS IS WRONG — but the black letters had faded to pale gray.

Kim Weaver was in his kitchen, drinking a glass of iced tea. When he came in, she stood up tall and kissed him.

"You got paint in your hair," he told her.

"Did I?" she said.

"You got some on your arm too, and on your shirt."

"I knew about that."

"And quite a lot of it ended up on my door."

"What do you think?"

"It looks good."

"It's not done yet. I'll do another coat tomorrow."

"You don't have to," he said. "It's not your responsibility."

She gave him a candid look. "Maybe not. But it shouldn't be yours."

Jack had been puzzled about the source of the message on his door, but Kim had understood the first time she saw it. "It's Doug," she'd said. "He keeps telling me he wants to get back together, and I keep saying no. So now this is him, acting out. I'm sorry. I don't know how he found you. I never told him your name. He must have followed me here one night."

Jack had offered to have a talk with Doug, but Kim insisted on handling it herself. She spoke to him, and he was apologetic. He promised not to do it again. Jack had doubts about the value of the man's promises. He had spotted him in the neighborhood once, on a Tuesday afternoon; he recognized him from a photo on the website of his real estate company. Jack had come out of his apartment building, and there was Doug, standing on the corner by Marcus Market. When Jack tried to approach him, he got into his car and drove away.

Another time, a few days later, there'd been a knock on Jack's door late in the evening. He'd been dozing on the sofa, and by the time he got to the door, there was no one there.

He had discussed these incidents with Kim, but they didn't worry her. Doug might act like a child, she said, but he was harmless. Jack was willing to let things be. He had given Kim a key to his apartment, and he saw her three or four nights a week now. He knew she spent her days working in an office in the Fisher Building, doing something that involved credit checks and loan approvals. He had given her some space in his closet and a drawer in his dresser, because she was pleasant company and he liked waking up next to her. It made him feel normal.

Now she finished her iced tea and kissed him again and went to take a shower. He heard the water running as he sat on the sofa and put his feet up. He closed his eyes and tried to process what he'd learned about Alex Cavanaugh, a boy who liked to take risks, who liked to get into places where he didn't belong and take things that weren't his. Was that what had gotten him killed? Had he stolen something from the wrong person?

Jack considered other possibilities. Virgil Parker claimed never to have acted on his attraction to Alex. But suppose he had. That can be tricky when you're seventeen. He imagined the two of them meeting up at the Sturridge house on an August night. Virgil works up his courage, makes a pass at Alex. It's unexpected. Alex isn't ready; he's not mature enough to handle it with grace. He gets angry, shoves Virgil away. Now they're fighting. Virgil picks up something sturdy, something you might find outside an abandoned house. A rake, a broom. He knocks Alex over the head.

If Virgil Parker was a murderer, he was awfully cool about it twenty years later, talking casually about his victim over milk and cookies.

Jack set the possibility aside. His mind skipped around to other things, as it often did when he was tired. Kim came to him a few minutes later, dressed in fresh clothes, running a brush through her hair.

She said, "I'd give a lot to know what you're thinking."

He made room for her on the sofa beside him.

"I've been thinking about a bunch of different things."

"Name one."

"Black-and-white cookies."

Her face brightened. "I love black-and-white cookies, but I can never find them."

"I know a place."

"What else — besides the cookies?"

"This and that," he said. "Weird little connections that don't mean anything."

"Such as?"

Jack had grown used to keeping his thoughts to himself, but he made an effort to respond. "Black-and-white cookies made me think of black-and-white photographs," he said. "My wife was a photographer, and she worked a lot in black-and-white." He gestured toward the photos on the wall. "I see her work here every day, and sometimes

I see it out in the world. That ad, right there, the one she shot for Motor City Keys —"

"The one with the piano and the hands."

He nodded. "I've always loved it. It has so many small details, all in black-and-white, down to the signet ring on the finger of the left hand, which has a chess motif, black and white knights, side by side. Motor City Keys has a blowup of that ad in their window. I see it when I walk by."

"What does it mean?"

"It doesn't mean anything," he said. "But Olivia was a photographer, and another victim, Alex Cavanaugh, he was too. The night he died, he was taking pictures of an abandoned house."

"You think they were killed because they were photographers?"

"No, but it's a connection. Some connections are important, and others aren't, and you have to sort out which is which. Here's another one. Olivia was killed on the shore of the Huron River, and Alex was killed in Belleville. The Huron River runs right through Belleville. Belleville Lake was formed by damming the river."

"Was Alex killed near the water?" Kim asked.

"No. The river's just there, sort of in the background. It's all over southeast Michigan; it winds around; it flows past too many cities and towns to count. If you went looking, you could find lots of people who were killed in the vicinity of the Huron River."

"So it's a coincidence. You're not searching for a killer who gets around by boat."

"I don't think so," Jack said.

"Or one who only kills photographers."

"No."

Kim looked at the images on the wall. Her brow furrowed. "What if they took a picture of him — Olivia and Alex? They took his picture, and he killed them, because he didn't want it getting out. Because, I don't know, he's wanted by the FBI."

Jack considered the possibility. "That's good. It's creative. But I think things like that only happen in the movies. Unless this guy is living in seclusion, people see him all the time. He can't kill everyone he meets. Besides, if he killed both Olivia and Alex — if I believe that — then it's possible he's killed other people too. Paul Rook's mother, for one. And she wasn't a photographer."

"Did she die near the Huron River?"

"She died in Dearborn. The Huron River doesn't flow there."

Kim nodded. She turned sideways on the sofa and put her legs on Jack's lap.

"Does it make your head hurt, trying to

keep all this stuff straight?" she said.

"Sometimes," said Jack.

"I bet it does." She waited a beat. "He was here, by the way."

"Who? Paul?"

"He came by with a girl with yellow hair."

"Jennifer."

"That's right. She brought you a pie her mother made. Apple. I put it in the fridge. They were sorry to miss you. They were going out to dinner, and to the Bronx Bar after. They said we should meet them there. I told them we would."

Jack frowned. "Why would you tell them that?"

"Because they're your friends."

"Not really," he said. It sounded harsh. "Maybe," he allowed.

"They brought you a pie. They asked you out for a drink. I'm sorry to have to tell you this, Jack, but you have friends. I hardly know them, but I like them. They're cute together."

"I don't feel like going out."

"Why not?" Kim said. "The Bronx Bar is at the end of the block. How much of an ordeal could it be? If you don't like it, we'll come right back. What are you afraid of?"

"I'm not afraid."

"Good. Then we can go."

Jack looked at the case file on Alex Cavanaugh, lying open on the coffee table.

"I have work to do here," he said.

Kim withdrew her legs from his lap. She sat up and leaned close to him. Rested a hand on his knee.

"Say yes to me. All this stuff will still be here when we get back."

Before he had a chance to answer, she got up on her feet. "They're probably at the bar now," she said. "I'll put on some makeup and head down to meet them, tell them you're on your way. You can wash up and change your clothes. You'll feel better."

She retreated to the bedroom and Jack looked at the Cavanaugh file, and the others all around him, all the dead he'd been spending his time with.

He decided he could afford a night away from them.

He made the shower hot and stayed in it a long while. He shaved afterward. Brushed his teeth. When he came out, Kim had gone. He found a note from her on his dresser. *Wear something cotton. I like you in cotton.*

He picked out a cotton button-down shirt. A pair of black jeans. The Bronx Bar wasn't fancy. He grabbed a blazer from the closet. His keys, phone, wallet. He stopped in the doorway of the bedroom and looked down at the wedding ring on his hand.

Kim's words came back to him. *Say yes to me.*

She was offering him something. A kind of life that, if you asked him, he would have said he wanted. A life with a lover. Nights out with friends. The kind of life he'd had once.

Jack took the ring off his finger and laid it on a corner of the dresser.

It didn't look right there. He tried it in a drawer out of sight. That wasn't right either.

He brought his key chain out of his pocket. A plain steel ring with nothing on it but the key to his apartment and the key to his car. His life pared down to a minimum. He added the gold ring to the steel one.

Kim had left the apartment door ajar. He pulled it shut when he went out, figuring the paint was dry enough. He locked up and went down the stairs. His phone rang before he got to the bottom.

It was Keely Tanager.

When he answered she said, "When's the last time you saw Ed Cavanaugh?"

Jack drove into Belleville under a starry sky and a moon that was nearly full. Turning onto Hull Road, he saw the lights of Ed

Cavanaugh's house from a long way off. Keely Tanager's cruiser was parked in the driveway. Jack pulled in beside it. He listened to his own footsteps in the gravel as he crossed to the house.

He climbed onto the back porch and called out. Keely told him to come in. She was on her phone in the kitchen. She held up a finger while she finished her call. "All right, Sully. Thanks. No, that's fine. I don't need you here."

She tucked the phone away and said to Jack, "I've had my officers looking for Ed in his usual haunts. Those would be various bars around town."

"No one's seen him?"

"Not tonight. Not for the past week."

"Who reported him missing?"

"A neighbor from across the road," Keely said. "Lady named Maylene. A friend of Ed's late wife. She doesn't talk to Ed much, but she's used to seeing him around. Puttering in his yard, mowing his grass. She realized tonight she hadn't seen him in a while. She walked over here to check on him and found the door unlocked. So she came in to look around, thinking maybe he had a heart attack. That's how his wife went. When she didn't find him she called me."

"Have you talked to his other neighbors?"

"Most of them aren't much help. One of them said he saw Ed a week ago Sunday. Ed came out of his house dressed in a suit. Looked like he was going to church — except that it was twilight and Ed doesn't go to church. He backed the truck out of the driveway and drove off. You said you saw Ed that Sunday."

Jack nodded. "In the afternoon."

"What did you talk about?"

"I told him about what happened with Irene Vernen. I apologized for not being able to tell him anything definitive about his son."

"What was his mood?"

"He was kind to me. He seemed calm, peaceful."

"Did you talk here in the house?"

"We sat at the picnic table out past the stone wall. Then we came back here."

"You didn't go anywhere else?"

"No. Why?"

Keely leaned against the kitchen counter. "I walked out to the spot where Alex died, behind where the Sturridge house used to be. There's a kind of memorial there."

"I've seen it," Jack said.

"There was a blanket on the ground next to it, and some photographs of Ed's wife and sons."

"You think he went there last Sunday?"

"I can't be sure when. But we know Alex was on his mind. I imagine they've all been on his mind lately, ever since Danny hung himself. Was Ed drinking when you saw him?"

"We each had a beer in front of us. But neither of us drank much."

"If he was sober — that's not necessarily a good sign. Also," she said, pointing to the refrigerator door, "I don't like the look of that."

There was a pad stuck to the door with a magnet. Each page preprinted with the heading TO-DO LIST. The top page held a shaky handwritten message: *Nothing left to do.*

"What do you think it means?" Jack said.

He regretted the question as soon as he asked it. Keely didn't respond. The answer was obvious. Still, he didn't want to believe it.

He said, "That Sunday, Ed gave me his gun."

"What gun?" Keely asked.

"A Smith & Wesson revolver. He wanted me to have it. But that's good, isn't it? If he gave it to me, he couldn't have shot himself with it."

"You're assuming Ed Cavanaugh only

owned one handgun," Keely said. "But let's not get ahead of ourselves. No one reported a gunshot, and I think if he wanted to kill himself he would have done it here, or at the spot where Alex died. He might simply be traveling, though I couldn't guess where. I can put out a bulletin on his truck."

She turned quiet for a few seconds, then moved past Jack, heading for the door. "There's one other place I'd better look," she said. "You can go — or come along."

Jack went along. He stood on the porch while Keely turned out the lights and pulled the door shut behind them. The air outside was cool and still. They walked together through the yard in the moonlight, aiming for the gap in the stone wall. A rough trail through the tall grass led them back to the dry creek bed, and they followed it until they arrived at the clearing with the picnic table. Keely went to the oak at the edge of the clearing, switched on a penlight, and aimed the beam up at Ed Cavanaugh's deer blind.

Cavanaugh had built a makeshift ladder out of lengths of two-by-four bolted to the tree trunk. Keely planted a foot on the lowest rung, reached for another above her head.

Jack said, "I could go up."

"I've got it," she said.

She climbed with the light clipped to her collar. Jack watched her progress from the ground. She stopped once and uttered a soft curse.

"What's the matter?" Jack said.

"Loose rung."

"Come down and we'll get a ladder."

"It's only a little loose."

She soldiered on and made it to the top. Jack saw her aiming the light into the blind.

"Jesus," she said.

"Is he there?"

"No. I got a splinter the size of a match stick. There's nothing here but a lot of Slim Jim wrappers and empty bottles. I'm coming down."

She made a slow descent and they headed back to the house. As they skirted along the creek bed, Jack thought he heard something moving in the grass. He put a hand out to stop Keely and held a finger to his lips. She indulged him for a moment, both of them standing frozen in the night. The sound did not repeat itself. Keely clicked on her light and swept it over the ground ahead of them, and the beam caught a flash of red: a fox tearing across the path. She laughed and clicked off the light, and they went on with just the moon.

When they reached the stone wall, her cell phone rang. She answered it without breaking stride, listened for a few seconds, and said, "Goddamn it. All right. I'm on my way."

"What happened?" Jack asked her. "Is it Ed? Did they find him?"

Keely started walking fast toward her cruiser. "It's not Ed. It's Jerry Diaz."

Jack didn't know who she meant at first, then made the connection. Jerry, the kid from the station house. The one who didn't do it.

"Is he making trouble at the Frosty Boy again?"

"He's having a fit at the Walmart," Keely said. "I have to go. He knows me. I can calm him down."

They reached the driveway and she looked toward the house.

"There's nothing more to be done here tonight," she said to Jack. "I'll let you know if I find out anything about Ed."

She got into her car without another word. The engine turned over and Jack watched as she backed out to the road and sped off in a spray of gravel.

28.

Jack stood in the driveway after Keely had gone. The Cavanaugh house looked lonely and plain, the white clapboards washed out to a pale gray in the night.

He wondered what the house might tell him.

He had never been in there alone, in the place where Alex Cavanaugh once lived.

Climbing onto the porch, Jack took hold of the doorknob and tested the door. As he'd suspected, Keely had engaged the spring lock when she pulled it shut.

But she'd had no key to turn the dead bolt.

Sometimes you can open a spring lock with a credit card, but it tends to ruin the card. Jack found something else in his wallet: a laminated ID from a gym he'd once belonged to. He slipped it between the door and the frame and wiggled it in, bending it one way and then the other. He leaned his weight against the door as he felt the lock yield. The door swung inward.

He stepped into the kitchen, then the living room, switching on lights as he went. Familiar objects all around him: The box of photographs on the sofa. The chair where Ed sat on that first night when they talked. The chessboard on the end table by the chair, with the pieces set up for a game. Nothing out of the ordinary.

Still, there was something eerie about being in the house alone.

Ed kept the place reasonably clean, but when you looked close you could see things he had neglected. Dust on lampshades, cobwebs in corners. The air had the stale smell of a place closed up too long.

Jack could only guess at the house's age. Had it stood for seventy years? Eighty? There were clues to be found: the ornate metal grilles that covered the heating vents; the floors that creaked with every step he took. The doors between the rooms were heavy wood and they opened on black metal hinges. The knobs were of the same black metal. The keyholes were the kind you could see through, the kind that would take skeleton keys.

Jack ascended the stairs, one hand on the smooth-worn banister. He felt the steps bow under his feet. At the top he flipped a switch, and an overhead light showed him a hall with four doors. The first opened into a bathroom. Rust stains in the tub. Water dripping from the faucet in the sink.

He moved down the hall to what must have been Ed's bedroom. Covers thrown back on one side of the king-size bed. Thin paperbacks on the night table: Zane Grey westerns. A wide dresser against one wall. Drawers overstuffed with old sheets. Combs and lipsticks and bottles of nail polish tucked away, tokens of his wife he couldn't bear to part with.

The remaining two rooms would have belonged to Ed's sons. One held a sewing machine now, and an ironing board, and a long table with an unfinished jigsaw puzzle and rolls of wrapping paper. All of it covered with a layer of dust. Jack guessed that this had been Alex's room, given over to other purposes after he died. He looked in the closet, thinking he might find something personal that Alex had left behind. But there were no papers or letters, no yearbooks, only a baseball glove and an old telescope and some matted photographs. The photos were mostly winter scenes: bare trees with their branches limned in snow; close-ups of icicles melting from the eaves of a roof.

Jack moved on to the last room, the one that would have been Danny's. It had a twin bed with a metal frame pushed up against a wall beneath a sloped ceiling. A casement window beside the headboard looked out into the backyard. This was the vantage point from which young Danny would have watched his brother sneaking out at night.

Jack sat on the edge of the bed and imagined Danny living here. He'd been thirteen when Alex died. A kid who wanted to be a writer. This house would have been the most familiar place in the world to him. It wasn't hard to see how he had used it. He had written it into his novel; he had turned it into a maze of hidden rooms and winding hallways, the place where the man in the crooked hat lived.

There were cardboard boxes piled in a corner, full of hardcover copies of Danny's novel, *The House on Night Street.* Jack thought that Ed Cavanaugh must have brought them here from Danny's house in Corktown. He recognized something else from that house: the desk from Danny's office. He got up from the bed and walked over to it. He had looked through it before, more than two weeks ago, but now he opened the drawers again one by one.

In the bottom drawer on the right-hand

side, he found Danny's laptop. He brought it out and laid it on the desk. He was about to close the drawer when he spotted something else, something he hadn't seen before: a tan envelope with the seal of the Detroit Police Department. On the front someone had written: *Personal Effects — Daniel Cavanaugh.*

The police would have given it to Ed after they concluded their investigation of Danny's death and determined it had been a suicide. Ed must have stashed it here.

Jack opened the envelope and shook the contents onto the desk. It wasn't much, just the things the police had found in Danny's pockets. A leather wallet with a driver's license, three credit cards, and fifty-eight dollars in cash. A small Moleskine notebook with a pen clipped to the cover. Loose change amounting to seventy-two cents. And a souvenir key chain embossed with the silhouette of the state of Michigan.

Four things on the chain: two house keys, a car key, and a woman's diamond ring.

An odd thing to find on a key chain, but Jack was not surprised. Ed Cavanaugh kept his late wife's engagement ring on his key chain. Jack had noticed it on the day they met.

You think I should be more careful with it,

Cavanaugh had said to him. *I should lock it away.*

But he hadn't locked it away. He had kept it with him. Danny must have done the same. His wife had died of leukemia, and he had put her ring on his key chain so he would always have it with him.

Jack had a ring on his own key chain right now: his wedding band, to remind him of Olivia. He drew it from his pocket and held it in the palm of his hand.

Ideas can be contagious. Jack had picked up the idea of putting a ring on a key chain from Ed, and Ed had gotten the idea from his wife. Jack remembered the story: Ed had met his wife in high school, and he had given her his class ring after their second date. She had kept it on her key chain all her life.

And here was Danny Cavanaugh's key chain with a ring on it. That made three Cavanaughs with the same habit.

What about a fourth?

Jack left Danny's room and walked slowly down the hallway, his mind jumping from thought to thought.

When they found Alex Cavanaugh's body, his wallet and keys were missing.

What did he have on his key chain? Not a wedding ring. He wasn't married; he was only seventeen. He had no car. He would have had a key to his house. Just that? Nothing more?

No. There would have been something more.

There would have been a ring. Alex had died long before his father started carrying a ring on his key chain, long before his brother Danny did the same. But Alex would have seen the ring on his mother's key chain. He could have picked up the habit from her.

That's what he had done. Jack knew, even though he couldn't really know.

Alex and Olivia were murdered by the same man, almost twenty years apart. There had to be a connection between them.

Jack descended the stairs to the living room. He stood by the end table next to Ed Cavanaugh's chair and looked down at the chessboard. He picked up a white knight, and a black one.

Some connections are important, and others aren't, and you have to sort out which is which. Alex Cavanaugh had carried a ring on his key chain. His killer had taken it from his body. But Jack saw the ring every day. Because Olivia had taken a picture of it.

29.

On Tuesday morning, in the kitchen of his bakery on Monroe Street, Virgil Parker pulled trays of brownies from an oven and set them on a rack to cool. Two of his assistants worked nearby, assembling the tiers of a wedding cake.

"That's an unusual question, Mr. Pellum," Parker said. "But the answer's yes, Alex kept a ring on his key chain. I'm trying to picture it. There were tiny horses on it, I think."

"Could they have been chess pieces?" asked Jack. "The knights look like horses' heads."

Parker nodded, remembering. "Of course they were," he said. "Alex's grandfather taught him to play chess. That's who he got the ring from. He wore it to school after his grandfather died. It was a bit too big for his finger. Then someone made fun of him for wearing it, because high school boys are idiots. After that, he put it on his key chain."

Jack showed Parker Olivia's ad for Motor City Keys: a close-up shot of hands playing a piano, a ring on a finger of the left hand. The ad was on glossy paper; Jack had torn it from a copy of *The New York Times Magazine.*

"Could this be Alex's ring?" he asked.

Parker leaned in to examine it. "I think so. Yes." He frowned. "Those aren't Alex's hands."

"No. This photo was taken long after he died."

A trace of doubt showed in Parker's eyes. "I can't be sure it's his ring, of course. There could be other rings like that."

"That's possible," Jack said.

"But you don't think so."

Jack shook his head.

Parker considered the implications. He looked troubled. "If that *is* Alex's ring, then it shouldn't be there, should it?"

"No," Jack said. "It really shouldn't."

Ken Wellner lived in a subdivision of cookie-cutter houses on the outskirts of Perrysburg, Ohio, a suburb of Toledo. He had a fenced-in yard and a barbecue grill and a big, friendly yellow Lab. He had a swing set and a slide and a four-year-old daughter who giggled as she ran around on the grass

340

getting chased by the dog.

Wellner was tall and hardy-looking, like a grown-up frat boy, with wide shoulders and thick biceps and no sign of flab around the middle. You could call him handsome, if you were willing to overlook a few imperfections: a ruddy nose, a heavy brow, a pair of prominent front teeth. You would never mistake him for a model, Jack thought — unless you focused on his hands. His hands would look good doing anything. Pouring a drink. Catching a football. Playing a piano.

He smiled when Jack showed him the Motor City Keys ad.

"I've got copies of that somewhere," Wellner said. "When it came out in *The New York Times,* my wife and I bought half a dozen. It was kind of a hoot, thinking about all the people who would see it. We still joke about it. I only got that gig because I worked for Glen and Laurie. Are they still in business?"

"They are," Jack said. Glen and Laurie Holland were a pair of aging hippies who ran Motor City Keys out of a renovated dry cleaner's shop on Second Avenue in Detroit. Jack had gone to see them earlier in the day, after he left Virgil Parker's bakery, and they had sent him here, to Wellner.

"I was there the day they first met with

the photographer," Wellner said. "They were throwing around ideas at that point. Brainstorming. They brought her back to the workroom and showed her the pianos, and Glen asked me to sit at one and play. The photographer — what was her name?"

"Olivia," Jack said.

"That's right. She got her camera out and started shooting different angles. I guess she liked the way my hands looked on the keys, because a week or so later she came back and set up her lights and we shot it for real."

"Who was there for the shoot, just the two of you?"

"Glen and Laurie checked in now and then, but mostly it was me and Olivia. We took our time with it, tried it a bunch of different ways."

"And the ring on your finger in the picture, where did it come from?"

Jack was watching Wellner's face when he asked the question. He thought he saw a reaction, a narrowing of the eyes, but it passed quickly.

"That was my ring," Wellner said. "I happened to wear it that day. I was going to take it off, but she liked it. She told me to keep it on."

"Do you still have it?"

Wellner looked away, at his daughter lying

on her stomach on one of the swings, pretending to fly. The dog was with her. She reached out to pat its nose.

"Maybe you should go," Wellner said.

"What's the matter?" Jack asked him.

Wellner turned so he was standing between Jack and his daughter.

"Look," he said. "I don't know you. You showed up here wanting to talk and I agreed because you look harmless and you said you know Glen and Laurie. To be honest, I thought it was about a job, another modeling gig. Which I would do. But if it's really about that ring, I'm not interested. I don't have it anymore. I don't know anything about it."

"What happened to it?" Jack said.

Wellner stood up taller, put an edge into his voice. "Are you messing with me?" he said. "I don't want any trouble."

Jack showed Wellner his palms. "You've got the wrong idea. There's no trouble here. But I need to know about the ring."

Wariness in Wellner's expression, and anger and fear underneath it. Sometimes people work themselves up, and they have a hard time calming down. But Wellner managed it. He let out a breath, shrugged his wide shoulders, and said, "I sold it."

Jack nodded to encourage him. "Who did

you sell it to?"

Another shrug. "To a guy. I don't know."

"What did he look like?"

"I never saw him. He called me on the phone. Told me he'd seen the ring in the ad and wanted to buy it."

"When was this?"

"I don't know — a few weeks after the ad ran in the *Times*."

"About a year and a half ago."

"That sounds right. He offered me five hundred dollars for it, which sounded ridiculously high. And when I didn't answer him right away, he bumped it up to a thousand. So I agreed and he wanted my address so he could send the money. That made me nervous at first. Paranoid. Like it was all a trick to get my address. But honestly, if a stranger wanted to find me, there would have to be an easier way."

"So you gave him your address," Jack said.

"I did. The next day I took the ring to a jeweler, because I was curious. What if it was worth more than a thousand? The jeweler told me the knights were made of quartz and the band was gold-plated, and the whole thing would have been worth a couple hundred if it was in mint condition, which it wasn't. Two days later the money came in the mail, and it was ten hundred-dollar bills. And again I'm thinking something is off, because who sends cash in the mail? But what the hell, I sent him the ring."

"Where did you send it?"

"He put his address on the envelope with the money. It was in Detroit, I think."

"But you didn't keep the envelope."

"No."

"What about his name?" Jack said. "There must have been a name to go with the address."

"Sure. It was John S."

"You're saying his last name started with *S*?"

"I'm saying *S* is all he gave me. Another reason to think he wasn't exactly aboveboard." Wellner looked around to check on his daughter. She was picking dandelions by the fence, the dog tagging along. He turned to Jack again and said, "The truth is, when you started asking about the ring, I thought you might be him. I didn't know what kind of game you were playing."

"I'm not him."

"You want to tell me what this is about?"

It was far too much to explain, Jack thought. He kept it simple.

"I'm a detective, and I'm trying to track down that ring."

"Why?" Wellner asked. "Was it stolen?"

"At some point it was. Where did you get it?"

"I didn't steal it. I bought it from a lady in Detroit, at Eastern Market. She had a stall where she sold jewelry."

"Do you remember her name?"

"I'm pretty sure it was Betsy, or Bitsy. She was one of those middle-aged artsy ladies. Wore a scarf and a lot of chunky bracelets."

"You don't know her last name."

"Sorry."

Wellner put his hands on his hips, ready to bring the conversation to an end.

"One more thing," Jack said. "The guy on the phone, did he ask where the ring came from?"

"Sure he did. It was the first thing he wanted to know, even before he offered to buy it."

"And you told him."

A look of concern passed over Wellner's face.

"I told him what I just told you," he said. "Was that a mistake?"

30.

The Eastern Market district covers several blocks about a mile northeast of downtown Detroit. Its centerpiece is a public market that's open every Saturday of the year: part farmers' market, part street fair. Forty thousand people might come through over the course of a few hours, shopping for fresh produce, for meat and eggs and cheese. There are artists too, selling their creations, and you can see jugglers and puppeteers and musicians playing for tips.

During the week, there's less activity, though you can still find farmers manning some of the stalls, selling in bulk to businesses and restaurants. Jack drove there on Wednesday morning and parked his car in a lot on Wilkins Street. He walked through the neighborhood around the market, stopping in at galleries and gift shops and boutiques, asking if anyone knew a woman named Betsy or Bitsy who sold jewelry. He could have waited until Saturday and gone looking for her among the stalls, but he thought he'd try this way first.

He went into five shops and struck out five times. The sixth was a place that sold vintage clothes and costume jewelry. Jack went up to the clerk working the counter and launched into his routine. Halfway through, as he recited Ken Wellner's description of Betsy/Bitsy — "a middle-aged artsy lady who wears scarves and chunky bracelets" — he realized that the clerk herself was a middle-aged artsy lady wearing a scarf and a chunky bracelet.

"Let me stop right here," he said. "Would you be Betsy, by any chance?"

The woman regarded him coldly. "My name is Evangeline."

"Oh. I apologize —"

"But I suppose all us middle-aged ladies are interchangeable."

"I really didn't mean —"

Evangeline turned away from him, moved to a curtained doorway behind the counter, and called to someone on the other side. "Do we know anyone named Betsy who sells jewelry?"

"Or Bitsy," Jack said.

"Betsy or Bitsy," Evangeline called. "Could be either one, as long as she's artsy."

A moment later she stepped back from the doorway and another woman drew the curtain aside and came through. Also middle-aged, Jack noted, and wearing a scarf and a chunky bracelet of oversized beads.

The newcomer said to Evangeline, "You don't remember Bitsy?"

"Should I?"

"Bitsy Patterson?"

"Doesn't ring a bell," Evangeline said, "but this gentleman is asking for her."

The newcomer looked at Jack and her expression turned grave.

"Were you a friend of Bitsy's?" she asked.

Jack shook his head. "I didn't know her."

"Well, I'm still sorry to have to tell you. Bitsy passed away."

The main avenues of Detroit radiate from its downtown like the spokes of a giant wheel: Michigan, Grand River, Woodward, Gratiot, Jefferson. Follow Woodward northwest for two miles and you come to Jack's neighborhood in midtown. Follow it for another nine miles and you reach the suburb of Royal Oak, where Bethany Patterson, known as Bitsy, once lived in a cozy-looking A-frame house on a quiet street lined with cherry trees.

Jack found the house on Wednesday afternoon. He stepped onto a porch hung with wind chimes and knocked on the door, and the woman who answered was brown-haired and plump-cheeked and about seven months pregnant. She'd never met Bitsy but she loved the house and she was eager to show Jack all the little touches that the woman had left behind. Birdhouses nestled in the trees, painted in bright colors. Crystal globes in the garden. An old weathervane on the peak of the garage roof. "And a fairy door," she said. "Have you ever seen a fairy door?" Without waiting for an answer, she led him to a corner of the house's stone foundation, where Bitsy Patterson had fashioned a miniature door out of pebbles and bits of shell glued to a piece of balsa wood. The doorframe was made of woven twigs, and there were acorns at each of the four corners.

The brown-haired woman had bought the house with her husband less than a year ago. Did she remember the name of the seller? She didn't, but it would be on the paperwork, and she was sure she could find it in a jiff. It took longer than a jiff, it took twenty minutes, but she finally dug up the name: Seth Patterson.

Seth was Bitsy's younger brother. He lived

on a slightly sketchy-looking block of down-town Royal Oak in a tiny apartment over a karate studio. The walls held Ansel Adams prints and the air smelled of cigarettes, with an underlay of marijuana. The furniture was junk but there was a flat-screen TV and a top-of-the-line stereo system with a turntable and half a dozen plastic crates full of old LPs. Seth lifted one of the crates off a chair so Jack could sit. He was a scrawny guy with a sad face, and he moved slow, as if the world had done him in. But his energy picked up when he talked about his sister.

"Bitsy just about raised me herself," he said. "She was fourteen years older. We had the same father, different mothers. Our dad had a hard time holding on to his wives. Bitsy's mom ran out on him when Bitsy was five. She was a waitress from some little town in Tennessee, and she took up with our dad because she wanted a little excitement. Dad was twenty-two and he and a buddy were riding across the country on motorcycles. But that can only go on so long. Eventually he brought her back home to Michigan and took a job as a carpet sales-man. Have you ever met a carpet sales-man?"

"No," Jack said.

"They're not real exciting. So she left and

Dad raised Bitsy on his own until he hit it off with another waitress — that was my mom. She married him because he convinced her he had ambitions. I think he did. He liked working on motorcycles. He let me help him fix up a secondhand Harley once. I think he dreamed about selling them, opening his own dealership. But it never happened. My mom hung around until I was six and then took off with a drummer she met at a jazz show at the old State Theatre — they call it the Fillmore now."

Seth paused for a moment, as if he had lost his place. Then he found it again.

"So Bitsy took care of me," he said. "She dropped out of college, though I don't think she minded. College wasn't really her thing. Our dad paid the bills, but Bitsy worked too — part-time jobs during the day so she'd be home when I got out of school. When I was older, she taught herself how to make jewelry. She did a lot with semiprecious stones at first, agate and sodalite, the kind of stuff you could buy at craft stores. But that bored her. So she got into metal work: silver, copper, tin. She was a whiz with a soldering iron. She experimented. She'd take apart an old clock and use the gears to make earrings. She'd make you a charm bracelet out of keys from an antique typewriter."

He smiled, but on his face even the smile looked sad.

"She started selling stuff to friends," he said, "and then she got a stall at Eastern Market. She couldn't make things fast enough, so she would go around to thrift stores and pawnshops and buy cheap jewelry and sell that too. She could buy something for a couple bucks and clean it up, and then tell you a story about it — how she got it as a gift from a German duke who wanted to leave his wife for her, but she wouldn't let him — and you'd pay her ten times what it was worth, just because she was so damn charming."

His voice broke on the last line. He was sitting across from Jack on a ratty sofa, and now he slumped forward and covered his eyes to hide tears. Jack looked around for tissues but didn't see any. He watched Seth's shoulders tremble and didn't speak. Muffled sounds came up through the floor from the karate studio below. Sounds of sparring. People stomping and grunting and getting thrown onto mats.

Eventually Seth wiped his face on his sleeve. "I'm sorry," he said. "I miss her."

"I understand," said Jack.

"I think about her in that house, the house where we grew up. That's where she died. She lived alone there. Our dad was gone and I moved out when I was twenty-five, because at a certain point you're too old to be living with your sister. If I'd stayed, she might still be alive."

Jack thought there might be more tears, but Seth held them back.

"Could I ask you how she died?" Jack said.

"It was an accident," said Seth. "She was doing laundry, carrying a basket down the stairs. The washer was in the basement. She lost her footing and fell and hit her head. They say she was bleeding in her brain. And there was no one to help her."

Jack searched for something original to say and came up empty. He settled for, "I'm sorry."

Seth barely seemed to hear him. "I had to sell that house. I couldn't live there. Now the money's sitting in the bank. I don't know what to do with it. Bitsy always said I was a late bloomer. I just needed to try things until I found something I wanted to do. *Try anything,* she said. *You never know what the right thing is gonna be.* But none of the things I tried worked out. Can I tell you something?"

"Sure," Jack said.

"Even if it's awful?"

"Tell me."

"I used to look down on her. Because she was alone. She never got married. Even though she never seemed unhappy, I thought she must have been. Now I see people who remind me of her, walking by themselves on the street or in a store, and I get scared. Sometimes it's hard to breathe. Because I know where I'm headed. I don't have anybody. I'm thirty-six and I work in a coffee shop."

"You still have time," Jack said.

Seth Patterson dropped his head and dragged his fingers through his hair.

"It doesn't seem that way."

That night Jack stopped at Slows for a sandwich and ate it at his apartment. He synced his iPod with the stereo and set it on shuffle, but all the songs that played were either too peppy or too gloomy and he had to shut it off. He checked his messages and there were none from Kim Weaver; he hadn't heard from her since Monday night when he called her to let her know he had to go to Belleville and wouldn't make it to the Bronx Bar.

Her clothes were still in his closet. He took that as a positive sign.

He sat on the floor by the sofa and tried to clear his head. There was a photo of Bitsy Patterson on the coffee table; he had gotten it from her brother. She had curly hair and wore funky glasses and big loopy earrings. She looked happy.

The man in the hat was on the table too, staring up at Jack from a flyer.

He picked up a pen and pulled the flyer toward him and scribbled over the words at the top: *Have you seen him?* He wrote new words to take their place: *I am close to finding you.*

He turned the flyer over and started writing on the back: *I can see you. You took the ring from Alex Cavanaugh's body but then, somehow, you lost it. You didn't know who had taken it, or you would have gone to retrieve it. Maybe you thought you would never see it again. Then it reappeared, in the ad for Motor City Keys. You saw it when it ran in the Detroit papers, or in* The New York Times. *It was a beacon that only a few people would recognize. You had to make a decision: let it go, or do something about it.*

Thirteen-year-old Danny Cavanaugh saw you the day his brother died. Grown-up Danny saw you again one morning on his front lawn. Why? You were checking to see if Danny subscribed to the newspaper. The ring was weighing on your mind. You were afraid of being exposed. You decided to try to get it back.

The first step was Olivia. You knew her name. It was right there in the ad: PHOTO BY OLIVIA MAKINNEN.

You followed her to a park one day in October, and she gave you the name of the man whose hands appeared in the ad, the one who had brought the ring to the shoot. Then you killed her — either because you wanted to or because you felt you had to.

You were more cautious when it came to Ken Wellner. If you killed him, the police might link his death to Olivia's, and you didn't want that. So you contacted him by phone and arranged to buy the ring without ever seeing him.

What would you have done if he refused? Best not to think about it.

You offered him much more than the ring was worth, to make sure he would agree. And he gave you something else you needed. He gave you Bitsy.

The ring alone wasn't enough. You needed to know who had taken it.

Did you think Bitsy took it from you? The middle-aged artsy lady? No. But you tracked her down and went to her house, the one with the crystal globes in the garden, with the fairy door, because you needed to know where she got the ring.

And she told you, didn't she?

She told you, and you pushed her down the stairs.

Jack dropped the pen on the coffee table. He had withheld the truth from Seth Patterson: his sister's death was no accident. He didn't want to add to the man's grief. But there was no other way to look at it, given the sequence of events.

Olivia had died the year before last, on the tenth of October.

Bitsy Patterson had died the very same month, on the twenty-third.

The man in the hat's call to Ken Wellner had fallen somewhere in between. Jack had phoned Wellner on the drive back from Royal Oak, trying to narrow down the date, and Wellner's best guess had been mid-October. He remembered that he had taken a weekend getaway with his wife near the end of that month — and had used the money from the ring to pay for it. If Jack had been able to access phone records, he could have fixed the date more precisely; he could even have found the number the man in the hat had called from. But he was sure it would have led nowhere. The man in the hat had been careful to conceal his identity. He would have used a pay phone or a burner cell phone.

Jack got up from the floor and paced around the room. He opened a window. The smell of Seth Patterson's apartment had stayed with him: cigarettes and marijuana. He had gotten away from the place as soon as he could; it made him uncomfortable, like lingering in a sickroom. He had the irrational fear that Seth's sorrow might be contagious.

Before he left, he had shown Seth the Motor City Keys ad, on the off chance that he might recognize Alex Cavanaugh's ring and be able to say where Bitsy had acquired it. But Seth only looked at it blankly and shook his head. Jack showed him the image of the man in the hat as well, and got the same reaction.

Now Jack stood by the window, breathing clean air. Bitsy Patterson was beyond his reach. She couldn't tell him what he needed to know. But he still had options. He had not yet come to the end of the line.

He sifted through the mess of files on the coffee table, gathering together the ones that Paul Rook had brought to him — the ones Paul had collected because he believed that the murders they described were committed by the same man who killed his mother.

Jack had discounted them all along. They

covered a large span of time, and there was nothing to tie the victims together. There were fourteen victims in all: eight women and six men. Their ages ranged from seventeen to sixty-four. They came from different income groups and worked in different occupations. One was a bus driver, one was a chiropractor, one sold shoes.

Paul had chosen these cases because in each of them a witness had described seeing a man in a hat in the vicinity of the victim or the crime scene in the days leading up to the murder. Jack had never believed that the same man was involved in every case; the odds against it were astronomically high.

But now he sorted through the files, looking for one in particular. He had remembered it on the drive home from Royal Oak. The victim was a black man named Everett Stillman. He was fifty-eight when he died. He'd been tied to a chair in his basement and cut with a knife repeatedly. Eventually his killer grew tired of tormenting him and sliced open his throat.

Everett Stillman had died the year before last, in November — a month after Olivia, two weeks after Bitsy Patterson.

Jack had read about the case at the time. He had discussed it with his former partner,

Carl Dumisani, and they had decided it had nothing to do with Olivia.

But now Jack had found a connection.

He believed that the man in the hat had gone to see Bitsy Patterson, to ask her how she had come by Alex Cavanaugh's ring. And Bitsy had told him.

Bitsy made her own jewelry, but she didn't make the ring.

She couldn't make things fast enough, her brother had said, *so she would go around to thrift stores and pawnshops and buy cheap jewelry and sell that too.*

That was the connection. It had to be.

Everett Stillman had been a pawnbroker.

31.

Leonard Stillman wasn't sure he wanted to talk about his brother.

"I talked to the cops when Everett died," he said. "They wanted to hear all about his life, and the people he knew, and how he spent his days. I sat in a room with them and drank coffee and told them everything I could think of, because I was eager to help. Around seven or eight hours in, they asked me what Everett was like as a boy, and how he and I got along back then, and how we'd been getting along lately, and I finally put two and two together. They didn't care about all the details they were getting out of me. They didn't need to know what my brother ate for lunch every day to work out who killed him. They had already decided who killed him. Me.

"The way they saw it, I was the one with a motive. Everett and I each owned half this place, and he didn't have a wife or kids, so if he died, I would inherit his share. They figured I must have killed him so that all this would be mine."

"All this" was Stillman Brothers Pawn, an ugly brick building on Greenfield Road with weeds growing in the cracks of the parking lot. There was an old jukebox on display in one of the front windows, a drum kit and a trombone in the other. Shelves along the walls to hold TVs and computers and sports equipment. Aisles of locked glass cases for the jewelry and smaller electronics.

"Once I caught on, I shut up and asked for a lawyer," Leonard Stillman said. "The cops had to look for somebody else to pin my brother's murder on. They never found anybody."

"I'm not a cop," Jack said.

"You said you were a private detective," Stillman countered. "I don't see a big difference."

"The difference is, anything we talk about is just between us."

"That sounds nice. But why should I trust you?"

"Because I don't think you killed your brother."

Stillman was perched on a stool behind the counter at the back of the store. His hair had gone white at the temples and he wore steel-framed glasses that rested low on his nose. He looked at Jack over the rims.

"Why do you have an opinion, one way or the other?"

"I've done some research on the case," Jack said. "You told the police about a man who spoke to your brother the day before he died. A white guy who wore a hat."

"That's right. He talked to Everett in the parking lot."

"Not inside the shop?"

"No, it was in the evening, after we closed. That's why the cops never believed me. If he had come inside, we would have caught him on tape." Stillman pointed at a video camera mounted near the ceiling in a corner of the room. "But since it happened in the lot, there was no proof. The cops thought I made him up."

"How long did he talk to your brother?"

"A few minutes. I carried some trash to the dumpster and locked the metal gates at the front of the store. Then I sat in my car for a minute and watched them, because you have to be careful in this neighborhood. But he didn't look like a threat — the guy in the hat. Everett seemed at ease with him."

"You never asked your brother about him?"

"I didn't give it another thought, until

after Everett died."

Jack had a flyer ready. He laid it on the counter. "Could this be the man you saw?"

Stillman studied it. "Hard to say. It's been a while, and I never looked at him close." He tapped his fingers on the paper. "This fellow here, I don't know, I guess it could be him. But the hat's not right. The guy I saw wore a ball cap."

This was a detail Jack already knew. It was one of the reasons he had originally decided that Everett Stillman's murder wasn't connected to Olivia's.

"I'm trying to find this man," Jack said. "He's a suspect in another murder — in several, actually. I think he had a purpose when he came to see your brother. He was interested in a ring that might have been sold from this shop."

"A ring?"

Jack brought out a copy of the Motor City Keys ad. "This ring," he said. "Do you recognize it?"

Stillman held the page at arm's length, then took off his glasses and brought it close to his face. He shook his head. "Sorry. We get a fair number of rings coming through here."

"I think you might have sold it to a woman named Bethany Patterson," Jack said. "Her nickname was Bitsy." He laid her photo on the counter, the one her brother had given him.

Stillman nodded. "The name doesn't mean anything, but I think she came in here a time or two. Not lately."

"It wouldn't have been lately," Jack said. "She died around the same time as Everett."

Stillman rubbed his eyes and put his glasses on again. "You're saying the fellow in the hat got her too? Because of some damn ring?"

"I think so."

"Why would he care so much about it?"

"I think someone stole it from him, and he wanted to know who. If Bitsy Patterson bought the ring here, would you have a record of it?"

"You don't have to give your name if you're buying," Stillman said. "But if you're selling, or pawning, then there's a record. You'd be in our system."

"So you could run a search for the seller?"

"I could, if you knew his name."

"His name is what I'm looking for," Jack said.

"Do you know the date when he's supposed to have brought this ring in?"

"No."

Stillman had another look at the Motor

City Keys ad. "Well, we enter a description of every item we take in, with a serial number if it has one," he said. "No serial number for a ring, of course. I could try a keyword search." He rolled his stool over to a computer. "It's going to depend on who was working that day, how much effort they put into the description."

He tapped the space bar on the keyboard and the monitor came to life. "Those are knights on there, aren't they?"

"Yes," Jack said.

"Okay, I'm trying 'ring' and 'knight' — and I'm getting nothing."

"What if you try 'ring' and 'horse'?"

Stillman nodded and tapped the keys. "Nope."

" 'Ring' and 'chess'?"

"No luck. Do you know what it's made of?"

Jack recalled what Ken Wellner had told him. "The stones are quartz," he said. "The band is gold-plated."

Stillman frowned. "We generally wouldn't bother with a gold-plated ring. Or with quartz. Whatever we take in, we need to be able to resell at a profit." He worked the keyboard. "I'm not seeing anything here."

"But it's possible you bought it and it wasn't entered correctly into your system."

"It's possible."

"You don't remember it. But maybe your brother bought it. Would he have done that, if he liked the way it looked? Or to give someone a break, even though it wasn't worth much?"

Stillman rose from his stool and faced Jack across the counter. "Everett wasn't known for giving people breaks. He wasn't the friendliest man I ever knew. But I suppose he might have bought it. Say someone brought it in with some other jewelry. He might have offered them one price for the whole lot, rather than picking and choosing. That could explain why I didn't find it in the system. If he was entering several items at once, he might have skimped on the descriptions. It could be listed as a ring and nothing more."

"So there's no way to track down the seller," Jack said.

Leonard Stillman's glasses had slipped to the end of his nose again. His eyes looked tired.

"I'm afraid not. Like I said, we get a lot of rings coming through here."

Jack drove away from Stillman Brothers Pawn around ten thirty on Thursday morning, thinking about Carl Dumisani.

In their early days riding together, when Jack was still learning the job, Carl delighted in passing along bits of wisdom. *Listen to your doubts* — that was one of his sayings. *Most detective work is a waste* — that was another. *You have to do it anyway,* Carl would add, *in order to make sure it's a waste.*

Jack's conversation with Leonard Stillman left him doubting himself. What if the man in the hat had nothing to do with Everett Stillman's death? What if the person Everett spoke to in the parking lot was someone else? What if Bitsy Patterson hadn't bought the ring from Stillman Brothers after all?

Listen to your doubts. Jack spent the rest of the day driving to other pawnshops, and then to thrift stores. He canvassed clerks, showing them his picture of the ring. He got nothing for his trouble. The effort was a waste, but at least he knew it was a waste.

It was close to eight o'clock when he arrived on his street. No place to park along the curb. Jack found a spot in the parking lot of the market on the corner. Stepping out into the mild evening, he saw a familiar car, a rusted white Chevy.

He opened the passenger door and slid in beside Paul Rook.

Paul had the radio tuned to an alternative station. John Darnielle of the Mountain

Goats singing a song about love.

"How long have you been sitting here?"

"Twenty minutes," Paul said, turning down the volume. "Maybe closer to forty."

"How long did you intend to wait?"

"I wasn't waiting for you. Sometimes I come here, just to see."

"To see?"

"To see if *he* shows up."

No need for more. The pronoun was enough.

Paul stared out through the windshield. "It's a habit now. Sometimes I go to the house in Dearborn, the place where my mother died. I park in the alley for an hour. Or Danny Cavanaugh's house in Corktown. I went there yesterday."

"That's a bad habit, Paul."

"It's for sale now — Danny's house. They fixed the ceiling in the living room, painted the walls. It's like nothing ever happened there."

Ed Cavanaugh would have put it up for sale, Jack thought. Of course. What else would he do with it? He probably did the painting himself. Jack had grown used to thinking of him in a certain way: as the colorful drunk he first met, climbing down a tree dressed in camouflage, or as the kindlier version he knew later, the one who listened to his story about Irene Vernen. But people have their own lives, their own business to attend to, even when you're not watching.

He asked Paul, "Have you ever talked to Danny's father?"

"No. Why?"

"He's missing. No one's seen him for more than a week."

Paul turned to him. "Is that why you went to Belleville the other night? Monday, when you were supposed to meet us."

"That's why."

"What do you think happened to him?"

"I don't know," Jack said. "He could be traveling."

Paul's mouth made an impatient line. "If he's traveling, then why are you worried?"

"I didn't say I was worried."

"Then why did you have to run off to Belleville?"

Jack could offer no good answer. He surrendered and shifted to another topic.

"I found something out," he said. "In Belleville. Something important. A link between Alex Cavanaugh and my wife." He spent a few minutes filling Paul in about the ring and Olivia's ad, about Ken Wellner, Bitsy Patterson, and Everett Stillman.

He tried to get a read on Paul's reaction.

There was something in his eyes that might have been anger. It came and went and left an emptiness behind. He looked wounded.

"The last time we talked," Paul said, "you pretended you were ready to give up."

"I wasn't pretending," said Jack.

"Now this. Why didn't you tell me sooner?"

"I've been working. I haven't told anyone."

"I could've helped. You've never wanted my help."

"Paul —"

"It's fine. Let me ask you something. Where does my mother fit in? Have you figured that out yet?"

"I don't know if she does," Jack said. "She was murdered years after Alex Cavanaugh, and years before Olivia and the others. I can't see the connection."

"What about the obvious one? Chess pieces. There were *knights* on Alex's ring. My mother's name was Bonnie *Rook*. You think that's a coincidence?"

Jack blinked. Somehow he had never associated the name Rook with chess. It was obvious to him now that he should have — and that it wouldn't have made the least difference.

"It has to be a coincidence," he said. "What's the alternative? I'm assuming the man in the hat has reasons for what he does. He didn't kill your mother just because of her name."

Paul scowled but didn't respond. He slumped in his seat, staring at his own hands on the steering wheel. Sulking. Jack tried to think of a way to smooth things over. He looked out at his apartment building across the street, at the neon sign of the Bronx Bar on the corner. Music murmured on the radio, the volume so low he couldn't make it out.

The door of the bar swung open and a man stepped out. He wore a suit and tie and carried a briefcase. His hair was impeccably combed. He walked east along the sidewalk, passing Jack's building at a leisurely pace.

Paul broke his silence. "I've seen him before. He keeps doing that. Strolling by."

"For how long?" asked Jack.

"As long as I've been here. I thought it was *him,* at first. The height seems like a match, and the build. But he's probably not old enough, and there's something about his face."

"It's the nose," Jack said.

"Exactly. He's got quite a beak. My mother would have called it a schnoz. It's not the nose of the man in the hat."

"No."

The man with the briefcase walked all the way to Cass Avenue. He stood on the corner beside the stop sign.

Paul said, "What's he doing?"

"Let's see," said Jack.

Steady traffic on Cass Ave. The briefcase man made no move. Then a break in the traffic and a woman crossed the street, carrying a shopping bag in either hand. Jack recognized her as one of his neighbors. She had a fast, clipped walk. The briefcase man fell into step behind her.

She came to the apartment building and put down one of her bags so she could punch in a code on the keypad at the entrance. She struggled a little with the bags and the door, until the briefcase man helped her.

He let her go first and followed her inside.

"Does he live in there?" Paul asked.

"No," said Jack.

"Should we do something then?"

"Let it be. He's not gonna hurt anybody."

"How do you know?"

"He's gonna knock on my door," Jack said, "and when he doesn't get an answer he'll come out again and go away."

"You know him."

"Yeah. He's doing this because he's frustrated. And mad at me."

"Why?"

"Because I've been sleeping with his wife."

Paul's eyebrows went up. "That's Kim's husband?"

Jack nodded. "His name's Doug."

"I didn't know she was married."

"They're getting a divorce."

"You don't think you should talk to him, tell him to stop coming around?"

Jack made a sour face. "I don't want to provoke him. He might hit me."

"Is he violent?"

"It's not him I'm worried about. If he hits me, I'm afraid I'll hit him back. Better to avoid the confrontation."

Paul looked doubtful, but whatever he wanted to say he kept to himself. Two minutes later the door of the apartment building opened and Doug Weaver came out with his briefcase. He walked to Cass Avenue again but this time he didn't stop. He disappeared around the corner.

"See?" Jack said. "Problem solved." He nodded toward the Bronx Bar. "How about you and I get a drink?"

32.

A drink at the Bronx Bar turned into two drinks and then a walk to an Armenian restaurant on Woodward. Lamb kebabs and pilaf and stuffed grape leaves. Jack parted from Paul around ten o'clock and climbed the stairs to his apartment. Before he saw the door, he caught the chemical smell of spray paint.

Doug Weaver had left him a new message, a variation on the first:

THIS
IS NOT
FAIR

He'd made a neat job of it until he got to the end. The final stroke of the *R* trailed off the door and over the frame and onto the wall.

Jack opened a window at the end of the hall to let the smell dissipate. He opened more windows inside his apartment. He went from room to room looking for signs that Kim had come by. He found nothing. Her clothes still hung in his closet.

He called her, got no answer, left a message on her voice mail. He let her know about Doug's visit and invited her to call if she felt like talking.

Standing in the kitchen, he drank a tall glass of water from the tap. He felt sluggish from the Armenian food. A can of white semigloss paint rested on a folded newspaper on the counter. A paintbrush beside it — the one Kim had used to paint the door. She had cleaned it thoroughly so she could use it again. Jack could use it now to paint over Doug's words, to put everything back in order.

It would take a while; the drying would take the longest. He would have to leave the door open while it dried. Maybe he should go to bed. Tackle it in the morning.

The Armenian food wouldn't let him sleep. He knew.

He locked up and made his way down to the street, to the lot where he'd left his car.

He drove west past dark buildings and empty sidewalks, plumes of steam rising out of grates. He took Trumbull Avenue south, saw the lights of MotorCity Casino, saw a homeless man camping out on the concrete slope of the underpass beneath I-75. Then the old Tiger Stadium on his right, just a field under the night sky. He drove through Corktown and found Danny Cavanaugh's street.

The colors of the houses were muted in the dark. Here was Danny's, red with white trim. Curtains closed. No lights. A for sale sign on the lawn, just as Paul had said.

Jack left his car by the curb in front. He drifted down the sidewalk, taking in the sounds of the neighborhood. The slap of a screen door. The patter of a sprinkler watering a lawn. A television laugh track through an open window.

Here's a jump rope tied around a tree. Here's a skateboard left out on a lawn. Here's an empty trash can someone neglected to take in. Here's a boy on a porch swing, kicking his feet, his mother telling him to come in and go to bed.

And here, down the block from Danny's house, there's a truck parked on the street, a Dodge pickup in faded silver. Jack recognizes it. He drove it once. It belongs to Ed Cavanaugh.

Danny's neighbor was awake. She answered the knock on her door in a tracksuit, curlers in her white hair. She told Jack she knew Ed. She'd seen him working at Danny's house, clearing things out, painting. But that was weeks ago.

Did she know his truck was parked down the street? No. These days she didn't walk around the neighborhood like she used to. She got her exercise on her treadmill, or she drove down to the river and walked there, for the view.

Jack asked her if Ed might possibly be staying in Danny's house. She didn't think so, but if he wanted to check she still had her key. They looked through the place together, top to bottom. The rooms had been stripped down to a few pieces of furniture. The closets and cupboards were empty. Nothing in the fridge. Not even a toothbrush in the bathroom. No one was living here.

Jack checked the backyard by himself, then the alley behind the house. He thought he might be looking for a body. He didn't find one. He circled around again and called Keely Tanager from Danny's front porch.

She answered on the third ring. "This is not a good time."

"I found Ed Cavanaugh's truck."

"Where?"

He told her.

"Ed's not in it," he added. "I've had a look for him in the house. He's not here."

There was silence on the line.

"Are you still with me?" he asked.

"I can't come there now," Keely said. "It really is a bad time. I'll call the Detroit police and ask them to impound the truck. That's the best I can do right now." Her voice sounded strained.

"Don't worry about it," Jack said. "I'll call them myself."

"Are you sure?"

"Absolutely.

"Thank you."

"What's going on?"

"It's just . . . bad. I have to go."

Nothing more. She had ended the call.

Jack stepped down from the porch. A gust of wind stirred the leaves on the trees. Lights went out in a house across the street, people turning in for the night. He felt wide-awake.

He scrolled through his contacts and called Carl Dumisani.

On a clear night you can make good time on Interstate 94. There are three lanes in either direction around the airport, to accommodate travelers eager to get home or get away. You drive west and the planes swoop down right in front of you, coming in from the north to make their landings. Sometimes they're so low it's surreal.

Everything is crisp and well defined: the white lines that separate the lanes, the red taillights of the semi you're following. Then the night turns strange. You look up and see your own name on a billboard: JACK PELLUM INVESTIGATIONS. Tasteful black letters on a pale gray field.

Jack hit the Belleville exit after midnight. He crossed the bridge over the lake and rolled down Main Street to the police station. If something bad had happened they would be talking about it there. He meant to go in and learn what he could, but in the end he didn't need to. Crime scenes draw crowds, and this one was easy to spot. It was across the street from the station, in the park where he had walked once with Keely.

The police had strung yellow tape around to keep people back, and there were screens set up to prevent them from taking pictures. The screens were white cloth panels on metal frames and there were three of them arranged at the foot of a slide in the center of the park.

In the movies, crime scenes are full of bustle and excitement: paramedics rushing in, techs gathering evidence, cops cracking jokes. In reality they can be dull. There are procedures to be followed. Few things happen fast. There's a lot of waiting around.

Jack saw no sign of Keely. He counted five uniformed cops, all of them there to safeguard the scene. There had to be a body behind the screens — that was their purpose, to hide a body. The cops were waiting for the medical examiner, who would need to sign off before the body could be removed. Procedures. Medical examiners are busy people, not to be rushed.

There were around thirty civilians looking on from outside the tape. A few of them kept to themselves, but the others gathered to talk. Jack stood on the periphery and listened.

"Did they arrest anybody yet?"

"How should I know?"

"You've been here longer than me."

"All I know is, there's a dead kid in there."

"It's not a kid."

"I heard it was a kid."

"It's a playground. It's logical that it would be a kid."

"Did you see a kid?"

"I can't see a damn thing."

"What are they doing?"

"It's not really a kid, is it? That would be awful."

"It's awful either way."

"But it would be a *tragedy.*"

"It's not a kid. I saw his feet."

"When?"

"When they were putting up those barriers. I saw his sneakers. He's a size eleven at least."

"Thank god."

"Hold on. A kid could wear size eleven shoes."

"Not a little kid."

"A teenager, though."

"Well, if it's a teenager, that's one thing. But if it's a little kid, that's worse."

"No it's not."

"Sure it is."

"That's the dumbest thing I ever heard."

"How about you two shut up? It's not a little kid. I don't even want to think about a little kid dying."

"That's what *I'm* saying."

The debate went on, but Jack's attention was drawn to the other side of the park, to a bald man in a windbreaker carrying a leather satchel. The medical examiner. One of the uniformed cops lifted the yellow tape to let him duck under.

A voice at Jack's elbow said, "About time. It's getting cold."

Jack turned and saw an elderly lady in a

long skirt and a sequined blouse with a string of pearls around her neck. He knew her. She'd been at the police station on the afternoon he came to meet with Keely — there to complain that someone had been driving her car without her permission. He tried to remember her name.

"Eugenia Abernathy," she offered, as if she'd read his mind.

"Jack Pellum," he said.

She spoke to him softly, confidentially. "You must be curious about the young man who died."

"I am."

"But you haven't engaged in speculation. Not like these scavengers hovering about, these chatterboxes."

"No."

"I take that as a sign of good manners. I despise chatterboxes." She gestured in the direction of the white screens by the slide. "Would you like to know his name?"

"If you'd like to tell me."

"I wouldn't tell these others. It would only encourage them. But I don't mind telling you. His name was Jerry Diaz. Did you know him?"

Jack shook his head. "I only met him once."

"He was a troubled young man. This is all

384

a formality, of course. No one's going to be arrested. He did it himself."

"I see."

"In a larger sense, I suppose we're all responsible," Mrs. Abernathy said. "I believe a civilization ought to be judged according to how well it treats the less fortunate. Wouldn't you agree?"

"Yes."

"But he's beyond our help now. All that's left is to bear witness." She touched the pearls at her neck. "I do wish they'd move him, though. It's not right to leave the poor child out in the cold."

Jack nodded his agreement. On the other side of the park, Keely Tanager stepped out of her cruiser, ducked under the yellow tape, and walked toward the slide. When she reached the white panels, she conferred with two of her officers. After a few minutes, the medical examiner came out from behind the panels and joined them.

The crowd moved closer in a futile effort to overhear. A uniformed cop came and waved them back, told them to go home. A few of them did. Most of them stayed to watch the denouement: the stretcher rolling behind the white panels and then out again, bearing Jerry Diaz's body in a black bag. The attendants lifting the stretcher into the ambulance, the ambulance driving away.

The ME was the next to depart, leaving Keely and her officers. Someone in the crowd said, "I guess that's it." They split into twos and threes and ambled off in different directions. Jack accompanied Eugenia Abernathy to her car and held the door while she got in. When she'd gone, he stood by his own car, leaning against the fender. He watched the crime scene turn back into a park: the panels broken down, the yellow tape rolled up. The cops left one by one, Keely Tanager last.

The others went into the station house, but Keely got in her cruiser and drove down Main. Jack thought she might pass him by, but she stopped in the middle of the street and rolled her window down.

"You didn't have to come," she said.

He shrugged. "I didn't like the way you sounded on the phone."

It was something a friend would say. He watched her trying to decide if they were friends. Her eyes were steady and clear and alive. She made up her mind.

"Follow me," she said.

33.

They drove to the north shore of the lake, to a cottage with a view of the water. There was a patio in back: red paver bricks with sand in between. Two chairs with thick cushions and a wide metal firebowl. A small table covered in colored tiles. Wooden crates turned on their sides to serve as footrests. Keely put Jack to work building a fire while she locked away her gun and shed her jacket and her shoes and her socks. He filled the bottom of the bowl with crumpled news-paper and arranged the wood in a pyramid on top. He touched a match to the paper and the flames spread.

He sat and watched them and she came out and offered him a glass of wine.

"I don't want to talk about Jerry," she said.

He took the glass. "We won't talk about Jerry."

"I don't think I *can* talk about him. Not right now."

"Just sit and relax and look at the water. This was a rotten day, but it's over. Let it go. Put your feet up."

The smoke of the fire rose into the cool night air. Wisps of cloud hung in the sky like mist, with patches of stars in the spaces between them. Jack sipped his wine and balanced the glass on his knee.

"When I was a kid we had a cat," he said. "A skinny little thing, black stripes over brown. She used to sleep under my bed. She used to climb up inside the box spring. If there was a storm, she would hide in the back of my closet. You couldn't get her out of there. She wouldn't come out even to eat. Some cats'll curl up in your lap, but not this one. She liked to lay at the top of the stairs. I think it made her feel safe, having the high ground. There was one thing she would do: if you sat at the bottom of the steps, if you were patient, she would come down and sit next to you, barely touching you."

Keely had been resting with her eyes closed. Now she opened them.

"Why are you telling me about your cat?"

"No reason," Jack said.

"You're trying to soothe me."

"Maybe. Is it working?"

"Not really. Tell me about Ed Cavanaugh's truck."

"That can wait."

"Tell me."

Jack took a breath that smelled pleasantly of smoke. He let it out again, surrendering. "I called someone I used to work with and he arranged to have it towed. I stayed with it until the tow truck came. They'll keep it in the impound lot until you're ready to look at it."

"You didn't touch anything?"

"I didn't even open it up. I looked in through the windows. Nothing seemed out of place. If something happened to Ed, I don't think it happened in the truck."

"Then where did it happen?"

"That's the question. There's no evidence of violence in the house. Or the yard. I can go back tomorrow, start talking to people in the neighborhood. Someone may have seen him."

"I'll go with you."

"One thing occurs to me," Jack said. "The Detroit River is less than a mile from Danny's house. Ed could have walked there."

Keely touched the rim of her wineglass to her chin. "You think he drowned himself?"

"Isn't that what we've been assuming all along — that he wanted to end it?"

"Someone would have noticed a body floating in the water."

"I thought so too. But if you wanted to die that way, you'd weigh yourself down, wouldn't you? Otherwise it would take a lot of willpower to stay under. So if you were serious, you'd fill your pockets with stones. Or something. That's what I'd do."

Keely took a drink and put her glass on the tiled table between them.

"You're like Danny," she said. "You've worked out how you'd drown yourself. That's something he would do." She looked at the fire. A log cracked and sparks drifted up with the smoke. "When I heard about how he killed himself, the steps it took — cutting open the ceiling, drilling a hole to run the rope through — it sounded just like him. He would have pictured it beforehand, planned it all out. That's how his mind worked."

"You were close to him," Jack said.

"I don't want to talk about Danny."

He gave her a gentle smile. "I could tell you more about my cat."

She rolled her eyes at him. Had another drink of wine to fortify herself. The sparks hovered in the air like fireflies.

"Danny was a weird kid," she said. "A loner. Never went anywhere without a book.

His head was full of trivia. He could tell you that a lightning bolt is four times hotter than the sun, or that eyeglasses were invented in Italy in the thirteenth century. That's if he bothered to talk to you at all. He grew up in the shadow of his older brother. Alex was the outgoing one, the athletic one, the one who planned to become a cop like their father. Danny was the smart one, and people knew he was smart, so in school, if he got something wrong, the other kids would pounce on it, they would laugh at him. So he almost always knew the answers, but he never raised his hand. He wanted to be invisible.

"We went to the same schools from kindergarten on, but I didn't really know him until after his brother died. Danny and I were in an exclusive club, because I had an older brother who died too, around the same time. When that happens, it marks you, especially at that age. We were both thirteen. We started spending time together. He understood me in a way that no one else did. We were going through the same thing — we were living in haunted houses. He was living with the ghost of Alex, and I was living with the ghost of Ryan."

Jack leaned forward in his chair. "How did your brother die?"

"He was out at night riding his bike, on Savage Road east of town. There's a place where the shoulder is narrow and there's a steep drop-off. He strayed too close and went over. Landed in a ditch headfirst. His neck more or less buckled. His airway was crushed and he suffocated. They found him the next morning."

"This was the same year Alex Cavanaugh died?"

"That's right. Ryan died in the spring, Alex in the summer."

Jack held his glass with two hands, his elbows resting on his knees. In the firelight, the wine looked almost black.

"You don't think someone could have run your brother off the road?" he said.

Keely kept silent for a moment, then chuckled softly. "You're really something. You want everything tied together. Your crazy killer, he definitely gets around. He runs a cyclist into a ditch. He bashes a teenager's head in. He waits twenty years and goes to a park —" She broke off suddenly.

"Go ahead," Jack said. "Say it."

"No. I'm sorry."

"You can say it: he goes to a park and strangles a photographer."

"I wasn't thinking. I didn't mean to be

callous." She bit her lip. "But I don't buy it. He can't be everywhere all the time."

She stared at the fire through her glass. "I'll let you in on a family secret," she said. "My brother was bipolar. And he was drunk the night he died. Mental illness and alcoholism often go hand in hand. When people think of bipolar disorder, they think of manic episodes followed by depression. Highs and lows. But it's possible to have both at the same time — it's called a mixed state. Mania gives you poor impulse control. Depression leaves you hopeless. If Ryan was in a mixed state that night, riding over the edge might have seemed like the thing to do."

She went quiet. Jack braced a heel on the rim of the firebowl. The heat came through the sole of his boot.

"It was the same with Jerry," Keely said after a while. "He was bipolar."

"I didn't know," said Jack.

"He had other problems too. Anxiety disorder. That's not uncommon. I saw you at Ed's — when was it? — Monday night. That's when Jerry had an episode at Walmart. There was a bird in the store. You know how they fly in sometimes and then can't find their way out. Well, Jerry wanted to help that bird. It was his mission. He couldn't believe no one else was worried about the bird. He started yelling at them — the customers, the employees. He wouldn't let up.

"I calmed him down and took him to the hospital, Saint Joseph Mercy in Ypsilanti. They kept him for forty-eight hours. But he was an adult, he was twenty-six. They couldn't keep him longer unless he posed a threat to himself or others. And when you've been through the system enough, you learn to give the doctors the answers they want to hear.

"Tonight Jerry went to the park and opened up his wrists with a piece of a broken bottle. It was his first try, and he got it right. You want to cut along the length of the arm, not across. He lay down on the end of the slide and bled out. The woman who found him had been at the park earlier in the day with her kids. She lost her sunglasses and came back to look for them."

Keely's face was pale in the firelight. "I had to tell Jerry's parents. They knew as soon as they saw me, but it didn't make it any easier. That's the part of the job I hate. I used to work homicide in Lansing. The guy I was partnered with, he always wanted me to take the lead when we notified the next of kin. He said I was better at it, but that's because he didn't want to do it. No one's good at it. What you're doing is telling them their life is ruined. You can dress it up. You can talk about finding justice, you can offer comfort. At the end of the day their life is still ruined."

She put her empty glass aside. "That's one reason I took this job. Smaller city, fewer people dying, fewer of those conversations. But it's not any better. In Lansing they were all strangers. But I knew Jerry."

34.

Michael Underhill has only a few clear memories of his father.

The earliest dates back to when he was seven years old. Late November, the day before Thanksgiving. After school he stayed with a neighbor until his mother came home from work. His mother fixed dinner: hot dogs and boiled potatoes.

Outside, snow fell in tiny flakes that disappeared when they hit the ground. A car pulled into the driveway after dark. His mother went out, telling him to wait inside.

He heard their conversation through the half-open door.

What do you want?

How about a smile, darlin'? That'd be a start.

You can't just show up here. Not after five years.

Are you turnin' me away? I've been on the road ten hours.

You can get right back on it.

Aw, that hurts, darlin'. You're breakin' my heart.

More wrangling and his mother relented. His father came in with a duffel bag and a package wrapped in brown paper. He was lanky and curly-haired and unshaven. Young Michael recognized him from pictures, but looked to his mother for confirmation.

"Give your dad a hug," she said.

The package was a present, though it was a month till Christmas. Michael tore away the paper and found a chemistry set. The box promised "101 Experiments." He opened it and saw a beaker and test tubes, measuring spoons and safety goggles. There were ten plastic bottles of chemicals, most of them with labels that said, WARNING!

"What's the age limit on this?" his mother said.

"It's for kids," said his father.

His mother looked at the instruction manual. "It's for ages twelve and up," she said.

"There's kids on the box."

"Yeah. They're twelve." She picked up one of the bottles. "Half this stuff is probably poison."

"He's not gonna eat it," his father said. "You're not gonna eat it, right, bud?"

His mother started putting things back in

the box. "I'm sorry, Mike, you can't have it."

"Oh, come on," his father said.

That night, Michael had a hard time falling asleep. There was music coming from his mother's bedroom, loud enough that he could feel it pulsing when he put his hand against the wall. He went down the hall and tapped on his mother's door to ask them to turn it down, but no one heard him.

In the morning, his mother woke him early. They got on the road at eight o'clock. "We're going to Indiana to see your grandma and grandpa," she said. He was confused, because his grandma and grandpa lived a few blocks away. There was no reason for them to be in Indiana, especially on Thanksgiving. Then he realized they were going to see his father's parents.

The drive took almost four hours. Michael had the backseat to himself. He had crayons and markers and coloring books. He had the safety goggles from the chemistry set; the rest of it was back home, on a high shelf in a closet.

The scenery on the Ohio Turnpike got dull fast. Michael put the goggles on and looked at people in the other cars. A teenage girl with pink hair smiled and gave him a thumbs-up. Then she was gone and the passing lane was empty. He unbuckled his seat belt and got on his knees to look out the back window. He waved at the car behind them. There was a bald man driving, a big dog in the passenger seat.

His mother noticed what he'd done. "Mike, put your seat belt back on."

"Sweet Jesus," his father said. "Give the kid a break."

By the time they crossed into Indiana, the goggles were making his face sweat. He took them off, settled into his seat, and dozed with his head against the door beside him. When he woke up, his mouth was dry. His mother and father were talking. He closed his eyes again and listened.

"You won't get anything," his mother said.

"I'll get something," his father said. "It's a question of how much."

"Not from them."

"*He* won't want to give me a dime. But she's easy. She can't resist her baby boy."

"The way I remember it, *he's* the one with the checkbook."

"True. But she'll be on my side — if we play it right. If I'm a bum, I'll get nothing. But I'm not a bum."

"Ha."

"I'm a man with responsibilities. I've got a wife and a kid. I'm trying to do right by them. I'm done running around —"

"Ha."

"— and now what I want is a happy family. My mother wants me to be happy. That's all she ever said to me, all my goddamn life. So what we have to do is act like we're happy. Are you happy?"

"You bet."

"Me too. We're happy as all get-out. All we need now is a little boost to help us along."

"A *little* boost?"

"Or a big boost. We'll see. Depends how well we play it. It'll help if they like the kid."

"Why wouldn't they like him?"

"I'm just saying. It'd be nice if he showed a little personality. Like if he talked. Does he ever fuckin' talk?"

It was noon when they arrived in South Bend, Indiana. The house was crowded with cousins Michael had never met. His grandmother was a heavy woman in an apron. She fussed over him, asked him if he was hungry, gave him a blueberry muffin. She took the turkey from the oven to baste it and said, "This bird is bigger than you were, the last time I saw you." She laughed, and he laughed too. It wasn't hard to believe. The turkey was enormous.

His mother stayed in the kitchen. All the

women were there, talking and drinking champagne. Michael stayed there too. His grandmother gave him a glass of grape juice.

An hour passed and the turkey was still roasting. The little red button had not yet popped up. Michael's father came in, breath smelling of beer. "Come on, bud, the game's on. You like football?"

"Not really," he said.

His father drew him away from the women. "You don't have to like it. Just sit next to Grandpa and pretend you like it. Can you do that?"

He nodded.

"Good," his father said.

They started for the TV room but before they got there his father took away his grape juice.

"Sorry, bud," he said. "But if you spill this on the rug, we're sunk."

Michael's grandfather had the biggest belly he had ever seen. It was bigger than a football, definitely — bigger than the Thanksgiving turkey, almost certainly. It was spherical like a balloon, like a planet, barely contained under a white dress shirt with the tails untucked. The man slouched on the sofa, as if his belly had fallen on him, as if he was trapped beneath it. His folded hands rested on it. It was a wonder he could see past it to the television.

Michael sat next to him and tried not to look at it. He focused on the game. He didn't know the rules, but he knew what a touchdown was. It was when a player threw the ball down at the ground and jumped in the air. He knew that was good, unless it was the team you didn't like. Then it was awful. In this game, one team wore blue and the other white. He didn't know which team his grandfather liked, so he waited and watched.

The players ran around and bumped into each other, and then the ball flew through the air and a player in blue jumped up and caught it and came down again, and Michael's grandfather's hands pumped in the air and everyone cheered. Michael raised his hands too, and hollered. He shrieked with joy, and his grandfather slapped a hand down on his knee and shook it. His father, on the other side of him, tousled his hair.

He remembers that as a high point of the trip. Afterward he had to eat his dinner at the kids' table, in a whole different room from his mother. He ate too much and later in the afternoon fell asleep in the back room where everyone had left their coats. He remembers kissing his grandparents good-bye. Waving at cousins and aunts and uncles who hadn't spoken a word to him.

He remembers driving away in the dark, his mother and father quiet up front. Then his father holding up a check and his mother turning on the dome light to see it.

"Well, I guess it's something," she said.

"Could be worse," said his father.

Driving east toward home with snow falling on the interstate. His father behind the wheel, cruising along in the passing lane. Michael was wide-awake now. His mother tried to find a station she liked on the radio. He got out of his seat belt and leaned forward between the two front seats. She gave him a look but didn't say anything. The road curved and he could see long lines of cars in both lanes, brake lights flaring. His father slowed down. Came to a stop. Mumbled, "Well, shit."

When traffic started moving again, it moved at a snail's pace. His father drummed the steering wheel impatiently and the car crawled along for what seemed like an hour. When they came to an exit, his father took it. "This'll be better," he said. His mother unfolded a map from the glove box, and with her navigating they motored along back roads through barren towns, the snow falling steadily. She turned up the heat and his father cracked his window and Michael unzipped his coat. The road stretched on, gray and slick in the glow of the headlights. They passed through a town called Seyberts and one called Howe and another called Mongo.

They rode across a bridge over the Pigeon River and wound up on a long, straight county road. Trees on one side, fields on the other. Michael's father pulled the car over and put on the blinking hazard lights. "Tell me we're still going east," he said.

His mother nodded. "I think so."

"I'd rather you knew."

"I'm pretty sure. You want to look at the map?"

His father sighed and opened his door. "I gotta take a leak."

The door slammed shut and Michael's mother twisted around to him and said, "You okay?"

"Yeah."

"You need to pee?"

He hesitated. "No."

"I think you do," she said. "Now's the time."

And this is the part he remembers best. Not the hours they had left to go. Not getting home and wading through eight inches of snow to the house. Not waking the following morning to find his father gone.

He remembers standing at the roadside next to his father, the low rumble of the car idling beside them, the smell of the exhaust. He remembers peeing into a shallow ditch, swaying from side to side to make patterns in the snow. His breath visible in the air.

He remembers asking his father a question: "Where are we, Dad?" And his father looking around, surveying the white field that stretched out into gray in front of them. Saying, "This is Indiana, Mike. It's the ass end of nowhere. If we dropped dead out here, nobody would ever find us."

He remembers, because it's the only time his father ever called him by his name.

He went back there a week and a half ago. First he let Ed Cavanaugh's drowned body dry in his bathtub overnight, then he wrapped it in green trash bags, three layers held together with duct tape. He carried it to his garage and loaded it into the trunk of his car.

He drove two hours from Chelsea to Mongo, Indiana, then a little south and east. He found the same spot, or one very much like it: a straight piece of county road with a field on one side and woods on the other. In the daylight he had a long view in either direction. There was no one to see him carry the body into the woods. He kept walking until the road was out of sight, and left Cavanaugh in a small depression beside a fallen tree. He cut through the bags and the tape with a carpet knife to let bugs and animals in. There was no ID on the body; he had emptied the old man's pockets. The driver's license and credit cards had already gone through the shredder in his office at home.

Back to his car and in two hours Michael Underhill was in Chelsea again. Cavanaugh's pickup truck remained on his street. He waited till nightfall and drove it to Detroit, arranging for Henry Tanager to meet him in Corktown and drive him home. Tanager was nervous. He kept sweeping his silver hair back from his brow. His skin was damp with sweat. He didn't ask what had happened to Cavanaugh, and Underhill didn't tell him.

Since that night, Underhill's mind has been mostly untroubled. He believes he has done the best he could with Cavanaugh's body. With luck, it might not be found for years. But the pickup is another matter. A truck is harder to hide than a body. If he could have made it vanish, he would have. Leaving it in Corktown seemed like the next best choice. Ed Cavanaugh might be expected to visit his dead son's house. If the police found his truck there, they would look for him there. When they didn't find him — well, they would tell themselves that there are many ways for an old man to come to harm in Detroit.

Still, it would be better if the truck were never found. There are places Underhill could leave it — poor neighborhoods where it might get stolen. Would that solve his problem?

Sometimes he thinks it would, and other times he thinks he should stop second-guessing himself and leave well enough alone. On Friday evening he drives to Corktown to see where things stand. He rolls down Leverette Street, mixing with the commuters coming home. The pickup truck is gone. Underhill feels a sweet relief. The decision is out of his hands.

Then he spots Keely Tanager, talking to a woman who's watering her lawn. And there's Jack Pellum with a notebook in his hand, knocking on someone's door.

They don't see him. He doesn't linger. He lets momentum carry him along, and soon he's out of Corktown and driving north.

It makes sense that Keely's there. Ed Cavanaugh has gone missing from her city; it's her responsibility to find him. Jack Pellum's presence is more alarming, but not entirely unexpected.

Underhill has given a great deal of thought to Jack Pellum. He killed Olivia Makinnen without knowing that her husband was with the police. He considers it the worst of his mistakes.

He knows about Pellum's interest in the murder of Alex Cavanaugh. Henry Tanager informed him shortly after Pellum turned up in Belleville. And he knows where Pellum's investigation led him; he has followed the news about the Vernens and their son Dylan.

Underhill has considered killing Pellum. If he were impulsive, he would have done it by now. But he has already taken too many risks in his life. To kill an ex-cop, the son of a federal judge, would be a desperate move. He won't do it unless he has to.

Right now he drives to midtown. He thinks of it as a reconnaissance mission; he needs to know how big a threat Pellum poses. He parks his car on Canfield Street in the historic district. There's a small pry bar in the trunk. He takes it with him, carrying it under his jacket. He paces along the cobblestones of the street, stopping to admire the intricate wood trim on the old Victorian houses.

Pellum's apartment building is only a

short walk away. Underhill is there in minutes. He watches it from across the street, having second thoughts about whether to go in. But if he's going to try, he should do it now, while Pellum is in Cork-town. He crosses the street as one of the tenants is coming out. A good omen. He catches the entry door before it closes, and slips inside.

There's a directory in the foyer. He scans the names and finds PELLUM/MAKINNEN. The apartment number is 301. When he reaches the top floor he realizes he won't need the pry bar. Pellum's door is standing open — not all the way, but there's a gap of several inches. The door is covered in a fresh coat of white paint.

Underhill stands in the hallway, indecisive. Jack Pellum can't be here, but someone has been painting. Either they're inside or they went out and could be back at any moment.

Quiet in the hall, but there's a sound coming from inside the apartment. Running water. A shower.

Underhill touches the knob of the door with a knuckle. Pushes it open.

There are newspapers on the floor to keep the paint off the carpet. He steps around them.

Inside, the sound of the shower is clearer.

He approaches the bathroom door and listens. Now he can hear humming too. A woman's voice.

She took her clothes off in the living room. They're on the floor: jeans and blouse, bra and panties. Underhill steps over them and comes to the coffee table.

He has seen Pellum's flyers before, and here's one now. He knows the face beneath the hat is supposed to be his, but it's like looking in a mirror through gauze and fog. He doesn't see himself there.

The flyer has writing on it: *I am close to finding you.*

There's more on the back, and it's not good. *You took the ring from Alex Cavanaugh's body but then, somehow, you lost it. . . .* Pellum knows more than he should. He knows the ring wound up in the Motor City Keys ad. He knows about Ken Wellner and Bitsy Patterson. He has even made the jump from Bitsy to Everett Stillman. He has a file with Stillman's name on it — it's there on the table with the flyers.

I am close to finding you.

Underhill feels a numbness in his cheeks. His heart is thumping in his chest. He can recognize panic. He doesn't mind it. He knows he can get it under control.

You may be close, he thinks. But you're

not there yet.

He folds the flyer and slips it in his pocket. He can feel his heart settling down. He knows what he wants to do. He's not afraid. He has time.

He doesn't rush. Not even when the shower shuts off.

35.

Kim Weaver liked Jack Pellum for his towels. They were big and plush and soft. She wrapped one around her body and used another to pat the water from her hair.

She wiped the steam from the mirror and thought about how she had resolved to stay away from Jack after he stood her up at the Bronx Bar. She told herself her resolve was still intact. She hadn't come here to see him. She had come because her husband was a child, scrawling messages on Jack's door. The least she could do was paint it over.

"Liar," she said aloud, to her image in the mirror.

She liked the way Jack held her, and the way he kissed, nothing casual about it. She liked his quiet intensity, even though she knew it had to be wrapped up with having a wife who had died. She knew the wife didn't bode well for her. The pictures on his walls — every one of them was a warning. Here was a man who was still holding on to his past.

Kim didn't care about the warnings. She had married Doug and it had gone terribly wrong. Whatever she did now would probably go wrong too. If she took her chances with Jack, it would at least be a new wrong thing.

She ran a brush through her hair and opened the bathroom door. When she stepped into the living room something seemed off. She turned to look at the apartment door and it was as she had left it: slightly open so the paint could dry. Careless, leaving it that way. Now she was spooked, wondering if someone had come in. She called Jack's name and got no answer.

No place for anyone to hide in the living room, except behind the sofa. Kim looked there, and in the kitchen too. By the time she checked the bedroom, she thought she was being paranoid. Then she saw her clothes piled on the bed. She knew she had left them on the floor in the other room. Her handbag was on the bed too; she had dropped it there when she came in. But now her wallet was out and lying on top. And her driver's license was on top of the wallet.

She was puzzled and a little afraid. She

dug in a pocket of her bag where she kept a canister of pepper spray. Armed with the spray, she looked under the bed. Nothing but dust.

One last place she hadn't tried. The closet. Two folding doors. She swept them open, both at once.

And laughed in relief when she saw only clothes.

She was reading on the sofa when Jack came home an hour later — a week-old copy of the *Detroit Free Press.* Jack got very serious when she showed him the tableau on the bed. She had dressed in fresh clothes from the closet and left everything undisturbed.

"This is bad," he said. "You were in the shower?"

"Yes."

"You can't do things like that."

"Take showers?"

"Not with the door open. What were you thinking?"

Anger in his voice. Kim touched his arm, trying to defuse it.

"Hey," she said. "I get it. I won't do it again. I'm safe. Nothing happened."

"You think this is nothing?"

"I think it's a prank. It was probably Doug. I'll talk to him."

Jack took hold of her wrist. "This isn't Doug," he said. "Doug sprays messages on the door. This is different. It's *him*."

"Who?"

"It's *him*. He was here. And he wanted me to know he was here." Jack pointed at her driver's license. "He put that there for a reason. It's a threat. Are you a child? You don't recognize a threat when you see one? I don't understand people like you. I don't know what sort of world you think you're living in. This is *his* world. He's in it. You can't leave doors open. He'll come right through."

Kim tried to draw away, but Jack wouldn't let go of her wrist.

"You need to wake up," he said. "You think the worst that can happen is you marry a guy and he runs around on you? That's nothing. You think this was a prank? *He* doesn't pull pranks. You think you're safe? He knows about you now. He knows your name and your address. That's the threat. He was here today. He could have choked the life out of you. That's what he does. That's just one thing he does. Should I tell you another? He bashes your skull in. That's another. Or he slices your throat."

"All right," she said softly. "Enough."

Jack looked down and realized how tightly

he'd been holding on to her. He let her loose. Said, "I'm sorry."

He backed away until he was standing against a wall. She followed him. He had tears in his eyes. She touched his cheek with the back of her hand.

"I can't have that happen to you," he said.

"I know."

"I can't. You need to get away from here, and stay away."

"I'll do whatever you want."

She felt his hands on her waist. He closed his eyes.

"Promise me you'll stay away," he said.

36.

Michael Underhill still has the safety goggles from the chemistry set his father gave him.

He never got any use out of the rest of it. The box sat on a closet shelf for years, and when he was old enough his mother took it down and opened it. Some of the bottles had leaked; the chemicals smelled foul. She threw it all away.

But not the goggles. He held on to those. Strange, the things we keep.

He has them in the back of a drawer in his desk. He thinks he'll want them if he ever has a son. He and Anna Haley have talked about having children. It's always been casual talk. Light and airy. *What if? Maybe someday.*

But Underhill would like a son, and if he ever has one, he knows one thing he'll do. He'll give the boy the goggles. He'll say, *My father gave me these.*

The day after Thanksgiving, when he was

seven, when he woke up to find his father gone, he thought he would never see the man again. He was mistaken. His father turned up every year or two; he stayed for a few days, sometimes as long as a week.

When Michael was eighteen his father appeared in late August. It was a lazy summer afternoon, and in a few days Michael would leave home for his freshman year at Ohio State. His mother had been in a mood for weeks. She wanted him to sit with her and watch television in the evenings; she cooked him special meals. She bought him presents: clothes and sheets, a desk set. Stationery and postage stamps — *So you'll remember to write to me.* It occurred to him that she would miss him when he went away. He wondered if he would miss her. He didn't think so.

She had grown old, he thought, even though she was only in her forties. She had streaks of gray in her hair that she didn't bother to color. She drank wine at the end of the day and read romance novels, and she had started to feed stray cats. There was one that she had tamed and brought into the house, and two others that she fed out in the garage. She never closed the garage door all the way anymore; she left a gap of half a foot so the cats could go in and out.

Other animals took advantage of the gap. Raccoons had started getting into the garbage. Michael had started strapping the lids on the cans with bungee cords. On an August afternoon he carried a bag of trash from the kitchen across the yard to the garage. He raised the door and stowed the bag in a trash can. He stepped outside again and began to lower the door and saw a tow truck pull up in front of the house. His father climbed out of the cab and the truck drove away.

Michael watched the man approach, a duffel bag slung over his shoulder. He was taller than his father now, by three inches at least.

"Here's my giant," his father said. "Are you six feet yet?"

"Five eleven," said Michael.

"Well, you'll get there. Where's your mother?"

"Still at work."

"Isn't she always?" his father said, turning toward the house. "I need a shower. Maybe you could fry me some eggs. I haven't had anything but coffee all day."

He shrugged the duffel bag off his shoulder as if Michael might take it from him. When it didn't happen he lugged it into the house himself, with Michael trailing behind him. In the kitchen he slipped off his shoes. Michael watched him climb the stairs to the second floor. There was a hole the size of a silver dollar in the heel of one of his socks.

Michael heard the door of the bathroom closing, the sound of water running through the pipes. He found the eggs in the refrigerator: four left in the carton. He dropped them one after another into the sink and washed them down the drain, shells and all.

He left the carton on the counter.

His car was parked out by the curb, an old Ford compact his mother had bought him for five hundred dollars. He drove into town and cruised aimlessly through the streets until he wound up at the movie theater. He bought a ticket and sat in the dark, surrounded by empty seats. The movie was about soldiers committing war crimes in Vietnam. The details of the plot faded from his mind two minutes after he walked out.

He snuck into another movie without paying, this time a road-trip comedy. He dozed off in the middle and woke to the credits rolling. Outside, it was dusk.

Back in the car, Michael zigged and zagged through the streets of town. Norwalk, Ohio — east of Toledo, west of Cleveland. He stopped for a Coke and two slices of pizza. He drove out to the reservoir and circled back to the golf course on the other side of town. He passed the house of a girl he knew: Debbie Pinckney. The first girl he ever slept with, and the only one so far. They did it on the couch in her father's den, on a weekend when her parents were out of town.

There were lights on in the house, but Michael kept driving. He came to the high school and left his car in the lot. Walked across a deep-green lawn to the baseball diamond. There was a party going on in the home-team dugout: a dozen teenagers and a cooler full of cheap beer.

He knew them all. He had been around them all his life. One of them yelled his name: *Mike! Mike's here!* A kid named Rory, filled with drunken enthusiasm.

Michael fished a can from the cooler and cracked it open. Rory got an arm around his shoulders and asked him how the hell he was, and what the hell he'd been doing all summer. Michael slipped away from him as soon as he could, and took his beer out to the pitcher's mound.

More people showed up. One of them had a boom box blasting Guns N' Roses. A girl climbed onto the roof of the dugout and said she wanted to jump off. She was look-

ing for volunteers to catch her. A fight broke
out over whether she should be encouraged
or talked out of it. Michael watched from a
distance.

Around ten thirty, Debbie Pinckney arrived with a group of her friends. By then
Michael was working on his second beer
and had walked out to the right-field wall.
Debbie split off from the others and came
out to see him.

"What's the matter?" she asked him.

"Nothing," he said.

"Sure. Don't tell me. I enjoy the chal-
lenge. I'll work it out on my own."

"I'm just having a beer."

"You don't even like beer."

"Everybody likes beer."

"You're not everybody. What happened?"

"Why do you think something happened?"
he said. "Just because I'm out here" — he
nodded toward the dugout — "instead of in
there?"

"I didn't expect to see you here at all,"
she said. "It's not your scene."

He sipped from his beer. It had turned
warm. "What's my scene?"

She leaned against the wall beside him. "I
don't know, Mike. I don't have you all
figured out."

The sound of laughter and music came

across the field, but it was muted. Michael could hear Debbie Pinckney's breathing. She was too thin and her hair was dyed pink and cut too short and she had a habit of biting her nails. She crossed her arms and her elbow brushed against his. She smelled of fresh soap and coconut shampoo.

"He's in town," Michael said.

"Now it comes out."

"He showed up this afternoon."

"What does he want?"

"What does he always want?"

"Maybe it'll be different this time."

Michael started to bring the beer up to his lips. Stopped suddenly. Tossed the can away.

"It probably won't be different," Debbie said. "I mean, he's probably the same. But you don't have to let him get to you. How you respond to him — that's up to you. That's in your control."

"I know."

"You *say* you know, but I wonder if you *really* know. You should talk to somebody. I think it could really help you."

Michael had heard this before. Debbie was heading to Penn State to study psychology. She'd been in therapy since she was thirteen.

"Maybe I *will* talk to somebody," he said.

"You won't," she said. "But you really should. I know you hate it when I say stuff like this, but you're bound to have issues around abandonment. That's just for a start. I mean, it's obvious."

"Right."

"And I wouldn't be surprised if you had an attachment disorder. Because you didn't get everything you needed when you were a little kid. It's not your fault. That's what you have to understand."

"Right."

She turned to face him. "Now you're giving me monosyllables. Which is one step away from the silent treatment. Because you're angry and you're afraid of what you might say."

He looked down at his feet. "I'm not angry."

"It's okay to be angry."

"I know. But I'm not."

She started to respond, but he spun toward her suddenly and kissed her on the mouth, pushing her up against the wall. She returned the kiss eagerly, her arms around his neck.

When they came up for air, she laughed. "Mike," she said softly. "Just because we're making out doesn't mean you're not angry."

He pushed her against the wall again.

Covered her mouth with his so she wouldn't talk. His hands moved under her shirt. He could feel her ribs. Her skin was soft and warm. He pushed his knee between her parted legs, and she clamped her thighs around him. He felt her fingers in his hair, against his scalp. He took her lower lip between his teeth.

She pushed him away, laughing again. "Jesus, Mike. Okay. We can do this. But not here, all right? Take me somewhere. Somewhere without other people. And go easy on me, will you? You're gonna leave bruises."

He could feel her hands on his wrists now, underneath her shirt. He had a tight grip on her waist. It took an effort to relax it. He released her and stepped back. Smoothed the front of her shirt.

"I'm sorry," he said.

She peeled herself away from the wall. "It's okay. Let's go somewhere."

She sounded bright and eager in the dark and he knew he should want to go with her. He knew it would be all right. He might be rough with her, but he wouldn't hurt her. But he knew something else: he wouldn't feel anything. He hadn't felt anything when he kissed her.

"No," he said. "Not tonight."

He left her and set off across the field,

listening for the sound of her following footsteps in the grass, hearing only his own. She called his name once, kindness in her voice. But that was all.

He reached his car in the lot and got out of there. Home was the only place he had to go, but he put it off as long as he could, riding aimlessly through deserted streets. Coming to the edge of town and turning back. He rolled into his driveway with a flash of white fur in the beam of his headlights — one of the stray cats slipping through the gap under the garage door.

A yellow bulb burned on the porch to welcome him. In the kitchen he smelled fried steak and onions. The frying pan was in the sink, along with a heap of dishes. A bottle of vodka stood on the counter, mostly gone.

He knew the sound of the ticking clock, which showed him it was after midnight. He climbed the stairs, hearing each familiar creak. He passed the closed door of his mother's bedroom on the way to his own. No sound behind it when he listened.

He opened the window in his room and lay awake on top of the quilt on his bed. He tried to remember the scent of Debbie Pinckney's hair and the smoothness of her skin and the hardness of her ribs, but everything eluded him. He put his arms at his sides and stared at the ceiling and made himself lie still until he fell asleep.

In the morning Michael found his mother in the kitchen dressed for work. Clean dishes arranged in the drainer by the sink. She was scrubbing bits of onion from the frying pan.

"I'll make you pancakes," she said, without looking at him.

"You don't have to," he told her.

"I'll put blueberries in them, the way you like."

"I don't want pancakes. Is he still asleep?"

The scrape of the sponge in the pan. Water running.

"Yes."

"How long is he staying?"

"I don't know."

Something wrong with his mother's voice. It sounded thin, and weak.

He went to stand beside her as she rinsed the pan and turned off the faucet. She didn't want to look at him but eventually she did. Red around her eyes, as if she'd been crying.

"What did he do to you?" Michael asked.

"Nothing," she said.

"What did he say? What does he want?"

She dried her hands on a towel. Her movements were mechanical.

"Never mind, Mike," she said. "It's between me and him."

That day he was alone in the house with his father. They mostly stayed away from each other. Michael went through his closet and the drawers of his dresser, gathering things that he would take with him to college. He filled a box with old schoolbooks and notebooks that he wanted to get rid of.

He carried the box out to the garage in the afternoon. It was cool and gray for August, and a light rain was falling. His father was lounging in the shelter of the back porch, wearing blue jeans with grease stains on them, a cotton shirt unbuttoned to bare his pale chest. He held a glass of vodka with two hands, the bottle within reach on the porch railing.

Michael sat down beside him on a folding chair.

"Let's hear the story," Michael said.

His father looked at him glassy-eyed. "What story?"

"There's always a story. You got dropped off here by a tow truck. What happened to your car?"

"It gave out on me. Two towns over. In

Clarksville."

"Clarksfield."

"Whatever."

"So you need money to pay for repairs," Michael said. "Is that it?"

His father put his feet up on a plastic crate. "Nah. That car shit the bed, kiddo. Mechanic said it wasn't worth fixing. I need a new one."

Raindrops plunked on the tin roof of the porch. Michael listened to them and studied his father's face: the pouches under his eyes, the broken capillaries in his nose and cheeks.

"So you're not leaving here," Michael said, "until you get a new car."

"I don't see how I can."

"And you expect Mom to buy you one."

His father shrugged. "That's something she and I are gonna work out. It's not your business, kiddo."

"She can't afford to buy you a car."

A hint of anger in his father's face. The glassy eyes were suddenly focused and alert. "What did I say? It's not your business."

Michael stared at his father. Seconds passed, with only the sound of the rain to mark them.

His father sipped vodka. Said, "What are you, seventeen?"

"Eighteen."

"Eighteen. You have no idea what the world is like. You're living in a bubble."

"Am I?"

"You don't have to answer to anybody. You have no responsibilities."

Michael couldn't help laughing. "What responsibilities do *you* have?"

"Don't talk to me like that," his father said. "Like a smart-ass." The sharp edge of his voice was a threat. "There's a woman I've been seeing," he said. "Down in Pensacola. She's gonna have a kid. A girl. You'll have a little sister. So, yes, I have responsibilities."

Michael took that in. He felt himself frown. "Wait," he said. "Are you expecting Mom to give you money for some other woman's kid in Florida?"

His father traced a finger around the rim of his glass. "I don't expect anything from your mother, except what I deserve."

"What do you think you deserve?"

"I already told you, kiddo: it's not your business."

"I don't see how you deserve anything."

"That's where you're wrong. Your mother and I, we have a history. It's complicated. Everything's complicated. Nothing's simple. She owes me."

"What?" Michael said. "What does she owe you?"

"I did her a favor," said his father. "When we broke it off. I let you stay. I didn't want to kick the two of you out into the cold."

"What are you talking about?"

His father looked around and waved his hand in the air. "This. All this. Your mother and I bought this house together. I own half."

Michael felt a prickle of heat along his spine. "But she's been paying the mortgage," he said. "It's her house."

"Doesn't matter. Both our names are on the title."

The heat reached the back of his neck. "Do you think you're going to live here?"

"No," his father said. "Of course not."

"Then what? She's supposed to sell it, and give you half the money? Where would she live?"

His father brought his feet down off the crate. Shook his head impatiently. "You sound like her now. Don't be such a goddamn drama queen. She wouldn't have to sell. Just refinance. People do it all the time."

Michael felt his cheeks flush. "I can't believe you."

"She wouldn't even have to refinance," his father said, "if she would just part with some of the money she's got squirreled away."

"What money?"

"Don't be naïve," his father said bitterly. "She's got money. With that cushy job she's been working."

Michael knew his mother's job wasn't cushy. She worked for an insurance agent. His father knew it too. Michael didn't need to say it, but he said it anyway: "She's a secretary."

His father smirked. "She makes good money. Don't try to bullshit me. I'm not the bad guy here."

Michael Underhill remembers this: his father reaching for the vodka bottle. Topping off his glass as if the conversation was over, as if everything had been settled. He remembers trembling as he stood up, and wondering if his father could see it. He remembers wanting to knock his father's chair over. And not having the courage to do it.

He remembers his father looking up at him and saying, "Go on. Get out of here. Don't act like I'm a thief. My name's on the title. I'm only asking for what's mine."

Michael went inside then. Upstairs to his room. He surveyed his possessions: the things he'd been packing to take to college.

Clothes and books and CDs. Souvenirs: arrowheads and old coins, a geode he'd gotten as a birthday present. He hefted the geode in his hand; it was as big as half a cantaloupe. The hollow inside lined with fine blue crystals.

He tossed it onto his bed. Went to his dresser and pulled out the bottom drawer. There was an envelope taped underneath, thick with money he'd saved from summer jobs. He peeled off the tape. Took the envelope with him.

Down the stairs, through the kitchen, out onto the porch again. He dropped the envelope on the plastic crate in front of his father. Took his car key from his pocket and placed it on top.

"What's this?" his father said.

"There's around seven hundred dollars there. It's all I have. You can take my car too. I want you to leave. In the morning. And if you come back here I don't want you asking her for money again."

His father scowled. "Seven hundred's not gonna be enough for me, kiddo."

"It'll have to be," Michael said. "She's not going to sell the house. She's not going to refinance. You're not going to take another dime from her."

"I'm not?"

"No. If you do, you and I are done. You won't see me. I won't talk to you again. Ever."

To Michael, his own voice seemed strong, and firm. But the threat seemed small. It hung in the air between them. His father locked eyes with him, but only for a moment. Then he turned his attention back to his drink.

Michael left him there. Back in his room, he put on music: U2, *Rattle and Hum.* He went on with his packing. When the album ran out, he put on another: Soundgarden, *Louder Than Love.* His mother came home from work and made dinner, but Michael didn't eat. He stayed in his room with the door closed. Being alone was easier. When anything went wrong, his first impulse was always to retreat. He wondered what Debbie Pinckney would say about that.

Hours went by. He listened to Dire Straits, Van Halen, The Cure. When it got dark he lay down on his bed. He convinced himself that if he stayed in this room, everything would go the way he wanted. In the morning his father would leave. He wouldn't have to see the man again.

He drifted off to sleep around midnight. Woke up an hour later, needing to take a pee. He passed his mother's room on the way to the bathroom. The door stood partway open. On the way back, he looked inside. A filmy curtain fluttered on the breeze from an open window. His mother's bed was empty.

Michael descended the stairs. No voices in the house. No television. The kitchen light was on. The dinner dishes had been cleared from the table. Through the screen door he could see the porch. His mother was standing out there with her back to him. She was dressed in her nightgown.

A white cat posed like a statue on the railing of the porch. One of the strays. It jumped down when Michael opened the door. His mother didn't move. He went out and stood beside her. His father was in the same chair where he'd been in the afternoon. He was sleeping, his head tipped back. A second vodka bottle stood on the railing now.

Michael stepped in front of his mother so he could see her face. She noticed him finally.

"Mike," she said. Fragile, as if she'd just woken up.

"What are you doing out here?" he asked her.

"I thought you were asleep."

"I was."

"I don't want you to see."

"Mom —"

"I have to, Mike. I've given him so much. You've no idea how much I've given him."

"I know —"

"So much. And it's never enough. I can't give him any more. I can't."

Her nightgown was gray in the light seeping out from the kitchen. Her arms were down at her sides. Her right hand held a knife with a long blade. Michael recognized it. It was the one she used for chopping vegetables.

He looked at his father. The open shirt. Chest rising and falling with his breath. No marks on him. No blood. She'd done nothing yet.

"He always comes back," she said.

"I know," said Michael.

He reached for the knife and she let him take it. He stepped inside and returned it to a kitchen drawer. When he went back to the porch, his mother hadn't moved.

He touched her shoulder. "Stay here," he said.

She nodded.

The envelope of money and the key to Michael's car were on the crate where he'd left them. He picked them up and stepped down off the porch. Raised the door of the garage. The white cat was in there by the food bowl. He shooed it out.

His car was in the driveway. He started it, pulled into the garage, rolled the windows down, and shut it off again. Got out and left the driver's door open.

Rain on the grass from earlier in the day. Hardly any moon. He crossed the yard to the house. Went back onto the porch. His father was snoring softly.

"We shouldn't," his mother said.

"We didn't do anything," said Michael. "He did it himself. That's what we'll have to say."

His mother's mouth was set in a pained line.

"He'll wake up," she said.

"I don't think he will. He's been drinking all day."

The white cat was crouched on the lawn, watching.

"He came here to see me," Michael said. "Because I'm going away to college. He didn't ask you for money. You didn't argue about anything. He didn't seem upset or depressed. You don't know why he did it. That's what you say."

His mother's hands clutched the fabric of her nightgown. Her eyes were downcast.

"That's what you say," Michael repeated.

"All right."

Michael pushed the crate out of the way and plucked the empty glass from his father's lap. The glass went on the railing.

"You'll have to help me with him," he said to his mother.

They hauled him up from the chair, got his feet under him. He was half-awake going down the steps. His feet dragged, crossing the lawn. Michael took over in the garage, wrapping his arms around his father, lowering him to the driver's seat, moving him through a quarter turn to position him properly behind the wheel.

His father's left shoe fell off in the process. Michael slipped it back on. And shut the driver's door.

His mother was waiting in the driveway. He took her by the arm and led her back to the house. Told her to go in.

"Are you sure?" she said.

"I'm sure."

She went in. He picked up the glass from the porch railing and filled it halfway. He carried it to the garage, the white cat watching.

Michael entered the car from the passenger side. Put the glass in the cupholder between the seats. Switched on the dome light.

His father stirred. Groggy. He smiled. "There's my giant."

"That's right," Michael said.

"My kiddo," his father said. "My bud. You weren't gonna talk to me anymore. But I knew you didn't mean it."

"No. I didn't mean it."

His father reached for the vodka glass, took a drink, slotted it back into the cupholder. It only took him two tries.

He leaned his head against the headrest and closed his eyes. Michael waited, listening to his breathing. Two minutes passed, then five. Michael turned the key in the ignition to start the car. His father didn't move.

It was easy, slipping out, closing the passenger door. The white cat was sitting on its haunches outside the garage. Michael walked toward it, thinking it would run. It let him get close, then it turned and strolled away with its tail held up.

Michael stood in the driveway and looked around. He saw the light on in the kitchen, and another in his mother's room upstairs. He smelled wet grass and exhaust. He heard the low hum of the engine.

No movement in the car. A peaceful night. He lowered the garage door, all the way down.

■ ■ ■ ■

Michael Underhill remembers the rest of that night. His mother standing in the hallway when he went upstairs.

He couldn't think of anything to say to her.

She touched his brow. Said, "You're a good boy, Mike."

He remembers lying awake, waiting for the morning. Thinking it wouldn't come.

Then the sunlight. Soft at first. Growing. Streaming through his window.

Just like now. He's not that boy anymore. He's a man. It's Saturday and Anna Haley is naked in his bed. Sunlight pours through his bedroom window onto the white sheets.

"You give me hope," he says.

Anna is lying on her stomach, her head turned toward him, strands of flaxen hair falling across her cheek.

"Why do I give you hope?" she asks him.

He rests a hand on the small of her back. "It's chiefly because you're a good person, I think."

"Am I?"

"Well, let's see," he says. "What did you do at the hospital yesterday?"

She purses her lips, trying to remember.

"There was a man who came in for surgery," she says. "He needed a valve repaired in his heart. But his surgeon was running behind. This poor guy, he must have been in his seventies. He had to wait for five hours. There was no one to wait with him. His kids all live far away. A neighbor had brought him in, and the neighbor had gone home."

"So you stayed with him," Underhill says.

"Not the whole time," says Anna. "But part of it. We sang Paul Simon songs together."

Underhill takes hold of the flesh of her hip and rocks her back and forth.

"That makes you a good person," he says.

Outside, a cloud passes over the sun. The shadows in the folds of the sheets fade and then darken again.

"That's why you give me hope," Underhill says. "Because if you're a good person, and you love me, that means *I* must be a good person. Doesn't it?"

Anna turns onto her side. "Maybe I like bad boys," she says.

"Do you?"

"I used to date a guy who rode a motorcycle."

"Is that all it takes to be a bad boy?"

"He used to drink too, and when he

drank, he'd yell."

"He yelled at you?"

"Sometimes."

"Give me his name. He'll never yell at anyone again."

Anna laughs. "Let's not worry about him. He's long gone. I'm with you now, and you're good. Of course, sometimes you're mysterious."

"How?"

She rolls onto her back, adjusts the pillow beneath her head. "In little ways," she says. She points to a spot on the wall across the room, the spot where Ed Cavanaugh's gun made a dent. "You never told me how that got there."

"Maybe I have a temper," Underhill says. "Maybe I got angry and punched the wall."

"I've never seen your temper."

"Maybe I hide it."

"I don't believe you."

Underhill leans close to her and kisses her chin. "Maybe I was vacuuming in here. Maybe the vacuum cleaner tipped over and the handle hit the wall."

"I don't believe that either."

"How come?"

"I've never seen you vacuum."

She gives him a deadpan look that turns into a grin. Something about the moment makes him pounce on her and tickle her ribs. There's some tussling and some kissing. The kissing turns more intense. Underhill slips inside her and she pushes her hips up to meet him. Her eyes close. He keeps his open. He likes to watch her face, the little movements of her mouth. He finds a rhythm and stays with it and after a time her nails dig into his back and she cries out and he feels himself let go.

Eventually they break apart. Underhill scoots around and lies on his back with his head on her stomach. He braces the bottoms of his feet against the wall beside the bed. He listens to her breathing and tries to get lost in it. Sometimes he can, but not today. His mind wanders in directions he doesn't like. He tries not to follow, but it's no use.

Anna nudges his shoulder. "What are you thinking, Mike?"

He doesn't answer. Not right away. He can't tell her the truth. He's been thinking about the warning he left for Jack Pellum. He has a feeling it won't be enough. Pellum won't stop. Underhill is afraid of what he'll have to do. He doesn't know what Pellum might have told Keely Tanager. If he kills Pellum, he'll have to kill her too. If he kills her, he'll have to kill Henry Tanager. That's three. Three more. Can he do three more, and still be a good person? He wants to believe that the ones he's done already haven't changed him. Is that wishful thinking? What if they all leave something behind? What if there's a mark, a stain? What if it comes with him, into the new house where he's going to live with Anna?

She nudges him again. "Mike?"

He pulls his feet from the wall and twists around so he's looking into her eyes.

"We should get out of here," he says.

"I was thinking the same thing," she tells him. "I'm hungry."

"No," he says. "Listen. We should move. We should get out of this town. Out of this state."

She smiles. "Where will we go?"

"Anywhere," he says. "We can go to New Orleans. I've never been to New Orleans."

"What will we do there?"

"We can do what we do here. They have hospitals in New Orleans. They have houses that need fixing up."

"What if I want to do something different?" she says.

"You can do anything."

"Can I be a torch singer, in a nightclub?"

"Yes."

"Can we live in the French Quarter?"

"Yes."

"And will I be very famous?"

"You will."

Her smile grows wider. "All right then, I'll go with you. But only if you can guarantee that I'll be famous."

Underhill gets a sick feeling in his stomach. She thinks it's a game. She thinks he's joking.

He takes her hand. "Anna, I'm serious. I want to go. I want you to come with me."

Her smile fades and something changes in her eyes. He can feel her retreating from him.

"I don't know anyone who lives in New Orleans," she says.

"It doesn't have to be New Orleans," he says. "We can pick another place."

"But I'm happy here. Everyone I know lives here. My family —"

"You'll be with me. We'll make each other happy."

"What about our house?" she says. "We're building our house here."

"We can build one somewhere else."

She smiles again, but now it's uncertain. "Mike, I like the life we have."

He lifts her hand and presses it against his cheek. "I'm asking you this one thing. Do you love me?"

"You know I do."

"And you'd still love me if we had to move somewhere far away. You said that once."

"I remember," Anna says. "And it's true. I would. But we don't have to move. Do we?"

Underhill blinks. He takes in a sharp breath through his nose.

"No," he says. "Of course not."

His voice sounds flat to him. Unnatural. She notices it too.

"Is something wrong?" she says. "You can tell me."

He gets himself under control. "Nothing's wrong."

"Are you mad at me?"

"No."

"For a second, you looked mad."

He smiles and kisses the palm of her hand.

"I'm not mad," he says. "I could never be mad at you."

37.

It's a beautiful place, the spot where Jack's wife died.

Hudson Mills Metropark, an hour's drive west of Detroit, covers fifteen hundred acres. It has a golf course, softball fields, tennis courts. There are picnic tables and pavilions and miles of trails, both paved and unpaved. Some of the trails run through the woods and some along the shore of the Huron River.

At a bend in the river, there's a tall tree on the shore. Jack doesn't know what kind, but the leaves are broad and some of the roots run right along the surface of the ground all the way to the water. Grass grows around the base. You can sit there with your back against the trunk and hear the current. You can be alone, even though there's a bike trail less than twenty yards away.

Jack went there on Saturday in the late afternoon. Kim had vowed to stay with a friend. Her husband was away for the weekend, visiting his parents in Traverse City. If the man in the hat went to their house, he would find it empty.

Jack and Keely had spent several hours on Friday talking to people in Danny Cavanaugh's neighborhood in Corktown. They'd learned nothing of use, except that Ed Cavanaugh's truck had been parked on the street for more than a week.

Now Jack sat with his back to the tree, knees up, feet in the grass. Out on the river, a trio of college kids paddled by in kayaks, oars cutting smoothly through the water. When they had passed, Jack said, "I got an e-mail from him today, the man in the hat."

His voice didn't travel far, but it didn't need to. He was talking to Olivia, even though he knew she wasn't here, and couldn't really hear him.

"He came to the apartment," Jack said. "That was yesterday. He took one of my flyers. I didn't think to check my e-mail until this morning. He kept his message short, one line: *She's a beautiful bird, Kim Weaver.* He's telling me to back off.

"I'm not backing off. I'm going to find him. His e-mail address won't help. He used a Gmail account, with a string of random letters as the username. I could try to trace it, but he's not stupid. That's not how I'm going to get him. I have other ways. Like today, I spent hours looking for a thief.

"See, I've been thinking about Everett Stillman. The pawnbroker. I've been assuming that he sold Alex Cavanaugh's ring to Bitsy Patterson. Stillman must have bought the ring from someone, but his brother couldn't tell me who.

"So now I have to use my head. The man in the hat tortured Everett Stillman — tied him to a chair and cut him with a knife before he killed him. He was looking for information, just like I am. He wanted to know who sold Stillman the ring. Let's assume that Stillman told him. The man in the hat got an answer. He got a name, and he tracked that person down, and in all likelihood killed him. This was the person who stole the ring from *him* in the first place. So all I need to do is look for a dead thief.

"I know what you're thinking. What good will it do me to find a dead thief? He won't be able to tell me anything. Okay. But simply knowing who he was might help. Or it might not. I haven't been able to find him anyway. I've been looking at murders in and around Detroit, in the weeks after Stillman's death, looking for a victim with the right kind of criminal past, and I've come up empty.

"But am I defeated? Not yet. Your Jack's a detective, darling. I realized I was missing something about Everett Stillman. I put myself in his place. I'm in my basement and someone's cutting me, wanting to know who sold me a ring. Why do I resist? Why does he need to cut me at all? Why don't I give him the name right away — if it's just some thief who doesn't mean anything to me?

"So there it is. I hold out because I'm protecting someone. So maybe the man in the hat never got his answer. Maybe the thief who stole the ring is still alive, and it's someone Everett Stillman cared about. That's good. A live thief is better than a dead one.

"But I still have to find him. I went back to the pawnshop today and talked to Stillman's brother again. A delicate conversation. I was basically asking him if some friend of his brother, or maybe a member of the family, might be a thief. I didn't put it that way, of course. I said the person Everett was protecting might have gotten the ring from someone who stole it, and might not even have known it was stolen. Which could be true. But our talk didn't go well. Stillman's brother was insulted. There are no thieves in his family, and they don't hang around with thieves, and Everett didn't make friends with thieves. And I could fuck off.

"I know. I should have been smarter about it. More diplomatic. But I have to be on the right track, don't I? The man in the hat tortured Stillman, because Stillman wouldn't answer his question. He wouldn't answer because he was protecting someone. Right? What's the alternative?

"The alternative is, Stillman bought the ring but didn't remember who he bought it from. Because a lot of rings went through his shop. But that doesn't help me. I can't do anything with that.

"You're laughing now. This is funny. You always thought it was funny: Detective Pellum spinning out theories, listing all the alternatives. Okay. It *is* funny.

"I'll keep going. I can do this all day. Maybe Everett Stillman didn't answer the question because he didn't know what the hell the man in the hat was talking about. He didn't know about any damn ring. A gold-plated ring with knights on it? He never sold anything like that. Not to Bitsy Patterson or anyone else.

"Bitsy was wrong about where she bought

the ring. She made a mistake. Or she lied.

"Why would Bitsy lie? The man in the hat didn't torture her. He pushed her down the stairs, but that happened at the end of their conversation. Early on, he might have been friendly, or tried to be. But maybe he scared her. Either on purpose or unintentionally. A stranger shows up at your door, asking odd questions. Suppose he didn't feel right to her. So she lied to him about where she got the ring.

"What did she hope to gain by lying? Darling, I've already answered that one. She wanted to protect someone she cared about."

38.

Jack found Seth Patterson at the Bean & Leaf Café in Royal Oak, early on Sunday afternoon. Seth was outside on a break, smoking a cigarette in the alley between the café and a restaurant called Hibernia.

There was a moment when he saw Jack and looked like he might drop the cigarette and run. The moment passed. He took another drag instead, and waited for Jack to close the distance between them.

He blew smoke from one side of his mouth. "I don't think I told you where I work."

"You said a coffee shop," Jack said with a shrug. "That was enough."

Seth examined the ash of his cigarette. "I know why you're here."

"I imagine you do."

"You're here about that ring."

"Yes."

"It's been on my mind. You never said why

453

it was important."

"We can talk about it now. Why don't you go first."

A pause. The ash grew longer.

"I should have told you," Seth said. "I gave that ring to Bitsy."

"Yeah?"

"I bought it at the Salvation Army store. I thought she would like it."

"At the Salvation Army. Here in town?"

"That's right."

Jack shook his head. "No."

Seth flicked the cigarette with his thumb, and the ash broke and fell away.

"You don't believe me," he said.

"I don't," said Jack. "If you bought it, you would have told me before. There's no shame in buying a ring. No reason to hide it."

"Maybe it slipped my mind."

"No. It didn't."

Seth leaned against the brick wall of the café. "You're right," he said. "But that's what I told Bitsy — that I bought it. She didn't know the truth."

Jack watched him draw on the cigarette, then prompted him.

"What's the truth?"

Seth let out a stream of smoke. "I probably shouldn't say."

"Why not?"

"It would be . . . confessing to a crime."

"I'm not going to arrest you."

"You still haven't told me why the ring is important."

Across the way, the back door of the restaurant opened and a pair of waitresses came out. Jack gave them a look and they moved off down the alley.

He turned back to Seth and said, "The ring belonged to a boy who was murdered."

Disbelief in Seth's eyes at first, and then he took it in.

"I didn't know," he said softly.

"There's more," Jack said. "Someone came to Bitsy and asked her where she got the ring, but she didn't tell him. She didn't want him going after you. If he had gone after you, you'd be dead, like her. If you care about what happened to her, you'll help me."

Seth's disbelief turned into confusion, and fear.

"What are you trying to say? Bitsy fell down the stairs. It was an accident."

"No," Jack said.

Seth's face froze, and when he spoke, his voice was barely more than a whisper.

"She fell. The police said so."

"Stay with me, Seth. She was murdered.

You need to realize that."

"You're serious?"

"I'm serious. The only thing to do now is tell me the truth."

A moment passed and Seth didn't move. His mouth was open; his eyes looked blank. Jack thought he'd lost him. But wherever he had gone, he came back. He cleared his throat and looked around, as if he were searching for something.

"It's hard to know where to start," he said.

"Start at the beginning," said Jack.

"Right. . . . There used to be a girl who worked here. She was sweet and quiet, always reading a book. . . . I liked her, but I figured I had no chance. I mean, graphic novels are about my speed, and she was reading *The Brothers Karamazov*. Honestly. But I wanted to try. You have to try things, or you never get anywhere."

Seth paused. Dropped his cigarette on the ground. "So I bought a book by Dostoyevsky. *The Brothers Karamazov* was too long, but I found an abridged version of *Crime and Punishment.* I thought I could handle that. I brought it in and let her see me reading it on breaks, and I thought it would start a conversation, you know? I thought she might even come to me. She'd say, *You like Dostoyevsky too?* and we'd be off. But it

never happened. She got a better job somewhere else, and I haven't seen her since."

He frowned. Maybe at the memory.
Maybe because he realized he was rambling.
Jack waited patiently.

"The book was interesting, though," Seth
said. "It's about a poor kid who works out a
plan to kill an old lady and steal her money.
Even though it seems immoral, he convinces
himself that it's right, because she's crooked
and miserable, and he intends to use the
money to do good things, so it'll balance
out in the end. . . . I never bought that,
because he's still a killer. But it made me
think. About stealing and how you could
justify it."

He looked down, saw the cigarette still
burning, crushed it with his shoe.

"There was a guy who came around here,"
he said. "You could tell he had money. He
drove a BMW. Parked it right in this alley.
If you stole from a guy like that, what harm
would it do? I'm not talking about hurting
him. You wouldn't kill him. But you could
take from him, and whatever you took, he
wouldn't even miss it."

Seth crossed his arms over his chest. "So I
kept seeing him, and I kept thinking about
it," he said. "One time he was driving away
as I got off work, and I got in my car and

followed him home. I watched his house, and it looked like he lived alone. I started planning. I kept track of when his car was here, in the alley. If he was here, I could go there and break in, and it would be safe. He wouldn't get hurt, and I wouldn't get caught."

Another pause. Seth's tongue ran over the front of his teeth. "One night I just did it. I drove to his house and broke in through a window. No one was there; I made sure. But I was shaking anyway, because I knew what I was doing was wrong. I didn't leave, though. I'd already done the hard part. I decided to gather what I could and get out.

"To tell you the truth, it was frustrating. It was too big a job for one person. He had a huge flat-screen TV in his living room, but I would have needed a crew and a moving truck to haul it out of there. I found a smaller flat-screen in his bedroom, and I took that. I took his stereo equipment and his laptop. I took some watches and a little cash he had on his dresser. Not much, really. A few hundred dollars. I thought there should be more. I kept looking and found a cigar box on a shelf in his closet. I opened it up and saw a big roll of bills: hundreds and fifties. That was it. I took the box and got out of there.

"I opened his garage door and drove my car in and closed it again so I could load everything up without being seen. When I left I didn't have any way to close the door behind me, but I didn't care. I had gotten away with it."

Hollow voice on the last line. Seth took out his cigarettes and tapped one from the pack. Set it between his lips. Brought out his lighter.

Jack said, "What about the ring, Seth?"

He got the cigarette going. Waved at the smoke.

"Right," he said dully. "I drove back to my apartment and opened the cigar box to count the money and there was a key chain in there too. It had one key on it — and the ring."

"Did you keep the key chain?"

Seth shook his head. "I threw it away. But the ring made me think of Bitsy. I thought she could make up a good story about it and someone would buy it. . . . I didn't know."

His voice was fading, his eyes turning blank again. Jack touched his shoulder to keep him from drifting away.

"The house you broke into, where was it?"

A shrug. "The address? I don't remember. It was about forty minutes from here, in

Belleville."

"And the man, what was his name?"

"I don't know."

"Come on, Seth."

"I don't. But it shouldn't be hard to find out."

"How?"

Seth raised the hand that held his cigarette and pointed across the alley.

"He owns that restaurant. I heard he owns one in Belleville too."

39.

On Sunday afternoon, Main Street in Belleville was more or less deserted.

There were a few cars in front of the Bayou Grill and Tanager's Pub. Jack parked there himself, behind a black BMW. He had no doubt about the identity of the BMW's owner. He had asked Seth Patterson for a description, to make sure.

"He's probably sixty," Seth had said, "with slick silver hair and better suits than I'll ever own."

So, Henry Tanager.

Jack could go into the restaurant and talk to him now. He certainly had questions. He thought he had a good grip on the pieces, but not on how they fit together.

He decided it was too soon to talk to Tanager, and the restaurant was the wrong place.

He took out his cell phone and made a call. Then he looked up two addresses. One of them was Tanager's. He drove to the other one.

Eugenia Abernathy lived in a small but well-appointed house on High Street, a stone's throw from the lake and not far from the public library. She sat Jack on a divan in her front room and insisted on making him tea. She brought it on a silver tray with milk and sugar and honey.

She told him the funeral for Jerry Diaz had been scheduled for Tuesday and wondered if he would come. "You should," she said. "The poor child, I don't know how much family he has."

She gave Jack the name of the church, and he told her he'd come if he could. He admired a vase she had on her mantel. It was blown glass stretched out into a tall, irregular, twisted shape and infused with color. He listened to her talk about the artist, a woman from Seattle she had known in her school days. When she stopped for a sip of tea, he got to the point of his visit.

"I understand you've been having trouble with your car," he said. "Someone's been driving it without your permission."

Mrs. Abernathy smiled. An enigmatic smile rather than a happy one.

"You're well informed, Mr. Pellum. But

that's been resolved."

"Has it? I'm glad."

"I have a woman who comes in and cleans for me. She's lovely, really, very conscientious. She has a seventeen-year-old son; I've known him since he was a little boy. Well, now he's got a girlfriend up in Plymouth. He was, how shall I say it, *borrowing* my car to go and see her. His mother didn't know. She was mortified when she found out, and told me right away. Wanted to pay me for the gas he'd used. I wouldn't let her, of course."

"That's generous," Jack said. "I don't know if other people would have handled it the same way. But you've had that sort of trouble before — your car going missing."

Mrs. Abernathy tilted her head, as if she were intrigued.

"I have, yes. Over the years."

"I wonder if it might have happened twenty years ago, in the spring," Jack said. "I'm thinking of a particular night. You might remember it. It was a sad occasion. A teenage boy died. He ran his bike off the road into a ditch. Ryan Tanager."

She nodded. "I remember. I left my car in the driveway that night. I was involved with a charity back then, collecting books and clothes and household things to give away.

The garage was full. I happened to look out before I went to bed, and the car was gone."

"Did you call the police?"

She looked sheepish. "It was late, and I was embarrassed, because it had happened before. It was my fault for leaving a key in the glove box. I thought I would wait until the morning to make the call. In the end, I didn't have to."

"You didn't?" Jack said. "Why not?"

"Because in the morning I looked out again, and the car was back in the driveway. I half believed I'd dreamt the whole thing."

"So you don't know who brought it back."

"No."

"Was there any damage?"

"Not a scratch."

Jack sat in silence for a moment, then returned his tea cup to the silver tray.

"I should go," he said, rising. "I appreciate your talking to me."

Eugenia Abernathy looked disappointed. "You mustn't go yet, Mr. Pellum. You should finish your tea first."

He hesitated. "I'm sorry. I didn't mean to be rude."

"I'm not criticizing your manners," she said. "But if you finish your tea, my sense of déjà vu will be complete."

Jack's eyes narrowed. He sat down again

slowly. "Pardon?"

"Déjà vu," Mrs. Abernathy said. "This is the second time today I've had this conversation. The first was with our chief of police, and she finished her tea before she left." She paused, touching the string of pearls she wore at her throat. "The two of you seem to be on the same wavelength. She wouldn't tell me what it was all about. I fear it's not good. Perhaps you'll come back when it's over and satisfy my curiosity."

"I will," Jack said. "If I can."

"Well, that's fair. Good luck to you, Mr. Pellum."

When Jack went out to his car he found it hot from sitting in the sun. He cracked the windows and ran the air conditioner and drove east and south. He passed Tanager's Pub and saw that the black BMW was gone. He made a U-turn and headed for the north shore of the lake.

Henry Tanager's house was tucked behind three big willow trees that brooded over a wide green lawn. The number of the house was carved into a hunk of granite at the end of the driveway, but even without the number Jack would have found it. Keely Tanager's cruiser was parked in the shade across the road.

He drew in behind her, cut his engine, and got out. Keely had her windows down and he could see her watching him in the side mirror. He went around to the cruiser's passenger side and climbed in.

"I just came from Mrs. Abernathy's house," he said.

Keely turned and met his eyes, nodding once to acknowledge him. Hard to read her mood. She slouched a little in her seat, her hands resting on the steering wheel, fingers spread. Maybe relaxed, maybe resigned. She'd left the clips out of her hair today. It flowed down past her shoulders. She didn't look like a chief of police; she looked like someone's daughter.

She lifted a hand from the wheel to gesture at the willows. "I used to play under those trees," she said. "When I was a kid, maybe four or five, my brother would play hide-and-seek with me. When I hid under the trees, the leaves hung down so far I couldn't see him. I thought it meant he couldn't see me either. He played along. He'd call out to me, 'Keely, where are you?' " She went quiet, then added something more. "When I got older I would pick mint leaves for my mother. Mint grew wild on the lawn. She would chop them and sprinkle them on the pork roast on Sunday. . . . I miss her."

"When did she pass away?"

A rueful smile. "She's not dead, Jack. She lives in Florida. It gutted her when Ryan died, but she stuck it out until I went away to college. Then she went south. She's remarried now to a retired engineer. They play golf. I talk to her every couple months."

Keely leaned across and opened the glove compartment. Took out a plastic evidence bag and dropped it in Jack's lap.

"I got around to searching Ed Cavanaugh's truck yesterday," she said. "They had it waiting for me at the impound lot, like you said they would. I didn't find anything worth noting — except for two leaves in the footwell on the driver's side. I'm guessing Ed tracked them in. One willow and one mint."

Jack drew the obvious conclusion. "Ed came here before he disappeared."

Keely nodded. "It set me thinking about why Ed would come to see my father. We know Ed's sons were on his mind. My father had a dead son too. I thought about the other night, the way the wheels started turning in your head when I told you about Ryan. You wondered if someone had run him off the road. Your crazy killer with the hat. But it wasn't him."

"No," Jack said.

"It was Alex Cavanaugh. I've always thought of him as a victim. As innocent. But that kind of thinking can trap you."

"I made the same mistake," Jack said. "Twice. I made it with Dylan Vernen, and again with Alex. Alex wasn't innocent. I've talked to his friends. He used to sneak out at night and break into places: the high school, the library. He'd try the doors on parked cars, and if they were open he'd steal something."

"And one night he tried Eugenia Abernathy's car, and found the keys in the glove box," said Keely. "That's a big temptation. Too much for a reckless teenager to resist. He took the car for a joyride out on Savage Road. Where Ryan was riding his bike."

She stared at her hands on the steering wheel. "So I've been sitting out here and thinking that my father had a reason to want Alex Cavanaugh dead. Revenge. But I don't want to believe it. Maybe it's not true. There are gaps in the narrative. How would my father have known that Alex was responsible? Did Alex confess to him?"

"He wouldn't have to," Jack said. "Have you ever taken a car for a joyride?"

"No."

"It's no fun if you're alone. I think Alex had company that night."

"Who?"

"A kid named Bobby Wilson. They were close. I've talked to Bobby's sister. He was never the same after Alex died. He left home as soon as he graduated high school and rarely came back, even to visit. An interesting thing about Bobby: as a teenager he had a part-time job washing dishes. I called his sister today and asked her where. He worked at the Bayou Grill. That puts him two doors down from your father's pub. If he was in the car with Alex, maybe he's the one who confessed."

Keely looked thoughtful. "Maybe."

"Bobby Wilson lives in an RV now," Jack said. "Moves from place to place. When I first heard, I assumed he didn't want to be tied down. His sister calls him the black sheep of the family. But now I think he keeps moving because he's afraid."

Keely let out a bitter laugh. "You think he's afraid of my father?"

"Not your father," Jack said. "Do you think your father killed Alex Cavanaugh himself? Do you think he killed my wife?"

No laugh this time. Keely closed her eyes and shook her head. "Let's try to stay grounded in reality," she said. "I'm not convinced yet that my father is guilty of anything. What I've got right now is a couple of leaves and some guesswork. It's not enough. Even if it were, I don't see any reason to bring your wife into this."

Jack looked away from her and back again. "She's in it," he said. "There's something I haven't told you. Something I've been working on. Alex kept a ring on his key chain, and the same ring showed up in a photograph my wife took." He laid it out for her: the ad for Motor City Keys and the steps he'd taken to trace the ring, ending with Seth Patterson in Royal Oak. "There's no room for doubt," he said. "Seth admitted that he stole the ring — from your father's house."

It was a lot to absorb. Keely was silent for a long while, staring off down the road. Her fingers drummed the steering wheel and then went still.

Finally she turned to Jack and said, "What do you expect me to do now?"

He nodded toward the house behind the willows. "Is your father home?"

"Yes."

"Then we'll go see what he has to say."

"Why would I let you talk to him?"

"Because you know I'm not going to let this lie. And right now you're trying to figure out how you're going to keep him out of prison. One way would be to kill me.

Are you going to kill me?"

Keely's fingers drummed the wheel some more. "No. I suppose not."

"Then maybe we can figure out another way."

40.

They found Henry Tanager standing on the deck behind his house. White shirt with the sleeves rolled up, dark slacks, sandals on his feet. When he caught sight of them, he was raising a glass of Scotch to his lips. The glass froze in midair, reversed course, and wound up on the railing of the deck.

Tanager's shoulders fell. The life went out of his face. When Jack and Keely were close enough to hear, he said, "Turn around and go back. That's the safest thing to do."

They talked in the house. Tanager slumped in the middle of a big leather sofa with Keely beside him. Jack thought it best to stay out of the way; he settled into an armchair in a corner.

"He seemed harmless," Henry Tanager said. "That's the thing you have to understand. His name was Michael Underhill and he looked like he should have been in college. I think he was twenty-five when I first met him. He would come into the restaurant and buy a drink at the bar and nurse it. He would speak if you spoke to him first, but mostly he listened. He never bothered anyone.

"Some nights he'd stay till closing. I got used to him. He happened to be there once when I was short-staffed, and he helped clean up. I offered him a job and he took it. He'd been working at a carwash. He made a good employee. He'd do whatever you asked him: bus tables, help out in the kitchen. He could tend bar in a pinch. The other staff liked him well enough.

"And that was it," Tanager said to Keely. "I forgot about him. He was just around. Until your brother died.

"That spring — you remember how it was. Your mother was like a sleepwalker. I did the best I could, but I was hollowed out inside. People at the restaurant didn't know how to behave around me. Nobody knows, really, at a time like that. One minute they're telling you how sorry they are and asking what they can do. The next, they're looking away when you walk by, or cutting off their conversations suddenly, and you wonder if they were talking about you.

"Mike Underhill handled himself well.

The first time he saw me after Ryan died, he acknowledged it. Shook my hand and said it was a shame. Then he went back to treating me the way he always had. I appreciated that. For a while there, I didn't want to deal with things, I dreaded going home at night to face your mother. I'd stay at the restaurant after closing. Sometimes Mike would keep me company. I got to know a little about him. He came from Ohio. His father had run out when he was a child. His mother had raised him. We'd talk about sports or movies or television. Nothing important. That was fine by me.

"One night in the summer everything changed. Mike had been hanging out with a kid who worked nearby, at the Bayou Grill. They would run into each other during breaks, out in the parking lot behind one restaurant or the other. This kid, Bobby Wilson, he was carrying a burden. He had a secret, and I guess it got to be too much for him to keep. So he confided in Mike.

"I could see how it would happen. A guy like Mike, who's quiet, you can project anything you want onto him. He comes across as a good listener. As sympathetic. Maybe he was. Bobby Wilson talked to him. Told him a story about the night Ryan died. And Mike told me."

The story was the one Jack and Keely had already worked out. Bobby and Alex Cavanaugh had stolen a car and taken it for a ride on Savage Road.

"Alex was driving," Henry Tanager said. "Doing sixty out there where the limit is forty-five. Bobby was the one who spotted Ryan. He didn't know it was Ryan; he just saw a kid on a bike. He told Alex to slow down, but Alex laughed and honked the horn and sped by.

"Ryan must have panicked. Lost control of the bike. Bobby Wilson thought he saw Ryan go into the ditch but he couldn't be sure. He made Alex turn around and go back, and when they did, all they saw was empty road."

"You heard all this secondhand, from Underhill?" Keely asked.

"That was only the start," Tanager said. "The next night, he brought Bobby into the restaurant and I heard the whole thing again. Bobby filled in some details. He wanted to stop and look for Ryan. Maybe they could climb down and help him. But Alex wouldn't stop. He drove Bobby home and dropped him off. That night Bobby lay in bed, thinking they were going to get caught. He was worried about one thing in particular. The night had begun with Bobby and Alex riding their bikes into town. They had chained them up behind the library while they went prowling. Bobby was feeling paranoid: he was afraid someone would see the bikes and start asking questions.

"The next morning — it was a Saturday — Alex showed up at his house. He had remembered the bikes too. They walked into town together and found them right where they had left them. Bobby asked him about the car, and Alex told him it was okay. His father had helped him return it. He had left Bobby out of it. He told his father he was alone. As long as they both kept quiet, they'd be fine."

"When you heard all this," Keely said, "you didn't go to the police?"

Tanager sighed. "It wasn't so simple. Ed Cavanaugh *was* the police. I knew it wouldn't be easy, accusing his son. I talked to my lawyer, and he said the first thing to do would be to get a signed statement from Bobby. But when I went back to Bobby he refused. He said he'd made a mistake; it didn't happen; he made it up. I don't know if he talked to Alex in the interim, or if he decided on his own that it would be smarter to keep quiet.

"So then I had no witness and no evidence. The stolen car had been returned, with no damage. I had nothing. I thought of marching into the police station anyway, making a lot of noise, throwing around accusations. But what would be the point? I fantasized about catching Alex Cavanaugh some night on his bike, driving after him, not to kill him, just to scare him. One day I was at an intersection and I saw Ed Cavanaugh in his patrol car. I almost rammed into him. I wanted to."

Tanager looked at Keely. "I had no one I could talk to about any of this," he said. "I couldn't tell your mother. It was tearing me up; I knew what it would do to her. All I had was Mike Underhill.

"I was stuck in a feeling of futility. Alex Cavanaugh had killed my son, and there was nothing I could do. Every bitter thought I had, I shared it with Mike: If there were any justice in the world, Alex wouldn't be walking around free. He should suffer. If he got away with this, he'd think he could get away with anything. He'd go through his life that way, recklessly, never taking responsibility. The consequences would fall on other people, not on him. He was a menace. He needed to learn. Someone needed to teach him a lesson.

"I wanted him to be afraid. I thought about how Ryan must have been afraid, that night when the car sped past him. I wanted Alex to feel that kind of fear. I must have said it a dozen different ways on a dozen different nights, and Mike Underhill was listening every time. One night he called me on it.

" 'That's not what you really want,' he said.

" 'What do you mean?' I asked him.

" 'You know what you really want. You can say it. It's just the two of us here.'

"He was calm and mild and matter-of-fact. I knew exactly what he meant.

" 'I can't think about that,' I said.

"He stared at me for a few seconds and said, 'You can *think* about it.'

" 'But I could never do it.'

"He nodded. 'It would be dangerous for you. You wouldn't want to take the risk. You have too much to lose.'

" 'That's right,' I said.

" 'But you could get someone else to do it. That's what I'd do, if I were you.' "

Tanager paused. He seemed to sink deeper into the leather sofa. "I should have laughed it off," he said. "But it was all make-believe anyway.

"I asked Mike, 'Do you know someone?'

" 'I could probably find someone,' he said. 'If you want.'

"We finished our drinks then and went home, and it would have stayed like that. Idle talk late at night. But a couple days later I saw Alex. I stepped out of the restaurant for a breath of air, right around dusk. He rode by on his bike, gliding fast down the middle of Main Street, and he saw me, he turned to look at me, and there was no recognition, no remorse. I might as well have been a bum on the sidewalk. I was nothing to him.

"That night I told Mike I wanted to go ahead and do it."

"And he found a killer for you to hire?" Keely asked. "How did it work?"

Tanager rubbed his face. "You have to remember what I said about Mike. You could project anything onto him that you wanted. He was this poor kid from Ohio. You could believe that maybe he knew someone who would kill for money. I never questioned it too closely. I didn't want too many details. We never talked about how it would happen, or exactly when. We settled on a price: ten thousand up front, and another twenty after it was done.

"I gave the ten to Mike and didn't see him the next day, or the day after. I thought he had run off with the money, which would have been a relief, because the more I thought about it, the more unreal it seemed. It was crazy. I tried to call him and put a stop to it, but he didn't answer his phone at home, and this was before everyone carried cell phones.

"Then he showed up here at the house one morning. He'd never been here. You and your mother were sleeping. I didn't let him in. I took him out to the deck and told him I'd changed my mind. I didn't want the money back; I didn't want to hear anything else about it. I wanted it to be over. But he said it was too late. It was done.

"I didn't believe him. He said to wait, I'd be hearing about it. In the meantime he had something for me. A souvenir. He tossed it to me, out there on the deck. It was Alex Cavanaugh's key chain, with that damned ring."

"Did you pay him the rest of the money?" Keely asked. "The twenty thousand?"

Tanager nodded. "It took some time to get the cash together, but I gave it to him. I wanted him to go away. I was afraid of him. I knew by then that there wasn't any hired killer; that was a story. There was only Mike. He was the killer. I could see it in him. I knew it the moment he tossed me the key chain."

Jack broke in. "Why did you keep it?"

Tanager turned to him slowly, as if he had forgotten he was there. "It's hard to explain. I was in a daze at first. Time went by, and they found Alex's body, and one afternoon I reached into my pocket and the key chain was there. I'd been carrying it around. I wanted to throw it in the lake. But I couldn't stop thinking about what I'd done, and I half believed that everyone I saw knew I was guilty. I thought the police might be watching me. They'd see me toss it away, and they'd send divers into the lake, and they'd have me. They'd have proof.

"So I hid the key chain out of sight. I tried to forget. More time went by. No one came looking for me. No one suspected me. The key chain stayed in my closet. For years. I never forgot about it, but sometimes I would go for days without thinking of it. Sometimes weeks. I got used to it being there. It didn't seem urgent anymore. Then I had a break-in, about three years ago."

"I know about that," Jack said.

"It shook me," said Tanager. "But when I thought it through, I wasn't worried. The key chain, the ring — no one would know who they had once belonged to. I might even be better off, because I didn't have them anymore. Then the ring showed up in that advertisement."

"You saw it?" asked Keely.

"*He* saw it. Mike. He brought it to me. He wanted to know what the hell had happened. He blamed me for keeping the ring, and for letting it get stolen. I told him to calm down. There was nothing we could do. There were a limited number of people who might recognize it: Alex's family, maybe a few of his friends. I thought we were safe. I told Mike not to do anything." Tanager turned to Jack. "I didn't know what he would do. I swear to you."

Jack said nothing. Tanager got up from the sofa. He crossed to a liquor cabinet on the other side of the room, picked up a bottle, put it down again. He turned away from it to face Jack and Keely.

"There's one other thing you have to understand," Tanager said. "About Mike, how dangerous he is. After Alex, after I gave him the twenty thousand, he left here. He moved out west. I was glad to be rid of him. I hoped he would stay away forever, but that's not the way it went. He came back about eight years later. His mother had died, and he spent some time in Ohio and then moved up here — he ended up living in Chelsea. He would come to me now and then, asking for money. A few hundred dollars at a time. I gave it to him, just so he would leave me alone.

"I guess it only encouraged him. He got an idea in his head — he was going to start his own business. Buying houses and fixing them up and reselling them. He needed capital. That's what he said. Like he wanted me to invest in him. He knew I'd been doing well. He wanted a hundred thousand dollars.

"I refused him. He said I should think twice. He knew my weakness, he said. If I was smart, I wouldn't test him. I thought it was an empty threat. What could he do? He could tell the police I'd paid him to kill Alex, but that would hurt him as much as it would me."

Tanager sat on the sofa again and touched Keely's arm. "He had something else in mind," he said. "This was nine years ago, right around the time you started working on the police force in Lansing. About three weeks after Mike told me to think twice, he came back to me and showed me two things. One was a photograph of you in your uniform. It looked like he had taken it himself on the street. The other was an obituary clipped from a newspaper, for a woman who'd been murdered in Dearborn. Her name was —"

"Bonnie Rook," Jack said.

Tanager and Keely turned to him in surprise.

"I know her son," Jack said. "He saw him. He saw Underhill a few days before his mother died."

"Who was she?" Keely asked her father. "Did you know her?"

"No," Tanager said.

"So Underhill killed a random woman?"

"It wasn't random," said Tanager. "It was because of her name."

Jack remembered the message he'd received from the man in the hat about Kim Weaver. *She's a beautiful bird. . . .*

"They're both bird names," he said. "Rook and Tanager."

"That's right," said Henry Tanager. "That's how Mike's mind works. He killed that poor woman just to make a point. To warn me. He got what he wanted. I gave him the hundred thousand."

41.

When Jack left Henry Tanager's house, he sat in his car for a minute in the shade and used his phone to look up Michael Underhill's address in Chelsea. He knew he could be there in a little more than half an hour. All he had to do was get on I-94 and head west.

He started the car and drove out and when he reached the interchange for I-94 he headed east.

They had settled on a plan.

Jack and Keely had gone out on the deck by the lake to talk. Henry Tanager trailed after them but stayed on the lawn, pacing in the grass, hands in his pockets, a man awaiting judgment.

"He'll have to wear a wire," Keely said.

Jack was quiet beside her. Both of them leaned on the railing and stared out at the water.

"He can arrange to meet with Underhill," she said. "He can say he's nervous, he's worried about you, that you're getting too close to the truth."

"Okay," Jack said.

"He can say he's thinking about leaving the country, living abroad, and Underhill should consider doing the same, for his own good. He'll wear a wire and get Underhill talking. That could work."

"It could," Jack said.

"If he can get Underhill to admit to the murders, even to one of them, then we'll have something. Otherwise all we have is a story, and no evidence."

Jack glanced over his shoulder at Tanager. "You'll need to coach him," he said.

"I know," said Keely.

"Some of it he'll have to improvise. It's unavoidable. But he should have an idea of what he's going to say. A plan. He'll be afraid. Do you think he'll hold up?"

"I think so. I won't do anything until he's ready. There'll be one chance at this. I'm not going to rush it. And he'll be protected. That goes without saying. I'll bring in the state police, if I can."

"Good."

On the other side of the lake, some kids climbed into a boat and pushed it away from the dock. Jack watched them raise a white sail.

"This is the way to go, right?" Keely said.

"Absolutely."

"It has to be. I'll talk it over with him, get him used to the idea. Then I'll make some calls in the morning and get things rolling."

"Good," Jack said.

Kim Weaver woke from a nap in the late afternoon.

She was staying with a friend from work, a woman named Rita who lived in Allen Park outside Detroit, in a three-bedroom house with a husband and a German shepherd. Kim tried to stay out of their way. She was in a small room on the second floor with a bed made up for guests and a copy of *Watership Down* on the nightstand. She'd started reading it and had fallen asleep.

Now she got up and went to the window. She looked at the rusted white Chevy parked on the street. Paul Rook was out there watching over her. Kim had noticed him earlier in the day, and had gone down to ask him if he wanted to come inside. He thought he should stay where he was.

Jack had sent him, of course. Jack felt responsible for her.

As she watched, a car rolled up the street.

Jack's car. As if she had summoned him. He parked behind the white Chevy and stepped out. She saw him raise his cell phone to his ear.

Behind her, on the bed, her own cell phone rang.

She picked it up. "Are you coming to see me?"

A strange silence. Then he said, "I wish I could. I'm in Belleville."

Kim's first instinct was to call him on it, but her pride won out. She let him have the lie.

"When will you be finished there?" she asked.

"It's hard to say. I probably won't see you tonight."

"That's fine. If that's the way it has to be."

"Are you okay?"

"Don't worry about me," she said. "Rita and her husband have an alarm system. They also have a shotgun and a big dog. I feel safe."

"That's great. I should go. I just wanted to hear your voice."

He sounded sweet and wistful. She wanted to open the window and call down to him.

She didn't. She said, "Take care, Jack," and they said good-bye, and she watched him put his phone away. He walked around to the passenger side of Paul Rook's Chevy and climbed in.

Ed Cavanaugh's revolver was on the passenger seat. Jack picked it up and got in and closed the door.

"You probably shouldn't leave this in the open," he said.

Paul had been listening to NPR. He switched off the radio. "I had it in the glove compartment for a while," he said. "But I wondered how long it would take to get it out."

"I guess it's been quiet," Jack said.

"Yeah."

"I didn't mean for you to stay all day."

Paul looked at his watch. "It hasn't been all day yet."

"You should head home. You've done enough."

"I could manage a little longer."

Jack rested the revolver on his knee. "Do you think he's going to come here?"

"No."

"I don't either. But I'm glad you kept watch. You're a good friend."

An unexpected compliment. Paul's face flushed. He took a sudden interest in a robin on a lawn across the street.

Jack let a moment pass and said, "You

were right about him, Paul. He killed Alex Cavanaugh and your mother and my wife."

Paul turned to him eagerly. "You found him?"

Jack nodded. "I've been trying to figure out the next step. If I told you his name, what would you do?"

Darkness in Paul's eyes. "I'd ask you to give me that gun back."

"That's what I thought. Maybe there's another way. What I found out today is that someone hired him to kill Alex."

"Who?"

"Just wait," Jack said. "This person, he could wear a wire. He could try to get him to confess."

"You think he'll confess?"

"I don't know."

"He won't. You know he won't."

Jack felt the weight of the revolver on his knee. He felt a tension in every muscle in his body. He let the tension go. "You're right," he said.

Paul leaned toward him. "Give me his name, and give me the gun."

"No," Jack said. "We'll do it together. Tonight. We'll wait until he's sure to be asleep. Go home now and get some rest. Meet me at my apartment at two a.m. We'll leave from there."

"Where are we going?"

"I'll tell you tonight," Jack said. "We have to do it my way. I don't want you going there on your own."

From the window, Kim Weaver watched Jack get out of the white Chevy. She watched Paul drive away.

She thought Jack might surprise her — might come to the house and ring the bell. But he only walked back to his car. She turned away from the window as he drove off.

She never saw the revolver. Jack had tucked it in his pocket and covered it with his shirt.

Jack headed toward the interstate on streets of washed-out gray. The traffic lights were against him, as if they wanted to slow him down.

He turned on the radio and found the NPR station Paul had been listening to. The news was about violence in far-off places. The voices droned. Jack turned it off.

"You got a little mushy back there," he said to himself. "*You're a good friend.* For a second, I thought you might hug him."

He saw a pothole up ahead. Skirted around it.

"You'll go at two in the morning," he said. "That's good. The two of you can dress all in black and wear your night-vision goggles. Jesus."

A green light turned yellow. Jack pushed the accelerator and went on through.

"Well, what was I supposed to tell him?"

He came to the on-ramp for I-94 and drove west toward Chelsea.

42.

Sunday. Michael Underhill walked alone through his unfinished house. The house had windows now. It had a skylight in the master bedroom. The electricians had installed the wiring, and an inspector had checked the work of the electricians.

Underhill descended from the second floor to the first. Sometimes he had doubts about his contractor, a thick-armed, beer-bellied man named Kirkpatrick. He seemed honest but disorganized, more lackadaisical than Underhill would have liked. The man had started to hang drywall in some of the rooms, but he had done it haphazardly. In some places, the walls rose to eye level and stopped. There were doors in a few of the doorways now, but none of them had knobs or locks, even the ones that led to the outside.

The workers Kirkpatrick hired were careless. They tracked mud into the house. They dropped things and never bothered to pick them up. Underhill moved through the downstairs rooms, sweeping up with a push broom. He collected the larger bits of trash in a paper grocery bag. He used a piece of cardboard to scrape a wad of chewing tobacco off the floor.

Down in the basement, the workers had framed in the utility room and a half bath. The air smelled of clean wood and sawdust. Underhill gathered some tools they'd left behind: a pair of wire cutters, a small handsaw, a cordless drill. He put them in a corner where they'd be out of the way.

There were pieces of one-by-eight lumber scattered on the floor. Underhill picked one up. It had started out around two feet long and had been broken down the middle. The two halves were held together by splinters of wood. They came apart in his hands.

He noticed another piece of one-by-eight screwed to a pair of studs in the framed-in wall of the utility room. It hovered right around waist level. When Underhill got closer, he could see that someone had cut a notch from the top edge of the board to the bottom. The notch was about half an inch deep. There was writing on the board in pencil: KUNG FU PRACTICE AREA.

Underhill scowled and raised his right foot

and kicked at the board with the heel of his boot, right along the notch. The board split in two. He pried the pieces from the studs.

He made a neat pile of the scraps of one-by-eight and carried them up the stairs, along with his bag of trash. He went out through the garage and tossed everything into the dumpster.

Michigan in late May. The days were long and getting longer. The blue sky had started to fade to gray, but there was still plenty of light. The ground behind the unfinished house was marked with the treads of earth-moving equipment. The sun made shadows in the treads. Underhill left his own boot prints in the loose dirt as he walked to the chicken coop at the back of the lot.

The birds clucked their greetings.

He opened the wooden bin that held their feed corn. Scooped some out and tossed it through the wire. He bent over the bin and reached down into the corn all the way to his elbow. His fingers touched the grip of Ed Cavanaugh's Colt .38.

The gun was the only thing Underhill had left of Cavanaugh's. He had dropped the man's key chain down a storm drain in another city. He had removed the diamond ring from it first. The ring went down a different storm drain.

These Cavanaughs and their rings.

Alex's ring was gone too. After he bought it from Wellner, Underhill had broken it with a hammer and taken the pieces for a drive in the country. They had wound up in a wheat field.

Underhill knew he should get rid of the gun as well, but he thought he might need it. He left it buried in the feed bin.

From the coop he walked to the backyard of his temporary house. The glass slider let him into the kitchen. Unwashed dishes on the counter. Anna Haley had stayed over the night before and he had made her pancakes for breakfast. She had forgotten his talk about moving to New Orleans. Or he thought she had. You couldn't always know what was going on in other people's heads.

She had left around noon without making any plans. It bothered him a little. They usually made plans for Sunday night.

She was on his mind as he crossed to the front door, unbolted it, and went out. A short walk to the street. His mailbox was full of Saturday's mail. He leafed through it as he came back in, sorting out the junk.

He neglected to lock the door behind him.

Through the living room and down the hall. Underhill came to the room he used as his office and put the bills in his in-box. The rest went in the trash.

He stood by his desk and looked down at the papers there. Parchment stationery. Pages of a letter he'd spent part of the day writing.

The letter was addressed to Anna. He wanted to explain himself to her. If she knew what he had done, if she *understood* it, then she might understand why he would want to leave this place. It might make sense to her. She might agree to go with him.

But it was no good. Maybe you couldn't put it down on paper, he thought. There at the desk by the window, Underhill picked up some of the pages and read them to himself:

. . . I never meant to go through with it, but I couldn't help *thinking* about going through with it. I had the ten thousand dollars that Henry Tanager had given me, more money than I had ever seen at one time. I felt rich. The first thing I did, I went and bought a new car. Not *new* new. Secondhand. But new to me. Better than anything I'd ever owned.

It cost me half the ten thousand. Gone. Suddenly I felt less rich, even though I hadn't lost anything. And I started thinking

about the other twenty thousand dollars —
the money Tanager had promised me,
once Alex Cavanaugh was dead.

Once I did the thing that I never intended
to do.

I started wanting that twenty thousand.

I thought about Alex. I didn't know him. I
knew about one thing he had done. I knew
he deserved to be punished. I couldn't
quite make myself believe that he deserved to die. But I could come awfully
close.

If I were on a jury — this is something I
thought about — if Henry Tanager killed
Alex himself, and got caught and went on
trial, and if I were on the jury, would I vote
to convict him? I didn't think so. I would
have sympathy for Tanager. A lot of people
would.

But Tanager was a grieving father. I
wasn't. If I killed Alex, those same people
might take a different view. But maybe
they'd be wrong. Wouldn't they be wrong,
if I was doing it for Tanager, if it was what
he wanted?

I knew Alex Cavanaugh by sight. I'd
seen him hanging out with Bobby Wilson.
As I drove around in my new car, thinking
about the money I had and the money I
didn't have, I told myself I should take

another look at him. I thought it would help me decide.

I found Alex's address and drove by his house on Hull Road. I don't know what I expected, maybe to see him in the yard. The yard was empty. I drove by again a few minutes later and saw the same scene. No Alex. The third time I tried, I heard a shuddering noise at the back of the car, a thumping. I passed the Cavanaugh house and pulled over to the side of the road. My tire was flat, the rear one on the driver's side.

I had a spare in the trunk, and a jack, and there was nothing to do but go to work. I pried the hubcap off and loosened the lug nuts and before long I was sweating in the August sun. I worked the jack and almost had the flat tire off when a kid rode by on his bike. At first I thought it was Alex, but he came back and watched me from a little way off. He was too young, but there was a family resemblance. I was looking at Alex's kid brother.

He didn't speak to me, didn't stay very long. I finished and stowed the old tire and the jack in the trunk. My clothes were soaked through with sweat and I drove off with every window rolled down. I went back to the room I was renting and started to pack. I figured I'd leave in the morning. The flat tire was an omen, and the kid was an omen, and they were telling me to take what I had and be happy with it and get out.

That was my plan when I went to bed. But I couldn't sleep. I was thinking about the tire. I would need to have it patched. Things wore out and you needed money to fix them, and when I left in the morning, I'd be leaving twenty thousand dollars behind.

I turned over in the dark and looked at the numbers on my clock radio: 2:21.

Alex Cavanaugh would be in bed. Unless I planned to break into his house, I should forget about him and go to sleep.

Except that he might not be in bed. I knew from Bobby Wilson that Alex sometimes snuck out at night. Sometimes he went to an abandoned house — the Sturridge house.

This is the truth, I promise you: I didn't believe he would be there.

But I went there, just to see. The houses on that road were few and far apart. The Sturridge house had no electricity. No lights. Nothing but moonlight on broken windows.

I drove by and saw Alex in the shadows

of the yard. A quarter mile on, I killed my lights and found a grassy place to park.

I walked back to him.

I had nothing with me, no weapon, I swear to you. That has to tell you something, doesn't it? I didn't plan to do it.

Alex was taking pictures. The camera looked expensive. The tripod too. I stood in the dark and watched. Listened to the click of the shutter, the ratchet sound when he advanced the film.

I stepped into the weedy driveway of the house. Alex heard me and spun around.

Nervous laugh. I'd scared him. But he played it cool.

"Are you enjoying the show?" he said.

I moved closer. "It's late," I said. "Should you be out here?"

He laughed again, not so nervous. "Who's asking?"

"You don't know me?"

"No. Why don't you get lost."

"You don't live here," I said.

"Nobody lives here."

"So I have as much right to be here as you."

"What are you, a lawyer?"

"No."

Quiet out there in the dark. Not even crickets. Time stretched on and Alex and I stood staring at each other. If it was a contest, he lost.

"What do you want?" he said.

"I wanted to see what you were like."

"What does that mean?"

"You're only a kid after all," I said. "You're not so bad."

"Who the hell are you? Why are you here?"

"I'm here about Ryan Tanager."

That got his attention. He took half a step back from me.

"What about him?" he said.

"Is this what you're gonna do?" I said. "Play pretend?"

"I don't know what you want."

"You know what you did to Ryan Tanager. And so do I."

Alex might have been afraid, but he wasn't giving in to it. I watched something change in his face.

"I recognize you now," he said. "I've seen you with Bobby. What did Bobby tell you? You can't believe what he says."

"You're pretending again," I said. "We're not gonna pretend."

Alex smiled. A con man's smile. "You can't listen to Bobby. He gets worked up over nothing."

"So it meant nothing, when you ran Ryan

off the road?"

"He's got problems. Bobby does. He makes up stories."

"He didn't make it up," I said.

Alex's expression hardened. "I don't have to talk to you."

"I thought you might want to explain," I said.

"Why should I?"

"I'd like to hear your side of it."

If he'd been afraid, he had it under control now. He smiled again.

"Oh, you would?" he said. "What, are you a cop now?"

"No."

"You're nobody," he said. "If you were a cop, I'd know you. My father's a cop. You want to hear my side? Ryan Tanager had an accident. He rode his bike into a ditch. I'm not gonna cry about it. It's not my fault he couldn't ride a bike. Is that what you wanted to hear?"

I didn't respond. Alex took my silence for weakness.

"Good," he said. "You can go away now. I'm busy here. I'm done talking to you."

He turned his back on me. That was part of it. I saw him clearly, as an arrogant child who would grow up into an arrogant man. Even then I would have left him alone. But as I turned to go, I stepped on something. A length of wood, a handle broken off a shovel or a rake. It lay on the ground as if it had been put there for me.

You're nobody, Alex had said. Such a casual insult. Here was the answer.

I bent down and picked it up.

Underhill laid the pages on the desk. He had intended to write more, to explain about the other people he had killed. But he had written enough to know that none of it would do any good. He couldn't show the letter to Anna. She wouldn't understand. She wouldn't want to move away with him and start a new life somewhere else. That was fantasy.

If he was going to solve his problem, it would have to be the other way: he would have to kill Jack Pellum and Tanager and Keely. Three more. Then it would be over. Underhill could do three more. He had to. He wouldn't give up Anna.

There was a shredder on the floor beside the desk. Underhill switched the power on and started feeding the pages through, two or three at a time. He listened to the hum and the crunch of the machine and felt the breeze that came through the parted curtains of the open window. As the last of the pages disappeared, he had a stroke of good fortune. He knew the letter hadn't been a waste of time, because if he hadn't written it he wouldn't be standing here now. He wouldn't be seeing the car that drew up to the curb across the street.

He would have missed this: the driver's door opening, Jack Pellum stepping out.

43.

Jack approached the house carrying Ed Cavanaugh's revolver. It felt light; he was barely aware of it.

Part of him knew he should be more cautious. He didn't listen to that part. He had been waiting a long time, and he wanted to set eyes on Michael Underhill. He had no plan for what would happen after.

The house was a disappointment, too small and plain to be the lair of a killer. Cracked sidewalk, concrete stoop. The front door had a brass handle with a thumb latch. Jack pressed the latch and the door opened for him.

He looked around, felt the emptiness of the place. Beige walls, ugly carpet. He moved through the living room and down a hall. Glanced into a bathroom with a towel left on the floor. A bedroom with an unmade bed. An office with a file cabinet and a cluttered desk.

The ordinariness offended him.

He moved back through the living room and into the kitchen. Dirty dishes on the counter. Sliding glass door with a crack in one corner. Through the glass Jack could see into the backyard. He saw a figure in the distance, moving away, crossing into another lot beyond the yard.

The man was wearing blue jeans and an untucked white shirt. No hat or peacoat. Jack couldn't see his face, but he knew him from his gait, from the set of his shoulders. He knew him from the October night when he had followed him on the street, three days before Olivia died.

The glass door slid open smoothly. Jack stepped through. In the distance, Underhill stopped at an outbuilding. Some kind of shed — no, a chicken coop. The sound of the chickens carried across the yard. Underhill scooped feed from a bin and tossed it to them.

Jack began a slow march across the yard, the revolver held down by his hip. Underhill left the coop and walked on through the far lot, toward a house that was under construction.

A flutter of noise and movement from the chickens as Jack reached the coop. Stunted wings flapping. Up ahead, Underhill walked past a dumpster to the side of the house and into the garage.

Jack went on over the soft earth. He tacked left to keep the dumpster between him and the garage. He covered the final distance in a crouch, ducked into the garage, and found it empty.

A wooden ramp led up to a door. Still crouching, Jack eased it open. He had a long view into the house. Bare plywood floors and half-finished walls. Clods of dirt from Underhill's boots made a trail that lasted a few feet, then petered out.

Jack stood straight and brought up the revolver. There was a closed door on his right. He stood at one side of the frame and pushed the door lightly. It swung open by degrees. Nothing in the room beyond.

He moved through the ground floor, slow steps with no sound but the plywood creaking under his feet. A lot of it was open space, pale light coming through the windows.

There was a foyer at the front of the house. Two sets of stairs nearby, one leading up, one leading down. Jack started to go up, but before he reached the top he heard sudden music coming from below. He stopped and listened. Notes from a piano. A Billy Joel song: "Just the Way You Are."

Don't go changin' . . .

Jack returned to the ground floor and stood at the top of the basement stairs. There were four steps down to a landing. He took them silently, the revolver leading him. He rounded the landing and the stairs switched back on themselves. He saw a dozen more steps. A cell phone rested on the second one from the bottom. The music was coming from the phone.

Open air on either side of the steps. Jack squatted on the landing, trying to get a sense of what waited for him below. No artificial light down there, only what was coming in through the windows. A large expanse of gray concrete floor. Steel support beams here and there. Jack couldn't see as far as he wanted. He moved one step down, then another. The view was better. There was Michael Underhill, his back to the stairs, working a push broom across the floor.

Jack moved to the third step down from the landing, then to the fourth. The music covered his descent.

When he put his weight on the fifth step, it broke away beneath him.

44.

Underhill heard the crack of the step over the music and turned in time to see Jack Pellum tumble down the stairs. Pellum landed rough on his back on the floor, and his revolver fell from his hand. He reached to retrieve it and Underhill swept it aside with the broom.

Pellum rolled over stiffly and tried to rise, and Underhill kicked him in the ribs and sent him sprawling again. When Pellum sat up, Underhill jabbed the broom in his face.

"You shouldn't be here," Underhill said.

Pellum scrambled backward, crablike, his palms and boot heels sliding over the concrete floor. He came to the framed-in wall of the utility room and braced his back against it. The handsaw was lying nearby, the one the workers had left behind. Underhill had dropped it there after using it to cut a notch in the underside of the step. Pellum grabbed it up and held it in front of him. He waved it like a talisman that might protect him.

The head of the broom swiped through the air, and the saw went flying.

Pellum got his feet underneath him and began to ease himself up. Underhill shifted the broom to his left hand, drew the Colt .38 from his pocket, and aimed it at Pellum's heart.

He watched Pellum sink back to the floor and sit still.

The music played on. One Billy Joel song changed over to another. Rambling piano notes followed by whistling — the opening of "The Stranger."

"I warned you," Michael Underhill said. "I understand what you want. I'd want it too, if I were in your shoes. But I can't allow it. You can see that, right? I thought I made it clear."

Pellum had a scrape along his jaw. Blood leaked from a corner of his mouth. Underhill thought the fall might have loosened some of his teeth. It might hurt him to talk.

Pellum managed it. "You warned me," he said.

"But you came here," said Underhill. "This is my home. I don't want you here. You're . . ." He searched for a word. "You're poison."

Pellum wiped the blood from his mouth with the side of his thumb. He swallowed. Said, "My wife —"

"Your wife," Underhill said. "Your wife was afraid of me. I asked her a question, about the ad she shot. Where the ring came from. She didn't want to answer — and I needed an answer. She was definitely afraid of me, I could tell. I don't know why."

Pellum glared at him. Underhill could see hate there. It pained him. It didn't belong here.

"This is my home," he said again. "I'm going to live here. You should have stayed away."

He lifted the gun, aiming at Pellum's head. His finger was on the trigger. He thought of the noise. He thought the neighbors might hear.

Holding the Colt steady, Underhill planted his left foot on the head of the push broom. He twisted the handle, unscrewed it. When it came free, he kicked the broom head aside.

The music was playing. The same song or a different one, Underhill didn't know. It was in the background. He hardly noticed it. Until it stopped in the middle of a verse.

The silence jarred him.

He stepped back from Pellum and risked

a glance over his shoulder.

Anna Haley was standing at the bottom of the stairs.

45.

Jack was preoccupied with the gun. He didn't see the woman until she turned off the music.

He had fractured a rib during the fall, at least one, he was sure. He could feel it as he breathed. His left elbow had taken a hit and he had scraped his shins and battered his knees. Every part of him felt bruised.

He should have made a move. When the music stopped and Underhill turned his head, Jack knew he should have lunged for the gun, but he didn't have a lunge in him. He stayed put. He didn't want to get shot.

The woman clutched Underhill's cell phone and said, "Mike, what's going on?"

Underhill moved toward her, his attention divided. He took small backward steps and kept the gun trained on Jack.

"Anna," he said. "I wish you hadn't come."

"Are you okay?" she asked him. "You're

scaring me."

"I don't want that," Underhill said. Tenderly, Jack thought. "I don't want you to be scared. I can fix this. I can fix everything. Do you believe me?"

"But what happened?" Anna said. "Did he attack you?"

She touched Underhill's shoulder. Underhill kept his back to her. He held the broom handle like a staff in his left hand, the gun in his right.

"Yes," he said. "But I'm all right. I'll take care of it. You should go back up. Go to the other house and wait for me."

"I want to stay here," she said. "I don't want to leave you."

Jack spoke up. "You really should do what he says."

Anna stared at him but didn't speak to him. She asked Underhill, "Who is this?"

"No one important," Underhill said. "He's someone with a grudge against me." He let go of the broom handle and it clattered on the floor. His free hand found hers and raised it to his lips. The gun never wavered. "Go on now," he said. "I don't want you to get hurt."

"But he's not dangerous, is he?" she said. "He can't do anything. You've got a gun."

"He's still dangerous," said Underhill.

"I'll call the police," Anna said. "They can arrest him."

Underhill shook his head. "We can't call the police."

Anna touched the screen of Underhill's phone. "Why not? He's not supposed to be here. He's trespassing. And he attacked you. He started it, right?"

Jack could see the frustration building in Underhill's face. He watched Underhill turn and reach for the phone. Anna kept hold of it. Jack planted a palm on the floor and rolled onto his knees. The pain wasn't so bad.

"Anna," he said. "Listen. You don't know him. You need to get away."

It happens fast, in the time it takes Jack to stand. Underhill, with the gun in his hand, struggling with Anna for the phone. The two of them twist around so that all Jack can see is Underhill's broad back. Then the gunshot and they turn again like dancers, Underhill going down, down to his knees, carrying Anna down with him.

He lays her on the floor gently, cushioning her head. Her eyes are open wide. Underhill's white shirt is stained red, but the blood is hers, not his. It's on her blouse too. And on her hand. The little finger of her right hand is mostly gone. All that remains is a stub. The bullet took the rest.

It didn't stop there. Underhill lays the gun on the floor. It clicks against the concrete. He opens Anna's blouse, delicately, to look at the wound in her belly.

"Put pressure on it," Jack says.

Jack is on his feet now. He takes his phone from his pocket and dials 911. The operator seems unnaturally calm. She talks slow like she's speaking to a child. She needs to know his location.

"What's the address here?" he asks Underhill.

Underhill recites it and Jack passes it along. "Tell them it's the house under construction," Jack says to the operator. "We're in the basement. They should hurry."

"They will," she promises him.

Underhill has his shirt off. It's folded in a square. He's pressing it against Anna's wound. The fabric is red and getting redder.

"Mike," Anna says. "It hurts."

"Don't let up," Jack says. "Even if it hurts."

Underhill keeps one hand firmly on the shirt. With the other, he moves a lock of Anna's hair away from her eyes.

"I'm sorry," he says. "I didn't mean it."

"I know," she tells him.

"I'll make it right," he says. "I'll make everything right."

"My finger," she says. "I don't want to look. Is it bad?"

Underhill smiles at her and caresses her cheek. "It's not bad."

Jack walks in a half circle around them, taking it easy, favoring his left knee. He passes the foot of the stairs. Ed Cavanaugh's revolver is on the floor by the wall.

Anna is still talking to Underhill. "I came here to tell you," she says, "we can go anywhere you want. It doesn't matter where we live, as long as we're together."

"We'll stay here," Underhill says. "This is our house."

Jack picks up the revolver. He holds it loosely by his side.

"I don't know, Mike," Anna says. "I don't feel right."

"You're okay," Underhill says. "I've got you."

"It's not right," Anna says. "I feel like I'm dying."

Her face turns pale. It's noticeable to Jack, even from a distance, even in the fading light. Her eyelids flutter and close. Her head tips to the side.

A sound comes from Underhill, half groan, half whine. Something you'd hear from a wounded dog.

"Keep the pressure on," Jack says. "There's an ambulance on the way."

Underhill, kneeling over Anna, bows his head until it touches her chest. He comes up again, stares at her face. His fingers brush her lips.

He's quiet now, close to immobile. But not quite. He moves sluggishly, by fractions of inches. He takes his gun from the floor, holds it between himself and Anna. He studies the barrel as if there might be a message written there.

He shifts around on his knees to face Jack. Raises the gun.

Jack brings up the revolver and shoots him three times in the chest.

46.

The Chelsea police kept Jack well past midnight. A patrolman drove him to the station, handcuffed, and deposited him in a cramped interrogation room, not much larger than a supply closet. Two sergeants questioned him, one after the other, both of them clean-cut men called away from their families on a Sunday.

The first sergeant kept the cuffs on and tried to pick away at everything Jack said. The second one apologized for the first. He unlocked the cuffs and brought Jack to a bigger room. Gave him coffee. His questions were friendlier, more sympathetic. At first, Jack thought the two of them were playing games with him. Then he began to suspect that the second sergeant had figured out who his father was.

Jack told both of them the same story, most of it true, part of it invention. In the end, he was left in an office crowded with piles of cardboard boxes. He sat on a lime-green sofa and waited to talk to the chief of police. He tried to sit still so his ribs wouldn't hurt. It wasn't easy. He kept having to scratch his neck. The shirt he was wearing was flannel, and the collar itched. He had it on loan from the patrolman who brought him in. His own shirt was ruined. He had used it to keep pressure on Anna's wound, after he shot Underhill. He had held it in place until the paramedics came.

She'd had a pulse. He had felt it himself.

Jack didn't know what had happened to her after the paramedics took her away. He had asked the second sergeant, who promised to find out what he could.

The man must have been true to his word, because when the chief of police came in, the first thing he said to Jack was: "I understand you were asking after the young lady, Anna Haley. They had her in surgery last time I checked. The nurse I spoke to said she's expected to come through."

"Thank you," Jack said.

The chief dragged a padded chair from behind a pile of boxes and sat down on it.

"Michael Underhill, on the other hand, is deceased," he said. "Three shots to the heart in a nice tight group. Pop, pop, pop. But that's not news to you."

Jack said nothing. The chief had calm eyes and gray hair combed straight back from his forehead. He was a big, lumbering man, thick in the stomach and the chest. He looked as if he'd been roused out of bed and had thrown on the first clothes that came to hand: black sweatpants and a navy blue sweater.

"Seems like people get hurt around you, Mr. Pellum," he said. "I read about those old folks in New Boston. The Vernens. They got shot too."

"Not by me," Jack said.

"No, not by you," the chief agreed. "Now, as for Mr. Underhill, I'm still trying to make sense of him. He's the one who shot Anna."

"That's right."

"Was that on purpose, do you suppose, or an accident?"

"I'd say it was an accident. He was trying to get a cell phone away from her. I didn't have a clear view of it."

"So the trouble was over the phone."

"She wanted to call the police," Jack said. "He wanted to stop her."

The chief nodded. "Well, we do like to be called when there are criminals in our midst." He picked idly at the sleeve of his sweater. "Now at some point Underhill aimed his gun at you."

"Yes," Jack said.

"But he never got off a shot."

"I didn't wait for him to pull the trigger," Jack said. "I was in fear for my life."

"I can believe it," said the chief. "You were already injured. He rigged one of the steps in the basement so you would fall. That suggests he saw you coming, and knew who you were. And meant you harm, obviously. When you went to see him, you thought he might be the man who killed your wife. Have I got that right?"

"Yes."

"And not only her. A boy from Belleville too, from twenty years ago."

"Alex Cavanaugh," Jack said.

The chief picked again at his sleeve. Tugged a thread loose. "Cavanaugh, yes," he said. "That name jogged my memory, and I went looking through a pile of bulletins on my desk. There was an Edward Cavanaugh who went missing from Belleville two weeks ago."

Jack nodded. "Ed is Alex's father."

"So you know him. Would you say you're friendly with him?"

"Yes."

The chief looked thoughtful. "Well, maybe that explains it then."

"Explains what?" said Jack.

"We ran the serial number on your gun. It came back registered to Edward Cavanaugh."

"He gave it to me, as a gift."

"And you used it to kill his son's killer," the chief said. "There's a word for that, isn't there? Poetic justice. It's almost as if you planned it."

Jack held himself perfectly still. "I didn't plan it."

"No, of course. Remind me, Mr. Pellum, what brought you to Underhill's door in the first place? How did you know to look for him here in Chelsea?"

"I got an anonymous tip. Someone saw a flyer I put up and contacted me. They thought the image on the flyer looked like Underhill."

The chief turned his attention back to the thread on his sleeve. "That's right. That's what you told my sergeants. You got a tip. You came here to check it out. You didn't seek out Underhill in order to kill him. Even though you thought he might have murdered your wife."

"I didn't know anything for sure," Jack said. "I only wanted to talk to him."

"But you brought a gun along."

"For protection."

"For protection. Good thing too. Seeing

as he tried to shoot you." The chief looked up. "Do you know where Underhill got his gun?"

The question caught Jack off-guard. "How would I know that?"

"We ran it through the system, of course. A fine gun, a Colt .38. Would you like to guess who it was registered to?"

Jack leaned forward, his fractured ribs burning in his side. "I don't know," he said.

"Edward Cavanaugh. It makes me wonder if that one was a gift too. Do you suppose it was?"

The burning gave way to a sour feeling in Jack's stomach. "No."

"Then how could Mr. Underhill have come by it?"

"There's an obvious answer," Jack said. "Underhill killed Ed Cavanaugh and took his gun."

"That's an answer," the chief allowed. "I don't know if it's obvious. It's convenient for you. It would reinforce your story that Underhill was a murderer. It would make it easier for me to believe that he tried to kill you, that you were justified in shooting him. But if I were skeptical, I might think you brought both guns with you. I might think you intended to kill Underhill with one and plant the other on his body to make it look like self-defense. But it didn't work out the way you planned. He got the Colt away from you, after you took your header down the stairs. Maybe it happened that way."

"It didn't," Jack said.

"And maybe he wasn't aiming the Colt at you when you shot him. Maybe he wasn't holding it at all. Maybe you shot him because you wanted to."

"You don't believe that."

The chief fixed his eyes on Jack's. "No? Why not?"

"Because you're an intelligent man," Jack said, "and I'd like to believe you think I am too. If I came here to kill Michael Underhill, I would have planned to do it without getting caught. I wouldn't have needed to make it look like self-defense. But if I *did* want it to look like self-defense, if I intended to plant a gun on him after I killed him, I would have brought one that could never be tied to me, not one that could be traced back to a friend of mine."

Jack paused for a breath. The sourness in his stomach was fading. "No, it makes more sense to assume that Underhill killed Ed Cavanaugh, and that's how he got the gun. And if he did, odds are it happened either here or in Belleville. So the first step is to start talking to people. Maybe you'll find someone who saw them together —"

The chief interrupted him with a raised hand. "You can stop there, Mr. Pellum. I know how to conduct a homicide investigation. If I discover anything useful about Ed Cavanaugh, I'll share it with the proper authorities. That's not your concern." He bent closer to Jack as if to study him. "You're right that I think you're intelligent," he said. "I don't really believe you brought the Colt with you. I think you were surprised when I told you it belonged to Cavanaugh. But that doesn't mean I believe everything you've said to me — or that I like what's gone on here. Do you know what's going to happen to you now?"

"I hoped you'd tell me," Jack said.

"Nothing's going to happen to you. You're a respectable man from a distinguished family, and the evidence I've seen is consistent with your claim of self-defense. We'll interview Anna Haley as soon as she's able to talk. As long as she doesn't tell us anything that contradicts your story, I don't believe you'll face any charges. I can't decide if that's good or bad. Homicides are rare in this town, so I don't have to think too much about killers and what goes on in their minds. It's just as well. I'm not a deep thinker. But it seems to me, in this case, that two different things could be true at the same time. You came here to murder Michael Underhill. And you wound up killing him in self-defense. Am I wrong?"

Jack kept silent. He held his hands in his lap and interlaced his fingers. The chief hauled himself up from his chair.

"You don't have to answer me," he said. "It's better if you don't. Your father's waiting outside. I promised him I'd fetch you. It's late. You can come back tomorrow with a lawyer and make a formal statement. Good night, Mr. Pellum."

Jack left the station house by a side door. He walked out into a gentle wind and a clear night. The silver Town Car was waiting for him, his father behind the wheel.

Pain like a shard of glass in Jack's side as he folded himself into the car. It was all right when he stopped moving. He would be fine, if he didn't have to move.

His father observed him without comment, then started the engine and pulled out onto Main Street. The man's black suit looked freshly pressed. His tie was knotted flawlessly.

"Tell me how it works," Jack said. "You know someone in every police station in every town in this state? I could get arrested anywhere, and the cops would call you?"

His father kept his eyes on the road, his hands at ten and two on the steering wheel. "The police didn't call me," he said. "One of them called a reporter. The reporter called me."

Main Street was a straight black line, blocks of houses on either side. Up ahead, a traffic light blinked yellow.

"If you turn left here," Jack said, "I can pick up my car."

His father didn't slow. He kept on, due south, toward the interstate. "I'll send someone for your car tomorrow. Right now, I should take you to a hospital. You don't look well."

"I'm fine."

The creases of Alton Pellum's stern face went slack. His voice too. "I don't think that's been true for a very long time," he said, "but I won't argue with you. You were always an obstinate child, and you're a grown man now. You'll do as you will. You've proven it tonight. I've heard the tale twice, once from the reporter and once from the chief of police. Would you care to give me your version?"

"I imagine they got it about right," Jack said.

Alton Pellum kept his chin up, his eyes

forward, his back straight. "Sometimes I comfort myself with the thought that I'm your father and you're my son — that you realize you can trust me and confide in me. I believe I'll hold on to that notion for a while longer. One day it might prove true. In the meantime, I can only hope you're satisfied and this business is at an end. Shall I take you home then?"

They had an hour together in the car. On I-94, Jack's father drove precisely at the limit, seventy miles an hour in the right-hand lane, ignoring the cars and trucks that overtook him and left him in their wake. Jack watched the mile markers go by, green rectangles glowing in the dark. He wanted to sleep, and knew he wouldn't. They passed the Belleville exit and the airport. Jack thought about whether he was satisfied. The moment when he shot Michael Underhill was already receding into the past. He didn't believe it had given him any satisfaction. He couldn't remember feeling anything in particular. It was a thing that needed to be done, and he had done it.

His father took the exit for Woodward Avenue, and soon they were on Prentis Street. The Town Car rolled to a stop in front of Jack's building. Jack felt the shard of glass in his side again as he levered himself out. He willed it away, but it returned when he bent down to look in through the open door.

"Good night, Dad," he said.

"Good night, Jack."

The car drove off and Jack was alone. A scrap of paper skittered up the middle of the street, carried along on a current of wind. The neon sign of the Bronx Bar floated above the corner. Jack punched the key code at the entry of his building and went in.

The stairs were endless. He held the rail, dragging himself up, listening to the echo of his heavy footsteps. His breath felt ragged by the time he reached the top.

Paul Rook was sitting on the hallway floor. Dressed all in black.

He got to his feet. "Where've you been?" he said. "What happened to you?"

Jack limped to the door of his apartment. "I'm sorry, Paul."

"You went without me."

"I shouldn't have," Jack said. "But I did." He wavered a little. The hallway lights seemed very bright. "He's dead, Paul. I shot him."

Paul's mouth set itself in a straight line and his eyes were hard to read. They looked cold, maybe angry. Jack braced himself for what might come. The lights dimmed and the floor tipped ever so slightly, but he managed to stay upright. His knees ached and the glass in his side broke into little pieces that ground against each other, but he kept a distance between himself and the pain. He endured it, even when Paul reached for him and pulled him into a hug.

47.

The funeral mass for Jerry Diaz was held at Saint Anthony's Church in Belleville on Tuesday afternoon. Jack arrived late and sat in a pew by himself. The turnout seemed large; he counted at least a hundred. Afterward, a smaller number drove with the family to the cemetery. Jack followed them and watched the graveside ceremony from a distance. Eugenia Abernathy spotted him when it was over, raised a hand in greeting, and went on her way.

Keely Tanager stood close to the grave and was one of the last to leave. She wore a black blouse and a gray skirt and her hair was back up in its clips. She picked her way through the sunlit grass and came to Jack where he was sitting on a long stone bench.

He thought she might ease into things, maybe start off with something about Jerry. But she didn't.

She said, "You look like hell."

Jack had a bruise and a scrape along his jaw from falling down the stairs. He wondered if she was reacting to that, or something more. He thought all his other bruises were hidden away.

"You look nice," he said.

Keely sat, leaving a space between them, and stared out at the lake. The bench was at the top of a slope that fell steeply down to the shore.

"I don't feel good about this," she said. "Any of it."

A big white cloud drifted over the water. Jack watched its progress. "That was part of the deal, I think. That you wouldn't feel good about it."

"We didn't make a deal," Keely said.

Jack nodded. "That was part of it too — that we didn't make it."

Down below them, a mother duck waddled along the shore. She glided out into the water, followed by a troop of ducklings.

"We had a plan," Keely said. "My father was going to wear a wire."

Another nod. "I remember. You were going to arrange everything. You were going to make all the necessary calls — first thing in the morning. When I heard you say that, I knew we were on the same page."

Splashing sounds from down below. The

ducklings were trying out their wings.

Keely watched them, frowning. "We were never on the same page, Jack."

"How many of those calls did you make?" he said.

Her eyes closed briefly. "In the morning I saw the news. I never got a chance."

Out in the middle of the lake, the big white cloud left its reflection in the water. A motorboat cruised through it, dividing it neatly in two.

"I told the Chelsea police some things about Underhill," Jack said, "but only as much as I needed to. I told them I believe he killed my wife and Alex Cavanaugh. The chief of police there is hard to read. He might do nothing. Or he might get curious about just how bad a man Michael Underhill was. He might take it on himself to look into it. I wouldn't be surprised if he got in touch with you."

Keely's fingers worried at a chip in the stone bench. "He already has," she said. "Just as a courtesy. He told me he'd recovered a Colt .38 that belonged to Ed Cavanaugh. Underhill had it."

Jack nodded. "I know. It has to mean that Ed's dead, doesn't it? Underhill killed him. I don't see any other way to interpret it."

Keely was silent beside him. Her eyes

looked empty.

Jack said, "I never mentioned your father to the police, in case you're wondering. I didn't tell them that he confessed to paying Underhill to kill Alex. I don't intend to. That's my end of the deal."

More silence. Keely didn't protest anymore that they hadn't made a deal. Out on the lake, the motorboat came around again and sliced through the cloud. The wake from its first pass reached the shore. The mother duck led her babies out of the rough water and onto land.

"I'm curious about him, though," Jack said. "Your father. I'd have questions for him, if I ever got to talk to him again. Some of the things he told us seemed a little too easy and self-serving. Like the idea that he wanted to call off the hit on Alex but couldn't, because it was too late."

"It wasn't a *hit,* Jack. He's not a mobster."

"Sorry. You're right. That was rude. The other thing I wonder about is what happened when Ed Cavanaugh came to visit him. You kept him away from that subject when we talked to him the other day."

"I didn't keep him away from anything," Keely said.

"Maybe not. But you didn't lead him *toward* it either. You didn't want to know."

Keely hung her head and looked down at the grass for a long time. Jack couldn't tell what she was thinking. He watched her, and then watched the blades of grass bending in the wind. After a while, he stood. Keely stood too. They were the last ones left in the cemetery.

She brought a hand up to shield her eyes from the sun and moved close to him. Face-to-face.

"I need to know that my father's safe," she said.

"I think he is," said Jack. "The chief of police in Chelsea might get curious, like I said. He might want to know for himself exactly what Underhill was guilty of. But even if he decides to look into Alex Cavanaugh's death, I doubt he'll get very far. The only person who can connect your father to Alex's murder is the thief who stole Alex's ring — Seth Patterson. He won't talk to the police. I could barely get him to talk to me."

Jack was ready to turn away, but Keely brought her hand down from her eyes and tapped him once on the chest.

"I need to know that my father's safe from *you,* Jack."

His instinct was to laugh. He didn't. He let a moment pass, so she would understand that he took the matter seriously. Then: "He's safe from me."

She left him without saying anything more. He stayed by the bench and watched her walk across the cemetery lawn.

EPILOGUE

Twelve weeks later

"I saw her the other night."

"Who?"

"Anna Haley," Jack says.

It takes a beat for Eleanor Brannon to recognize the name. "The woman who was with Michael Underhill," she says. "The one who was shot."

"She's a musician," says Jack. "I saw her perform at a café in Chelsea. She plays guitar, and sings. She has a beautiful voice. She played some covers, and then a few songs she must have written herself. One of them was about him. It had to have been. It was about a lover who had gone away, and there was a house in it, a house without walls."

"Did you speak to her?" Dr. Brannon asks.

"I didn't go in. It was a warm night and the café door stood open. I could hear well enough from outside."

"Do you think it would have been wrong to go in?"

"I can't imagine she'd want to talk to me."

This is not quite true. Jack listened to Anna for an hour from outside the door, and when her show wound down he crossed the street and watched her from the corner. He could see her clearly through the windows of the café. The small crowd drifted away and eventually two or three loyalists were all that remained. Anna lingered until the owners started turning out the lights. She put her guitar in its case and snapped it shut.

And she saw him. She looked up from the case and saw Jack. No mistaking it. She came out the door carrying the guitar and looking straight at him. She stood on the sidewalk and they faced each other across the empty street.

It seemed as if they stood there a long time. Long enough for Jack to wonder what he would say to her, if she came closer. Long enough for him to shuffle through some possibilities.

I'm not sorry. You can't expect me to be sorry.

I don't regret it. He was a terrible man.

I didn't know about you. I never meant for you to get caught up in it.

You didn't lose anything when he died. Not anything worth having. You may think you did, but you didn't.

I know about loss.

You and I are not alike. We're not.

All these thoughts remained unspoken. Anna stayed on her side of the street, and Jack stayed on his. After a while he turned away. She didn't call to him or try to follow. He walked to his car without looking back.

Jack tells none of this to Eleanor Brannon, and they move on to other subjects. They talk about Underhill, but not very much. It's territory they've already covered. When he told her the story, she had little to say about the right and wrong of it. Instead she prodded him with vague questions: *What's different now? What's changed?* It took some time for him to get the message: she wanted him to realize that killing the man who killed your wife doesn't solve all your problems.

Today she wants to know if he's thought about his future. She has gone on a kick lately about the importance of making decisions.

It's five blocks from Dr. Brannon's office to Jack's apartment. Jack has healed enough to walk them without aching. He has no trouble climbing the stairs. It doesn't hurt to breathe anymore.

Inside, he locks the door behind him. His living room is strangely barren now. He took down the pictures of Alex Cavanaugh and Tim Caslake and Dylan Vernen. All the files that once occupied him are gone. Some of them went back to Keely, others to Paul.

There are no flyers on his coffee table. Or in his neighborhood either. Jack searched them out and tore them down, every last one. He took them to the old Tiger Stadium on an evening in July and burned them on a bare patch of ground on the edge of the outfield. He stirred the ashes into the dirt.

He put away Olivia's photographs around the same time, the ones she'd taken and the ones he'd taken of her. He stripped them from the walls and gathered them in craft-store boxes and put them in his closet. Only one of them is left: a framed five-by-seven of Olivia looking at him from their bed. She's lying on her stomach with her arms resting on her pillow, her chin resting on her arms. The photograph is black-and-white, but he likes the way it captures her eyes.

Jack could lose himself in those eyes. He could let them draw him back into the past. It would be easy. But it's only a picture.

He focuses on the frame and is struck by the smallness of it. It makes the wall around it seem vast. It reminds him of the walls at Danny Cavanaugh's house in Corktown. These days he finds himself thinking about Danny. About his last words.

Not *There's a killer, and he wears a crooked hat.*

The other ones: *What's so great about any of this?*

Jack writes those words now on a yellow Post-it note and puts them on his wall.

He has decisions to make. His father wants him to go to law school. He still has an offer of admission for the fall semester at the University of Michigan. The deadline for claiming it has passed, but Jack is sure the deadline won't matter, not for Alton Pellum's son.

That's one option. There are others. He could go back to the Detroit police. He knows the work, and they would take him. He could partner up again with Carl Dumisani.

Or he could make use of his private investigator's license. He still has his billboards; he still receives calls from would-be clients. Most of them leave voice mails. Jack has gotten into the habit of deleting them. He could start responding to them instead.

Decisions. There's another he's been putting off. He hasn't talked to Kim Weaver, not since Underhill. She called him once — the day after — but he was sleeping and she left no message.

He didn't return the call. At first, he wasn't ready. He didn't know what he would say. Then, as time passed, he started to believe that he had waited too long. Kim wouldn't want to hear from him. He convinced himself that she'd left no message because she didn't know what to say to him either. He was a killer. She wouldn't want to be with a killer, even a righteous one.

Best to forget about her.

But Jack hasn't forgotten. Sometimes he walks to the DIA and sits on the steps where they first talked. He thinks he might see her again. She might come up and sit beside him.

He thinks of something she said to him, here in his apartment: *Say yes to me.*

He writes the words on another Post-it note, and puts them on the wall, next to the others.

The words were an offer. Maybe the offer still stands.

Some of her clothes are still in his closet. She never came to take them back. She kept his key.

Jack pulls his phone from his pocket and finds Kim's name among his contacts. He touches her number to make the call, and waits to see if she'll answer.

ACKNOWLEDGMENTS

I'm grateful to my editor, Sara Minnich Blackburn, whose insightful notes on this novel led to changes that made it much stronger. And to my agent, Victoria Skurnick, for believing in me even when the story took a long time to tell.

I'm thankful for the support of my family: my parents, Mike and Carolyn Dolan; my brother, Terry; and my sister, Michelle.

Thanks also to Ivan Held, Alexis Sattler, Tom Dussel, David Chesanow, Melissa Rowland, Lindsay Edgecombe, Elizabeth Fisher, and Miek Coccia.

ABOUT THE AUTHOR

Harry Dolan is the nationally bestselling author of *Bad Things Happen, Very Bad Men,* and *The Last Dead Girl.* He graduated from Colgate University, where he majored in philosophy and studied fiction writing with the novelist Frederick Busch. A native of Rome, New York, he now lives in Ann Arbor, Michigan.